"CAT! THEY SURE NAMED YOU RIGHT. YOU'VE GOT ALL THE INSTINCTS OF A CAT AND ALL THE MORALS."

She couldn't hold back her tears. "Please, Duke, don't try to hurt me. We've hurt each other enough."

"The only thing you care about is that Jebediah in my jailhouse. You don't give a damn about me. Tell me, honeychild, how many times have you spread for him?"

"Don't say that."

"And you think you could be a lady. As if a bitch in heat, a goddamn rutting animal could ever be a lady. Because that's what you are, my dear, no better than a French Alley whore."

Cat raised her eyes and drew back her lips. Her breath hissed between her teeth. "And that's just the way you love it, don't you, Duke? Bitch-hot and barnyard filthy. But not with your wife, oh no . . ."

"Bitch," he yelled. "You hellcat!" And he lunged for her . . .

HELLCAT OF SABREHILL

RAYMOND GILES

FAWCETT GOLD MEDAL • NEW YORK

A Fawcett Gold Medal Book
Published by Ballantine Books

Copyright © 1982 by H.R.J., Inc.

ISBN 0-449-12382-0

Printed in Canada

First Edition: January 1983

To
those wild, wonderful Ritter girls
Helen
Mildred
Marion
Bertha
Louise
and their brother
Harry

One falsehood spoils
a thousand truths.

—*Ashanti proverb*

ONE

MR. DUKE

⊷⊶{ I }⊷⊶

AFTER THE BIG BLACK bastard had run away the fourth or fifth time, Wingate said to hell with him. He had paid a good price for the boy because he was such a beautiful piece of prime field hand, but it was time to cut his losses. When the patrol brought him in to Charleston, Wingate didn't even bother to whip him. By his own lights, the planter was not an inhumane or unreasonable man, and besides a newly cut back or some broken ribs would hardly bring up the slave's price. So he left the boy in the work-house for a few days, allowing him to rest and regain his strength, and then told him that he was an ungrateful wretch who didn't appreciate a good master when he had one and that he would be sold the next morning.

As Wingate turned away from the cell, he could smell the nigger's hatred like the stench of death.

When he returned before dawn the next day, the guards had the boy ready: wrists tied behind his back and his ankles spanceled with a stout length of cord. All Wingate had to do was mount his horse, yank the leash that was tied to the slave's wrists, and say, "You lead, Jebediah. I reckon you know where we're going." And they set off through the chill of the February morning.

It wasn't far: a block south from Magazine Street to Queen, then five or six blocks east till you came to the street called Vendue Range, just before the wharves. The slave dealers on the Range were already hard at work, hiring out their people for the day. Until they were sold, the dealers wanted them to earn their keep.

Wingate dismounted, tied his horse, and shoved the slave ahead of him through a narrow archway into a torchlit courtyard. A few white men and a number of blacks stood about. A couple of black guards had whips. A white man was sitting at a deal table, some lamps and writing equip-

3

ment before him and his clerk at his side. As Wingate approached, he stood up.

"By God, he *is* big!" The man was in his middle forties and heavyset, with innocent brown eyes under heavy brows.

"Like I told you, Avery. And about as strong as any two of my drivers."

Sam Avery's smile was not so innocent. "And he stands proud, don't he? Too damn proud. Nigger, don't you know to lower your eyes in front of a white man?"

The black, head high and shoulders back, gave no sign of hearing.

Avery laughed. "I could have told you this one was a runner. Thought you knew how to cure a runner, Mr. Wingate."

"Evidently not."

Avery took a lamp from the table and looked more closely at the slave. He frowned. "You said he was only 'bout twenty-two years."

Wingate's voice took on an edge. "He is."

Avery shrugged. "Sure as hell looks older to me. Bring him inside."

Avery picked up a hunting crop from the table and pointed to a doorway. He led them to a small barren room with barred, unglazed windows in the wall and the door. One of the whip-carrying guards followed them in and untied the slave's bonds.

"What you say his name is?" Avery asked.

"Jebediah. Jebediah Hayes."

"All right, Jeb, shuck down. Boots and all. Show us your ass."

The slave's eyes closed, his head lowered, and his shoulders slumped, and in that instant Wingate understood his hatred. Jebediah Hayes was, as Avery had said, a proud man, prouder than any nigger had a right to be. And yet the thought hit Wingate, *By God, in his place I hope I'd have the guts to run! And damn well never give up!*

The slave's eyes opened. His head came up again, and his shoulders squared. With a casualness that was a measure of his contempt, he began pulling off his clothes.

Avery's inspection was thorough but mercifully quick, as he sought any flaw from bad teeth to hemorrhoids to poorly mended bones. At the touch of the dealer's hands, the slave's face tightened with strain and his body quivered like that of a race horse, but he maintained a stoic silence.

"Well, he seems fit enough," Avery said, when he had finished, "but I don't know how I'm gonna get any kind of price, what with that bad-nigger back. Don't know when I last saw such a mess of whip cuts."

"I bought him," Wingate said, "so will somebody else."

"And lookee here." Deftly, before the slave could move, Avery slipped the leather loop at the end of his hunting crop over his genitals, tightened it with a twist, and lifted the entire phallus. His eyes widening with shock, the slave uttered an involuntary cry and brought up his hands to protect himself. Without thinking about it, Wingate reached for the small pistol he always carried in his pocket. The guard raised his whip, and the slave froze, his face twisted by hatred and fear.

"Look at this," Avery said, as if he had noticed nothing. "He ain't even got much for breeding."

"He's cold and he's scared," Wingate said, trying to control his anger, "and I'll thank you to take that goddamn thing off of him. He doesn't belong to you yet."

Avery laughed, as if amused by Wingate's sensitivity, and let the loop slip away.

"Give you two hundred for him."

"Two hun——!" Wingate broke off in shock. "Jebediah, get your clothes on."

"Now, wait a minute. We can do business. But you got to realize that I'm gonna have me a problem with that back."

"You'll have to do better than two hundred."

"I can do a mite better. Let's just go to my office for a minute. You can leave your boy here."

The light faded as Avery and the guard left the room, taking the lamp with them. In the doorway, Wingate took one last look at his slave.

"You could have had a pretty good life at my place, Jebediah," he said, "but God only knows what you've got to look forward to now. Only one thing's certain—sooner or later, you're going to have a master who'll break you."

The door closed, leaving the room completely dark. A bolt snapped home.

The slave, still naked, did not move. His heart pounded as if to break through his chest, and Wingate's parting words reverberated through his mind: *". . . you're going to have a master who'll break you."*

The hatred he had felt for so long burned higher, like a fiery cauldron within his own interior darkness.

Never! Jebediah Hayes swore silently. *Never!*

Leduc Avery, usually called Duke, was awakened at dawn by a soft clatter and a splashing sound. He knew at once where he was—in Jessie's quarters—and he smiled, desire stirring, as he remembered the previous night. In the six months since he had purchased Jessie, there had been a number of such nights, but at nineteen he still came to each of them as if it were the first.

After a moment he opened his eyes and looked at the girl in the gray light. Her naked brown body, slim and lithe, was bent over the washbasin, her breasts swaying as she threw water on her face. Straightening, she tossed water on her breasts and belly, then washed herself slowly and thoroughly. Again, desire stirred, and he fought it, knowing he should leave. Sam, his uncle, would already be at work up on Vendue Range.

But the temptation to remain right where he lay was great. Still unaware of his gaze, Jessie began to towel herself, and it seemed to him that nothing in the world could be more lovely than the rise and fall of her breasts as she moved her arms.

When she was finished, she carried the basin to the door, opening it just wide enough to throw the water out into the courtyard. Then, turning, she saw for the first time that he was awake and watching her. A broad smile flashed across her face. Setting the basin down on the table, she hurried around to the other side of the bed and slipped under the covers into the curve of his arm. Her head settled on his shoulder, and her arm slid across his bare chest.

"Jessie, honey, I got to go now."

"No, not yet," she crooned, as she snuggled up against him. "Soon is soon enough. You jes' stay here a little while."

"Aw, Jessie . . ."

He smiled and sighed and closed his eyes again. He didn't like to have the servants see him leaving, but, hell, what difference would a few more minutes make? He worked down into the bed and drew Jessie closer still.

Sometimes he actually felt a thrill of fear when he thought of how easily he might never have met her and what might have happened to her then—of how different his life and hers might have been and how neither of them, surely, would have known this happiness. If he had not been walking along Elliott Street on that hot afternoon last June. . . .

Quite simply, if he had taken Broad Street as usual, instead of Elliott, he would not have encountered Madam Lareina Gomez, and he might never have met Jessie.

Later, feeling older and wiser, Duke could smile about that afternoon and his naiveté. He had never before been with a woman, and though he had heard tales about Madam Lareina, he honestly believed that the only thing she had in mind when she coaxed him into her shop— "Before you get sunstroke, Mr. Avery! Now, you come in here!"—was his health. He thought the same thing when she insisted that he accompany her upstairs to her bedroom, where she could bathe his face in nice cool water. She had actually pulled off his shirt and, as he bent over the washbasin, was tugging at his belt buckle before it occurred to him that she *might* have something else in mind.

The shock was almost too much for him, and failure seemed imminent. But Madam Lareina, a tall, full-figured, darkly handsome woman at least twice Duke's age, was experienced and patient and knew exactly how to get what she wanted, and before the afternoon was over, Duke was convinced that he was the most accomplished and satisfying stud that Charleston had ever known.

Thereafter, he returned to the shop—and the bedroom—

at least two or three times a week, and he soon became
aware of Jessie. He became aware, in fact, that, in addition
to Madam Lareina's other assistants in her dressmaker's
shop, she had three of the most beautiful young maids he
had ever seen, not to mention the handsomest houseboy.
To Duke's eye, Jessie was beyond measure the most beautiful of all, and before long it was she whom he most wanted
to see when he visited Madam Lareina's establishment.

"Can't keep your eyes off her, can you?" Madam asked
one afternoon when Jessie had brought them coffee while
they still lay in bed—a custom that embarrassed Duke,
although Jessie always averted her eyes and pretended to
see nothing.

He shrugged, feigning indifference.

" 'Course you can't. That's why I bought her—'cause I
figured she'd turn out to be about the best damn fancy I
ever raised. She'll bring a pretty penny, believe me."

Duke had hardly spoken to Jessie, but he felt a sick pang
at the thought that she might vanish from his life into the
life of another.

"You mean you'd sell her?"

" 'Course I'd sell her. What do you think I bought her
for?"

Madam Lareina was lying back against a great heap of
pillows, the sheet drawn up over her thighs. While Duke
stared at her, she sat up and, raising her arms over her head
and arching her back, stretched luxuriously, showing off
her full, ripe figure. Duke was dimly aware that she had
brought up the subject of selling Jessie because she felt a
certain jealousy of the slave girl.

"But you wouldn't sell one of your own servants."

Madam lay back on the pillows and rolled to face Duke.
Her dark eyes were suddenly hard.

"Why wouldn't I?"

"Nobody sells their own servants, not if they can help it.
At least, nobody decent."

"Decent? Are you saying I'm not decent?"

"No, but—"

"Who the hell are you to say I'm not decent? Your
daddy and your uncle have the biggest slave trading firm in

Charleston, and you work for them. You buy and sell every kind of nigger—"

"It's a necessary occupation—"

"It's a trade, and to most people it's the lowest kind of trade, and *you're in it!* So don't you get self-righteous with me, young Mr. Avery."

This was what Duke hated most in all the world: the special scorn that was reserved for the slave trader, no matter how good his family name might once have been. He had felt it often, and his temper, always near the surface, surged: How dared she?

Somehow he controlled himself, and his anger faded. "Lareina, I just said your own servants—"

"Anyway, they're not really servants, not the way you mean."

"Then what the hell are they?"

"They're my fancies. They're my stock in trade—the slave trade. You mean to tell me--you've never heard of Madam Lareina Gomez's fancies?"

He had heard of them, but he had thought, if he had thought of it at all, that the reference simply meant that her servants were handsomer than most: Many people preferred fancies for servants. He had also heard that Madam Lareina dabbled in the slave trade, but he had assumed that meant she invested in one of the local firms.

"I didn't know you were in the trade."

"Well, I am. Fancies only, and fancies come high. So if you're thinking of spreading that wench, remember it's going to cost you."

"I wasn't thinking of that, Lareina."

"Ha!"

"How did you get into the trade?"

"Been in it for years. I've always had an eye for good-looking niggers—I can spot them while they're still young and you can get them cheap. I always try to have at least two or three wenches and one young buck on hand. I treat them good and make them earn their way. I teach them to keep house and to cook and sew and to talk tolerably well." Madam gave Duke a defiant look. "I also teach them everything I know about pleasuring a man—and I don't reckon anybody knows more about that than me."

She waited for Duke to raise some objection. When he said nothing, she went on. "That's one reason I always have a good-looking houseboy around—to help teach them. I don't let them spread for him if I can help it, because I don't want them knocked up, and besides virgins sell for more—God only knows why. But they still learn what a man likes, and you can bet that that boy has more fun than just about any other nigger in town."

Duke's face felt stiff and drawn, as he thought of what those words meant. "Are you saying that he and Jessie have . . ."

"Why not? She's got to learn somehow. Anyway, the older ones help train the younger ones, and by the time a wench has been here three or four years, I've got a full-trained fancy. And even if she doesn't turn out as fancy as I hoped, I still have a trained housemaid who'll fetch a good price."

"Who buys your fancies?"

"You'd be surprised at the fine gentlemen who claim to be looking for a housemaid when they really want a bed wench. And one of my best-paying customers is Mr. Antoine Bellesort. He visits France every three or four years, and on his way home he always buys one or two of my gals."

"What does he do with so many?"

"What do you think? He just happens to own the three best whorehouses in New Orleans." Sipping her coffee, Madam gave Duke a sly look from the corner of her eye. "Yes, come to think of it, Mr. Bellesort is due back here next fall. Reckon he'll pay me more for Jessie than he's ever paid for a wench before. Wouldn't be surprised if she was the highest priced fancy ever sold."

The thought of Jessie being sold into a New Orleans brothel sickened Duke even more than the thought of her being "trained" on the houseboy. And as for the latter . . . what the hell, he thought, niggers were niggers, and everybody knew they couldn't hardly help themselves from taking their pleasure. Like animals. Even Madam Lareina, who couldn't be more than one-eighth black. Of course, she claimed to be pure Spanish, but everybody knew that half of those spics had nigger blood, and anyway, she sure as hell didn't fuck like a white woman.

"Are you sure that boy of yours never got into her?"

"He hadn't the last time I inspected her, a few days ago. And he knows that if I found out he did I'd beat his balls off."

At that moment, Duke made up his mind to buy Jessie.

That evening he considered how best to go about it. Fortunately he had some money. Sam, his uncle, had urged him to do some trading on his own—"Nothing'll teach you to judge black flesh faster than risking your own money on it"—and he had not done badly. His father would not approve of his buying a bed wench, but he could put her to work as a maid, and, although he disliked the dissemblance, pass her off as an investment: simply a well-trained fancy he had bought for a good price, expecting her to bring him a profit. And then somehow he just never would get around to selling her.

The purchase was not that easy, however. When a day or two later he told Madam Lareina that he would like to inspect Jessie, as he thought he had a buyer for her, she gave him a long, hard look.

"I don't split my profit with anyone. I get the top price, and I keep every dollar."

Duke shrugged. "Anybody you sell to has the right to sell again. If you don't like my price, just turn it down."

Madam's stare never wavered or softened, but a crooked grin slowly spread over her face.

"You want her for yourself, don't you?"

Duke flushed. "If I did, I'd say so."

"I told you, if you want to spread her, it's going to cost you."

"Name a price."

"Make an offer."

"If she's really fancy under that dress, I might go to a thousand."

Madam threw back her head and laughed. "Duke, if you weren't so young and stupid, I'd consider that downright insulting."

"A thousand is pretty good for a young, half-trained house servant—"

"Yes, she's young, not seventeen yet, and that means she's got a lot of years left as a fancy. But the only way she's half-trained is that she's still got her cherry, and we both know that's part of what you're buying. And you're not going to get that for *twice* your thousand dollars!"

Duke suddenly realized that Madam Lareina was angry: She knew she was losing her lover, and losing him to a younger woman, and to a black at that. That did not bode well for his purchase of the girl.

"I'm sorry, Lareina," he said, trying to sound friendly and reasonable, "I only meant it as an opening bid. But I'll open at twelve hundred, if you like."

Madam's dark eyes sparked. "I said not for *twice* your miserable thousand dollars, and I meant it!"

Duke was fully prepared to go to fifteen hundred or even higher, but it had never occurred to him that he might have to pay over two thousand.

"All right," he said slowly, "how much do you want?"

"Thirty-five hundred," Madam snapped, "and not a penny less!"

Duke had had no experience with fancies, but the price struck him as fantastic: It was about what he might charge a planter for five or six prime field hands. But he saw some of the wind go out of Madam Lareina's sails, as she realized that she had committed herself and wished she had not. That meant she would never lower the price.

Nevertheless he said, "That's ridiculous."

"I'm not going to dicker with you, Duke. Bring the money today, and I'll let you look at her. But if you try to talk me down even one dollar, the deal is off."

"You know I can't bring you the money today. My bank is already closed."

"All right, tomorrow. Madam Lareina's one-day special."

That night he could hardly sleep. He knew that if there

was anything he didn't need, it was a thirty-five-hundred-dollar fancy. He would be spending most of his savings. Furthermore, he hardly even knew the wench. And he had no idea of what he would do with her when, at some future date, he returned to college. Yet the idea of not going through with the purchase was unthinkable, and he began to realize what an obsession Jessie had become with him.

The next day Madam Lareina seemed to have become reconciled to the situation. "I know you think thirty-five hundred is high, Duke, but I figure I could sell her to Mr. Bellesort for as much or more. But what the hell, I get attached to my girls, and I'm sure she'll be happier with you than in a whorehouse. Now, shall we look at her?"

The inspection took place in Madam Lareina's bedroom, and whatever experience Jessie had had with the houseboy, it had left her no less shy about taking off her clothes in front of Duke. Twice the girl broke out in sobs, and Madam Lareina had to take a moment to soothe her. But dear sweet Jesus, Duke thought, she was beautiful! Full-chested, long-limbed, narrow-waisted, barely hirsute, every line graceful. He could see that, even as she whimpered and tried to huddle away from his gaze.

"Good eyes, good teeth, no hernias, and a good tight ass," Madam Lareina said. "But you look for yourself. And I'll show you she's still a virgin—or at least she was this morning."

Duke hated what they were putting the slave girl through. "No need," he said, turning his back to her. "Jessie, honey, pull on your clothes. I'm not going to look at you anymore."

Madam Lareina was more sanguine. "Jessie," she said cheerfully, "you've always known you weren't going to stay with me forever. But how would you like to stay right here in Charleston? See me now and then if you get homesick? See the other girls, as long as they're with me? Would you like that?"

"Yes, ma'am."

"How'd you like to live with Mr. Duke? He's a kind, thoughtful gentleman. You think you'd like that?"

Duke turned back to Jessie, who was now clutching her

dress to the front of her body. Their eyes met. Jessie's lips formed a wisp of a smile.

"Yes, ma'am."

If it was possible for a white man to love a colored girl, Duke thought, at that moment he loved Jessie.

He and Madam Lareina parted on friendly terms, knowing their affair was over, and he took Jessie home with him that afternoon. He had no difficulty in inducting her into the household. He introduced her as the new maid to the butler, the housekeeper, and their daughter, the chief housemaid, and made clear that the lines of authority and supervision were to remain undisturbed. Jessie's demure manner and competence soon won their praise, and within a few days she was completely accepted. As for his father, Duke simply announced that he had invested in a fancy who would be earning her keep as a maid, and his father nodded. Since Duke had returned from South Carolina College the previous spring, Ben Avery had increasingly left the household decisions to him.

Finding quarters for Jessie was no problem. The Avery house was a large Georgian "double house" on King Street, on a property that extended ninety yards west through the block to Legare. To the south and west of the house lay the lawns and gardens, and to the north lay the side courtyard and service lane and a long line of outbuildings. The farthest of these from the house had been used as storerooms in recent years, and Duke had the servants clear out and clean the very last of them. Its small fireplace seemed to be in good repair, and he had a bed and a few other pieces of furniture installed. Some of the servants might grumble at Jessie's having all this space to herself, but that was just too bad, he thought, let 'em. He wanted Jessie to live alone.

Ten days passed before Duke could bring himself to visit Jessie in her little room at the end of the lane.

Madam Lareina had assured him that the girl knew what was expected of her. But was that really true? Duke kept remembering her sobs and the fear in her eyes when Madam had made her strip naked in the bedroom.

He also remembered her beauty.

At the end of ten days, he could wait no longer. He was sick with desire, his mind flooded with images of Jessie.

He waited until the last light was out in the servants' quarters. His father had long been asleep. In shirt sleeves, he quietly left the house and followed the moonlit lane to its end. He stood before Jessie's door for a full minute before he could bring himself to knock. He heard a slight rustling sound inside.

"Who that?"

"It's me. Mr. Duke."

The door slowly opened. Moonlight struck Jessie's face, brightened her eyes, revealed her shy smile. She stepped back, and Duke followed her into the darkness of the room.

The door closed.

The months that followed were the best of Duke's life. Although he and Jessie were discrete, he thought the other servants knew about their relationship, because sooner or later servants knew everything. But they said nothing and showed no discontent over any extra privilege he might give Jessie, because she was always cheerful and helpful and never shirked her household duties. She had indeed been well trained.

And she was intelligent. After that first night, when they had thought of nothing but their ravenous desire—and Jessie's seemed every bit equal to Duke's—he found that in the sweet interludes between pleasure he could talk to her, tell her his plans and dreams, and she would listen with interest and sympathy.

"It's a funny thing, Jessie," he said one night as they lay together in her bed, "these gentleman planters, they buy and sell slaves all the time, and they don't think they're any less gentlemen. But we buy and sell and broker slaves *for* them, help do what they need to get done, and they figure that makes us dirt."

"People feel bad 'bout something, Mr. Duke, they want to put the bad of it off on somebody else."

"That's right, Jessie. That's certainly right." Jessie lay with her head on his chest, her shoulders and back burnished by the lamplight. "But they're not always going to think of me like that, Jessie."

Jessie was silent, her hand gently, pleasurably stroking him in the way she had been trained.

"I've got it all figured out, Jessie. I'm going to get a good education, maybe even read some law, so nobody can ever say I'm just an ignorant slave trader. And one day I'm going to have land. That's the real secret—to have one of the finest plantations in the state. 'Cause that's one thing everybody respects. And they'll never again forget that the name of Avery is one of the oldest and best in Carolina."

But there was one part of his plan that he hesitated to tell her. It was she who brought it up.

"Mr. Duke, what you going do with me?"

Once again her head was on his chest, and she raised it to look into his eyes. Everything about that face—the high, strong cheekbones, the broad yet delicate nose, the wide mouth—grew more precious to him each time he was with her.

"What do you mean, Jessie?" His fingertips traced the contours of her face.

"You go back to the school, you get tired of your Jessie, you meet some nice white gal . . ."

There it was: some nice white gal, the unspoken part of his plan.

Duke shook his head. "Honey, I don't know yet what I'm going to do about school. But I do know I'm never going to get tired of you. And as for a white gal . . ." He wanted to be honest with Jessie. "You're right. Sooner or later, I'm going to hitch up with some white gal. She's got to come from a good family, one that nobody can help but respect, 'cause that's so important. And I reckon I'll love and respect her the way a white man should love and respect his wife. But, Jessie, honey, that won't ever make any difference between you and me!"

Slowly Jessie lowered her head to his chest again, and suddenly her thoughts seemed impenetrable.

"Jessie? Understand, honey?"

"I understand, Mr. Duke."

And she did, he was certain she did, for they continued

to share their own little world, a world of affection and pleasure such as Duke had never before known.

Oh, God, he thought, his arm tightening around her, as they continued to lie abed on that February morning, *God, I love her!*

He immediately thrust the thought away. Of course, he didn't *actually* love her. A white man didn't love a colored wench, not the way he loved a white woman. But by God, he thought, he did delight in Jessie, he treasured her, he cherished her, whatever word you wanted to use. He *cared* for her. And after six months, her little room was still paradise.

"Jessie," he said, reluctantly, for desire still stirred, "I think I'd better go now."

"Aw, no!"

He felt her hand move over his thigh to hold him, and at once he became fully aroused. He moaned and gave himself up to her touch for a moment, then forced himself to brush her hand away. "Jessie, honey, there isn't time!"

Hurriedly, before she could caress him again, he slipped out of the warm bed and into the cold morning air. He poured water from the pitcher into the basin and began washing.

"Jes' a little while," Jessie crooned temptingly behind him, her voice low and dulcet. "Jes' a little while."

He glanced down at his swollen flesh, now achingly hard, but he forced himself to say, "No, Jessie! Now, I mean it!"

But by that time Jessie was on her knees behind him on the bed, her hands moving up and down his bare back. Her lips moved lightly across his spine, and he felt the flicker of her tongue.

"Jessie, please—"

"Jes' a little while."

He nearly cried out as her hand moved around his waist and down over his quivering belly, nearly cried out again as her other hand moved up between the thighs, did cry out as the hands met on tender flesh to cup and fondle and caress him. He was no longer resisting when she turned him to face her, and as she drew him back down into the bed, he didn't care if he never left the room, no, not ever again.

Gray dawn crept into the small locked room where the slave sat huddled and shivering in a corner. He had found his clothes—tattered and ill-fitting shirt, pants, and jacket and worn brogans—and put them on again in the dark. He had not been fed at the workhouse last night or this morning, and his hunger was painful.

Survive, he commanded himself. Endure and survive.

He had had three masters. The first had sold him into the fields. The second had brought torture and death to his family. The third had tried and failed to break him. He had survived them all, and a new master meant new opportunities to escape.

To escape north to freedom.

The dawn light grew stronger. He could hear talk, shouts, laughter beyond the walls of the little room. Rising to his feet, he flexed his muscles to warm them, and went to the door. It was bolted, he remembered, but it did not look very substantial. He thumped on it, then seized the bars in its small window and shook it hard. Yes, he could break through it easily. But what then? A thousand obstacles would still stand between him and freedom. He shook the door again.

"You stop dat, you hear me?" came a rasping voice. "You leggo dat door 'fore I bus' your finger off!"

Looking through the bars, Jebediah Hayes saw a young black man carrying a whip. He slammed a hand against the door again, harder and louder than before.

"Listen, you ass-licking, toad-eating, cock-sucking little son of a bitch, you get me some food and get it here damn quick, or I'm coming through this door and stick that goddamn whip up your miserable ass!"

The guard's eyes widened with shock. He turned and ran.

Jebediah Hayes laughed.

Endure. Survive.

And never, never let the bastards break you.

THE MORNING WAS OVERCAST and gray, but nothing could dampen Duke's spirits. He gave Jessie a last kiss, made sure the lane and the courtyard were deserted, and hurried toward the house. In the pantry he encountered Raphael, the butler, but by then it didn't matter if he was observed.

Upstairs in his room he found that the bed he had so carefully rumpled the night before had already been made, a small fire burned in the fireplace, and there was hot water in the pitcher. As he shaved, the troubling question of what he would do about Jessie when he returned to school came back to him. He had no intention of leaving her behind, but how could he take her with him? As a body servant? Impossible! He already had a fifteen-year-old boy for a servant, and though the boy was not very satisfactory, to replace him with a wench—and, at that, with a wench who looked like Jessie!—was unthinkable. Yet somehow he had to find an answer.

After hurriedly changing his clothes, he went back downstairs. Raphael had seen to it that breakfast was waiting for him, and he gulped it down. He was on his way out of the house when his father called to him:

"Leduc."

Duke looked into the parlor. He was surprised that his father was awake and up at such an early hour. He sat in front of a crackling fire in the big marble-manteled fireplace, still in his robe and slippers and heavily wrapped in blankets. Each day, it seemed to Duke, his father became smaller, thinner, and grayer, until now he looked at least twenty years older than his fifty-odd years. His illness had kept Duke home from school this year, and Duke had made himself face the painful fact that his father would probably die within a few months. Perhaps he could have prolonged his life in a better climate, but he insisted that he

wished to die at home. The doctors said that, even if his
lungs didn't give out soon, the strain on his heart would
probably kill him.

"Leduc, sit down."

"I'm already late—"

"Sit down. I want to talk to you."

"Yes, sir." You didn't refuse your father—or a dying
man. Duke sat down in a chair on the other side of the fireplace.

For a moment Ben Avery stared into the sputtering
flames. When he spoke, his voice grated with fatigue. "You
didn't sleep in your own bed last night. Again."

So he knew. Or at least suspected. Duke said, "No,
sir."

"You're nineteen. You'll be married in a few years.
Couldn't you have waited?"

Duke had rarely discussed sexual matters with his father, and the thought of his father being aware of his
spreading Jessie made him cringe.

"Daddy, you know how it is," he managed to say, "how
a man . . . well, how he . . . how he can't hardly help . . ."

"I know. But many men do wait. And most women. Our
kind of women."

"But it's different for a man. Men are more . . . well,
more like niggers. White women just don't have the same
kind of feelings. I mean, they don't have them so godawful
strong."

His father's eyes, as gray as his skin, turned toward
Duke and widened. Candles seemed to burn within his
eyes, flickering but still bright. "Where the hell did you
ever get that idea?"

The question startled Duke: after all, everybody *knew*.
And the idea that everybody might be wrong was, when
you thought about it, frightening. As a fair-minded man,
Duke was willing to concede that the white male was not
as far above the black race as he liked to believe: Whatever
his superiority, he shared much of the same animal-like
nature. It was in the gentler sex that the greatest differences
between the two races were to be found. The white woman
was the repository and guardian of the virtues and values

of the white civilization. And how could she be that if her nature was the same as a white man's—or a black woman's?

My God, Duke thought, with a touch of panic, *if a white woman had the same needs and desires as a man, how could you ever be sure she was faithful?*

"Well," he managed to say, "they just *don't*."

His father stared at him. He shook his head and turned back to the fire. "I don't know. When I was your age, a man might have to work a little to arouse a woman's interest, but once aroused, she didn't necessarily show any lack of enthusiasm. But maybe there's something in what you say. It's hard to believe people change much from one generation to the next, but it seems to me you hardly ever meet a real woman anymore. They seem more prim and prissy every year. But if they are, maybe it's because we expect it of them."

Dyke stood up. He was eager to end this conversation as quickly as possible. "Daddy, I'd better go now—"

"No. Sit down."

Reluctantly, Duke sank back down on his chair.

"Son, I don't suppose I'm the one to moralize. I have to confess that, before I married, I gave in to temptation with more than one wench. But not often, thank God. And thank God I never had any yardchildren. And I don't want you to have any either. If there is any thought that sickens me—and should sicken you—it's the thought that you might have a child born into slavery."

"Daddy," Duke said, alarmed, "nothing like that is going to happen!"

His father shook his head. "You keep on spreading that little wench the way you've been doing, Leduc, and that's exactly what's going to happen."

"There won't be any yardchildren," Duke said miserably. "Jessie knows how to take care of herself."

"Son, let me tell you something. There *is* no sure way for a woman to 'take care of herself.' That wench can use the best plugs and douches ever devised, and maybe they'll work for a month or a year or ten years. But if she's fertile enough and your seed is good, sooner or later she'll likely conceive. And I just pray that I won't live to see the day."

Duke hunched forward in his chair. "Daddy, I wish you wouldn't talk like that!"

He could hear his father's harsh breathing, the rumble of tattered lungs.

"Christ, I hate slavery!" Ben Avery said after a moment, and Duke had never before heard such bitterness in his voice. "When I was a boy, honorable men still worked at the trade because we thought it was a necessity of the times. We thought it would eventually vanish. God, we were fools! And we learned nothing from the slave conspiracy back in 'twenty-two or the rebellion up in Virginia last year. Nothing at all—except how to degrade and brutalize ourselves further. Because make no mistake about it, Leduc, the slaves aren't the only victims. And they won't be the last. Because God is just!"

Duke didn't like his father's agitation. He got up again and went to him. "Daddy, don't you think you ought to be in bed?"

"Listen to me, Leduc." His father looked up at him with haunted eyes, the candles within burning higher. "I want you to get out of the trade. Get out as soon as you can. Go back to the land, where a gentleman belongs."

"Daddy, that's exactly what I plan to do."

"That was where we made our mistake, in ever leaving the land. You get yourself a plantation and take care of your people, instead of tearing families apart—husbands from wives, children from parents—"

"Daddy, that's just what I'm going to do!"

"Then you'll be able to find yourself a decent woman and settle down—"

"It's all right, Daddy!"

His father subsided into his chair as if releasing a burden he could carry no longer, and the light went out of his eyes.

"You're a good boy, Leduc."

"I try, Daddy."

"But remember, that wench is here, not out of any love for you, but only because she was bought and paid for."

Not true! Duke wanted to say, but he held back the words and forced himself to smile. "Well, I reckon you could say the same about many a fine white married lady, Daddy."

"Perhaps. But it's not quite the same."

"Daddy, I really better go now."

His father closed his eyes and nodded. His breath rumbled in his lungs, and he didn't move. Duke quietly left the room.

A fine plantation, a good wife, and the respect of the best people of Carolina—that was all he wanted.

That and, forever, Jessie.

He was still pondering the question of how he could take her with him on his return to South Carolina College, when he arrived at Vendue Range and his thoughts were interrupted by a shriek that seemed to express both grief and rage. As he entered the archway into the courtyard, a black man came hurling at him, collided with him, and nearly knocked him down. Over the man's screams, Duke heard his uncle, Sam Avery, yelling, "Grab that nigger, get him!" and he stretched out his arms. Fists beat against his chest and knees thumped against him, but he bore the writhing mass back into the courtyard. The black man was short and thin but wiry, and he nearly tore away from Duke before two guards came running and seized his arms.

"By God," Sam said, grinning, "he don't *never* give up, do he!"

Still held by the guards, the man sank to his knees on the cobblestones, and Duke realized that among his wild cries were words: "No, no, no! Please, sir! Please!"

"What the hell is wrong with him?" Duke asked. "Does he think he's going to be hurt?"

Still sobbing, the man looked up at Duke and answered for himself. "Please, sir. I ain't no slave! I was stole! They stole me from up north!"

Duke realized that the man's accent was indeed northern. "Sam, what the hell—"

"My name is Calvin Ames, and I ain't no slave, sir! Please! I got a wife and three children, need me in Philadelphia. But them slave catchers, they stole me! They stole me 'board ship, they stole me south—"

"Boy, what are you talking about?"

"I ain't no slave, I'm just a poor tailor from Philadelphia, but they say they kill me if I don't let them sell me! But my wife, my children, what they going to do without me? Please, sir! Please . . ." Unable to go on, the man slipped from the guards' hands and fell facedown, sobbing against the cold stones. Duke, feeling as if he had been unexpectedly hit in the stomach, stared at him.

"Sam, what's going on here?"

Smiling, Sam clamped a big hand on his shoulder and led him away. "Nothing for you to worry about."

"Could it be true, what he said?"

Sam shrugged. "Could be true, I suppose. But if a nigger tells me some wild story 'bout being a tailor from Philadelphia, you think I'm gonna take his word against the word of the white men who sold him to me?"

Duke followed Sam out of the courtyard and into the office, a room crowded with cabinets and scrivener's desks and dusty ledgers. "But if it's true, and that man isn't a slave, and he's got a wife and children somewhere depending on him—Sam, we've got to do something for him!"

"Aw, now, wait a minute." Sam propped himself against a high stool by a desk. His eyes were innocent, his smile benevolent. "Boy, you must know that if that little booger's story is true, I feel as sorry for him as you do."

"We can find out—"

"But he didn't say a word until his owners had sold him and gone."

" 'Cause he was scared they'd kill him!"

"The fact remains that the firm of Avery Brothers now has a lot of money tied up in that nigger, and I aim to get it all back. With a profit!"

"But, Sam we can't—"

"Oh, yes, we can. If it was up to me, maybe I'd let him earn out our investment and his keep and then let him go. Hell, maybe I'd even forego our profit and let him go in five or six years—"

"Six years!"

"—but that just ain't practical. So I'm gonna sell him, and maybe he can persuade his next owner that his story is true."

Duke stared at his uncle. In his experience, Sam was not a particularly cruel man. In most circumstances he could be as decent and generous as anyone else. But not now. Not where a black man and an investment and a profit were involved. At that moment Duke could understand why the chivalry held that trade, and the slave trade beyond any other, corrupted and brutalized a man. Yes, his father was right: The slaves were not the only victims.

Sam smiled and gave him a pat on the shoulder. "Aw, now, don't look so Holy Ghost, boy. Our little friend from Philadelphia ain't as bad off as he seems. I'll sell him to some planter, and a week or so later he'll likely run off for the North. Good chance he'll make it, too—it happens all the time. Northern niggers ain't protected from the evils of geographical knowledge the way ours are."

Duke shook his head. "Sam, I don't think my daddy would approve."

"Now, don't you go bothering your daddy 'bout this," Sam said sharply. "He's got enough to think about, being sick. You understand?"

"Yes, sir."

"Tell you what." Sam climbed off the stool. "Don't you give no more thought to that little fella. I got something else come in this morning I want to show you."

Sam led the way from the office, evidently determined to distract Duke from the tailor's plight. They went to a nearby room, where Sam looked in through a barred window in the door, then drew the bolt.

The moment they entered the room, Duke could feel the hatred, and when the black, sitting in the corner with his back to the wall, raised his head, his gaze was as penetrating as a sword thrust. Duke stood where he was, hardly breathing.

"On your feet, boy," Sam said.

The black slowly stood up. He was exceptionally handsome, Duke saw—a noble brow, a strong nose and jaw— but the clear brown eyes were hard with defiance.

"Now, ain't he something?"

Duke stared. The black was tall, as tall as Duke himself. His tattered clothes couldn't hide the fact that he was heavily but smoothly muscled. His shoulders were as broad as any Duke had ever seen, his hips were narrow, and his thighs threatened to burst through his thin pants.

"Where did he come from?"

"Wingate, the planter, brought him in. I got him cheap. He's twenty-two years old, sound as they come, and 'cept for some whip stripes, there ain't hardly a mark on him. Even his teeth are good. You ain't never gonna meet a nigger with a sweeter breath."

"If he's so good, how did you get him cheap?"

" 'Cause he's a runner and an insolent son of a bitch. Thinks he's too good for the fields just 'cause he talks good—better than most white men, truth to tell." Sam laughed. "You shoulda been here earlier. He just plumb scared the shit out of poor Muley!"

Duke's gaze was so locked with the black's that he was hardly aware of Sam's answers. Yet he dimly realized that they didn't quite make sense. The slave appeared to have been born and bred for the fields and to have spent years working in them. But field hands didn't speak white man's English. House servants might, but not field hands.

"What's your name, boy?"

"Jebediah Hayes." The voice was a full, rich baritone.

"You see?" Sam said, grinning. "No *sir*, no *massa*, just his name. Next he'll be asking you yours."

Jebediah Hayes's lip curled slightly, as if he couldn't have given less of a damn about Duke's name.

"Is it true that you speak well, Jebediah?"

"I speak as I speak . . . *massa!*"

The slave gave the last word a contemptuous ring, made it almost a curse. Sam's eyes hardened, but Duke listened fascinated.

"Jebediah, how does it happen that you speak as well as you do?"

"I speak as I was brought up to speak."

"But how were you brought up? Don't make me work for every word, goddamnit, just tell me!"

Jebediah Hayes took a deep breath, and the rents in his shirt tore a little further. "I was born on the Pinkham plantation," he said in a monotone. "My parents were the butler and the housekeeper. I was brought up in the big house as a companion to little Willy Pinkham. That's where I learned."

"You learned a hell of a lot better than most houseboys do. Can you read and write too?"

"No."

"He is also a goddamn liar," Sam said. "Wingate said he could read and write as good as you or me, and calculate as well."

Duke ignored him. "What happened, Jebediah?"

"Four years ago, Mr. Pinkham found himself in financial straits. He sold my parents and me as house servants to a Mr. Osborn. But Mr. Osborn didn't want house servants. He wanted my father and me for the fields and my mother for . . . for . . ."

For the first time, the big black man's voice shook with something other than hatred. He turned to the outside window and gripped the bars, his great muscles swelling. Sam took a step back toward the door, ready to call for help.

"It's all right, Jebediah," Duke said quietly. "Take your time."

Slowly the black man's body sagged. One hand left the bars, and he wiped his eyes.

"Jebediah?"

"My momma . . . my daddy . . . they died. I won't tell you how they died."

Duke could guess the rest.

"And you no longer had anything or anybody to keep you on the Osborn place, so you started running."

"You look at my back," the slave said fiercely, "and you'll see how I ran—*massa!*"

"Until Osborn sold you to Wingate?"

"And I kept on running!"

The room was silent. After a moment, Sam asked, "Seen enough of him?"

"No." An idea was beginning to form in Duke's mind.

"Well . . . I reckon he ain't gonna give you no trouble. I got things to do."

Sam left the room.

"Jebediah," Duke said, "I know it's not easy, being sold."

"Is that a fact, massa!"

"It's hardly ever easy. But we try not to make it any harder than necessary. We're not like some traders—you have to be inspected for sale, of course, but aside from that, we don't treat you like an animal—"

"Oh, don't you, massa!" The slave turned from the window long enough to throw one swift look of burning hatred through the doorway, then turned back to the window.

"Was it Sam?" Duke asked after a moment, hoping he was wrong. "What did he do to you?"

"Never you mind what Sam did to me!"

First the tailor, Duke thought, and now this one. And he had thought it was going to be such a wonderful day.

Well, maybe it wouldn't be so bad after all. Maybe he could do something for this one.

"I'm sorry," he said.

"Shit!"

Yeah, Duke thought sadly. Shit. He left the room, and once again Jebediah Hayes heard the bolt slide home.

He raised his head from the bars of the window to look at the sky through blurred eyes. The humiliation of the morning had been almost unbearable, and that white boy had made him remember too much. Tears continued to flood his eyes. But he forced an angry grin.

Still not broken! Never broken! Never!

The idea that had formed in Duke's mind grew more specific, and he gave it plenty of thought; in fact, he thought of little else all morning. He kept Jebediah Hayes isolated from the other slaves and several times paused to talk to him, trying to get a better impression of the big black. Gradually the rage in the man's eyes became more guarded, and Duke even detected an occasional glint of humor.

"Suppose we sold you as a house servant instead of a field hand, Jebediah. Would that stop your running?"

The slave looked at him as if he were a fool. "Do I look like a house servant?"

"You're damn right you do. You're the best looking—"

"Is this the hand of a house servant? Is this the arm of a house servant?"

Duke knew what he meant. Calling Jebediah a house servant wouldn't keep a master like Osborn or Wingate from putting him into the fields where that great strength might be most useful.

"But suppose you did get a chance to work as a house servant again. Could you learn to say *sir?*"

Jebediah smiled faintly. "I can easily say *sir* when it's called for. But being nothing but a fool darky," once again his lip curled with contempt, "I generally prefer . . . *massa.*"

Duke laughed. Jebediah was hardly the first proud black he had encountered, but he was certainly not the least of them.

By afternoon he had made up his mind.

"Sam, I don't want to sell the Wingate nigger. I want to keep him. For myself."

Sam, at his desk in the office, looked up in surprise. "What the hell for? You've got no use for a prime field hand."

"Not as a field hand. As a house servant. As my own personal body servant."

Sam shook his head in disapproval. "My God, boy, don't you have enough useless darkies loafing around that big old house? What about that boy you took off to college with you last year?"

"Like you said, useless. Sam, from what I gather, Jebediah Hayes is about as bright and well-trained a house servant as you'll ever meet. And I don't care how big and strong he is, it's a goddamn crime to take a boy like that, brought up in a house, and turn him out into the fields when he hasn't done a damned thing to deserve it."

Sam observed Duke shrewdly. "Now, how do you know he hasn't done a thing to deserve it?"

"I just don't believe he ever did."

"And of course Jebediah Hayes is going to be so grateful

for your kindness that he will immediately become your most steadfast and loyal nigger friend, beholden to you forevermore."

Duke flushed. Such thoughts had, of course, occurred to him. But he tried to be realistic. "Sam, I know perfectly well that when a nigger's gone bad, you're not going to change him overnight. But you've got to take into account the reasons he's gone bad. I figure this one is smart enough to know when those reasons no longer exist. It may take a little time, and he may give me a little trouble, but he'll learn."

Sam shrugged and laughed. "Suit yourself."

If it worked out, it was the perfect solution to the problem of what to do about Jessie when he returned to college, and he was surprised that he had not thought of it at once.

By next fall his father would probably be dead. Duke hated to think about that, and disliked himself for taking it into account, but the fact remained. His father would be dead, and Duke would be a fairly wealthy man. Not as wealthy as he would be if he were working at the business, and not wealthy enough to finance the kind of plantation he dreamed of, but wealthy enough for what he had in mind.

Instead of returning to college at Columbia with a single, male body-servant, instead of rooming and boarding with strangers, instead of living on a minimal allowance as he had done in the past, he would live in style.

He would simply move to Columbia and set up residence.

He would buy or rent a house. Nothing big or fancy, just a small house with a few outbuildings: kitchen, stable and carriage house, servants' quarters. Jessie would be his cook and housekeeper. Jebediah would be his factotum. It might be a good idea if he got Jebediah married to some handsome wench who could assist Jessie—then he would have a complete household staff. No doubt Jessie's beauty would draw some comments, but the situation would be sufficiently respectable. He would have a place to live, a place to entertain his friends.

And Jessie would be with him, in the house. God, Duke thought with delight, to have Jessie alone under the same roof with him every night!

Jebediah looked stunned when Duke spoke to him: "I'm not promising anything, but we'll try it for a month or two. If we don't get along, I'll sell you, but I'll do my best to sell you as a house servant. Is that agreeable to you?"

He could not imagine Jebediah saying anything but yes, but for a long moment the big black merely stared at him. Then he nodded, as if unwilling to trust his voice.

They left for Duke's house at once. As they walked through the busy crowds toward King Street, Jebediah looked about with dazed eyes, trying to take in everything: the Planter's Hotel, the city hall, St. Michael's, the guardhouse.

"Ever been to Charleston before, Jebediah?"

"Yes, sir. The Pinkham family spent half of every year here. It's like coming home."

The words touched Duke. "Well, I hope it will be home for you, Jeb. For a long, long time to come."

The rest of the day went quickly, for there was much to be done. Jebediah was introduced to the household, and, as with Jessie six months earlier, his position and the lines of authority were made clear. A place had to be found for him to sleep. Unfortunately, there was no place convenient to the main house, as Duke would have wished, but there was another storeroom, third from the end of the lane, that would serve. Duke rallied all of the younger household staff to clean it out and wash it down. A bed and a few pieces of furniture were installed. "Tomorrow, Jeb, we'll paint the place. And I know where there's an old Ben Franklin stove we can put in. You're going to be as comfortable as anyone else that lives here."

Darkness fell. The supper hour arrived. Jebediah ate with some of the other servants on the steps of the kitchen house. He had hardly said a word since his arrival, hardly lifted his head to meet the other servants' eyes. Goddamn,

Duke thought, you couldn't tell *what* the big boy was
thinking!

The last chores of the evening were completed. Duke
strolled across the courtyard to where Jebediah, looking
lost, stood in the light of the kitchen house.

"I'll bet that was the best meal you've had in a long
time, wasn't it, Jeb?"

"Yes, sir," the slave answered softly, "a very long time."

"There'll be a lot more of them. And tomorrow we'll
measure you for some decent clothes. We like our people
to look good."

"Yes, sir."

Duke gave Jebediah's shoulder a friendly squeeze. "I
don't need you tonight. Why don't you get some rest?"

"Yes, sir. Thank you, sir."

Duke watched for a moment while Jebediah walked into
the darkness of the lane. Yes, he thought, everything was
going to work out just fine. He went into the house.

Jebediah continued along the lane until he reached his
door. He looked about. Here and there, in the main house,
over the carriage house, in the kitchen, a candle or a lamp
went out. No one was in sight—no one to threaten him or
to lock him up for the night or to see that he didn't run
away. Except for when he was on the run or locked up in a
cell, it was the first time in months that he had been left
alone.

He went into the room, shutting the door behind him,
and felt his way through the darkness to the bed. He sat
down on its edge.

His head lowered, his shoulders hunched. He could hold
back no longer. He wept. Wept long and hard and painfully. Wept until it was done and he could wipe his eyes
and laugh again.

Laugh his low, mean, half-crazy, bad-nigger laugh.

He had done it: survived another month, another week,
another day. Survived the hazards of Vendue Range.

He laughed again and shook his head. For a little while
there he had felt almost grateful to the whey-faced son of a
bitch. But it was important to remember: Jebediah Hayes
owed the bastards *nothing!*

Jebediah Hayes was *owed*!

And one day, one way or another, Jebediah Hayes was going to *collect*!

Endure, he commanded himself. Survive. Whether you're out of the fields for good or back in them in a month, you are going to outlast the bastards, and one day you will shake the very pillars of their goddamn godless temples!

Because, Mr. Jebediah Hayes, no matter what happens, you are one mean, arrogant, crazy-bad nigger!

With a soft, childlike sigh, he lay back on the bed and slept without dreams.

No one awakened him the next morning, and Jebediah slept late, but he was up and washing when he heard the tap at his door. Opening it a few inches, he saw a girl, the one they called Jessie. Like all the Avery servants, she was well-groomed, her simple brown dress well-pressed and spotless and her head bound in a pale yellow kerchief. She had brought a plate of food, and the instant the aroma hit Jeb's nostrils, his stomach lurched with hunger.

" 'Morning, Jebediah," Jessie said, holding up the plate.

Her eyes were shy and her smile infectious, and Jebediah smiled back. "Good morning."

"Cook say I don't bring you this food now, you don't get nothing hot till dinner."

Jebediah took the plate. "It was kind of you to bring it, Jessie, and I thank you. Now, if you'll excuse me—"

"I got to come in."

"Pardon me?"

Jessie pushed against the door. "Mr. Duke say I got to measure you for new clothes."

"Oh. Well . . ." She was without a doubt the prettiest girl Jebediah had ever seen, and her gaze made him feel self-conscious. "If you'll wait a minute until I put on my shirt—"

"That don't make no never-mind to me, Jebediah," Jessie said, stepping into the room. "I'm jes' folks."

"I'd still prefer . . ."

Feeling shyer than he would ever have expected, Jebediah turned his back on her, set down the plate, and began pulling on his shirt.

"Mm," Jessie said softly, "your poor back. Reckon it's true what they say 'bout you."

"What's that, Jessie? What do they say?"

"They say Mr. Duke don't know it, but maybe he made

34

a bad mistake 'bout you. They say you one bad nigger, musta run 'way from that Mr. Wingate a hundred times."

Jebediah laughed. It was odd how quickly information traveled through the slave community, especially in the city.

He sat down at his table and began to eat: rice johnny cake, sweet potatoes, and fatback with some meat, all of it covered with a rich gravy. A substantial breakfast! At least they ate well in the Avery household.

"You finish that," Jessie said, as she started making up the bed, "and then I measure you. Jessie's going sew up your new clothes herself."

"You don't have to make the bed, Jessie."

"I want to."

He had first noticed Jessie soon after his arrival the previous afternoon. She had shown a quick and easy smile but had said almost nothing as she helped clean out his room. He had sensed that she enjoyed a special place in the household, but none of the others seemed to resent it, perhaps because no one worked harder or more cheerfully than Jessie. He had also felt her gaze on him when she thought he was unaware of it, but he was used to that. The wenches often stared at him.

"Do you have family here, Jessie?" he asked.

Jessie's hands, straightening a blanket, hesitated, and the smile left her face. "No," she said. "Ain't got no family."

"No momma, no papa, nobody? No brothers or sisters?"

She looked down and shook her head.

"Well, where did you come from? Just spring up in the flower garden?"

She threw him a brief smile, but all happiness had left her eyes. "My momma and my daddy died when I was real little. But 'least I had my aunt Flora and my uncle Ned. You know how it is on a big plantation—if your folks die, 'most always there's somebody to be aunt and uncle to you."

"I know."

Some of Jessie's childhood field-accent returned as she spoke. "That was on the McClintock plantation. Then when I was twelve, Mr. McClintock say he got too many lazy, useless niggers lay 'bout, not earning their keep, and he going get rid of them. Mr. McClintock say he ain't going break up no family, but I ain't got no family, so I got to go. My aunt Flora and my uncle Ned, they weep and they beg and they say, '*We* her family! She our chile! Don't take 'way our chile!' " Jessie shrugged and shook her head. "But it don't do no good. Mr. McClintock say they ain't my *real* aunt and uncle, and he bring me to Charleston and sell me to Madam Lareina. That's a dressmaker, likes to buy nice little gals and train them and sell them again."

"Why aren't you smiling, Jessie? Was she mean to you?"

"No," Jessie said slowly. She sat down on the edge of the bed near Jeb but didn't look at him. "No, she wasn't mean. She was strict and she make us work hard, but she teach us good. Teach us to cook and sew and," Jessie hesitated, "and how to please a man. I was there four years, and then 'stead of selling me to somebody like Mr. Bellesort for his whorehouses—"

"Whorehouses?"

Jessie nodded again. "She likes fancies so she can sell them for high prices, and she sells some to whorehouses, the real 'spensive kind. But she sell me to Mr. Duke, who is kind as can be, 'cept when he get mad, so I reckon I should be real grateful—"

He had not known he was going to slap Jessie until he did it; had not known until, the word *whorehouses* echoing in his brain and anger rising in his breast, he saw his hand shoot out and slap, not hard but sharply, against her cheek.

"Don't you ever let me hear you say that again!" Jessie fell back on the bed, looking up at him in surprise. "Don't you ever let me hear you say you've got reason to be grateful to a white man. Whorehouse, hell! You owe the bastards nothing! Remember that! You owe them nothing!"

Fear in her eyes, Jessie held up an arm to defend herself. The gesture immediately brought him to his senses. "Jessie," he said, "I'm sorry! I didn't mean . . ."

Christ, he thought sinking back into his chair, here he was in Charleston, with his best chance of escape in years, and he was going to spoil it. If the girl said anything about this to Duke Avery . . .

"Jessie, forgive me. It's just that the idea of some white bitch selling you into a whorehouse . . ."

Tears glistened in the girl's eyes, perhaps from his blow, but she wore a crooked little smile. "I think they right," she said. "I think Mr. Duke made a bad mistake 'bout you. I think you are one real bad nigger, Jebediah."

"No, Jessie, I'm not. And I'm truly sorry—"

"That's all right." Jessie sat up, rubbing her cheek. "That's all right, I *like* a real bad nigger. And I got a idea we going be good friends." She glanced out the open doorway. "Now I better hurry and measure you. Won't do for me to be 'lone with you too long."

From a small cloth poke Jessie produced a scrap of paper, a pencil, and a tape measure. As Jebediah stood self-consciously before her, she began measuring him, and despite her words, she seemed to be in no hurry. First she measured his neck. Then she measured both the width and the circumference of his shoulders, standing before him and reaching around him with both arms to do so, until Jebediah became uncomfortably aware of the closeness of her body to his. She measured his biceps and the length of one arm, and then, again standing before him and embracing him with both arms, she measured his chest.

"Jessie," he said, his voice thickening, "are all these measurements really necessary?"

"I know what I'm doing." Still holding the tape to Jebediah's chest, Jessie looked up at him, her eyes bright with mischief. "Jebediah, you like me?"

"I hardly know you, Jessie, but . . . yes, of course, I like you."

She smiled. After making a notation on her paper, she began measuring his waist, her fingers moving over him far more slowly than was necessary.

"I'm glad you like me. I been watching you all I could since you come here, and I think maybe you somebody I been waiting for."

Jebediah said nothing. He knew Jessie was purposely teasing him, as any healthy young wench might tease a buck who attracted her, and at one time, years before, he would have been pleased.

Jessie made her notation and began measuring his hips. Again her fingers moved slowly, and when they brought the tape to his front, they lingered, barely touching him.

"Would you like to know me better, Jebediah?" she asked, her eyes still bright.

He forced a smile. "Well, time will tell, won't it, Jessie?"

"Time ain't the only thing," she said, sliding her hand down over him, and she laughed as he slapped it away.

"That's enough, now, gal. You've got your measurements, and I haven't got time for fooling around!"

"Jes' two, three more measurements, and I'm done," she said, laughing, and before he could stop her, she had bent down and slipped the tape around his thigh.

"You don't need that!"

" 'Course I do! Jes' look how you nearly busting out of these here pants!"

With a moan, Jebediah allowed her to measure his thigh, though lightning shot through his flesh each time she touched him.

"Nearly done, Jebediah! All we got to do now . . ."

Kneeling, she held the tape to his ankle and slowly ran it up the inside of his thigh, and lightning struck again.

"Oh, my, would you *look* at that! You really *is* nearly busting out of these here pants! Well, I reckon I better measure this here too—"

She dodged his blow and rolled away, shaking with laughter.

"Jessie, you are a mean and wicked woman, rousing up a man like that!"

Jessie got to her feet. "That mean you don't like it?"

"Too damn much. Now, get the hell out of here and let me simmer down so I'm fit to go see Mr. Duke."

Jessie grinned wickedly. "Sure you don't want your little Jessie to help you?"

"Get out!"

Still chuckling to herself, Jessie gathered up her poke and the empty plate and went to the doorway. "I'm sorry, Jebediah," she said, turning back. "I guess I really am a mean and wicked woman. But only 'cause I like you."

"*Out!*"

Jessie blew him a kiss and left, closing the door behind her.

Jebediah threw himself on his bed, and as he willed himself calm, a sadness came over him. Jessie meant no harm. She was simply a pretty girl coming into season and looking about for the right man. Sometimes Jebediah wished he could be the *wrong* man, the wrong *kind* of man, the kind who took his pleasure where he found it, said to hell with the consequences for others, and refused to be tied down.

But he was not. And that was how a slave was so often held in bondage, he reminded himself. How much chance did a slave have of escaping to freedom with a wife and children in tow? Oh, he knew it had been done, but what were the odds? His mother, too frail to attempt escape, had died to give him a chance at freedom, and he would not let that sacrifice be meaningless.

No, he would remain free of all ties. Charleston meant a new and better chance of finding the Underground Railroad that he had heard so much about. It meant a chance to meet one of those sea captains who were said to smuggle runaway slaves north. And when his chance came, Jebediah would let nothing hold him back. Nothing.

Race Week, the culmination of the "gay season," with its many parties and concerts and balls, came late that year, and it was on a blustery afternoon in early March that Duke encountered Miss Amity Sabre at the Washington Race Course.

He was slightly acquainted with the Sabres, and he had spoken to Miss Amity's older sister, Lucy, and her uncle Joel in the grandstand earlier that day. Miss Lucy, a tall, blonde spinster with an aristocratic mien and so-blue eyes, had been politely distant. Mr. Joel, however, had, as always, been quite cordial. "Good to see you, boy, good to see you!" A chunky, graying man of about fifty, he had given Duke a spine-shattering thump on the back. "Say, those field hands you sold us last spring? Worked out just fine! Gonna need some more! Gotta see my jockey now—if that boy don't win the next race, I'm gonna flay him alive!"

Mr. Joel was proof to Duke that *real* aristocrats—and who in the South was more aristocratic than the Sabres?—could accept Averys on equal terms.

Still, he was hardly prepared for the honor that Miss Amity did him. He had come down out of the grandstand between races, intending to place a few bets, when she tore through the crowd toward him. Her blue-gray eyes were hard, her jaw was set, and her mouth was meanly twisted: his first impression was that she was about to shove him out of her path. But then she came to a sudden halt. Recognition widened her eyes, and her mouth resumed its usual pretty shape.

"Mister . . . Mister . . . ?"

"Avery, Miss Amity," Duke said, whipping off his hat. "Leduc Avery."

"Oh, of *course*, Mr. Avery!" Miss Amity's eyes were no less hard, as she touched his arm, but her voice was honeyed. "Of *course*! I hadn't forgotten you!"

"I do hope you're enjoying—"

Before Duke could finish, another figure tore through the crowd toward them, a handsome youth in his early twenties.

"Miss Amity, honey—"

"If you say one more word to me, Quentin Kimbrough, I swear I shall never speak to you again!"

"But Miss Amity, honey—"

"There! You have said it!" Miss Amity's fingers tightened on Duke's arms, and her eyes implored him. "Mr. Avery, would you be so kind as to see me home? I vow, this here rude creature—"

"Amity, goddamnit!"

"You hear him, Mr. Avery? You hear how he cussed at me?"

"Please, Amity, be reasonable!"

"Mr. Avery?"

Duke had been looking forward to the final races of the day, but not for the world would he have missed this opportunity. To see Miss Amity Sabre home! It was as if he had suddenly been favored by an angel.

"Why, Miss Amity, I'd be honored!"

He started to lead her away, but the dismissed youth stepped before them. "Amity," he said angrily, "do you know who this here *is*?"

"More of a gentleman than you'll ever be, Mr. Quentin Kimbrough!"

Quentin glared at Duke. "A 'gentleman' more acquainted with Vendue Range than with a civilized drawing room, I can tell you that!"

In an instant, blood pounded in Duke's head and he was ready to kill. Duels had been fought over far smaller insults, and if Quentin Kimbrough refused to exchange shots with the likes of Duke Avery, Duke was quite ready to beat him into the dust of the race course.

But Miss Amity was tugging at his arm. "Pay no attention to this here lowlife, Mr. Avery. He is unworthy of our further thought."

Quentin tried one more time: "Miss Amity, honey, you know I didn't mean—"

"Good *day*, Mr. Quentin Kimbrough!"

Quentin gave her a despairing look, threw a look of sheer hatred at Duke, and turned on his heel to plow away through the crowd.

Amity giggled. "And now, Mr. Avery . . ."

"Miss Amity, if Mr. Kimbrough did something to offend you . . ."

"Oh, that boy, he makes me so angry sometimes. Ever since I told him my baby sister, Dulcy, was coming home from the North this spring, it's been Dulcy-this and Dulcy-that and 'Oh, my pretty little Dulcy, she must be all growed up by now,' and 'She always was the prettiest little thing,' and 'I just can't hardly wait to see that little Dulcy!' It's gone on, Mr. Avery, until I have just about gone out of my mind! Now, don't you misunderstand me, Mr. Avery, I do dearly lo-o-oove my little baby sister! But to hear Mr. Quentin Kimbrough and some of his friends go on and on and on about her the way they do! Really, Mr. Avery, it all finally becomes the very height of rudeness, and I finally told Quentin Kimbrough, I said, 'Mr. Kimbrough . . .' "

Duke paid little attention to what Amity was actually saying. It was enough that she was babbling on about her personal affairs and feelings as if they were old friends, and the words swept over him like glorious music. She did remind him, however, that there was a third Sabre sister, or rather a young half-sister, who for some obscure reason lived in the North, and he dimly recalled a gangly fourteen-year-old girl, big-eyed, coltish, and darkly pretty.

As Amity climbed into his carriage, fetched from the nearby park, Duke was aware of the eyes that were on them. In fact, he felt as if they were being watched during the whole drive down to Lynch Street, where the big Sabre house stood. He, Duke Avery, was delivering one of the most prominent belles of Charleston to her house, and he felt as if all the world knew it.

"And will you be at the Jockey Club Ball this evening, Mr. Avery?" Amity asked, as he assisted her down from the carriage.

"Why, I certainly will, Miss Amity. I wouldn't miss it for anything in the world."

"Well, don't you forget to ask me for a dance. In fact, you might ask me for two or three, if you care to and, if you'll pardon my French, *to hell* with Quentin Kimbrough!"

"I'd be proud to, Miss Amity!"

Great balls o' fire, he thought happily as he drove homeward, why had he ever, even in his darkest hour, doubted that his every dream would come true? How had he doubted that he would fulfill his every plan? Slave trader he might be, but his name was good, and hadn't Amity Sabre clearly shown that she preferred him to Quentin Kimbrough? Yes, high-and-mighty Mr. Kimbrough, heir to Kimbrough Hall!

By God, there would be an Avery Hall one day, on an Avery plantation, every bit as grand as . . .

A new possibility occurred to him.

Sabrehill!

My God, he thought, *was* it possible?

There were three Sabre sisters: Lucy, Amity, and Dulcy. They had no brothers and were unlikely to acquire one. Their twice-widowed father, old Aaron Sabre, was unlikely to marry again, and their uncle Joel had never married at all.

But Amity would surely marry.

And so would Dulcy.

They would probably marry important planters and leave Sabrehill for their husbands' homes. But suppose one or the other of them did not. It stood to reason that if one of them married a man who *did not have* a plantation, that man would one day take over Sabrehill—one of the finest plantations in the entire South.

Not that such a man, if he were Duke Avery, would bring nothing of his own to such a marriage. With his inheritance and the fortune he intended to make—far from it! But married to a Sabre, he would not have to invest in his own plantation. He could simply invest in Sabrehill, making it bigger and grander than ever. And what bride could object to that?

Amity or Dulcy, he thought. Was there any chance at all that he might marry one or the other? Amity was about his own age and wasn't likely to wait until he was through college—not that he wasn't willing to forego college in order to gain her hand—but Dulcy was two or three years younger. And Amity had said she was coming home soon.

And he mustn't over look Lucy. True, she was eight or ten years older than he and unlikely to marry—gossip said she still pined for a lover who had jilted her years before—but she was beautiful and human, and Duke was not altogether without faith in his charms. Looking into a mirror, he had observed the thick brown hair, the strong nose and chin, and the chiseled lips, and he had understood why he drew admiring glances.

Amity, Dulcy, and Lucy Sabre. As he drove into the side courtyard of his house, Duke felt as if his fate lay in their hands. It was a damned fool idea, he told himself, based on nothing more than a pleasant conversation, a drive to Lynch Street, and Amity's invitation to dance with her that evening at the Jockey Club Ball. Realistically, the odds were a thousand to one against that leading to anything.

But it could. It just might.

"That is one happy man tonight," Jessie said, as she and Jebediah watched Duke close the courtyard gate and disappear into the shadows of King Street. "Going be the handsomest man at the Jockey Club Ball, too."

Jebediah closed and locked the front door. There was little left to be done. He made sure there was firewood in all the downstairs fireplaces, and Jessie extinguished the last of the lamps. Old Mr. Avery was already long asleep, or at least abed, with a boy sleeping near him in case he needed help. The other servants had left, and the house was quiet. Mr. Duke had said there was no need for anyone to wait up for him.

Jebediah and Jessie went out through the pantry and the side door and descended the stone steps into the side courtyard. The only light came from the cook's quarters, and even as they watched, it went out.

"Well, ain't I lucky," Jessie said, laughing softly, "got me a beau to see me home in the dark."

Jebediah didn't answer. During the past twelve days, he had developed a habit of smiling, respectful silence toward the other servants. He answered their questions, but asked no more of his own than necessary. He laughed at their little jokes, but offered none in return. He was always pleasant, always ready to help the others in any way he could. He didn't want them to think that, simply because he was Mr. Duke's "boy," he considered himself in any way superior to them, and without undue humility, he deferred to one and all as having seniority over him in the household hierarchy. Thus he remained apart without seeming aloof. But Jessie presented a special problem, and now he had to face it again.

With a little shiver, she pulled her shawl tighter around her shoulders, then proprietarily took Jebediah's hand and drew his arm around her. "There, now," she said, "ain't that nicer?"

A week earlier, Jebediah would have thrust her away. Now, with a feeling of helplessness mingled with desire, he drew her closer against his side.

"Jebediah," she asked, as they walked slowly along the moonlit lane, "why you always running 'way from me?"

"Am I running away from you now, Jessie?"

"Been running ever since you got here."

But not fast enough. It was all very well to tell himself that he must form no ties, but what was he to do when suddenly, after years, love was held out to him? When he learned that, in spite of all the brutality and pain and hatred he had suffered, he still hungered for the common affections?

Jessie had taught him that. Jessie, whose hands seemed to heal old wounds and whose sweet smile and mischievous eyes brought booming laughter up out of his depths in spite of all his efforts to hold it back. Whose behavior revealed nothing when they were in the presence of others, but who teased and mocked him, cheered and delighted him, whenever they were alone. She made a point of bringing his breakfast to him each morning so that they could share at least those few minutes. And the night the worst of his bad dreams had come—the one where he saw his mother's dead body lying in the field, while the buzzards descended upon it—Jessie had heard his cries and come running to him, allowing him to cling to her until his tears ceased and the dawn fog rolled in.

After twelve days, he had no doubt that if he had met Jessie in freedom she might very well have become his woman. Now he dared not love her.

When they reached her door, she turned and wrapped her arms around him, laying her head against his chest. "When you go," she whispered, "you take me with you?"

His heart seemed to pause for an instant. "Go where, Jessie?"

"I ain't forgot them scars. You still a runner, Jebediah."

"Twelve days can change a lot of things."

"You ain't going change in a hundred years."

"But Mr. Duke has been very good to me—"

"And I 'member you telling me I ain't got no reason to be grateful to no white man. 'You owe them nothing,' you tole me, 'nothing!' " She raised her eyes to his. "Don't you go without me, Jebediah."

"Jessie, I haven't any luck. I've never been able to get away on my own, and I could never do it with you."

"But I can help you! I go to Market Street and the wharves 'most every day! I know people, I talk to people—"

"Jessie, I'm mighty fond of you, but I don't want to hear anymore about running away, you understand?"

She stared into his eyes for a long moment as if trying to read his thoughts. She nodded.

"I'd better say good night, Jessie."

"Kiss me."

For all their increasing intimacy, not once had he kissed her. In fact, only rarely in his life had his lips pressed gently and lovingly against those of a woman he truly cared for, and he hardly knew how to go about it or what to expect. With one hand, he tilted her head back. He bent down over her. Uncertainly, tentatively, their lips met. And then, as one warm mouth moved on the other, there was no stopping the abrupt surge of his desire and the instant quickening of his flesh.

She, too, felt it, his and her own, and after a moment she drew her lips away. She sobbed, almost as if in pain. She was breathing hard, and her eyes looked blurred in the moonlight, but her body remained against his, rolling slightly and pressing rhythmically against him, and they kissed again.

This time, when her mouth left his, she stepped away from him. Her forehead fell against his chest. When she spoke, Jeb could barely hear her beyond the pounding of blood in his head.

"Ain't hardly nine o'clock yet, Jebediah," she said. "He won't be back for least four hours. That's plenty time. You want to . . . come in . . . ?"

He knew what she was offering, and he wanted desperately to accept. Even if he had not been fond of Jessie, he was a man of twenty-two years who had largely been deprived for the last four. But he knew that if he yielded to his desire, he would never be able to leave Jessie behind. That was her price, and even if it meant losing any last chance at freedom, he would have to pay it.

He forced himself to shake his head. With a little cry, Jessie threw herself back against him and sought his lips. "No, Jess . . ."

For a moment, he gave himself up to her again, but

when she began to fumble his clothes open, he forced himself to thrust her away. "Jessie, it can't be."

"Jes' for a little while—"

"No, Jessie!"

She stared at him as if, once again, he had struck her. Pain came to her eyes, but she quickly averted them. She went up the three steps to her door. She didn't look at him again until she was in her doorway.

"Jebediah, you say you fond of me. And you know I'm mighty fond of you too. But you think I ain't got my pride? I ain't going to ask you 'gain."

His voice stuck in his throat. "I'm sorry, Jessie."

She slowly closed the door.

In the darkness of his room, he quickly, angrily flung his clothes off. He opened the shutters of his window and pushed back the old dimity curtains Jessie had dug up for him somewhere. He put a couple of corn-shuck pillows against the wall behind his bed, then sat back against them, welcoming the cool evening air against his naked body. Passion was already beginning to curdle into sickness and pleasure into a pain low in his gut.

He was a fool, he thought. A fool not to take what Jessie offered, a fool to think he would owe her anything if he did. He could return to her room right now, and though she might protest, she would let him in.

And after he had got what he wanted . . .

No. He wouldn't be able to desert her. He already cared for Jessie too deeply, and he would never be able to betray whatever love she might have for him.

Then why didn't he stay here with her?

The thought came as a shock, and he wanted to deny that it had any meaning for him. But it came to him again.

Why didn't he forget his mad dream of freedom and simply stay here in peace and comfort with Jessie?

It was a denial of all he had lived by for four years. But wasn't he a fool to think he could ever find freedom? Hadn't he proved again and again that freedom was beyond his reach?

Jessie wanted him. He wanted her. Dear Lord, he thought, how he wanted her, and not just for a night. Even if he succeeded in gaining his freedom, he might spend the rest of his life searching and never find another Jessie. And he wanted . . . how he wanted . . .

He must have slept, however lightly. But the chink of metal, so distant as to be almost inaudible, brought him instantly awake: It was the wrong sound for that time of night. He would hardly have known he had slept if the moon hadn't set, leaving the room darker.

Mr. Duke, he thought. Mr. Duke had returned and had entered the side courtyard. But why not the front? The instinct for survival, developed in the field, kept Jeb listening.

Footsteps. No more than a soft grating on the cobblestones, but Jebediah heard them. Mr. Duke, if that was who it was, had not entered the house but was coming down the lane. But why, at this hour of the night?

Jebediah got up from his bed and hurried to the side of the window. And, yes, the dark figure that moved by could only be Mr. Duke. He seemed almost jaunty, as if the evening had exceeded his best expectations.

Jebediah heard a sharp double tap on a door. As he looked cautiously out the window, he saw the dark figure enter Jessie's room. He heard the door close.

No!

He felt so sick he almost sank to the floor. But surely Mr. Duke would leave at once. He probably only wanted to give Jessie some forgotten instruction. Surely there was nothing between them.

He waited, growing sicker by the minute.

After an hour, he returned to his bed. He did not sleep, but continued to stare at the open window. Only two walls separated his and Jessie's rooms, and it seemed to him that he could almost hear Mr. Duke and Jessie at their pleasures.

Now he understood why Jessie had said they had four hours. Of course: They had had *only* four hours. After that, she would become Mr. Avery's plaything again.

As she had tried to make him hers.

A growl of rage tore through Jebediah's throat, and he flung himself from the bed. He picked up a piece of kindling from the floor by the Ben Franklin stove. He would kill Mr. Duke Avery. He would charge into Jessie's room now, just as he was, naked, and he would kill the slaver and his nigger whore. He would kill them, kill them. . . .

But he knew he would not. He dropped the piece of kindling and threw himself back on his bed. Gradually his angry sobs eased.

He was still awake when, near dawn, Mr. Duke Avery walked back along the lane.

It didn't matter, he told himself. At least he was free of Jessie. Free to run. And he would stay that way.

⊸⊷ 4 ⊷⊸

FROM THE VERY FIRST evening, Jebediah had sensed that
Jessie enjoyed a special position in the household, and now
that he knew what it was, he cursed himself for a fool.
Why hadn't he realized from the very beginning? Surely
Mr. Duke Avery had made more than one visit to Jessie's
room in the last two weeks. He told himself he had no
right to be angry with Jessie, only with his own naiveté,
and yet as he dressed in the gray light of early dawn, he
found himself muttering *Bitch! Bitch! Bitch!* and feeling
the pain of betrayal.

He heard Jessie pass his room, and a few minutes later
she stood outside his door with two plates of food. She
gave him an uncertain smile and a soft " 'Morning, Jebediah," and he came outside and took one of the plates.

"Aren't you worried," he said, as they sat down on the
steps to eat, "that Mr. Duke will see us together and get the
wrong idea?"

She looked at him wonderingly, for he had never before
raised the question. "No harm in us eating together like
this. 'Sides, he trust me."

He couldn't hold back his short, ironic laugh. She stared
at him.

"You angry with me, Jebediah?"

"Why should I be angry with you?"

She didn't answer, but continued eating, slowly, as if her
food had lost its flavor. He should keep silent, he knew;
he had meant to act as if nothing out of the ordinary had
happened. But in spite of all resolve, pain welled up, driving him to speak.

"What right have I to be angry, Jessie? After all, what's
the difference between you and me? Me, a white man's
slave-lackey, and you, a white man's slave-whore?"

For an instant Jessie seemed to stop breathing. She put

50

down her fork and stared at her plate. "Reckon you didn't know 'bout me and Mr. Duke," she said after a moment.

"Reckon I was stupid."

"Maybe so," she said in the same soft, even voice. "But that don't make me . . . what you said."

Only pain could have wrenched the words from him: "No? Then what did you want from me last night? And how many others have you asked to spread you when he wasn't looking?"

Her long, grave stare seemed to probe him. Her eyes grew moist, but not a drop fell from them.

"I 'member that first day you come here," she said at last. " 'Member that morning you slap my face. I thought you was somebody special." She looked away and stood up. "Well, I was wrong. And you was right—a few days sure do make a difference."

She walked away unhurriedly, her back straight and her head high, leaving him in the bitter wasteland somewhere between hatred and love.

After that, she stopped bringing him his breakfast. Though she was never less than pleasant, she rarely looked directly at him, never spoke to him unnecessarily, and avoided being alone with him. It was just as well, he told himself; but still, conscience nagged at him until, after a week or so, he found himself alone with her in the pantry and could say: "Jessie, I've been wanting to tell you—I'm sorry!"

She smiled her usual soft, sweet smile. "Why, that's all right, Jebediah."

"No. I had no right to speak to you as I did. And, Jessie . . ." He knew he was unwise to speak freely, but he wanted to regain her respect, so he plunged ahead. "Maybe I haven't changed as much as you think. I've got stripes that you can't even see. Stripes that will never heal."

She nodded as if she understood. But, even so, she was not at his door with his breakfast the next morning, and their old intimacy was not recovered. As much as possible, he avoided thinking about her, and if Mr. Duke visited her in the night, Jeb was asleep and didn't hear his footsteps.

His days passed quickly and pleasantly enough, for his duties were light. He cleaned and pressed Mr. Duke's clothes and polished his boots. He frequently accompanied him about the city and occasionally on longer trips—to Georgetown and Beaufort and Savannah. He helped with housework—with dusting and minor repairs and shopping for provisions. He occasionally prepared a toddy for Mr. Duke's daddy in the evening. And when his day was done and he was no longer needed, he often retired for a quiet half hour in the jessamine-covered gazebo, far back in the gardens and away from the main house and the service lane.

It was there, one evening in early April, when Mr. Duke had left the city for a day or two, that Jessie came to him. The night was so dark that he didn't see her standing outside the gazebo until she whispered his name. When he answered, she entered the archway and sat down on the bench beside him, drawing his arm around her shoulders as if they had never quarreled.

In that moment he was drawn back to the hour before his disillusionment. He had wanted her then, and he wanted her still, and for a moment all his defenses dropped. Without a thought of what he was doing, he tilted back her head to kiss her. Their mouths met and, as boldly as if he owned her, he explored the softness of her body. With a little moan, she slid a hand over his thigh, and galvanic pleasure shot through him.

When their mouths finally parted, he leaned back on the bench, his mind reeling, and her forehead fell onto his chest.

"Jebediah?" she said after a moment, "you change your mind? You want . . . ?"

Why not? he thought hopelessly. Hadn't he learned his lesson? What chance did he have of ever being free? Why not give up and take whatever Jessie offered?

But she was not his woman and never would be. And, like her, he had his pride.

He pushed her away and sat up. "I shouldn't have done that. I don't share a wench with anyone."

"You don't have to. He don't come to me no more. Not since . . . that night."

Jeb found that hard to believe. "What keeps him away?"

"I tole him I don't do it in Lent. Not even on Sunday."

Thinking she must be joking, he tried to make out her face in the dark. In spite of himself, he laughed. "And you mean to tell me he doesn't *make* you?"

She shook her head, and he dimly saw her sweet smile. "Jebediah, you still don't understand 'bout Mr. Duke, do you? He don't like to *make* people do things. He comes to my bed 'cause he bought me for that and 'cause he likes me. And I let him, 'cause *I* like *him* and 'cause Madam Lareina teach me that's what I'm s'pose to do. But if I put him off, he ain't going *force* me!" In a low, soft voice, she added, "You don't want me to, Jebediah, I don't never do it with him again."

"And how are you going to put him off come Easter?"

"Tell him it's the wrong time of the month. And after that, tell him I'm sick. And after that," she smiled as if they shared a secret, "maybe you and me be gone by then, Jebediah."

He shook his head. "We aren't going anywhere."

"But maybe you wrong! 'Member I said maybe I can help you?"

He remembered that she had said something about inquiring among her friends on Market Street and along the wharves.

"Well, I think I found somebody can get us away! You see, for a long time I been hearing how some ship cap'ns that sail 'tween up north and here and the islands . . ."

Skeptically at first but with growing interest, Jebediah listened to her story. During her five years in Charleston she had made a number of acquaintances whom she thought she could trust, and for the last few weeks she had been carefully, discreetly questioning them, trying to find out who the slave-smuggling ship captains were. She had had no luck. But often she had been told to ask this or that other person, and finally she had realized that the person most often mentioned was a certain Aunt Ora—who worked for the Averys on Vendue Range.

At first she had thought that she was being teased, because Aunt Ora was just an old fortune-telling conjure woman who did menial jobs. But finally she had made overtures to the old woman. "Don't know what you talking 'bout," Aunt Ora had said. "Who tell you I know 'bout such things?"

Jessie had mentioned names.

"No, no, no, no, don't know such people. Don't know no sea cap'ns. You go 'way now, or I put badmouth on you."

"But everybody says—"

"Don't care. You jes' a silly gal anyway." Aunt Ora had frowned and given Jessie an evil look. "You know the one, the whip take his back and his momma strew the field with her blood?"

Jessie had thought of Jebediah's back.

"You send him to me and I conjure him 'way. I make him *imbisible*, and he fly 'way on the back of the brown dove."

"If I bring him, can I go with him?"

"I don't say no more." The old woman had pointed a bony finger at her and commanded sternly: *"You bring him!"*

The dark masked Jebediah's rising excitement. "On the back of the *brown dove*," the old woman had said. Evidently the words meant nothing special to Jessie—just conjure woman talk—but to Jebediah, as to many other slaves, they meant the Underground Railroad. For the Gullah word for the *brown dove* was *adaba*—and Adaba was said to be the name of a "conductor" who was notorious for taking slaves north to freedom.

For years, Jebediah had looked for the Underground Railroad, when he could, hardly believing that it—or Adaba—really existed. Now it seemed not only to exist but to be aware of him and to be reaching out to him.

"You take me with you, won't you, Jebediah?"

He was grateful to Jessie, but he was taking no unnecessary risks. Aunt Ora had made Jessie no promises, and the brown dove would be carrying only one passenger.

He affected a sneer: "An old conjure woman!"

"But I'm sure she can help us!"

"Fly us away on a brown dove?"

He could hear the pain and disappointment in her voice. "Then you won't talk to Aunt Ora?"

"To a crazy old woman? Jessie . . ." He tried to put his arms around her, thinking he could silence her with a kiss, but she moved away from him.

"Now maybe you like being Mr. Duke's slave-lackey?" She sounded on the verge of tears.

"No, but it's better than the fields and Mr. Wingate's drivers."

"Not in such a hurry to 'scape no more?"

Jeb was silent.

"No, not in such a hurry." Her tone of mockery deepened. "Get fed good every day, got good clothes, don't work too hard. Mr. Duke going have the tailor make you a nice new livery, so the wenches say, 'My, ain't that Jebediah handsome!' Then Mr. Duke say, 'Jebediah, that pretty wench you want? I buy her for you!' And he buy you a wench, and pretty soon she give you a pretty little chile, and ain't you proud! And ain't Mr. Duke proud of his big handsome houseboy and his new housemaid and their sweet little pickaninny! Oh, Jebediah, ain't you glad Mr. Duke buy you and settle you down, and you don't have to worry 'bout running 'way and going north no more!"

For a time, the only sound was that of their breathing. Common sense told Jeb to remain silent, to tell Jessie nothing. But her words had stung him.

"Don't have to run no more? What do you know about running? What did you ever have to run from? Have you ever seen your mother fighting off her master while he tried to spread her? Have you seen her tied naked to the post for defying him? To be whipped and raped by the worst of the drivers, while you and your father were forced to watch?

"Have you seen your father go mad after that? Seen him whipped raw and bleeding for seeking revenge? And then seen him dying in agony from the flux, while nobody lifted a hand to help him?

"After that, my mother begged me to run away. Begged

time and again. But she was too sick and weak to go with me, and I couldn't leave her behind.

"So she cut her wrists, Jessie. Bled to death. Killed herself so that I'd be free to run. And our master, Mr. Osborne, left her body to rot in an open field—as a lesson to the other slaves. . . .

"So don't you tell me I'm not going north. Sooner or later, I'll find the Underground Railroad. And I'm going. My mother paid for the ticket."

She was almost hidden in the darkness, but he thought he heard her weeping.

"Take me with you, Jebediah," she said after a moment.

"I've told you. I can't."

"You take me, I do anything for you. I be your woman long as you want me. Cook and clean for you, take care of you. And then go 'way when you say, and you never see me 'gain. But you don't take me, Jebediah, I think I die."

"Die, Jessie?" Jebediah laughed. "Why should you die? I'll bet you've never even been whipped, not once in your life. Why, I've seen white women that don't have a quarter of what you've got—they make you look rich. Why would you want to give all that up to go north and live like a common nigger, wear hand-me-down clothes, work your fingers to the bone, and maybe not know where your next meal is coming from? You're no field nigger with a crazy head and a heart full of hatred, Jessie. You're just a sweet little colored gal who doesn't know how lucky she is."

"Lucky?" came the voice out of darkness. "You think I'm *lucky?*"

"A lot of people would think so, Jessie."

"Oh, yes—'cause Mr. Duke, he treats me *so* good, tells me how much he likes me, and all I got to do is bed down with him now and then. Lot better'n going into a whorehouse. . . . 'Course, one day he's going get hisself a nice white wife, and he says he got to love and respect that wife like a white man should—but that ain't going change nothing 'tween him and me! You ain't nothing but a sweet little ol' animal jes' like me, Jessie, he says. Ain't no white lady like I can love and respect, but, honey, you sure is fun to spread!

"Then one day he going give me a baby. Ain't no way he ain't going do that. And maybe he find out he don't like me so good no more. Maybe he ain't going like seeing his own little nigger chile running 'round the yard. Everything in this world that he owns, he going give to his white babies—his black babies, maybe he sell them 'way so he don't have to think 'bout them. Jes' sell 'em—*my babies!*

"And me? You know his white lady going hate me, try send me 'way. And even if she don't, I'm going get old, Jebediah. *Old!* And one day he's going say, 'What that old nigger whore doing 'round here? Sweet Jesus, get rid of her!' " She sobbed. "Oh, yes, I'm so lucky!"

Suddenly she had returned to him and was pounding on his chest with both fists. "Take me with you, Jebediah! I don't want to be a slave no more! I don't want my babies born in slavery, to live and die and be sold like animals! I rather kill them first!"

She gave one last pain-filled sob, and ran from the gazebo.

Jebediah sat motionless.

He remembered something Jessie had said that first morning after he had come to this house: *"I think you are one real bad nigger, Jebediah . . . and I think maybe you somebody I been waiting for."*

He thought of how his affection for her had grown through the first weeks and had never really vanished, even after he had learned about her and Mr. Duke. He thought of the surprising pain he had felt that night.

And all the time, he thought, smiling to himself, though he felt more like crying, all the time she had had something more than his big brown body on her mind. Something far more important. He laughed aloud.

He got up and left the gazebo. He knew he was probably about to make one of the worst mistakes of his life.

He went to Jessie's door. When he tapped, she didn't answer. He went in anyway.

Amity! Duke thought, as he observed himself in his bedroom mirror and adjusted his cravat. *Amity!* The name had a melody all its own, and he must have sung it to himself a thousand times since the evening of the Jockey Club Ball. How long ago had that been? Over seven weeks? Seven weeks and more since he had held her blonde loveliness in the crook of his arm while they circled the ballroom to the waltz and she whispered: "Now, don't you dare forget me while I'm away at Sabrehill, you naughty boy. I'm going to *insist* that my daddy bring us back to town right after Easter. I do believe there's to be a charity ball, and I'll expect to see you there, you hear me, now?"

Oh, how he had heard, and for over seven weeks he had been looking forward to this evening.

"How do I look?" he asked anxiously, turning from the mirror. "You sure this coat isn't too loose?"

"Why, I think you look downright beautiful," Jessie said. "Don't he, Jebediah?"

Tilting his head one way, then the other, Jebediah looked him over: Except for his white silk shirt and his pearl waistcoat, Duke was dressed entirely in black, and his coat and trousers were of a simple but elegant cut. Jebediah smiled faintly and briefly and nodded his approval. "You look fine, Mr. Duke. My compliments to your tailor."

Duke flushed with pleasure. He had learned that Jebediah didn't give praise lightly.

"Well, I thank you both. And I won't be needing you anymore tonight, so . . ."

Before leaving the house, Duke went to his father's room to say good night. "Sure I can't do anything for you before I go, Daddy?"

His father, sitting up in bed, smiled and closed his book. "No, if I need anything, the boy will get it." The boy, already asleep on his pallet in a corner, snored lightly, as if in response. "You look mighty handsome this evening, Leduc."

"Why, thank you, Daddy."

"Yes, sir, I'd be surprised if some young ladies weren't mighty impressed."

"Oh, well . . ."

Somehow Duke's father seemed to be aware—and pleased—that Duke hadn't been paying nocturnal visits to Jessie for quite some time. Of course, Duke realized guiltily, he had no idea of the true reason for that, or that the long Lenten abstinence 'would soon be over—maybe this very evening. He merely assumed that his son, being young and healthy, had naturally begun looking for a more suitable object of interest, and he wondered who she might be.

"You wouldn't have any particular young lady in mind, would you, Leduc?"

"Oh, I don't know. . . ." *Amity.*

"Come on, now. You don't mind an old dog's curiosity, do you? Can't you name a possibility or two?"

Duke felt embarrassed and pleased at the same time. He shrugged elaborately. "I don't know, Daddy. I sorta promised . . . Miss Amity Sabre . . . I'd be there tonight."

"Amity Sabre!" His father raised his eyebrows as if he were truly impressed. "Aaron's girl, Amity? Well, now! And you say you promised her?"

"Sorta." Duke's face burned and he couldn't keep from grinning.

"Well, my goodness. I used to know Aaron and Joel Sabre very well. If you should see those fine gentlemen, please give them my very best regards."

"I'll do that, Daddy."

He bent down and gave his father a quick peck on the forehead, then escaped out the doorway and down the stairs. He was heading for the front door when he heard Jessie's voice from the parlor.

". . . know you got reasons to hate white folks . . . but Mr. Duke, sometimes he's so sweet, a body jes' can't help liking him. Now, ain't that so, Jebediah?"

"Yes, Jessie . . . yes, that's so."

They liked him. His people. Duke's heart swelled painfully, and he hurried out the front door.

When they heard the click of the door, Jebediah and Jessie looked at each other. They didn't have to say a thing. Excitement showed bright in Jessie's eyes. She bit back a smile as if she might burst out in delighted laughter at any instant, and Jebediah's entire body quivered in anticipation.

Quickly, but with no show of haste, they completed their chores. When they went out into the courtyard, a couple of lamps still burned, but none that they had to worry about. As usual, they walked into the darkness of the lane together, taking their time. Each moment made it less likely that some forgotten detail would bring Mr. Duke back to the house.

At his door, Jebediah touched Jessie's shoulder and whispered, "Soon." She looked up at him, her eyes and her smile sparkling in the starlight. She nodded and walked on to her own room.

Jebediah waited in his room for only a few minutes, though they seemed like an hour. Then, cautiously, silently, moving in shadows, he left the room again and went to Jessie's door.

Not a glimmering of light showed at her window, for she had draped it heavily. There was only the dimmest, briefest flash to the outside, as he opened the door, stepped into the room, and closed the door again.

She was already undressed and sitting on the edge of the bed, holding a blanket before her. Her eyes brighter than ever, she gave a little cry of delight.

He rushed to her arms.

The night was beautiful and it was only a short distance to the St. Andrews Society Hall, up on Broad Street, so Duke walked. As he strode along, he had a wonderful sense of life opening up for him and of every step bringing him closer to Amity. Outside the hall, he lingered for a few minutes, watching the arriving carriages and looking for her. When she didn't appear, he went inside, left his top hat with a cloakroom attendant, and entered the crowded ballroom.

Clearly the ball, the first big affair since Race Week, was going to be a great success. As soon as the last fiddle of the orchestra was tuned up, the city intendent, Mr. Pinkney, introduced the governor, Mr. Hamilton, and Mr. Hamilton thanked one and all for their contributions to the fund for indigent widows and orphans. The orchestra began to play, and the ball was formally opened.

But where was Amity?

A little self-consciously, Duke walked around the room. It seemed as if every young person but he almost immediately had a dance partner. He looked for someone to talk to and wished he saw more people he knew. Surely there had been far more such people at the Jockey Club Ball—but, of course, his attention then had been almost exclusively on Amity.

When he had been turned down several times by polite young ladies who had already promised the dance to someone else, he began to feel a little out of place. His hands became uncomfortably damp, and he took to frequenting the punch bowl in order to appear busy. He even allowed himself to become a little angry with Amity: She had almost begged him, had extracted his firm promise to attend this ball, and wasn't that virtually a promise that she would be here too? He had been waiting for this evening all these weeks. . . .

After an hour he was tempted to leave. He had danced very little and had had little conversation—no one seemed particularly interested in talking to him. He could no longer deceive himself that he was having a good time.

And then, suddenly, miraculously, there she was.

It was as if the ball, a poor, dreary thing until that moment, had suddenly come to life. The chandeliers glittered, the waltz had a joyous bounce and sweep it had lacked before, and the room was aswirl with gaiety and laughter. And it was all, all because of Amity.

Already other acquaintances had gathered around, and he hurried toward her. He had no idea of when she might have arrived, for she sat in a corner with her family as if they had been there all along. Her uncle Joel and her father, tall, silver-haired Aaron Sabre, stood behind her. Her older sister, Lucy, sat beside her. And the girl standing along side could only be her once-gangly younger sister, Dulcy, now grown to a dark-eyed seventeen-year-old beauty.

How did you ask one sister to dance without slighting the others? But surely they would understand that Amity, too, had been looking forward to this moment.

He stood before her and bowed. "Miss Amity—ladies—"
He had spoken in such a rush, he hoped he hadn't interrupted anyone. Amity, leaning to one side in her chair, seemed to be trying to see around him.

"Mr. Aaron, Mr. Joel—"

"Good evening, Leduc."

"Mr. Avery," Lucy said, "do you remember my sister Dulcy?"

"Why, I surely do, and she's grown up mighty pretty!"

"Thank you, Mr. Avery."

"Mr. Aaron, I wonder if I might ask these ladies—ask Miss Amity—"

"Why, certainly, Leduc."

The moment had come at last. Duke bowed again. "Miss Amity, I wonder if you would do me the honor of this dance?"

Amity, frowning, continued to look past him, until Lucy gently shook her arm for attention.

Amity glanced at Lucy. "What?"

"Miss Amity—excuse me—Miss Amity, I wonder if I might have this dance."

She looked up at him irritably, and with a shock he remembered how hard her blue-gray eyes could be. "What is it?"

The orchestra was, after all, rather loud, and he leaned down toward her. "I'm sorry. I said, I wonder if I might have—"

But Amity was looking past him again, and at his elbow, Duke heard a familiar voice: "Miss Amity, with your father's permission, may I have the honor—"

"Miss Am—"

Amity's eyes widened with pleasure and a smile came to her face. She stood up and brushed past Duke. He wanted to protest that she hadn't heard him, that she didn't understand, and without thinking, he laid his hand on her forearm.

She threw a quick, angry look at him.

Quentin Kimbrough, smiling, said, "Boy, don't *do* that," and brushed his hand away.

Pleasure returned to Amity's eyes and the smile to her face, as, looking adoringly up at Quentin, she slid into his arms and they moved out onto the ballroom floor.

He couldn't believe it. This wasn't happening.

But it was, for it had been witnessed. Aaron Sabre looked exasperated, Miss Lucy flushed with anger, Miss Dulcy looked stricken. Only Joel Sabre appeared to have noticed nothing.

Duke looked back at Amity and Quentin on the dance floor. And he understood.

He had meant nothing to Amity at any time, except as a means of arousing Quentin Kimbrough's jealousy. That was the only reason she had asked him to be here—in case she should need him. But she didn't need him, and when he had appeared before her, he had only been in the way. In fact, she had hardly recognized him—he was the least of her most casual acquaintances.

He was, after all, only Leduc Avery. A fool and a boor.

The ballroom turned into a vast blur before his eyes. He muttered an "Excuse me" to whomever might hear and hurried for the front portals of the room, heedless of anyone he bumped into.

In the reception hall, he asked the attendent for his hat. He was about to leave, when he heard a voice behind him.

"Mr. Avery ... Leduc ..."

He looked around. It was Miss Lucy, hurrying toward him, concern in her eyes. "Leduc, are you all right?"

"Why, of course, Miss Lucy," he said, forcing a smile. "Why wouldn't I be?"

"I want to apologize for my sister. She can be so thoughtless, so unheeding—"

"No need, Miss Lucy, no need at all!"

She took his arm. "Leduc, please come back."

"Oh, I can't, Miss Lucy, I really can't. You see, my daddy has been awfully sick, and I only stopped by for a minute, just for a minute to pay my respects." He was conscious of babbling, but he couldn't stop himself. "To represent our family, you might say. You see, we believe in supporting worthwhile charities—"

"Leduc, please, just for a little while. I know Dulcy would like to dance with you, and so would I."

Somehow her sympathy only made the pain worse. "I can't, Miss Lucy. Thank you, but I just can't! My daddy . . . sick . . ."

Pulling away from her, he hurried for the door. Behind him, he heard her soft, pitying voice: "Oh, Leduc . . ."

Outside, he hurried to the dark doorway of St. Finbar's Cathedral, only a few yards away. There he stood hidden in shadows for a few minutes, pounding on the door with his fist. It seemed as if all the once-promising doors in the world were slamming shut in his face.

But he remembered one that was still open.

He headed back home.

Whether Jebediah truly loved Jessie, or she him, he couldn't have said, and it hardly seemed to matter: On that first evening when he had gone to her dark room, they had pledged themselves to each other. He had entered the room and joined her on the bed, where she lay weeping. He had kissed her wet face, her eyes, her mouth. As her weeping subsided, he had loosened her clothes. Then he had shrugged off his own clothes and before long had gently, carefully taken her.

It had been like nothing else he had ever known, that coupling in the dark. He had had little previous experience, but when it was over, he had known that this was the way it should be and that, without a word being spoken, a mutual vow had been taken. For now at least, and perhaps forever, they were one.

The next day they had gone looking for Aunt Ora, but it was over a week before they managed to speak to her. He and Jessie were occasionally sent out to do marketing together, and on that particular morning they encountered her while she was buying victuals for Mr. Sam Avery. Amid the crowded, noisy shops and stands of the marketplace, surrounded by more black faces than white, they could talk discretely.

"Jessie tells me you can conjure us away on the back of a brown dove. Can you really do that, Aunt Ora?"

Aunt Ora shook her ancient head vigorously. "*You*, boy, *you!* Ain't going conjure for no no-good gal!"

"Don't call her no-good, Aunt Ora—"

"Mr. Duke no-good darkie gal! Aunt Ora know 'bout her same as 'bout you. The *loa* tell the *mamaloi*—"

"She's not Mr. Duke's, Aunt Ora, she's mine, and where I go, she goes."

Aunt Ora stared at him as if reluctant to believe that the voodoo spirits—or her sources of gossip—could be mistaken. "True?"

"True."

"I jes' got to go with Jebediah, Aunt Ora," Jessie said, "I jes' got to!"

The old woman still looked skeptical. "Maybe. Maybe. I conjure the brown dove, then you see."

"When will he come, Aunt Ora?" Jebediah asked.

"He come from far. I tell you when he come. Maybe soon."

This morning she had told him: She had "conjured" the brown dove to Charleston, and within a few days, if they were lucky, he would carry them away on his back.

"And we ain't never coming back here again, ain't that right, Jebediah?" Jessie said now, as she held him in her arms. She was lying back on her pillows in the dim lamplight, and his head was on her shoulder.

"That's right," he said, "we're going all the way to Canada and never coming back."

"I be scared to go without you, Jebediah."

"When we get there, honey, you'll never have to be scared again."

She laughed softly and he smiled. In all his growing years he had never conceived of the pleasures she had given him in the last few weeks, and he had done his best to return them all. He had also learned how pleasure, affectionately shared, could weld bonds far stronger and deeper than a mere blissful shiver or the thrust of a man's hard flesh.

"Jessie," he mumbled, half asleep, "what do you want to do when we get to Canada? Think you might marry me?"

She laughed again and kissed the top of his head. "If

that's what you want. Told you I'm your woman long as you want me."

"Good. Because I don't ever want to lose you."

Her arm tightened around him. "Then you ain't ever going lose me."

"I'll always take care of you, Jes—"

He heard the door flung open. Raising his head, he saw Jessie's eyes widen with shock. He rolled onto his elbow and looked around.

Mr. Duke was racing toward him. He was carrying a long black whip, the butt reversed so that he held it like a club. He raised it above his head. His face was twisted with anger and hatred.

In that moment, Jebediah felt all the futility of his dreams, all the unfairness of the universe, all the treachery of the gods. Once again he was being cheated, robbed, betrayed. He heard himself roar, as much out of rage at the injustice as out of fear of what was to come: *"No!"*

As he lifted an arm to protect himself, he saw the whip butt come smashing down.

⊸⊷ 5 ⊶⊷

THE WHIP CAME DOWN like a great claw that tore over his back from shoulder to buttock. He fought against his scream and, lifting himself with his arms, tried to drag his naked body over the paving stones in a futile attempt to escape. The whip came down again, clawing, tearing, burning, and he could hold back his scream no longer.

He looked wildly about. He was in the lane, with no idea of how he had got there: He had simply seen the whip butt descending, felt the explosive impact, and then, as his head cleared, felt the pain of the whip. A couple of torches now illuminated the lane, and some servants were cautiously advancing. He heard Jessie's cries, and, looking over his shoulder, he saw her in the doorway, clutching a blanket around her body.

"God damn you, nigger," came Duke Avery's voice from somewhere above him, "you stay on your goddamn belly!" and the claw came down again, as he scrambled like a wounded animal over the harsh, flesh-cutting stones; "God damn you, lie still for it!" and a boot slammed between his legs, bringing new agony—kicking, stamping, grinding, trying to mutilate his genitals.

"Leduc! Leduc!"

At first Mr. Ben's harsh voice was unrecognizable. Jebediah saw him coming out of the house, still pulling on his robe, and hurrying along the lane, but his approach only caused Duke Avery to bring down the whip with new fury—faster and harder—and each time Jebediah tried to rise up from the pavement, the great burning claw slashed him down again.

"Leduc, no more! I tell you, no more!"

"I'll kill them!" Duke Avery sobbed. "I'll kill them both! I'm going to geld this son of a bitch, and then I'll cut his guts out—"

67

"You'll do nothing of the kind!"

"—and then I'll cut up this whore's face so that nobody can ever stand to look at her again!"

Jebediah rolled onto his side just in time to see Mr. Ben hit his son across the face, a long sweeping blow, open-handed, that sounded like a board hitting a rock. Duke Avery reeled back and nearly fell.

Mr. Ben grabbed his shirtfront. "You'll do nothing of the kind!"

"I saved her from being sold into a whorehouse! I took him out of the field—"

"They owe you nothing!"

"He was spreading her! Screwing her like the goddamn whore she oughta been—"

Mr. Ben gave his son a hard shake and lifted his right hand as if to hit him again. "For God's sake, boy, grow up. They're not your goddamn toys! You're not their god! They've got minds and bodies and needs of their own! You can't buy fidelity, you can't even earn it! If they want each other, that's their business! They never asked to be your slaves!"

Duke Avery thrust his father away. "They turned on me! Like goddamn animals! And I'm going to teach them—"

Once again, Duke Avery raised the whip, raised the handle high over his head, and Jebediah shrank from the blow. But it never came.

"By God, Leduc," Mr. Ben said, his voice shaking with passion, "if you hit that boy again, you're no son of mine!"

Duke Avery's whip hand wavered. "Daddy, you get back from me!"

"You're no son of mine!" Mr. Ben repeated. "Christ, boy, I've tried to teach you! *You're* the one who made a whore of the poor bitch, and when she finds a man she really wants, you try to maim and kill him!"

Duke Avery's eyes still burned with hatred, but after a moment the whip hand slowly came down.

"I want you to promise me, Leduc, you'll do nothing more to hurt these two. No whipping, no hurt of any kind, you won't lay a hand on them. Now, you swear to me!"

"All right. I promise. But I'm going to lock them up so they can't run, and then by God I'm going to get rid of them!"

"Fine. You do that. And God knows, they'll be well rid of you!"

He had lost again. There would be no brown dove now, no flight to freedom. *Jessie,* he thought, looking down at the shackles on his wrists and ankles, *Jessie, I'm sorry.*

"So it didn't work out," Sam Avery said to Duke. Sam was circling Jebediah and looking him over, as they stood in the courtyard of Avery Brothers.

"No, it didn't work out. I told him that if it didn't I'd sell him as a house servant. But I wouldn't put this treacherous bastard in anybody's house."

Sam Avery laughed. "Well, I tried to tell you there must be some reason he'd been put into the fields. All right, Muley, lock him up."

Muley pushed him toward a door, but he couldn't go yet. He and Mr. Duke hadn't exchanged a single word that morning, but he had to know about Jessie. He forced himself to say, "Please . . . is Jessie . . . ?"

"Never you mind about Jessie, boy. Jessie is none of your business, not now or anytime. Sam, you can put him to work—the hardest work you can find. Make him earn his keep. And, boy . . ." Duke Avery gave him a long, hard look. "I promised my daddy I wouldn't whip you any more for anything that's already happened. But if you slack or shirk, that's a different matter. And ol' Muley here would just dearly love to have your ass."

The next day and every day thereafter, six days a week, he was hired out to the city of Charleston to work on the streets. It was hard, back-breaking work, as hard as any Jebediah had ever done—paving streets with ballast stones brought in by sailing ships; clawing up the paving stones of older streets, often with bloody hands, and then resetting them—and any faltering brought Muley's vengeful whip down on his back.

He worked a day, a week, three weeks. He lost count. He worked under a scorching sun and in pouring rain. He

worked from "day clean" to "first dark" on barely enough
mush and hog fat to keep alive. The city of Charleston
demanded value for its money.

The few weeks with the Avery household receded into
the past like a dream. They seemed like no more than a
few days, the briefest of respites in his years of labor, a
little rest between his last master and his next. Even Jessie
came to seem like a dream, an illusion of happiness that
could never have really existed.

Then one evening when he returned exhausted to Vendue Range—he thought it must be sometime in June—he
found himself confronted in the courtyard by Mr. Duke
Avery.

"Well, Jeb, boy," he said with a grin, "I've got news for
you. You've spent your last day wrestling paving stones.
Tomorrow you leave Charleston—for good!"

Coffle!

Every slave knew the word. Every slave feared it.

The next morning, before dawn, Jebediah was brought
out into the courtyard. There he and nine other male slaves
were handcuffed in pairs and fitted with padlocked iron
collars connected by chains. They made up the first section
of the coffle.

He couldn't see how large the coffle was—probably forty
or fifty slaves. Some of the women wore rope halters rather
than chains, and a few of the younger slaves were allowed
to walk unfettered, sometimes along side their mothers.
The supply wagon was driven by a pair of manacled slaves.

As dawn began to color the sky, they walked up King
Street onto the Charleston Neck. They had no idea of
where they were being taken—to Atlanta or Birmingham
or Columbus, perhaps. Jebediah's knowledge of geography,
like that of most slaves, was hazy; but he did know that
every year thousands of slaves were torn away from family
and friends and transported from Virginia to the Deep
South and from the eastern coastal states to the West. Now
he was part of that great forced migration.

The late fall and winter was the best time of the year for
coffles; this was very nearly the worst. As the day turned

hot and steamy, feet began to drag and the whip began to fall. There were, as far as Jebediah could see, only two guards, besides Mr. Duke, both of them on horseback; but they were enough to keep the coffle moving, for every slave who felt the lash urged the others on.

Every couple of hours they were allowed a short rest, and in the early afternoon they were led off the road to some nearby woods. There, still chained, they were allowed to relieve themselves, and they were fed dry cornbread, which they washed down with water from a nearby stream. They were told to rest, but it seemed to Jebediah that he had hardly closed his eyes when they were ordered back on their feet.

By late afternoon, they were marching through a kind of hell. The iron collar chafed Jebediah's neck, and his chains seemed to have grown a dozen times heavier. Though the guards called for silence, a constant moaning sound arose from the coffle. The only relief, and it was a small one, came with the lowering and setting of the sun.

Then, when it seemed they could endure no more, Jebediah realized the coffle was again leaving the road. They were led behind a large, ramshackled old building with a faded sign of a rooster hanging over the front door. Keegan's Roost, one of the slaves said knowingly, a bad place.

Mr. Keegan, a tall, fat, bald man with squinting eyes, seemed to have expected them and to be ready to make a dollar. With the help of his hatchet-faced wife, a couple of sullen slaves, and a slatternly white wench, he saw to it that they were served cold mush on shingles, to be eaten with unwashed fingers. Then, one group at a time, they were allowed to drink from the well, sharing a single cup. From there, they were led to a trench latrine to relieve themselves, and finally, still in chains, they were allowed to make themselves as comfortable as they could on the bare ground while they waited for morning.

At dawn the hell began all over again, and Jebediah knew it might well go on for weeks. Again, they were served mush on shingles—the same, unwashed shingles they had used the evening before. They were allowed to go to the well and to use the trench, and then once again they were on the dusty road.

The second day seemed even longer than the first. In the afternoon a sudden rainstorm burst. The guards and Mr. Duke could huddle under their slickers, but the coffle slaves, quickly soaked to the skin, could only wade on through the mud, while the whips urged them to cover another mile, and another, and another.

After an hour the rain stopped. The sun reappeared and began to sink in the west with agonizing slowness.

The stars had long been out when they turned south off the road. They went through an open gateway and followed a long, broad avenue, great oak trees on each side, up a rise toward a house. The night was too dark, and Jebediah was too weary, to observe much, but the house seemed to be a large brick two-and-a-half story place, crowned with a cupola. Lamps shone in some of the windows, and a portico at each end of the house led to a well-lit outbuilding. Jebediah guessed that, if the house conformed to the usual pattern, there would be a pillared piazza on the far side and a stretch of lawn sloping down to a river.

"Why, I 'member this here place," the slave at Jebediah's side said wonderingly. "Was here with massa long time ago."

"You were?" Jebediah asked. "Do you know where we are?"

" 'Course I know. This here, it call Sabrehill."

Now at last, Duke thought, he was going to have his vengeance, the vengeance he had hungered for from the moment he realized that Jebediah had become Jessie's lover. Now at last he was going to exact payment for all he had suffered and all he had lost on that spring evening. His father had made him promise never again to lay a hand on either Jebediah or Jessie for what they had done, and he would keep his word. But there were still ways.

After all, Duke thought, what business is it of mine what happens to them after they're sold?

The avenue from the road led to a circular courtyard,

from each side of which extended a service lane between the numerous outbuildings. The coffle had been expected, and Mr. Turnage, the overseer of Sabrehill, led it along the torch-lit east lane toward a large brick barn where the slaves were to spend the night.

"Don't worry about them," Mr. Joel said. "Mr. Turnage will see that they get fed and bedded down. You go on into the house—my nieces are looking forward to seeing you."

Duke was surprised. "I didn't think they'd be here at this time of the year."

"Oh, we're not much for city living—except maybe Amity. And after three years up north, Dulcy has been looking forward to being at Sabrehill."

Duke had no great desire to see the Sabre sisters—one of them the cause of his humiliation, the other two its witnesses—but Miss Lucy greeted him in the passage of the big house as if that incident had entirely slipped her mind.

"Mr. Avery! Leduc! How nice to see you again—we hardly ever see you here at Sabrehill."

"Well, Mr. Joel said something last winter about needing a few more hands. . . ."

"Leila," Miss Lucy said to a pretty colored wench, "is Mr. Avery's room ready for him? He'll want hot water for a bath. I don't suppose you've had supper, have you, Leduc?"

"Why, no—"

"Tell Momma Lucinda that Mr. Avery will want supper, Leila." Miss Lucy called through a doorway: "Dulcy! Come out here, dear. Mr. Avery is here!"

A hand appeared on the edge of the doorway. Then, slowly, dark hair, a sparkling eye, an impish smile. Dulcy Sabre stepped out into the passage, and though she was rather tall and thin, with a dark complexion, Duke thought she was about the prettiest thing he had ever seen.

"I don't think Mr. Avery wants to see me," she said, and even her voice had a kind of dark, soft music. "Last time we met, he wouldn't even stay long enough to dance with me."

"That was a bad mistake on my part, Miss Dulcy," he said, "and I apologize for my rudeness."

Holding up a hand, Dulcy came toward him. "Just don't let it happen again, Mr. Avery, or I don't know how I'll ever forgive you."

"Why, Miss Dulcy . . ."

Taking Dulcy's hand, Duke found himself unable to speak. He realized that Lucy and Dulcy were trying to make amends for what had happened at the ball. He also realized that they need not have bothered and that Dulcy, at least, was genuinely glad to see him for his own sake. Nothing else could have explained the pleasure in her eyes.

He bent forward and brushed her fingertips with his lips.

Amity Sabre chose that moment to come down the passage stairs. "Well, my goodness, do we have a visitor? Dulcy, why didn't you tell me my dear friend Mr. Avery was here, you bad—"

She broke off. For a moment neither Duke nor Dulcy bothered to look at her, but continued to gaze into each other's eyes.

When Duke did look around, Amity's blue-gray eyes were furious.

Well, turnabout, Miss Amity, he thought, *too goddamn bad.*

Miss Lucy beamed.

The evening, short though it was, turned out to be the most enjoyable Duke had spent since the Jockey Club Ball —and that one no longer counted. After he had washed up, he was served supper in the dining room. Amity soon wandered sulkily off: She was obviously a young woman who wanted whatever male attention happened to be available, and she was deathly jealous of her younger sister. Miss Lucy stayed with Duke and Dulcy a little longer, then she too left, telling Dulcy not to stay up too late. There followed a glorious hour in which he told Dulcy of his dream of owning his own plantation and she told him of some of her adventures in the faraway North. She was, he thought, quite simply the most marvelous person he had ever met, and he loved her and Miss Lucy both. When she left him, he was quite ready to go to bed, the sooner to see her again in the morning.

But there was one thing which, if possible, he had to do first.

Due to the arrival of the coffle, some of Sabrehill was up late that night. When Duke went outside, a light was still burning in the office, where Mr. Joel was at work, and Mr. Turnage was sitting on the little porch of the overseer's house at the head of the east service lane. Duke walked over to the porch.

"Something I can do for you, Mr. Avery?"

"Maybe something we can do for each other, Mr. Turnage. I think I've got something that will interest you."

"Oh? And what would that be, sir?" Turnage had a lean, bony face with high cheekbones, a strong jaw, and a heavy mustache. He was not altogether ill-favored, but his eyes were mean and sometimes, it seemed to Duke, just a little bit crazy.

"Last winter Mr. Joel told me he was going to need some more hands."

"Might could be. We're clearing some new land."

"I've got a nigger. A *bad* nigger."

"Oh?" Turnage at once looked interested, and it seemed to Duke that even in the darkness he could see some of the craziness come into the overseer's eyes.

"And whenever I've got a bad nigger, Mr. Turnage, I think of only one person. I think of you."

"Well, if you want a nigger tamed," Turnage said with a laugh, "you've come to the right man. What's the problem with this one?"

"He doesn't know his place. Arrogant son of a bitch. Probably because he's the best-looking black bastard you ever saw in your life. If you're looking for a stud, the wenches can't hardly keep their hands off of him."

"Is he sound? How old is he?"

"Twenty-two and sound as they come. The only thing is, when you look at his back, you'll know he's been whipped within an inch of his life. But he still hasn't learned."

Turnage looked doubtful. "He's got a marked-up back? Mr. Aaron and Mr. Joel ain't gonna like that."

Duke held up a placatory hand. "Nobody's going to like it, and I'll let him go cheap if I have to. There's even twenty dollars in it for you if you can get the Sabres to buy him."

Fresh interest came to Turnage's eyes. "Well, Mr. Aaron ain't here right now. Reckon I just might get Mr. Joel to go ahead and buy him if he's cheap enough."

"But I'll only sell him on one condition, Mr. Turnage. And you've got to swear to God that you'll keep to it."

"And what's that?"

"I want you to teach this son of a bitch that he's a nigger and nothing but a nigger and the lowest kind of nigger. I want you to break him."

Turnage licked his lips. His eyes seemed oddly uncontrolled as he looked about to be sure they were not heard. He tilted his head forward toward Duke and lowered his voice.

"You want him dead?"

Duke laughed. "Dead? That's the last thing I want—how can you hurt a dead nigger? No, I want the bastard to live a hundred years and hate every goddamn minute of it."

"Well, now!" Turnage looked delighted. His eyes shone. "I think we can arrange something like that. Why don't we just take a look at this boy of yours and then sluice him down and go talk to Mr. Joel?"

The sale took place in the plantation office, one of the outbuildings connected by portico to the big house. Mr. Joel was, of course, skeptical at first.

"I dunno, Turn," he said, walking slowly around the naked black, who stood silent in the middle of the room, his head hanging down. "He's big all right, but those stripes . . ."

"Wench trouble," Turnage said, shrugging the matter off. "He's old enough, we'll soon have him settled down with his own wench."

"It's just that Aaron isn't going to like those stripes. And another thing—he looks good, but he surely hasn't got much butt, Turn. And you've always said a first-class field hand should have plenty of butt and gut."

"Oh, that's true, mostly. But look at those arms and

those shoulders and the width of that back. Now, that more'n makes up for the lack of butt."

Duke let them talk it out. Any sale, he soon realized, would depend on the overseer's persuasiveness. He himself was only there to dicker over the price, and that was a distinctly secondary consideration.

He looked at Jebediah. The big black's downturned face was expressionless. Unlike most slaves in his place, he refused to show humiliation by trying to hide his nakedness with his hands, but stood in unbroken dignity, like some dark-skinned gladiator of old. *"I promised my daddy I wouldn't punish you for anything in the past,"* Duke had told him after he had been unchained, *"but if you do or say anything to stop this sale, by God you're going to be the sorriest nigger that ever had his ears cropped and his balls lopped off. So you just go in there and say 'Yes, sir, massa,' like any other stupid field hand and keep your eyes on the floor."*

Now the eyes slowly rose to meet his own.

It was the same gaze that Jebediah had given him in the first moment of their first meeting; only now more than ever it seemed to impale him, to defy him, to accuse him. It was a look that brought back all his scalding anger—that this treacherous black bastard should look at him as if somehow *he,* Duke Avery, were the guilty one!

In that moment he would gladly have foregone the sale. He would have broken his word to his father and kept Jebediah for the sheer pleasure of destroying him. But it was too late for that: He heard Mr. Joel saying, "All right, Turn, you can take this boy away now. Mr. Avery and I will see if we can't come to terms."

A price was reached quickly and easily before Jebediah had even dressed. Because the slave obviously had a "discipline problem," as indicated by his back, Mr. Joel refused to go higher than $450, but that was more than Duke had expected to get anyway. Cash changed hands. Duke wrote out a bill of sale, which Turnage witnessed, and Mr. Joel tossed it into a tin box on a cluttered desk. Turnage shoved Jebediah toward the open doorway.

"He's all yours, Mr. Turnage," Duke said.
And silently added: *Break him!*

Jebediah was so weary that, after the overseer had put
him back into the barn for the night, not even the thought
of the indignity of his sale had the power to keep him
awake. Striking it from his mind, he sank down on the bare
wooden floor and threw himself into the depths of sleep.
He stirred when he heard the coffle being awakened and
again when it departed, but he didn't awaken fully until a
boot toe prodded his ribs and he opened his eyes to full
daylight.

The overseer was looking down at him.

He sat up, wiped the remaining sleep from his eyes,
looked around. Duke Avery stood in the open doorway.

"Just thought I'd take one last look at you before I head
back to Charleston, Jebediah," he said. "Don't figure we're
likely to meet again."

Jebediah looked straight into his eyes but said nothing.

"On the other hand, who knows? Maybe I'll stop by
Sabrehill in a year or two if it's convenient and find out if
you've learned to behave yourself."

"Oh, he'll learn," the overseer said. "He'll learn so good
that in a year or two you won't even recognize this here
boy. Don't reckon you'll know him even a month from
now."

"You hear that, Jebediah? You have anything to say?"

Still Jebediah said nothing.

"Don't you even want to know about . . . ?"

Yes, he did want to know, and though he hated himself
for asking anything of Mr. Duke Avery, he couldn't keep
himself from saying her name: "Jessie . . . what have you
done . . . ?"

"Nothing much . . . yet. But I've got something in mind.
Maybe in a year or two, if I get back here, I'll tell you. If
either of us gives a damn any longer."

"I don't know who this Jessie is," the overseer said, "but
I can guarantee you that a few weeks from now the only
thing this boy is gonna give a damn about is his own
stinking hide—if he's still got any left."

"When that day comes, Jebediah, the day you're broken, I want you to remember what you did and all you lost. And then just ask yourself one little question. 'Was it worth it?' "

Duke Avery seemed to be waiting for a response, but Jebediah would give him no further satisfaction. Once again he was silent.

The overseer went out the doorway. Duke Avery gave Jebediah one long final look, and the door closed.

Never had Jebediah felt more desolate, more alone. Never had he felt weaker or more spent. The day he was broken, Mr. Duke Avery had said. Duke Avery could have no idea of how nearly broken he was already.

No!

From somewhere within himself he had to summon up the old madness and hatred that for so long had kept him going.

Regret nothing! Endure everything!

Survive!

You are not an animal!

You are the biggest, meanest, craziest nigger they will ever meet!

And one day, Mr. Duke Avery, one fine day . . . !

Outside the barn, where he stood talking with Mr. Turnage, Duke Avery thought he heard Jebediah Hayes laughing.

TWO

MR. JEB

⸻❧ I ❧⸻

DUKE DIDN'T EVEN RECOGNIZE Jebediah at first. It wasn't just that more than three years had passed since he had left the big black at Sabrehill—Jebediah had changed.

They met on Broad Street on a beautiful October afternoon soon after Duke's return from a trip up north. He was on his way to Vendue Range when he saw some blacks loading a wagon with goods from a nearby shop. It was one of those shops where a planter could get every kind of supply imaginable—from his Osnaburghs and Welch Plains to imported silks, and from harness to flour and sugar—and the wagon was piled high. The sight was common, and Duke would have gone on by, except that something about one of the blacks seized his attention. He was the tallest of the three and powerfully built, though he walked with a limp. He had a certain rugged handsomeness in spite of a broken nose and a whip blaze across the face. There was something familiar. . . .

Duke recognized him.

He stepped out of the way of the passing crowd and watched, fascinated, as Jebediah went in and out of the shop. In three and a half years, the pain of that spring evening had almost vanished. He had forbidden himself to think about either Jebediah or Jessie. But now he saw Jessie in memory as clearly as if he had taken her portrait out of a drawer, and with the memory came the ache of loss.

He watched as Jebediah inspected the load in the wagon, motioned the other two blacks to drive off, and then limped over to an empty carriage and stood patiently, as if awaiting his master or mistress. Duke knew that dignity would best be served if he simply walked away without saying a word but somehow he couldn't do that.

"Afternoon, Jebediah," he said.

Jebediah slowly raised his head. He looked directly into Duke's eyes but said nothing, and his scarred face was as impassive as if he had never seen Duke before.

Duke strolled closer. "So they let you come into town now, do they, boy?"

Still Jebediah remained silent and his eyes never wavered.

"You've got nothing to say, boy?"

Jebediah spoke at last, softly. "No, Mr. Duke. Nothing to say."

"Enjoying life at Sabrehill?"

"I . . . have no complaints."

"Well, I'm certainly glad to hear that. But haven't you learned to say *sir?*"

Jebediah's lip curled, and for an instant Duke thought he was going to spit out a contemptuous *"Massa!"* But his face went blank again, and he merely said, "Sir."

"That's better. I can see that Mr. Turnage has taught you a lesson or two."

Jebediah's gaze dropped. "Yes, sir. A lesson or two."

"Glad to hear it. By the way, don't you want to know about Jessie, Jebediah? Seems to me I remember promising you that when we met again I might tell you . . ."

A muscle twitched at the corner of Jebediah's mouth: He was not as indifferent as he perhaps wished to appear.

Duke shook his head sadly. "Ah, too bad about Jessie. I really took care of that little gal, you know. And if you hadn't come along, she'd have had a good life. But thanks to you, she lost all that. Sure you don't want to know what happened to her?"

Jebediah started to turn away. Duke grabbed his shoulder and whipped him back.

"Don't you turn away from me, boy. You look at me. You look me in the eye. Because I'm going to tell you. I sold her, Jebediah. Don't you want to know where I sold her?"

"No, sir, I don't—"

Duke felt the anger of that spring night returning. "Well, you're going to know. I sold the little bitch into a whorehouse, Jebediah. That's right, I sold her for the whore she was always meant to be. You and me, we broke her in, boy, but I reckon she's had a thousand others since. I reckon she's had so many, she doesn't even remember what you look like."

Now he had what he wanted. Jebediah's face suddenly went gaunt—the eyes wide and staring, the corners of the half-opened mouth pulled crookedly down, the brown skin ashen.

"Oh, don't take it bad, Jebediah. I'm sure she's happier there. I just sent you both back to where you should have been all along." He forced a grin. "Give my regards to Mr. Turnage."

He turned away. As far as he was concerned the score was settled. From the look of him, Jebediah had suffered the breaking he had deserved, and Duke needed never again give him a single thought.

At that moment, Miss Lucy came out of the shop.

He had not seen her or her sisters since he had delivered Jebediah to Sabrehill, but he had never forgotten that wonderful evening, and a hundred times he had recreated in memory that loveliest hour of his life, spent alone with Dulcy. Though he knew that it was most unlikely that Dulcy would ever be his, he could not give up that sweetest of dreams.

Miss Lucy walked toward her carriage. At first glance, she was as beautiful as ever: the large, searching blue eyes, the high cheekbones over thin cheeks, the firm jaw. But time and the world had taken its toll of her, as it had of Jebediah, and now she had a long scar down the right side of her face from temple to jawline. Her eyes moved over him without interest, as she crossed the sidewalk, then lit up with recognition.

"Why . . . it's Mr. Avery, isn't it?"

He took the hand she extended to him. "Yes, ma'am. Just arrived back in Charleston."

"My, but it's a long time since we last saw you!"

"Well, ma'am . . ." He explained that after his father had died, soon after Duke's visit to Sabrehill, he had almost at once left Charleston and had completed his education at the University of Virginia, rarely returning home. He didn't feel it necessary to explain that he had wanted to

live for a time in a place where his connection with the
slave trade was not generally known and he was treated
as a gentleman.

"Anyway, I'm home to stay now, and it's mighty nice to
see you. I hope all is well with your family?"

"Quite well, thank you. It's good to see you again, too,
Mr. Avery." Miss Lucy withdrew her hand and moved on
toward the carriage.

Almost fearfully, he asked the most important question.
"And how is Miss Dulcy?"

"Doing very nicely, thank you."

Jebediah gave Miss Lucy a hand up into the carriage,
then climbed up with her. Duke didn't want to appear
overly interested in Dulcy, but he looked for some way to
prolong the encounter, hoping to learn more.

"That's a mighty big boy, you've got there, ma'am," he
said, smiling. "I wouldn't mind having one like him. If
you're ever of a mind to sell him . . ."

He had meant the words only as a small, friendly joke,
but Miss Lucy's eyes became reproving and her voice
gently admonitory.

"Mr. Jeb is not a boy, Mr. Avery," she said. "Mr. Jeb is
our overseer. Good day."

At her nod, Jebediah flicked the reins, and the carriage
rolled away.

Duke stood where he was, unmoving, feeling as if he
had been suddenly and unexpectedly slapped.

"Mr. Jeb is our overseer," she had said. What the hell
had she meant by that? It was quite impossible. He had left
Jebediah in the hands of the meanest nigger-hating slave-
breaker he knew, and the big buck showed it: the whip
blaze, the broken nose, the limp. Then, just what did she
mean, Mr. Jeb was their goddamn overseer?

What had gone wrong?

It didn't matter, he told himself. It had all happened a
long time ago, and whatever else had happened to Jebediah
Hayes, he had certainly suffered at Turnage's hands. You
had only to look at him to see that. Besides, Duke thought,
he had probably misunderstood Miss Lucy. Black overseers

were few and far between, at least in South Carolina, and by law every slave, even a foreman, had to be supervised by a white man.

He settled into a chair in his uncle's office and looked around at the familiar desks and cabinets. It was the first time he had been in the room since the summer of 'thirty-two, soon after his father had died.

"Say, I ran into Miss Lucy on the way over here," he said.

"Miss Lucy?" Sam Avery asked, as he sat down at his desk. "Now, what Miss Lucy would that be?" As if he didn't know. Sam had always liked to tease Duke, in a good-natured way.

"Miss Lucy Sabre."

"Oh, *that* Miss Lucy. Only, you mean *Missus* Lucy Sabre."

"Missus?"

"Boy, you ain't been home long enough or often enough. I recollect that just before your daddy died and you left Charleston, you was all full of Miss Lucy. Her and Miss Dulcy, you couldn't say enough about how wonderful they was. Well, I'm afraid you're too late to latch onto Miss Lucy—she married a cousin of hers, Mr. Justin Sabre of Virginia, just last spring. To the relief of one and all, I might add."

"How's that?"

Sam feigned wide-eyed surprise. "Good God, boy, you really *have* been away these last three years! Haven't you heard any gossip from your friends since you left?"

"I don't have many friends in Charleston," Duke said impatiently, "and those I have, I'd just as soon be rid of."

"That's a hell of an attitude for a man in trade, boy."

"Just tell me what you're talking about, Sam. What do you mean, 'to the relief of one and all'?"

Sam shrugged. "Well, you might have heard that old Aaron got hisself killed off in a riding accident and Joel drowned—or maybe it was the other way around. Anyway, they both died, and there was Miss Lucy with a big plantation to run and a helluva passel of niggers to look after, and nobody to help her. Except this big nigger buck she took a shine to."

"Mr. Jeb is our overseer," she had said. The words re-echoed in Duke's mind, and he felt his face growing stiff.

"What about the overseer? There was a man named Turnage, the last time I was there."

Sam spread empty hands. "Can't say. I do recall hearing that Aaron was dissatisfied with his overseer. Seems he was a mean son of a bitch and getting worse all the time, so maybe Aaron and Joel let him go."

Goddamn! Duke thought. He had been so eager to punish Jebediah that such a possibility had never occurred to him.

"Anyway," Sam went on, "for some time, there was all this talk about how Miss Lucy was letting a fine plantation go to rack and ruin and her niggers was running wild and she ought to get herself a white overseer instead of relying on a big black stud who didn't know any more about running a plantation than she did. For a while there, people took to calling her the Whore of Sabrehill and 'that damn scar-faced bitch'—some nigger cut her up, I guess—and I don't know what all. Even talked about taking legal action."

The very thought that anyone should speak of Miss Lucy in such a manner was enough to anger Duke, but he kept his face impassive. "Why didn't they take legal action?"

"Guess she talked 'em out of it. And to give credit where it's due, somehow she and that nigger kept Sabrehill going until finally she married Justin. Which gave people something else to complain about."

"They don't like Justin?"

Sam's face darkened. " 'Course they don't! He's a goddamn abolitionist! Even worse than your old daddy! Oh, he don't preach it—he'd be tarred and feathered it he did. But you ask him, he don't make no bones about it either." Sam shook his head in bewilderment. "I swear, I don't understand it. Sometimes it seems to me that half of these abolitionist-minded fools are Southerners! Levi Coffin, from North Carolina. James Birney, from Kentucky. The

Grimké sisters, from right here in Charleston. Some of them even own slaves, or once did. Goddamn turncoats, the whole lot of 'em!"

"Have you heard anything about . . ." Duke hesitated to mention Dulcy and draw more of his uncle's teasing. "Have you heard anything about Amity Sabre?"

"Christ, boy, how should I know about her?" Sam was still caught up in his anger. "She died or got married or something equally final. Maybe she went north with her sister Dulcy. I dunno."

"Dulcy? She went back up north?"

Sam stared at him. Slowly a smile spread over his broad face. "You mean you ain't never heard about Dulcy? My God, mostly I don't pay no attention to gossip, but, Christ, even I heard about Dulcy!"

Duke's heart thumped a little harder. "Well, what about her?"

"She's a nigger."

For the second time that day, Duke had a sense of unreality, a feeling that the world had somehow gone askew and become something quite different from what he had thought it.

"What . . ." His voice faltered. "What do you mean?"

"Just what I said. That little gal turned out to be a nigger!"

"But how . . . how could . . ."

"It come out after Aaron died. His second wife, Miss Faith, was black. Oh, maybe only a quarter or an eighth or even less—but black just the same, and that was Dulcy's mother. I guess that was why Aaron sent her north the first time. She was growing up, and he didn't want any problems with her if the truth come out. Then after she come back for a visit and her daddy died, the whole goddamn thing *did* come out, so Miss Lucy sent her back up north for good." Sam leaned back in his chair and grinned. "Well, boy, what do you think of your sweet little Miss Dulcy now?"

Duke shook his head. He felt much as he had when he had found Jessie and Jebediah together. He felt betrayed.

"Well, then, I'll tell you what *I* think, Leduc. It don't

surprise me at all. It don't even surprise me that Justin Sabre is an abolitionist. 'Cause, hell, there's black blood running all through that family."

"Oh, no!" The words came out involuntarily. The fact that Dulcy was black was bad enough. The thought that Miss Lucy's blood might be tainted was intolerable.

"Oh, yes, there is. All through it. Like that other cousin of Miss Lucy's, that Mr. Lewis Sabre of Jessamine plantation, married a nigger girl some years back. You telling me their pickaninnies ain't niggers?"

"I don't know," Duke mumbled, disconcerted. "I forgot about him. I've seen their children, and they sure look white."

"Sure they do! Whiter'n you or me! But that don't make 'em any less niggers as far as I'm concerned. *White* niggers."

"Well, that may be true. But Miss Lucy sure as hell isn't a nigger. She's as fine a lady as any in South Carolina, and don't tell me she'd marry a man with black blood, either."

"Maybe not, but I still say half of them Sabres is black as the ace of spades." Sam got up from his chair and stretched. "Hell, I can't jaw all afternoon. I gotta turn a profit. Boy, are you really back for good this time?"

"I sure am. I want to make some money. A *lot* of money."

Sam nodded his approval. "That's just fine—you already showed you've got a knack for it. Aside from that, there's just a few simple rules you've got to remember. Don't trust banks too far the way your daddy did, so he lost 'most everything he had in the panic of 'nineteen. And don't go soft the way your daddy did. Hell, I know you don't want to put a black through any unnecessary misery, but you got to remember they're half animal anyway and business is business. Think you can remember that?"

"Yes, sir."

"Then we're gonna get along just fine, and you're gonna get rich. And that's all that matters."

Duke got up from his chair. His uncle was right. That was all that mattered. The past was past, and it didn't matter in the slightest that Miss Dulcy Sabre was a nigger or that Jebediah Hayes lived and apparently thrived and was now the overseer of Sabrehill. It simply didn't matter.

The hell it didn't.

"Jebediah? Are you all right?"

"Yes, ma'am."

"You look so . . . Did Mr. Avery say something?"

"It was Mr. Avery who sold me to Sabrehill, Miss Lucy."

"Oh!" The carriage rolled on, headed for Lynch Street. "I remember now," Miss Lucy said slowly after a moment. "He came to Sabrehill with a coffle only a few weeks before I became aware of you."

"Twelve days." The memory was sharp.

"Do you hate him so very much, Jebediah?"

"Hate him, Miss Lucy?"

Well, did he? Certainly he had devoted a great part of his life to hatred. But hatred was useful only when it helped you to survive or to protect those you loved. And though he *had* hated Mr. Leduc Avery, he had thought that he had left that behind . . . until this afternoon; until the slave trader had spoken of Jessie.

For a long time he had put her out of his mind: The thought of what might have happened to her was too painful. But when Mr. Duke had spoken of her, she had suddenly become real again, and he had remembered her tears, her voice, her cry of pain:

"I don't want to be a slave no more! I don't want my babies born in slavery. . . . I rather kill them first!"

But he had failed her, that slave girl with her secret dignity and her dream. And now, somewhere in Charleston or New Orleans or Natchez, or God alone knew where, she was just another fancy black whore. Or maybe not so fancy anymore.

"Yes, Miss Lucy. I hate him. But not for what he did to me."

Mercifully, Miss Lucy asked him no further questions, but merely patted his arm and left him to his thoughts.

He had to smile, remembering Mr. Duke's face when Miss Lucy said, *"Mr. Jeb is no boy, Mr. Avery. Mr. Jeb is our overseer."* But what he had had to survive in order that she might say those words! Turnage had managed to sic some of the meanest of the field hands on him—because he was supposedly "a snotty house nigger" who thought he could take all the wenches away from them—and the whip had descended on his back daily. It had taken Turnage only a week to drive him away—to make him bolt in mindless pain—and since he had had no idea of where he was running, the overseer had inevitably caught up with him. He remembered lying exhausted in a barn while Turnage bent over him.

"You're the kind of swell-headed, useless nigger that I just purely hate," he had said. "And if I work and run and whip the bejesus out of the likes of you, I sure as hell ain't gonna have any trouble with the others."

Turnage had leaned closer, and Jebediah's mouth had begun to work, gathering saliva.

"And if you want to get out of that, boy, here's what you go to do. You hang your head, bend your back, and work like hell. And remember you're a nigger. *Just a nigger.* And out in the field or in the quarters, you're not Mr. Aaron's nigger or Mr. Joel's nigger—you're *my* nigger. . . . And if you ever look down that snotty nose at *me*, boy . . . I'll pound it off your face with a whip butt. And then I'll run you off and whip you into your grave. You understand what I'm saying, Jeb?"

Jebediah's mouth had continued working, almost as if independent of his will. He would have spat in the man's face, even if it cost him his life. But Turnage had seen something in his eyes—hatred, pride, madness—and had backed off in sudden apprehension. "You bastard," he had muttered. "You stinking black bastard."

Well, Jebediah thought, *this stinking black bastard outlasted you, Mr. Turnage, sir. Outlasted, outhated, outfought you. Beat you into the dust and took your place. . . .*

With Aaron and Joel Sabre dead, there had been only Jebediah and Miss Lucy to see to the welfare of the people of Sabrehill—to see that they were fed and clothed and had at least a chance at some scrap of happiness in spite of their slavery. And somehow they had done it. Knowing nothing of how to manage a plantation, they had consulted neighbors, foremen, anyone at all who might advise them. They had poured over agricultural books, old records, copies of *The Southern Agriculturalist.* Jebediah had worked along side the hands, had improved their gang and task assignments, had worked out incentives for them. He had shown them that he was no ordinary "house nigger" and no Turnage, but a black man with a genuine concern for his own people. And one day when he was in the fields, a young three-quarter hand had addressed him, as if it were the most natural thing in the world, as "Mr. Jeb."

Other hands overheard, and the custom quickly spread. Even the white help Miss Lucy brought in often called him that. Of course, no white man would seriously call a black man "mister," and they tried to make a little joke of it, slurring it into a single word, "Missijeb," and they pretended he was really only Miss Lucy's or Mr. Justin's messenger boy. But in their hearts they knew the truth. He was the overseer of Sabrehill. He was *Mister* Jeb.

The Lynch Street residence was a spacious red brick house with white stone trimmings that gleamed in the afternoon sunlight. It was situated on two acres of tree-shaded, carefully gardened land, with most of its outbuildings neatly clustered together in a far-back corner. Jebediah drove through the open front gate, let Miss Lucy out of the carriage, and proceeded around the house to the service yard.

The supply wagon had already arrived, and Mr. Justin Sabre was supervising the transfer of its contents to a much larger wagon, which would carry the fresh supplies to Sabrehill. Once a year, sometimes twice, a supply expedition to Charleston and back was necessary, and it was always something of an event. The children in particular were always curious as to what delicious and delightful things might be hidden away in the wagon in preparation for Christmas, and a number of them, black and white, now stood about hopefully watching.

The three white children were Mr. Justin's by his first

wife. The oldest and youngest, Mark and Beau, paid little attention as Jebediah got down from the carriage, but their sister, eight-year-old Katie Anne, came running to him.

"Did you bring me a treat, Jebediah?" she asked. She was a skinny little thing with tawny hair and green eyes and an angelic, if often dirty face, and Jebediah thought her one of the prettiest children he had ever seen.

"Bring you a treat, honeychild?" He scratched his head and feigned puzzlement. "Why, I don't rightly recall."

"You promised me a treat."

"I did?" Jebediah patted his pockets. "Then I suppose I have something here somewhere."

He heard a giggle and looked around as a small brown hand thrust into his jacket pocket. "Damien, what in the world are you doing in there?"

"I found it, I found it!" Damien crowed in delight as he pulled out a small parcel. "I found it!"

Katie Anne's face, so innocent until then, instantly twisted itself into the visage of a small angry demon. *"That's mine!"*

Damien tried to run, but he hadn't a chance. Katie Anne landed on him, struggling with termagant fury to snatch away the package. "It's mine, it's mine, it's mine! Mr. Jeb promised me!"

"He promise me too!" Damien protested.

"It's mine! It's mine!"

"Honeychild," Jebediah said, "It's for both—"

The package burst, spraying candied fruit over the paving stones.

"Now look what you done!" Damien said tearfully.

"Share, children! You must learn to—"

"I get the apricots!" Katie Anne snatched a candy from Damien's fingers.

"You *always* take the apricots!"

"They're mine!"

Mr. Justin came over to them. "What the hell is going on here? Katie Anne, what are you up to now?"

"She ain't no Katie Anne," Damien said, weeping. "She a—a cat!—cat!—*catamount!*"

Everyone who had heard immediately burst out laughing

and echoed Damien: "She ain't no Katie Anne, oh, no! She a cat, cat, catamount!"

"I don't care," the cat said placidly, around a mouthful of candied fruit. "Long's I get my apricots. I just don't care."

Jebediah picked up Damien and held him close, hoping to comfort him. "How's my little friend?"

"I'm nine years old," Damien said. "I ain't little."

Nevertheless he was content to stay where he was and shed a few tears against Jebediah's neck. Jebediah's heart swelled. He was fond of Katie Anne, but Damien, orphaned, black, and a slave like himself, was naturally much closer to him.

The evening went swiftly. Mr. Joshua Greener and his son Paddy arrived, and their supplies were put in the large wagon along with the Sabrehill supplies. Mr. Greener owned a farm out beyond Sabrehill, and he and his son would serve as armed guards on the trip. Finally the big canvas top was mounted on the wagon, and, except for hitching up the six mules that would draw it, it was ready to go.

"Can I go with you tomorrow, Jebediah?" Damien asked, as they made a last inspection of the wagon.

"Oh, I don't think—"

Katie Anne at once hurled herself at him, throwing her arms around his waist. "Oh, please let us go with you tomorrow! Oh, please, Jebediah, please, please, please!"

"Katie Anne, I don't think your momma—"

"Oh, please, please, please, Mr. Jeb!" The little girl's face became a mask of suffering. "Please, I can't *stand* it, if I have to stay here, I can't *stand* it! Oh, please, please—"

"Catherine Anne," Miss Lucy called from the kitchen house, "will you kindly leave Mr. Jeb alone! Come get your supper!"

"Oh, I can't stand it," Katie Anne wailed tragically, as she released Jebediah and wandered off. "I can't stand it, I can't stand it, I can't stand it!"

The last rays of sunlight vanished and, though the moon lingered on low in the sky, the night thickened. Jebediah ate supper in the kitchen house with some of the household staff, then wandered back through the gardens toward the little room that he occupied on his rare trips to Charleston.

He was almost there when he heard a mockingbird.

He halted, not really knowing why, except that the call had come so abruptly and with a certain urgency. And was there something slightly *wrong* about it?

He looked around.

The call was repeated, even more urgently. It seemed to come from the middle of the garden, but he could see nothing, for the moon was behind a cloud. Hesitantly, peering into the shadows, he followed the sound.

He had almost convinced himself that there was nothing unusual about the birdcall, when he thought he saw a dark form sitting on a bench under a tree. He moved toward it.

As the cloud drifted, unveiling the moon, the figure became defined: a man's form, a black face with a muzzle of short dark beard, a grin. The man laughed softly. "You noticed that my mockingbird is slightly out of voice, old son."

"Adaba," Jebediah said.

The man put a finger to his lips. "Shush! Ain't no Adaba. He's just a tale they tell in the quarters—a hope, a dream."

A hope, a dream that Jebediah himself had had for years. One he had shared with Jessie. And then, ironically, when he no longer needed or wanted rescue, he had discovered Adaba hiding from his pursuers in the Sabrehill field quarters.

That had been almost a year ago, and Jebediah had been cooperating with the Underground Railroad ever since, but he still knew little about Adaba. He knew that the notorious "conductor," a man about ten years his senior, could speak like a common field hand, a house servant, or an intelligent, well-educated man. He knew that Adaba sometimes claimed to be an itinerant free-black carpenter, and perhaps he was—although most people said he was a runaway slave. When Jebediah had first met him, he had looked like a wilderness man, with his heavy clothes and boots, meant for wear, and his steel tomahawk slung at his side. But this evening he looked quite different: Even in the dark, Jebediah could see that he was wearing the well-tailored suit, polished boots, and stylish cravat of some wealthy free black of Charleston.

Adaba, observing his stare, chuckled. "My woman do like her Johnny Dove to dress up pretty from time to time."

Johnny Dove: So that was what he was calling himself.

"All right, Johnny Dove, if that's who you are, what are you doing around here? If the city patrol catches you after dark—"

"Ain't likely. I been slipping and sliding through the shadows, making fools of the patrol, since I was old enough to put on pants. Hell, it's a boy's game. You think the patrol is gonna keep old Johnny from calling on a friend?"

Adaba extended a hand, and Jebediah shook it and sat down with him. The Brown Dove's high spirits were infectious, and Jebediah found himself grinning back at him, but he doubted that the call was purely social.

"What can I do for you, Ad—Johnny?"

"Well, first of all, you can tell me what your plans are."

Jebediah shook his head. "The future's pretty uncertain. About all I can say for sure is that before long I'll be heading north."

Adaba stiffened. "What do you mean, heading north?" His countrified accent had vanished.

"Just what I said. I've already told Miss Lucy and Mr. Justin they should start looking for a new overseer. In January, when the new man takes over, they'll sell me north to a state where I can be freed—"

"I know how it works. But why would you want to do a thing like that?"

Jebediah looked at Adaba as if the latter were mad. "Why would I not! Do you think I want to stay a slave the rest of my life?"

"I'm not suggesting that you should. But look at it this way. A man must make a livelihood wherever he is, and you've got a job that most men, black or white, would give a year of their life for. And I need you here. And, Jeb, son, it gets *cold* up north!"

Jebediah smiled and shook his head again. "You don't need me. About all I can do for you is turn a blind eye and a deaf ear on the quarters when your people ship their black wool through."

"You can do more than that, and you know it. Like you're going to do tomorrow."

Jebediah made a guess: "You want somebody taken out of the city."

Adaba nodded. "Young fellow from Savannah. I couldn't get him on a ship—they're watching the waterfronts like hawks—so I want to run him through Sabrehill. All you have to do is get him there."

Jebediah considered: Was it possible? He didn't see how. "Johnny, I'm leaving in the morning, long before first light. I'll have two white men with me. There is no way I can get a runaway slave into that wagon and keep him concealed for two long days."

"You won't have to. When you came to Charleston to get your supplies, you brought someone with you."

"No, I came alone."

"You brought someone along to help you," Adaba insisted, "likely somebody Miss Lucy and Mr. Justin haven't even noticed back in the servant quarters. You write your own passes, don't you?"

"Yes. It saves a lot of bother."

"Good. You write a pass for yourself and this helper of yours. Tomorrow morning, soon after you leave this house, you're going to find your helper walking along with you. You'll go to Sabrehill, a trip like any other. When you get there, your helper will go to the field quarters. You'll never see him again."

Adaba made it sound so simple, but the very thought of such a trip made Jebediah sweat. A black overseer, after all, had enemies who hungered for his downfall, and so did his abolitionist master.

Adaba saw his hesitation. "Scared?"

"Not just for myself. For Miss Lucy and Mr. Justin. And for that slave from Savannah."

"Never mind that. Remember when *you* were on the run. Remember the hounds and the whips. Remember Mr. Turnage."

Jebediah remembered all that and more. He remembered his father's death agony . . . his mother's defiled body and her slit wrists. Even if he could have forgotten, he had sworn that he never would.

He nodded. "I'll do it."

◦═╡ 2 ╞═◦

"Now, ONCE AGAIN," ADABA said, "what's this about you heading north?"

"Just what I said. After I was sold to Sabrehill, Miss Lucy arranged for me to earn my freedom. Well, I earned it. She and Mr. Justin will sell me north any time I ask, and since I figure they don't need me anymore . . ." Jebediah shrugged.

"And what will you do when you go north?"

"I don't know. I reckon I can find work. Miss Lucy says some freed slaves give lectures. Maybe I'll do that."

"What will you lecture about?"

"Four years of hell in the fields," Jebediah said grimly. "Three years at Sabrehill, and a lot of that still more hell."

"Fine, fine. Are you going to tell them about the Underground Railroad?"

Jebediah hesitated. "I don't know much about the Underground Railroad."

"No, you don't. But before long, you're going to know a lot more. Because the Underground Railroad needs you, Jebediah."

"But I am just not going to be here, Johnny Dove!"

Adaba ignored his words. "Like tomorrow. I have to get my friend from Savannah away from Charleston as quickly as possible, and you're the only person I can count on for help. I understand that you travel between Sabrehill and Charleston two, three, four times a year. Each time is a chance to get another runaway slave out of Charleston."

"I'll do it this once. After that, you'll have to find someone else."

"And that's not the only reason I need you," Adaba went on. "The first time I was at Sabrehill, hiding in the quarters, I promised a lot of people up and down that stretch of river that sooner or later I'd steal them north.

100

Now, it's about time I kept that promise, Jebediah. And I'm going to need your help."

"I told you, all I can do is—"

"Turn a blind eye and a deaf ear on the quarters. But if you leave now, the Sabres will have to get a new overseer. And he'll be a white overseer—all he'll care about is turning a profit and keeping his job. Do you think *he* is going to turn a blind eye and a deaf ear?"

Jebediah felt a kind of sickness at what Adaba was asking, and the sweat on the back of his neck grew clammier. "Johnny Dove, I can't stay on here forever!"

"I'm not asking you to. Just for a little while." Adaba leaned closer to Jebediah, his voice low and almost pleading. "And what's a year or so out of your life? Why, you're practically a free man already. Think of those who may never be free if you don't help them."

"I'll help you tomorrow. But I don't see how I *can* help you after that!"

"Leave that to me. Jebediah, you can quit and go north any time you wish. And when you do, old son, I promise you I'll send you to some friends of mine—Mr. Garrison, Mr. Weld—who'll make sure you have a chance to give those lectures. You'll tell people up north all about those years of hell—and about the Underground Railroad, too. Beside," he added, "there's another good reason for you to stay and work with us here. One of the very best reasons you could ever think of."

"What's that?" Jebediah asked dubiously.

Adaba leaned closer still, until their faces were almost touching. His eyes widened. His teeth glistened in the moonlight.

"For the fun of it!"

The words were so unexpected that Jebediah almost jumped, and Adaba rolled back from him, smothering laughter. "Yes, for the fun of it, old son. My God, Jebediah, do you think we abolitionists and Railroaders don't *enjoy* what we're doing? Why, we're the merriest band you are ever going to be a part of! And think of the tales you'll have to tell!"

Once again, Jebediah found Adaba's spirit infectious,

but he clung to common sense. "Johnny Dove, no matter what you say, every day I stay here, I'm running a risk. If something should happen to Miss Lucy and Mr. Justin—if a fever should take them away at the same time, say—I probably never would get my freedom."

Adaba's face sobered. "Well, I can't tell you there are no risks—of course there are. But you've got to remember that you've got some big advantages over most slaves. You can not only write your own passes, I'm told that you know maps."

That was true. When he had first started running away, he, like most slaves, had had virtually no geographical knowledge. He had had hardly a glimpse of a map in all his life and little idea of how to read one. But at Sabrehill, after he had become overseer, he had memorized every map of the United States and Canada he could find in the library. Nothing in the world, not even Miss Lucy's promise of his freedom, could have kept him from that knowledge, not after what he had suffered because of the lack of it.

But he said, "That doesn't signify much when you're in chains."

"No, it doesn't. But most slaves are chained only by ignorance. The white man does his best to turn the black man into a timid, empty-headed beast of burden that can't stray ten miles before it's caught. But you—you're different."

"Not so different. I don't know how many times I ran, and I was always caught."

"That was before you learned certain things. And I'm going to teach you more. Jebediah, have you ever heard of Josiah Henson?"

"I've heard the name."

"Now, that's interesting. Because Josiah is a black man the white folks don't want you to know anything about. Some years back, you see, Josiah got tired of his master's lies and broken promises. So he asked himself, 'What for am I putting up with all this here shit?' And being a sensible man, he simply took his wife and child and—walked away!

"Oh, it wasn't as easy as that sounds, of course, and he had some help from the Underground Railroad and our Indian friends. But still, he did just walk away, with his family, all the way to Canada. And then he came back, came back again and again, to help other slaves do the same. So far, he's freed close to two hundred slaves. If my people and I can get a slave to Maryland, Josiah and his can get him the rest of the way to Canada.

"What I'm saying, Jebediah, is that for men like you and me and Josiah—and we are not alone—there is always hope. But for others, there is not, and we, by God, must help them!" Adaba clamped a strong arm around Jebediah's shoulders. "Now, you are going to stay, old son. I know you are going to stay!"

But he did not wish to stay. Only luck, great bodily strength, and mad determination had kept him alive this long. And he had the feeling that if he stayed in the South too long, he would not survive.

He said, "I'll think about it."

Adaba laughed softly in the darkness and squeezed his shoulder.

When he awakened the next morning he immediately thought of Adaba, of Mr. Greener and his son Paddy, of the slave from Savannah—of everything that might pose a danger for him until he reached Sabrehill. It was as if he had never really ceased thinking of them but had been considering, weighing, balancing them all the time he had been asleep.

When he left his room, it was still two hours before sunrise, but the service yard was already bustling with activity. No lamps showed in the windows of the house as yet, but the kitchen was bright, and a couple of boys were already bringing out the mules. Jebediah took the blanket roll he had found in his room last night—Adaba had said it would be there—and tossed it into the back of the wagon. The slave from Savannah was well supplied.

Mr. Greener and Paddy arrived and put their rifles into the wagon: There was no need to carry weapons in the daytime, but the Greeners would sleep in the wagonload with their rifles in hand at night. Mr. Greener, in his early forties, had a round, heavily freckled face and a short, slim knotty-muscled body, and he was inclined toward small, friendly jokes and smiling silences. Paddy was the same man, twenty-five years younger. Jebediah judged they would make good traveling companions.

By the time they had eaten a good, if hasty, breakfast, the wagon was ready and Jebediah's mule had been saddled. He suggested that the Greeners ride on the wagon, but Mr. Greener insisted that they would walk, at least until tired—"Make better time"—so Jebediah, in turn, insisted that they share his mule.

They were ready, then. Mr. Greener and Paddy led the mules and wagon through the open gate out onto Lynch Street. Jebediah followed, leading his mule. As he started through the gateway, he saw a motion in the deep shadows behind a large azalea bush, and he paused.

"All right," he said softly, "who's there?"

Slowly, hesitantly, the figure of a young black man emerged from behind the shrub. His voice was a whisper: "Je . . . Jebe . . ."

"Solon," Jebediah said, using the name he had given Adaba, "Solon, is that you?"

His eyes wide with apprehension, "Solon" came forward. "Yes, sir," he said. "Yes, sir, it's jes' me. S-Solon."

"Well, come on, Solon." Jebediah laughed and gave the youth an encouraging pat on the back. "You just danged near missed the train! Welcome aboard, Solon!"

They went east on Boundary Street and then up King, and by the first hint of dawn, they were well up on that peninsular stretch called the Neck. At this time of year, traffic was heavy, and before long, another wagon was always in sight, with people hailing them, as friendly travelers always did. They pushed on steadily, giving the mules a short rest every hour and a slightly longer rest every second hour. Traffic thinned until, by mid-morning, they were traveling alone. They had encountered no difficulty, and Jebediah began to wonder why he had even hesitated to accept this commission from Adaba.

Adaba. Who was he? Jebediah wondered, as he pulled

himself up into the saddle for his turn on the mule. Who was he and where did he come from? When Jebediah had asked him why he himself didn't conduct "Solon" to Sabrehill, he had smiled and replied, "Why, I'm sure a smart fellow like you can figure that out, son." "Are you slave or free?" Adaba had grinned. "I'm as much a slave as you, but maybe a little bit freer."

Adaba was legally a slave, then. Quite likely a Charleston slave who might be recognized as such if he attempted to escort a runaway. A Charleston slave who dressed better than was legally allowed. With the freedom to run loose. A rich white man's favored yardchild? His complexion seemed too dark for that. Even so, Jebediah tried to remember the gossip he had heard years earlier about wealthy Charlestonians and black mistress and—

As they went around a bend in the road, through a concealing grove of sweetgum trees, they saw four horsemen approaching them, less than a hundred feet away.

Jebediah knew them.

His first reaction was pure panic. They were all members of the patrol, and he remembered all too well their fists and boots and the hard leather paddle with the holes bored through it. He wanted to throw himself down from the saddle, tell Mr. Greener it was his turn to ride, beg him to mount the mule. But it was too late for that, even if he had given in to the craven impulse, and he hated the four white men all the more for having made him even think of doing such a thing.

He saw the first two riders straighten in their saddles and knew they had recognized him.

The leader was Balbo Jeppson, a planter from near Sabrehill. A craggy, barrel-chested, gray-haired man in his middle fifties, he was the most dangerous of the four. "*A nigger watcher, that's what I am,*" Jebediah had once heard him say. "*Why, I reckon I know more different niggers on more farms and plantations than any other man you'll ever meet. Know their names, know their husbands and wives, know their pickaninnies. Know 'em like Caesar used to know his legions, knew every soldier by his first name.*"

Jebediah thought of "Solon," walking behind him.

The other riders, all of them considerably younger than Jeppson, were Philo Bassett and the Carstairs brothers, Rowan and Caley. Of the three, Jebediah figured Bassett to be the worst. If Jeppson was a nigger watcher, Bassett was a nigger hater, and, illiterate himself, he hated a literate, book-reading nigger like Jebediah Hayes most of all. Moreover, some months earlier Mr. Justin had given one of the Bassetts a well-deserved beating for insulting Miss Lucy, and Jebediah had no doubt that the entire family was waiting for an opportunity for revenge.

When the four riders were only a few yards away, blocking the road, Balbo Jeppson raised a hand to signal a halt, and the wagon came to a creaking standstill.

" 'Morning, Jebediah," Jeppson said, with a thin smile. "What you doing in the saddle while a white man walks?"

"I don't know who you are, sir," Mr. Greener said, "but these here niggers is with me. Now, if you will kindly stop blocking the road—"

"I don't know who *you* are, sir," Bassett said, his lean, unshaven face twisting into a sneer, "but this here nigger ain't yours 'lessen he been sold, and I don't believe that. Get down off that mule, Jebediah. Take off your hat to a white man and show us your ticket."

Mr. Greener flushed with anger, and Jebediah was just as happy that the rifles were not within easy reach. Taking his time, he dismounted, took off his hat, walked to Jeppson and Bassett, took out his pass, unfolded it, handed it up between the two white men. "By God," Jeppson said, as he took the slip of paper, "you sure ain't in no hurry to go no place, are you, boy?"

Jebediah said nothing, allowed his face to show nothing. Jeppson read the pass.

"Says here you and Solon on your way back to Sabrehill." Jeppson nodded toward the Savannah slave. "That Solon?"

Jebediah nodded, his lips moving soundlessly.

"Say yessir or nosir, goddamnit," Bassett commanded.

"Yes, sir. That's Solon." Jebediah could only hope that Jeppson's memory for slaves' names and faces was not all he claimed. At one time or another, while riding with the patrol, he had probably seen every slave on his beat.

He frowned at "Solon." "Funny. I seem to remember that name but not that face. Jebediah, are you *sure* that there is a Sabrehill nigger?"

"All right," Bassett said, swinging his long, bony frame down from his horse, before Jebediah could answer, "out of your saddles, men. If old Balbo don't recognize a nigger, sure as hell something is wrong. We're gonna find out what it is, if we gotta take that goddamn wagon off its wheels."

"Now, just a minute," Mr. Greener said, his eyes widening with alarm as he moved to block Bassett, "you ain't gonna touch this here wagon!"

Bassett shoved Mr. Greener back and cocked his right arm and fist. "You gonna stop me?"

Young Paddy Greener tried to grab Bassett from behind. "Don't you do that, mister!"

That was all Bassett wanted. Spinning around, he threw his fist, catching Paddy squarely on the mouth and knocking him flying to the ground. In an instant, Mr. Greener was on Bassett's back. While Bassett struggled to throw him off, Rowan and Caley Carstairs jumped down from their horses and came running to his aid. When Jebediah moved toward them, he felt a big hand grab him by the back of the collar, and Jeppson said, "You just don't do a thing, Jebediah."

Rowan threw Mr. Greener aside, and Caley stood over Paddy, who was wiping blood from his mouth. The Savannah slave looked about in fear and confusion. Bassett, breathing hard, laughed. "Well, now!" he said. "Well, now, wonder what these here freckle-face nigger lovers is hiding in this here wagon. Reckon as good citizens, we just gonna have to find out."

"Mr. Bassett," Jebediah said, "that wagon and everything in it belongs to Mr. Justin Sabre and Mr. Joshua Greener, and you have no right—"

"No right!" Bassett took a few quick steps toward Jebediah. "No right! Ain't no nigger gonna talk to me that way! Ain't *no* nigger—" His open hand cut a fiery path across

Jebediah's face. Involuntarily, Jebediah raised his hands to protect himself. At once, Jeppson pulled up hard on his collar, and Bassett shot a fist like a battering ram deep into Jebediah's belly. Jeppson let go of the collar, and Jebediah, head down and fighting for air, dropped to his knees.

"Now we gonna find out just what Mr. Justin Sabre got hiding here," Bassett said, and Jebediah heard him clambering up into the wagon.

In spite of the pain in his guts and lungs, Jebediah managed to raise his head and look around. The Savannah slave was wisely keeping his distance. Mr. Greener looked helpless in the face of the much bigger, heavier Rowan Carstairs, and when Paddy Greener tried to get up, Caley Carstairs kicked him back down with a bootheel to the shoulder.

At the sound of tearing fabric, Jebediah looked at the wagon. Bassett was cutting the canvas cover with his knife and then tearing it away. "Now maybe we can see something," he said, when a third of the cover was gone. "Now maybe we can see just what's hid in here."

Bending down, Bassett picked up a bolt of cloth and threw it into the road. Another bolt followed it. He picked up a rifle. "You damage that there gun," Mr. Greener said, "and I'll kill you!" Bassett laughed and threw the rifle off the other side of the wagon. He picked up a wooden box and hurled it down into the road. The box smashed, and loaves of sugar rolled in the dust. Philo Bassett was having his day.

He ducked under what remained of the wagon's cover. Someone screamed—a child.

"Well, what we got here!" Bassett said. He dragged Damien up out of the wagon, while Katie Anne followed, crying, "No, no, no, no!"

"Ain't nothing in that pass 'bout a pickaninny, is there, Balbo?" Bassett asked.

"Nothing."

"Ever seen this boy before?"

"Not that I recall."

Bassett casually dropped Damien over the side of the

wagon. "You don't suppose that rascal Justin is trafficking in runaways, do you?"

"Wouldn't be surprised."

He picked up the sobbing Katie Anne by the back of the dress. "Now, this is what I call a real light-skinned nigger."

"I think that's Justin's daughter."

"Did I say she wasn't?"

He dropped Katie Anne out of the wagon, and both children ran to Jebediah's arms. He embraced and tried to comfort them while his strength returned. When he looked up, Bassett was still throwing bolts of cloth, boxes, the second rifle, anything he could get his hands on, from the wagon.

Cold fury helped to bring Jebediah's strength back. Releasing the children, he rose to his feet. He had a legal excuse for trying to stop Bassett—the man was damaging Sabre property, and the Greeners were witnesses. But at that moment, he didn't need an excuse. Bassett had laid his hands on Damien. And on Katie Anne, too, for that matter. Bassett would pay.

With each step he took toward the wagon, his strength seemed to grow. He came to a halt, feet apart and arms out from his body, and looked up at Bassett.

"Mr. Bassett," he called in something close to a roar, "you come down here!"

Bassett looked at him in surprise, then burst out laughing. "You better just mind how you talk to a white man, boy!"

"Mr. Bassett, I am telling you to come down here!"

Mr. Bassett's eyes widened. "Boy, do you know what you are saying?"

"Mr. Bassett, you come down here right now, or I am coming up after you!"

Bassett stared.

Jebediah had gone too far, and he knew it. It was unlikely that any black man had ever talked to Bassett in such a way before, and, if Bassett could help it, none ever would—and live. But the old madness was welling up in Jebediah, and nothing could stop him now.

Suddenly, lithe as a cat, Bassett leapt from the wagon, past Jebediah, and landed in the road in a crouch. Jebediah turned to face him, his own knees bent. He took a step forward.

Bassett stuck a bony forefinger out at him. "Don't you try it, boy, don't you try it!"

Jebediah was unaware of anyone but Bassett: Everyone else seemed to have disappeared. The madness pounded in his brain as he took another step. "You touched that boy," he said. "You touched Mr. Justin's little girl."

"Yeah," Bassett said, whipping out his knife again, "and now I'm gonna touch you. You have just sassed your last white man, nigger."

Still crouched, he began weaving from side to side in a graceful snakelike motion. The knife, always pointed at Jebediah, was like a natural extension of his arm. He circled to Jebediah's left, the knife always moving, always threatening.

Bassett laughed. "Think you can outrun me, nigger? It's your only chance."

The knife flashed in Jebediah's face, vanished, darted toward his belly. Jebediah jumped back from it. Grinning, Bassett advanced on him again, the knife moving gracefully through the air like a rattler threatening to strike. Again it darted at Jebediah's face. But this time Jebediah saw it coming. Instantly, his left hand swept it aside, and his right hand smashed into Bassett's face.

"He hit me!" Bassett's cry was more one of outrage than of pain. "You seen him, the nigger hit me!"

Before Jebediah could strike again, Rowan and Caley Carstairs were on him. Rowan's fist pounded into his face, and Caley tripped him, throwing him down onto his back.

"Hit me!" Bassett screamed, almost womanishly. "Nigger hit a white man!"

Jebediah raised a leg, trying to protect himself, but Bassett was already over him, coming down, the knife thrusting toward Jebediah's upper belly.

A pistol shot crashed through the air. Bassett rose up and reeled back as if he had been hit, but there was no mark on him. Rowan and Caley released Jebediah and moved back toward Jeppson and their horses.

Jebediah raised his head and looked about. Damien and Katie Anne were clinging to each other at the roadside. Jeppson was still on his horse. No one was moving.

Then he saw Justin Sabre. Mr. Justin had come around the bend of the road in his carriage and pulled up behind the wagon. He sat perfectly still for a moment, a small pistol in his hand, and the dark, deep-set eyes in the long, hard-jawed face seemed to take in every detail of the scene before him. Then he thrust the pistol into his coat pocket and lowered his rangy, broad-shouldered frame to the road.

"I'm sorry, Mr. Justin," Jebediah said, as he got to his feet, "but these people—this man—"

"I know," Justin said, "I heard and saw enough."

Without haste, he took off his coat, folded it carefully, and put it into the carriage. He took off his hat and put it on top of his coat. As he pulled on a pair of heavy, well-fitting leather gloves, he turned toward Bassett, and his mouth took on a scornful twist.

"Bassett, isn't it? Aren't you one of the Bassett clan?"

Forcing a grin, Bassett held up his knife and thumbed the blade. "*Mister* Bassett to you, nigger lover."

"I'm not armed, Mr. Bassett," Justin said, still strolling forward, while rolling up his sleeves, "not with a pistol or a knife."

Bassett laughed. He tossed his knife to Rowan Carstairs. He spat on both palms, lathered his hands, and made fists.

And Justin hit him.

Simply hit him squarely in the face with a big left fist, knocking him back against one of the horses. Grabbed him by the shirtfront, whirled him around, and hit him again, knocking him sprawling in the dirt of the road. Rowan and Caley started toward them, but held off as Jebediah stepped in their way and Mr. Greener pulled an ax handle from the wagon bed.

Justin picked Bassett up and threw him against the side of the wagon. "How many of you people do I have to make eat dirt," he asked, "before you learn to keep your hands off me and mine?"

And he hit Bassett again, pounded the bleeding nose and mouth, hit the eyes until they closed, refused to let Bassett fall, held him up long enough to crack a few ribs, then threw him on his back in the dirt again.

Jebediah ran to the weeping children and gathered them to him. When he looked around, Justin was down on one knee beside Bassett. He lifted Bassett by the shirtfront and slapped him, once, twice, three times with a heavy leather-gloved hand. Then, as Bassett gasped, he grabbed a hand-ful of roadside dirt and shoved it into his mouth.

"Now, eat that!"

Bassett made small bleating sounds and tried to spit the dirt out.

Justin grabbed another handful of dirt and shoved it into Bassett's mouth. "I said, eat that!" The gloved hand slammed across Bassett's face twice more. "Eat, Bassett, eat!"

Somehow, Bassett managed to swallow.

Justin let go of him. Stood up. "All right," he said, with a glance around, "get him on his horse. And then get the hell out my wagon's way."

Rowan and Caley Carstairs hurriedly and without a word, got the sobbing, bleating Bassett up on his horse, where he sat hunched over and barely able to hang on. Justin gave the horse a light slap on the rump, and it obediently continued on its way toward Charleston. Rowan and Caley quickly mounted their horses and fol-lowed after.

Jeppson grinned down from his horse. "Mr. Sabre, I'm sorry Philo got just a little out of line—"

"On your way, Jeppson, or you may find yourself eating dirt, too."

"You got no call—"

"On your way!"

Jeppson shrugged. He kept his grin but his eyes were hard. "I can see, Mr. Sabre, that you're a mite out of sorts today."

Jeppson rode on, and Jebediah watched as the four men disappeared among the sweetgums. He thought he must have been mad, even to consider Adaba's request that he remain in the South for a time. A crazy, unbroken, defiant nigger like Jebediah Hayes could not be allowed to go on living in South Carolina by these redneck buckra. For him to remain here was to die.

But at least Damien was safe for now. Damien and Katie Anne.

⊷ 3 ⊶

"CATHERINE ANNE," JUSTIN THUNDERED, "do you know how worried your new momma has been? If I hadn't guessed where you were—Damien, how could you worry Miss Lucy so? Oh, for shame, children, for shame!"

The children burst into fresh tears, *Wah, wah, wah!,* and Justin struggled manfully to keep a straight face.

Jebediah had a bad moment when Justin asked who the young black was; when Jebediah told him, Justin stared at "Solon" then at Jebediah again. Then he shrugged and shook his head and climbed into his carriage with the children to head back for Charleston. A man couldn't learn *all* the names and faces at Sabrehill in such a short time as he had been there, could he?

The rest of the trip was uneventful, and the next night, very late, the wagon rolled through the Sabrehill gateway and up the oak-lined avenue Jebediah had first seen more than three years earlier. Without stopping the wagon, he reached into the back, found the Savannah slave's blanket roll, and handed it to him.

"You know where to go now?"

"Johnny Dove, he say there a old voodoo house at one corner of the quarters—"

"You don't have to tell me. Good luck, boy."

He started to follow the wagon, but the slave called to him. "Mister . . . Jeb . . . I do thank you."

"No need."

"Johnny Dove, he say that what people here call you— Mr. Jeb. He don't say why. Now I know *why* they call you Mr. Jeb."

Jebediah watched as the slave disappeared into the darkness in the direction of the field quarters. Now that they had arrived safely at Sabrehill, all the trouble, all the risk, seemed worthwhile. He remembered Adaba's words:

114

"Think of those who may never be free if you don't help them."

He shook his head. He had as much right to freedom as any other black man. Maybe more, considering the number of white men—Bassett, Jeppson, Duke Avery—who would have liked to see him dead. He *couldn't* stay. Come January, he was heading north.

But what would happen to Damien after he was gone? Who would make him practice long division and teach him algebra? Who would see to it that he read the right books and understood what he read?

Jebediah couldn't help asking the questions, though in his heart he knew perfectly well that they were unnecessary. At the age of nine, the boy could read virtually anything in English that was put before him. He had access to the Sabre library and spent hours in it. Whenever Katie Anne and her brothers were tutored, he was allowed to attend the lessons, and he learned as fast as any of them. He reminded Jebediah of himself at the same age, back on the Pinkham plantation, getting more out of the lessons than little Willy Pinkham ever had.

Except that Damien's going to be smarter than I, he thought proudly. *If he keeps on studying, he's going to be smarter than I ever could be.*

"Jebediah, can I go play now?"

"*May* I go play now. Finish your problems first."

Damien, lying on a rag rug in the front room of the overseer's house, made a sound of frustration and wiped the last arithmetic problem from his slate. "I want to go play with Cat."

"Cat?" Jebediah was amused. "Is that what you call her now? Cat for Catherine?"

"Ain't for Catherine. She a catamount."

"Don't say ain't. She *is* a catamount."

"She sho-o-o' is!"

"Do your problems."

It was a chilly but bright Sunday morning in the middle of November, a week after the Sabres' return to the plantation. Jebediah, his borrowed copy of *Don Quixote* for a moment abandoned, slouched comfortably down in his chair and watched Damien scratch out another problem on the slate. With the advent of cool weather, Jebediah had procured a pair of pants for the boy to wear under his long-tailed shirt, but he still had trouble keeping shoes on him, and he resisted an impulse to reach down and tickle Damien's feet and then pick him up and embrace him.

The trouble, he admitted hopelessly, was that he loved the boy. A companion to the other children and to Katie Anne in particular, Damien had come down from Virginia with the Sabres the previous spring, and from the day of his arrival he had followed Jebediah about, like a puppy that attaches itself to a much older and bigger dog. It was difficult, Jebediah soon discovered, to resist the pleasures of a child's admiration, and when he realized how intelligent Damien was, those pleasures were redoubled.

"Mr. Justin," he said, soon after the family's arrival, "has anybody told you how bright that little fellow is?"

"Nobody had to tell me," Justin replied. "My children speak French fluently—we make them use it during their lessons so that they don't forget it. And Damien hadn't been attending lessons with them for six weeks when I discovered that he was speaking French too. By now, I'm sure he speaks it almost as well as they do."

"I hope, Mr. Justin," Jebediah said cautiously, "that maybe someday you'll find it in your heart to do something . . ."

"You mean it would be a sin to waste a mind like that by keeping it in slavery." Justin smiled. "Want to take him north with you, Jebediah?"

The suggestion startled Jebediah. "Why, I—I hadn't thought—"

"I'd let you take him, but I'm afraid he's too young. He still needs something more like a family around him. But when he's ready . . ."

"I'll be waiting."

It'll only be a few years before he comes north, Jebediah thought, *but if only I could have just a little more time with him . . . teach him the things he needs to know. . . .*

Damien squirmed on the rag rug, and his face wrinkled up.

"What's the matter, Damien?"

"Cat."

"Now, never you mind Cat. You didn't do your problems yesterday, and that means you have to do them today."

Damien's shoulders slumped and his head hung down, but he went back to work.

Of course, Jebediah reflected, Damien's near-constant companionship was in some respects a mixed blessing. For instance, he slept in a cot in Jebediah's bedroom almost as much as he did in the big house. Usually, this was fine with Jebediah. There was more than one wench at Sabrehill who would have liked to share that room with him, but he was increasingly convinced that a wife and children had no place in his plans for the future, and the presence of Damien helped keep the wenches away. Still, Jebediah was a young and vital man, and there were times when the need came on him so strongly that he wanted only to abandon all common sense and lie for a few hours in the arms of Leila, the housekeeper.

Lovely Leila, one of his oldest and dearest friends at Sabrehill. Jebediah smiled to himself. She had been a housemaid when he first arrived, and he had taken her for an empty-headed little piece of fancy good. But, as with Jessie, he had found out he was wrong. Leila was a woman struggling to maintain some inner freedom and dignity, no matter what the odds, and when he had needed her, Leila had been there. . . .

"Cat."

Jebediah recalled himself to the present. "Now, Damien . . ."

"Cat."

Something about the way Damien said the word arrested Jebediah. There was no note of pleading or complaining in his voice. He simply said it. And when Jebediah looked around at him, the boy was no longer squirming on the rug. He lay perfectly still, his head up, as if he were staring at something in the distance.

"Cat," he said again.

"What is it, Damien?"

"I don't know." The boy sat up and gave his head a hard shake. "Cat! Cat!"

Jebediah felt a chill sweep over him. "What about Cat?"

"I don't know! I don't know!" The boy pounded his heels against the floor in a rapid tattoo. "Cat! Cat! Cat!"

"Damien, if anything's wrong—if you'll just tell me—"

"I don't *know!*" The boy jumped to his feet and looked wildly around. "I don't *know*, Jebediah! I must find Cat!"

"If you only want to play—"

"*No!*" Damien looked genuinely frightened and on the verge of tears. "I *must* find Cat, Jebediah, I *must*, I *must!*"

Jebediah wanted to say, *Now, calm yourself, Damien— this is nonsense!* But somehow he knew it was not nonsense, and he heard himself saying, almost as if another person were speaking, "Then *find* Cat, Damien! Damien, *take me to Cat!*"

Again, the boy looked around, as if he had no idea of where to start. Then he darted out the door and down the steps into the courtyard. Jebediah followed him.

"Cat!" the boy called. "Cat!" But there was no answer.

Damien turned and ran down the east service lane, past the carpenter and blacksmith shops, with Jebediah close behind. As they went by the coach house, Zagreus, the stable master, came out and joined them. Damien called Cat's name again.

Somewhere ahead of them, Leila screamed.

The cry had seemed to come from beyond the stables. As they ran in its direction, they saw Leila standing by the paddock.

"That horse," she cried, "oh, Jebediah, that horse, he kill her!"

Then Jebediah saw: Katie Anne was in the paddock, near the other side, and before her, doing a kind of troubled dance, was a sorrel gelding. Being gelded had done nothing to gentle the horse down—in fact, it had grown more dangerous every year, and Jebediah suspected it was more than a little crazy.

"Katie Anne," Jebediah called, "move backward toward the fence! Slowly! Zagreus, I'll bust your ass! What's that horse doing out?"

"Jebediah, I don't know!"

As he climbed between the poles of the paddock fence, Jebediah saw that Katie Anne wasn't moving. She was staring at the horse as if mesmerized. He decided not to call to her again, but to avoid startling her. Behind him, he heard Leila explaining that Miss Lucy had sent her looking for the child, and . . .

Then he heard nothing more, as he advanced, concentrating entirely on the prancing, kicking horse and on Katie Anne. The horse had kicked out two stall doors since summer, and he wondered why the hell Mr. Justin didn't get rid of it before it killed somebody.

Like Katie Anne.

Suddenly the horse reared up, pawing the air and moving over the child. Leila screamed again. Jebediah ran toward Katie Anne, swept her up with one arm, whirled her away, and felt a hoof tearing down through his shirt-sleeve and scraping away flesh. "Out, Katie Anne, out!" he yelled, and she moved at last, running toward the fence. Jebediah realized that the horse was going to rear again. It was wearing no headstall, so he did the only thing he could at that instant—grabbed it by the head and one ear.

"Now, you son of a bitch," he snarled, "pick on someone your own size!"

Although the horse stomped and pulled and tried to bite and to rear, he managed to hang on until Katie Anne had climbed out of the paddock. Then he gave the horse the best kick in the shin he could manage, let go, and threw himself between the fence poles.

He lay in the grass panting until Zagreus and Leila came and helped him up.

"Katie Anne," he said hoarsely, "Cat—what were you doing in there with that mean old critter?"

"I didn't think he'd be mean to me, Jebediah," she answered innocently. "I *like* horses."

He laughed. She was eight years old and getting to be a

load, but not for him, so he picked her up in his arms to carry her back to the big house.

That was when he realized that he loved this one too.

What had happened on that Sunday morning? How had Damien known that Katie Anne was in danger?

Jebediah could only speculate. He had little belief in voodoo or in spirit influences, but he did know that sometimes people sensed things without knowing how they did it—as when he went out to the field quarters some evenings and knew there was trouble brewing without knowing *how* he knew. The place might be too quiet, or the sounds might be subtly wrong, or somebody might not be where he should have been. He might have no idea what it was—until later, perhaps—but he would know that *something* was amiss.

And then there were times when certain people developed a very special bond between them. When that happened, they might think the same thoughts and say the same words at the very same time. One of them might know, without thinking about it, what the other would want for supper that evening. Or that the other would already be home for supper if he weren't in trouble.

Perhaps the whole thing was that simple. Jebediah knew that Katie Anne and Damien were almost constantly together. She trailed after Damien in much the same way that Damien trailed after Jebediah, and in spite of their frequent childish quarrels, he had no doubt that there was some kind of bond between the two children. They knew each other's ways intimately. Wouldn't it be natural, then, for Damien to know, without really knowing *how* he knew, that Katie Anne would have come to join him in Jebediah's house by that time on a Sunday morning—unless she was in trouble somewhere? Might not that produce an increasing unease, and perhaps badly disturb the boy? And might not something in him know that her affection for horses had probably led her to the paddock?

And hadn't something in Jebediah *known* that Damien was not simply throwing a childish tantrum in order to go play with Katie Anne? Hadn't he heard that something-in-him speaking? *"Then find Cat, Damien! Damien, take me to Cat!"*

Or maybe all his common sense and his reasoning was mere self-delusion. Maybe what had happened really *was* voodoo and spirit messages and the way of Danbahlah.

He was still pondering the matter that evening, while he and Leila sat together on the porch of his house, when Damien approached. Inwardly, Jebediah groaned. The close brush with death that morning had done something to him: It was one of those times when he wouldn't have minded having Leila stay with him—Leila, who had so lovingly washed and bandaged his torn and aching arm.

Nevertheless, he smiled and said, "What is it, boy?"

Damien looked dubiously at Leila, then said, "Mr. Justin. He want you in the office."

"He *wants* me, Damien. Run tell him I'm on my way."

Damien looked at Leila again, and ran off toward the brightly lit plantation office.

"Do you want me to wait for you, sugar," Leila asked softly, as he stood up, "or am I wasting my time?"

"Pretty lady," Jebediah said, bending down to kiss the tip of her nose, "you do just as you please."

Justin was alone when he arrived at the office. The room, once the scene of his humiliation, had become almost comfortable through familiarity—the two desks and the table, the prints on the walls, the old, unreliable pepperbox pistol, half-hidden under a pile of papers. As Jebediah looked about, wondering if the tin box on one of the desks still held his bill of sale, Justin asked him to sit down.

"Jebediah, I have something important to discuss with you. But first of all, I want to tell you that, even if you hadn't long ago been promised your freedom, you certainly earned it this morning. I have no doubt that you saved my daughter's life."

Jebediah shrugged. "I did what I had to do, Mr. Justin. I couldn't let that little girl get hurt."

Justin let that go by. "Not that any man but a criminal should ever *have* to earn his freedom," he went on. "And furthermore . . ." Justin looked about the room as if avoiding Jebediah's eyes, and his face looked strained. "Furthermore, you've been told that you might leave here any time you wished. And that's what makes what I have to say so difficult."

Jebediah's breath stopped. His hands gripped the edge of his chair. He could only think, *Sweet Jesus, is it happening again?* He remembered his first master, Mr. Pinkham, so apologetic that he couldn't give Jebediah his promised freedom. *"But it'll only be a matter of time, Jebediah, and meanwhile you and your parents will continue as house servants."* And the horror that had followed.

Justin swung around in his chair and faced Jebediah. He looked puzzled for a moment, and then his eyes widened with shock. "Good God, Jebediah! You didn't think I meant—! You can leave here in the morning, if that's what you want!"

"I didn't know what you meant," Jebediah said weakly.

"I should think you'd know by now you could trust me. But then, why the hell should you?"

"I'm sorry, Mr. Justin. Of course, I trust you. What did you want to discuss?"

Justin shook his head and stood up. "I wanted to ask you a favor. But I've no right. I can't do it now."

"We're friends, Mr. Justin. You have the right."

Justin still appeared reluctant to say anything more, but he sat down again.

"In that case, I'll go straight to the point. Jebediah, we need you here. Oh, not forever, but at least for a little longer. You know how difficult it is to find a truly good overseer. Some of them are fine, but most of them are . . . well . . . one cut above a slave trader. We're planning to build a new overseer's house, a big one, fit for a whole family, and once that's done, maybe we can attract someone good, someone who knows how to handle the people the way you do. But meanwhile, if you could see your way clear to staying the next year . . ."

Jebediah felt his heart sinking. Another year. He had had the feeling that something like this was going to happen. Did Mr. Justin have any idea of what he was asking?

And if he stayed, it would mean falling in with Adaba's

plans. *"For the fun of it!"* the big black renegade had said. Jebediah shook his head and uttered a choked laugh, and Justin looked at him oddly.

Still, would it be so bad? A man must earn his livelihood somehow, as Adaba had pointed out, and actually Jebediah *liked* his work at Sabrehill. He was good at it. He was proud of it.

"Oh, I suppose it's too much to ask," Justin was saying. "People like Jeppson and the Bassetts and their kind resent you, and they're a constant danger. . . ."

Exactly. There were plenty of good reasons to stay at Sabrehill a little longer, and he trusted Miss Lucy and Mr. Justin as two dear friends should be trusted. The chances were that he would get through the next year at Sabrehill very nicely, even happily. But with ignorant buckra like Jeppson and the Bassetts ready to give him trouble at any opportunity, he'd be a fool to stay.

"But if you are willing, Jebediah, of course we'll compensate you. And be forever grateful. I hope you'll think about it."

Jebediah swung around in his chair to face the door and the darkness of the courtyard. One more year.

Damien came to the door. Smiled at him. *A little more time with the boy,* Jebediah thought, *a little more time to teach him. And why wasn't he in bed?*

"I've already thought about it, Mr. Justin," he said. "All right. I'll stay."

-⊰ 4 ⊱-

THE TRUTH OF THE matter, it slowly dawned on him, was that he *did not want* to go north.

For years he had told himself that the only thing he wanted on this earth was his freedom. He had told himself that he must avoid any tie that might keep him from attaining that end. But now that his goal was within his reach, he found that, like most other men, both slave and free, he had unwittingly formed innumerable bonds of affection, which conspired to keep him right where he was. There was Miss Lucy, with whom he had labored so closely for the last several years. There were Zagreus, the stable master, and his white-skinned woman, Binnie, who aided him in his Underground Railroad activities. There was Leila, who more than once had bound up his wounds. And Cheney, the chief driver, and Saul, the blacksmith, and how many others?

And now Damien and Cat. Perhaps Damien and Cat above all.

The truth of the matter, he admitted to himself with some astonishment, was that, in spite of every evil thing that had happened to him at Sabrehill, he loved the place. Or maybe he loved it, at least in part, *because* of all that had happened to him. At times his enemies had very nearly broken him, but in the end he had conquered Sabrehill and made it his own—the people, the land, the little house he lived in. They were his domain, as much as they were Miss Lucy's and Mr. Justin's, and he was damned if he was going to let the Bassetts and the Jeppsons drive him away.

But he knew they would. Sooner or later.

He and the Sabres had little to fear from most of the nearby planters—the Kimbroughs and Buckridges and Pettigrews and McClintocks. They might disapprove of Justin Sabre's abolitionist ideas, but at least Justin didn't waste his breath preaching them; and Sabrehill's having a black overseer troubled them somewhat less, now that Justin was in charge. And, after all, whatever residual disapproval there might be, the Sabres were of their own kind, aristocrats, members of the chivalry.

No, the danger came from the Jeppsons and Bassetts and Carstairses and their kind. Jeppson, of course, did own a large plantation, Redbird, just up the river. But the others had little or nothing—a small farm and a few slaves at most—and it was these who were most willing, even eager, to ride with the patrol and exercise its authority over the blacks.

The next spring, on returning from a trip to Charleston, Jebediah learned that they had formed a "special watch" on Sabrehill. They would take turns patrolling Sabrehill at night to see what they might detect passing through the quarters.

"How did you find out about it?" he asked Zagreus. Jebediah had arrived that night with four runaways, and after they were hidden away, he met with Zagreus and Binnie in their room over the coach house.

"Housekeeper at Redbird tell Binnie and me," Zagreus said. He was a tall, slim, dark man, a few years older than Jebediah, though he looked younger. "You know how they always been s'picious of Mr. Sabre and Sabrehill. And right, too. More'n one runaway's trail led to Sabrehill 'fore it disappeared—"

"Like he flew awa-a-ay on a bro-o-own dove," white-skinned Binnie drawled, smiling.

"And since last fall," Zagreus added, "that Mr. Philo Bassett will do anything he can to get you hung up and burned alive."

"Still, it could be just talk."

Zagreus shook his head. "I've seen them. They don't come every night, far as I can tell, but I been going out early and just sitting and listening and moving slow, and three times I've seen 'em—Mr. Rolly Joe Macon and Mr. P. V. Tucker and Mr. Philo Bassett." Zagreus grinned. "But they don't see me—till one night I say, 'Why, good evening, Mr. Rolly Joe, sir. You here looking for Mr. Justin? Be glad to take you to him, sir!' And, oh, my, ain't old shit-eatin' Rolly Joe friendly all of a sudden! 'Ain't no need, Zagreus, heh-heh-heh, ain't no need! Was just passing down the road and thought I saw somebody skulking 'round 'bout here! But ain't nobody here, heh-heh-heh, so ain't no need! No need to bother Mr. Justin!' "

"What you think, Jebediah," Binnie asked, "should we tell Mr. Justin?"

Jebediah considered the possibility and rejected it. "Best not. You know Mr. Justin's temper, and if he starts busting white-trash heads, that just means more trouble for us. No, what we have to do is send out word that this station is closed down for a little while. No more passengers to go through Sabrehill until we know it's safe."

Zagreus agreed. "And we'll be special careful, shipping out those four you brought here tonight."

This "special watch" might be an inconvenience, Jebediah reflected as he left the coach house, but he doubted that it would last long. Except perhaps for Balbo Jeppson, the kind of people involved simply didn't have the patience and discipline to keep it going.

When he reached his house, he saw that a lamp was alight, apparently in the bedroom. Damien? But if Damien had decided to spend the night here, he would have arrived earlier, and he wouldn't have bothered with a lamp.

Jebediah entered the house and crossed the sitting room to the bedroom.

Leila, deep in his bed, the blanket pulled up over her shoulder, smiled at him. "Well, 'bout time you got here, candy man," she said.

Jebediah put his fists on his hips and pursed his lips to show an exasperation he didn't really feel. Leila continued to smile, her lips moving invitingly.

He sighed, shook his head, dropped into a chair. "God-damnit, Leila," he said wearily, as he began pulling off his boots, "get out of my bed."

" 'Course, sugar," Leila said. "But it's a mite cool out tonight—thought I'd warm it up for you."

"I don't care what you thought," he said, dropping one boot and tugging at the other, "I've had a long, hard day—"

He broke off, as Leila slipped out of the bed. He had expected her to be wearing, if anything at all, her usual old shift or torn cotton gown. Instead, she was wearing a gown of gauzy black silk, trimmed with lace. As she moved toward him, the dim light of the turned-down lamp passed through it, clearly revealing her slim-waisted, high-breasted body, and he felt a hot rush of desire.

Leila smiled. "You like my gown?"

"Where the hell did you get that?"

"It was Miss Amity's, long time ago. I found it, and Miss Lucy let me keep it."

Of course. It was the kind of gown you weren't apt to see on a slave wench unless she was a rich man's fancy or had an appreciative and grateful mistress.

Jebediah was silent, as Leila pulled off his other boot and dropped it to the floor. He let her pull his shirt over his head and cast it aside. But when she knelt between his knees, slid her hands up his trembling thighs, and began unbuckling his belt, his hand closed on hers.

"No. Leila, it's not fair to you."

She closed her eyes. She was breathing harder, and he saw the rise and fall of her breasts under the lace. "It's been a long time, weeks and weeks, must be months since you was in me, Jebediah—"

"I've told you time and again, I'm going north. And I'm going alone. Because I don't know what it'll be like up there, maybe I'll starve—"

Her eyes opened slightly. "I know you ain't got love for me like I got for you. You still dreaming on some other wench?"

Laughing quietly, he leanced forward and kissed her. "No. I stopped dreaming of any other wench a long time ago."

"Then I don't care. Ain't gonna stop you going north if that what you want. 'Cause I know I can't. But while you here . . ."

Her fingers tugged at his belt again and began unfasten-ing buttons. He wanted to stop her, knew he should stop her, but his body responded with a will of its own. With a sigh, he gave up and helped her slip off the rest of his clothes.

Much later, when the lamp was out and Leila lay sleeping with her head on his shoulder, he wondered if he would ever reach the North. At that hour, with Leila in his arms, he hardly even cared.

The "special watch" on Sabrehill continued throughout the summer—longer than Jebediah had expected. It was not a constant watch, but once or twice a week, at irregular intervals, a Bassett or a Carstairs or one of their friends might be observed prowling about the plantation by anyone who cared to look. By the end of August, however, the "watcher" was as often as not found asleep, and thereafter no more were to be seen. By October, when Jebediah had to make another trip to Charleston, he felt reasonably safe in bringing back a couple of runaways with him.

In November, he saw that Mr. Justin was worried by the fact that he still hadn't found a satisfactory new overseer, though the new house which was meant to attract one was nearly completed. So he told Mr. Justin not to worry—he would stay on a bit longer. Mr. Justin sighed with relief.

Jebediah rarely saw Adaba. Sometimes a fugitive would arrive, guided by a conductor from a not-too-distant plantation. Sometimes one would arrive alone, carrying a forged pass. Jebediah always looked to see if it had an "accidental" scrawl somewhere on it: three wavy lines that, taken together, suggested an undulating sea—or a flying dove. One always had to beware of spies.

Of course, Jebediah observed with amusement, none of this activity disturbed the neighbors in the slightest, since they were quite unaware of it. Not even the occasional local runaway particularly disturbed them, since, without the Underground Railroad's help, he was almost invariably caught. Indeed, most slaves were so easily caught that they could be "sold running." Tired of chasing that slave that keeps showing his heels? Then the next time he does it, just sell him and let someone else chase him down. The more troublesome case was when a few thousand dollars' worth of property vanished and was never seen again.

That happened the following spring. The hounds tracked three slaves from the McClintock plantation to Sabrehill—and there the trail vanished.

Naturally, the pattyrollers raised more hell than they had in several years, but Mr. Justin kept them in control and nobody got hurt. And he convinced the neighbors that his abolitionist views had not somehow inspired the incident and that he had had nothing whatever to do with it—which was absolutely true.

Nevertheless, the incident did have an unfortunate consequence. The Jeppson crowd, as Jebediah thought of them, once again put a "special watch" on Sabrehill, and the station had to be closed down for most of the summer. But that, too, passed, activity was resumed, and in September Jebediah met a special passenger.

He waited until he thought Leila was asleep, but as he sat in the dark pulling on his boots, she sighed and reached for him. "Jebediah?" she called sleepily, when she failed to find him. "Jeb, honey?"

"It's all right, Leila. Go back to sleep."

She sat up and blinked her eyes. "Is it morning already? What you doing up?"

"No, you've only been sleeping a little while. I have to go check here and there, see that everything's all right, make sure the quarters are quiet."

"That ain't your job. Let Cheney do it—he's the chief driver."

"Now, Leila . . ." He went to her, laid her back on the bed, and sat down beside her. "This is just something I have to do every now and then, you know that. It's so the people will feel that I'm looking after them. You go to sleep and I'll be back before you know it."

He could barely see her frown in the dark. "Jebediah, you up to something again, gonna get you in trouble?"

It had been impossible to hide his activities from her altogether.

"No, Leila. I'm not going to get into trouble. I promise you."

She reached up and touched his face. "Sometimes you go out at night, and I get scared maybe I never see you again."

Her words gave him a pang. So often he had reminded her that eventually he must leave Sabrehill—alone—but the months and the years had drifted by, and still he had not left. And now it was September and, as far as he knew, Mr. Justin still had not found a satisfactory overseer. It was not surprising, really, considering the kind of man most of them were.

Well, did it really matter if he stayed another year? Or even another after that?

But how would he ever leave Leila then?

He leaned down and kissed her eyes, whispering, "You're not going to get rid of me that easily."

"Mr. Jeb," she murmured happily. "Candy man . . ."

He left his house and walked silently along the east service lane, keeping in the shadows. He entered the coach house and felt his way to the stairs that led to the overhead rooms. He mounted the stairs and knocked on the trap-door, a pattern of taps Zagreus would recognize. The door opened almost at once, and he ascended into Zag's and Binnie's room.

Even with but a single candle burning, it was a cheerful place, compared to most slave quarters. Zagreus had plastered and painted it, it had three glazed windows, and Miss Lucy had provided some furnishings and even a couple of pictures for the walls. But that was not what interested Jebediah now.

"Is he ready?"

As if in answer to his question, a short and thin but wiry-looking man came out of the next room, where he had been hiding for the last couple of days. He had his few belongings in a bundle under his arm, and he was smiling broadly.

"I just don't know how to thank all you people," he said with a northern accent.

"Oh, ain't no need to thank us, Mr. Ames," Binnie said. "We're only doing what we think is right."

"But after all this time . . ." Tears came to Calvin Ames's eyes. "More'n five years since I've seen my family . . . since they kidnapped me and sold me to them Avery people. You don't know what it was like!"

"I think I do," Jebediah said gently. "I was bought and sold by the Averys too, you know. It must have been about the same time."

"Five years," Calvin Ames said, shaking his head. "Five years down in Georgia. My children won't even know me."

"They'll know you, Calvin," Zagreus said. "They're waiting for you. Johnny Dove has talked to your family, and he says they're all well and waiting."

"Do you really think I'll be in Philadelphia before Christmas?"

"With any luck, long before," Jebediah said. "You're traveling on the Brown Dove Line, Calvin. It flies!"

Zagreus and Binnie gave Calvin Ames a last good-luck wish, and Jebediah led him down the stairs. The trapdoor closed behind them. When they went out into the lane, all was quiet, all serene. Jebediah could have wished for less moonlight, but at least the sky was clear and the air was cool—a good night for traveling.

He led the way along the lane. Calvin Ames was on his way home, and Jebediah Hayes would soon be back in his bed.

Damien listened to the sound of Mark and Beau breathing. He and Mark were together in the big bed in the boys' room, and Beau was alone in the little one.

He couldn't sleep. At first he thought it was because of the moonlight that flooded through the window, but then he realized that something was nagging at his mind. It was as if each time he started to drift off, someone whispered into his ear, *No! Don't! You mustn't!*

With a little moan, he turned over in the bed. Something was wrong. He had no idea what it was, but he felt it, and the feeling was growing stronger.

The trouble had to do with Jebediah, he decided. Jebediah had a secret again. Damien could tell when Jebediah had a secret almost as well as he could when Cat had one. He could see it in the way Jebediah stood a little straighter and looked at everything more carefully. He seemed to be *listening* for something. At times, Damien was amazed that *everybody* didn't know that Jebediah had a secret; yet nobody but he, and perhaps Cat and the other children, seemed to notice. Perhaps you stopped noticing things when you grew up.

Jebediah's secrets put him in danger. Damien sensed that, too. But he also sensed that Jebediah would not want him to tell anybody, not even Cat.

He moaned and rolled in the bed again, then remembered that he mustn't disturb Mark and Beau. If they awakened, he couldn't help Jebediah.

Help Jebediah. But what could he do?

He sat up in bed. The bad feeling was growing stronger, and somehow that made it hard to breathe. So he had to do something. Jebediah wouldn't want his help, but he *had* to help him!

He slipped off the bed and knelt, feeling about the floor for his boots. Jebediah said you should never go out at night without wearing boots. In fact, he said that little boys shouldn't go out at night at all. But Damien wasn't little—he was eleven now, wasn't he?

In his boots and nightshirt, he slipped out into the upstairs passage. He paused outside Cat's room, listening. She was sleeping with her baby brother, Macy Aaron. Damien sighed. Macy Aaron was over a year old now and *still* an awful lot of trouble.

Silently, he moved on, down two flights of stairs to the lower passage. He paused at the outside door. He knew he shouldn't be doing this. If Miss Lucy found out, she would be angry. And Mr. Justin and Jebediah would be angry too.

But he went outside anyway. He *had* to.

The moon was still bright and that made the night less scary. He followed the courtyard circle past the dark office and approached the overseer's house.

He stopped. He couldn't go in there.

Leila was in there. He knew. He wasn't supposed to know, nobody was supposed to know, but he almost *always* knew when Leila spent the night with Jebediah. First she would get kind of fidgety and look at Jebediah in certain ways, and if he acted in certain ways in return, that meant she would spend the night with him. Damien didn't actually remember seeing them act that way earlier, but they must have, because *he knew* Leila was in there.

But Leila wouldn't hurt Jebediah.

Then why did he feel that Jebediah was in danger?

Were the pattyrollers coming for Jebediah? Damien shivered at the thought.

No. No pattyrollers.

Jebediah wasn't in his house. Somehow Damien knew it. Then where was he?

Damien entered the east service lane. The dimmest of lights, a candle, flickered in an upstairs window of the coach house and went out. He was right, something was happening, something dangerous. And at the far end of the lane, he saw a shadow move and vanish.

Jebediah.

Whatever was happening, Damien had to watch. And help, if need be. He hurried along the service lane, silently following.

Jebediah led the way east a few hundred yards and then circled north, keeping as much as possible in the shadow of trees, until he and Calvin approached a grove on the far side of the field quarters. He observed the grove from a distance for a few minutes, expecting Adaba to see him and give a signal. When no signal came, he went alone to inspect the grove, then brought Calvin to it.

"Something the matter?" Calvin asked.

"Not a thing." Jebediah tried to sound more certain than he felt. "My friend's a little late, but it's a nice night, so we can just sit down and make ourselves comfortable until he gets here."

They found a comfortable spot at the edge of a small clearing within the grove and sat down on the ground.

Jebediah leaned back at ease against a tree trunk, but Calvin looked nervously about the clearing, trying to see into the surrounding shadows.

"You haven't told me much about your life down in Georgia, Calvin," he said, trying to distract the man. "Was your master very hard on you?"

"No, he wasn't a bad man most of the time—except twice when I tried to run away, and then he dang near killed me. But mostly Mr. Greavy treated his people good."

"What did he say when you told him you'd been kidnapped?"

"Madder'n hell. Said he'd paid for a first-class servant and tailor and he intended to get his money out of me. I told him to write to my family and they'd raise the money, but he wouldn't hear of it. Said I could consider myself his indentured servant. Said when he figured I'd earned what he'd paid and my keep on top of it, then he'd let me go."

"Do you think he would have?"

"Never. First time I ran away, after 'bout six months, he said in another month I would have been free, but now I had to start all over again to make up for all the trouble and expense I'd caused. So then I didn't run away for over two years. He kept saying, 'A little longer, a little longer.' When I finally tried to run away again, like I say, he just about killed me."

"What are you going to do when you get home, Calvin? Go to the law?"

"Sue him, you mean?" Calvin laughed. "How is a poor nigger tailor in Philadelphia ever going to get satisfaction from a rich planter down near Savannah? My only witnesses are his nigger slaves. And that white man that stole me away from Mr. Greavy, and he ain't even American."

Jebediah's unease was growing. Where was Adaba? He tried to keep Calvin talking.

"You mean Mr. Murdock."

Calvin nodded. "Gavin Murdock. Grizzled old geezer, with a beard. Said he was a Scotch-Cherokee Indian. Came prowling 'round the quarters on a Saturday evening. Asked if it was true what some of the other niggers said, that I was Calvin Ames who was kidnapped, and did I want to be free. I figured maybe he was just a nigger stealer, aiming to sell me, but if I didn't take a chance, I'd never be free."

"So you took a chance."

"That's right. The next Saturday night, Mr. Murdock and me just walked away. Kept on walking fast all night long. At first light we came to a farmhouse where they fed us. Then they put me in a wagon with a false bottom, and I slept most of the day, while a little white boy called Freddy Golden drove. Had a couple of hours to rest and relieve myself, and then another white man put me to running through most of the night." Calvin laughed. "With luck, Mr. Greavy didn't even miss me till Monday morning, and by that time—two nights and a day—I figure I was half-way to Charleston."

"Was someone with you all the time?"

"No, a couple of times I had to travel alone, and that was scary. I had a fake ticket, but I didn't figure it would do me much good if somebody stopped me. Anyway, I finally reached a plantation called Jessamine, and the people there sent me here, and—"

"Calvin," Jebediah said, "these names. Don't ever say them to anybody. In fact, it would be best if you just forgot them."

"Oh, I know that," Calvin said quickly. "Mr. Murdock told me right at the beginning. And if it was anybody but you—"

"It's all right. I was just reminding you."

Calvin shook his head. "Still can't hardly believe it. After all this time, gonna see my family."

"That's right. Johnny Dove has had people looking for you ever since he first talked to your wife and brother. Still, you were mighty lucky that Mr. Murdock found you. And now Johnny wants to deliver you to them personally." But where *was* Adaba? Jebediah rose to his feet. "Calvin, I think that just as a precaution I'm going to hide you away until he gets here—"

"Oh, no, you ain't!" Philo Bassett said.

The voice seemed to come out of nowhere, ripping through the soft fabric of the night, and instantly Jebediah was on his feet, aware that in the next moment he might have to kill—or die. Beside him, Calvin moaned with fright and climbed to his feet, clutching his little bundle.

"No, you ain't gonna hide nobody!" came the voice again, and with a crashing, splintering sound, Philo Bassett pushed through the brush and into the moonlit clearing. He had a rifle in his hands, held at ready.

"Mr. Bassett," Jebediah said, holding out his hands as if imploring, but in hope of grabbing the rifle, "Mr. Bassett, sir, you don't understand."

"Oh, I understand, all right!" Bassett said triumphantly. "I knew I'd get you sooner or later! I knew all I had to do was keep coming back again and again! And I heard it all, everything you said!"

"Mr. Bassett—"

"A nigger stole away by a white Injun, name o' Murdock! Carried off by a boy named Golden! Sounds like a Jew-boy—shouldn't be hard to find! And hid at Jessamine! And that's another Sabre plantation, ain't it—owned by Mr. Lewis Sabre, the one with the nigger wife! By God, ain't nobody ever gonna believe that Mr. Justin ain't helping steal niggers now!"

"Mr. Bassett, please!" Jebediah stepped closer, still holding his hands out.

"Don't you get close to me, nigger—I'll break your head!" Bassett swung the rifle in a fast series of butt and barrel strokes, and Jebediah leapt back.

"Mr. Bassett, sir, if you'll just let me explain—"

"Don't need no explaining. We gonna hang you for this, Jebediah—if I don't kill you for my own satisfaction first. And I reckon that there Mr. Greavy will pay me plenty to get this here nigger back—"

With a little cry, Calvin bolted. Bassett twisted toward him, leveling the rifle. In the same instant, Jebediah threw himself forward and grasped the rifle before Bassett could even draw back the cock.

Bassett looked up at him with shocked eyes, as if he could not believe that once again this black man was defying him and actually laying black hands on him. Then the eyes went mad, and with a scream of rage, he tried to slam a knee up into Jebediah's groin. Jebediah twisted to block the blow, but in the same instant, Bassett's right hand left the rifle, flashed to his hip, and returned with a knife. Jebediah let go of the rifle with his left hand and leapt back, but not fast enough: the tip of the knife ripped up through his left side.

The second time Bassett thrust the knife forward, Jebediah grasped his hand.

Releasing the rifle, he threw his right arm around Bassett's neck and turned the knife inward toward the man's chest. Bassett's eyes grew wide with alarm, and a keening sound came from his throat. He let the rifle fall to the ground, as he tried to claw at Jebediah's face.

With a single great effort, Jebediah forced the knife blade up into Bassett's chest.

Bassett's mouth flew open. As he started to scream, Jebediah released his neck, placed his hand over the open mouth, and tripped him. Bassett fell backward, and Jebediah went down over him, keeping his hand over the mouth and thrusting hard with the knife.

Bassett squirmed like an impaled insect, and his eyes, large in the moonlight, seemed to grow even larger.

Jebediah worked the knife.

Bassett's movements slowed, and a hopeless look came into his eyes.

He went limp, and Jebediah knew he was dead.

He removed his hands from Bassett's mouth and knife hand. He sat back, gasping for air. He hadn't realized that he was holding his breath.

He looked over his shoulder and saw Adaba holding Calvin as if to support him.

He looked at Bassett again, and his necessary anger began to fade. Poor, dumb Bassett. Got himself killed, and for what? If he'd had an ounce of brains or compassion, he might have had a long and happy life. But instead . . .

"I had to do it," Jebediah said.

"I know," Adaba said. "I reckon I got here about the same time he did. I was trying to get behind him when—"

"He made me do it. Why did he make me do it?"

He didn't realize he was crying until he felt Adaba pat his shoulder. "It's all right, son. I've had to do it myself. And there's no son of a bitch so mean or so low that sooner or later I didn't weep for him."

When Jebediah felt in control of himself again, he reached forward and closed Bassett's eyes. It was the least you could do for the poor bastard you had killed, he thought.

Adaba sighed. "I hate to say it, but I think it's about time you left Sabrehill, Mr. Jeb."

"I can't," Jebediah said dully. How could he leave Damien . . . Cat . . . the only family he knew? And Leila . . . he hadn't meant to hurt her. . . .

"You've got to. You've got too many enemies around here, too many people who are already suspicious of you. When they realize that Mr. Bassett has disappeared for good, maybe while spying on Sabrehill, they're going to raise hell. And they're going to remember that there was a lot of bad feeling between Mr. Bassett and you."

"But Mr. Justin still hasn't found the right overseer."

"That doesn't matter now. He'll find someone—who knows, maybe I can help him. But I didn't ask you to stay down here just to see you get yourself hanged, son."

The cut in his side burning as if it were on fire, Jebediah climbed wearily to his feet. "Never mind that for now. We've got work to do."

"That's right. We've got to get this fellow buried fast and deep, and it had better not be on Sabre property. He's probably got a horse or mule or carriage around here somewhere, and we don't want that found on Sabrehill either. And you've got to get that knife cut taken care of. I reckon you'd better hide Mr. Ames here for a few more days—"

"No. We don't know how soon they'll start looking for Mr. Bassett, but we do know they'll come looking here. You take Calvin away tonight, just as you planned. Zagreus and I will take care of Mr. Bassett."

Adaba hesitated. "If you're sure you're up to it."

"I'm up to it." Jebediah managed a smile. "At least I am if I don't get any more surprises."

"I'm afraid I can't promise you that. I came across something when I got here." Adaba called over his shoulder: "Boy, if you're still with us, you can come out now."

Damien stepped out of the shadows and into the moonlit clearing.

"I WANT TO HELP."

No, Jebediah thought, not Damien. He was too valuable to be put in danger. He was too young. He could do his part later, when he was grown, when he had gone north.

"Jebediah, I want to help!"

He looked so small, standing there in the moonlight in his nightshirt and boots, and Jebediah could see he was frightened. After all, he had just witnessed a killing, and the corpse still lay before him, practically at his feet.

"Tell me what to do, Jebediah!"

"Damien, you shouldn't have come here."

"I *had* to! I was scared for you!" The boy looked at Bassett's body and added in a shaky voice, "And I ain't sorry. I'm gonna do whatever you do, Jebediah."

Jebediah looked at Adaba, who was smiling at Damien as if foreseeing the boy's fate. Calvin Ames stared at him, as if he couldn't quite believe what he was seeing. Jebediah nodded. The boy was in. Of course he was in. He could not live with what he knew now and do nothing about it. Other children worked for the Underground Railroad—they were often invaluable—and who was Jebediah to say Damien was too special to do his part? Still, he was so damn young.

"You can help, Damien. Go to Zagreus. Tell him exactly what's happened. Tell him to bring a couple of shovels and a mule, in case we need it to help move Mr. Bassett. And tell him to bring something I can bind up this cut in my side with."

"I'll be back right away."

"No. Stay there and go back to bed. We'll talk in the morning. This is important, Damien—if you're going to help, you must follow orders exactly. Or we could all end up as dead as Mr. Bassett here. Now, go on."

Damien took a last look at Bassett and hurried off into the darkness.

"That's quite a boy," Adaba said. "I grabbed him in the dark and told him to keep quiet and not move, and he didn't try to yell out or get away or anything else. I knew he was scared, but he seemed to understand instantly that I was there to help you. And he didn't lose his nerve and run off when you killed your friend here either."

"He's a brave boy and he thinks fast," Jebediah said. "And now you and Calvin had better be on your way."

"You're sure . . . ?"

"I'm sure." He gave Calvin a reassuring slap on the back. "I'll be seeing you in Philadelphia, Calvin. Very soon!"

It was a long, hard night. Binnie came with Zagreus, and it was fortunate that she did. After binding up Jebediah's wound, she refused to return home and insisted on helping them find Bassett's mule and bury his body. It soon became apparent that Jebediah was too weak to help dig the grave, so she took over his shovel, while he led Bassett's mule off a few miles and abandoned it, along with Bassett's rifle. When he arrived back at Sabrehill and stumbled into his house shortly after dawn, he was almost too exhausted to stand.

Leila, up and dressed for her day's work, cried out in dismay when she saw his blood-sodden clothes.

"Help me, Leila."

"Jebediah, what happen—"

"It doesn't matter. If anybody asks, say that I was hanging up a scythe and I got careless. It fell and tore my side."

"But you been gone all night—"

"No. I've been right here. Please don't ask any more questions, Leila. Just help me get cleaned up."

Leila seemed torn between grief and anger, as she stripped off his clothes and the soaked bandages and washed his wound, but her fingers were always gentle. She didn't speak again until she was replacing the bandages.

"Who bind you up before?"

"It doesn't matter."

"You get hurt, you ain't got no right to go to nobody but me! I took care of you almost from the day you come to Sabrehill—from the day you got whipped for running away. Maybe you had other wenches here, but I was the first, and you ain't got no right . . ."

Her chin quivered, and for a moment he thought she was going to cry.

When she had finished replacing the bandages, she pulled a nightshirt over his head. "You ain't gonna work today," she said, in a tone of finality. "I think you got a little fever, and I ain't gonna let you die of lockjaw."

He smiled. "I do thank you for your consideration, Leila."

"Oh, Jebediah!" Then her arms were around his shoulders, as she leaned down over him on the bed, still careful not to hurt his wound. "Jebediah, what you been up to? Did somebody try to kill you?"

"Nobody but an old scythe."

"No!" Leila raised up so that she could put her hands to the sides of his head and look intently into his eyes. Her voice lowered. "Did you kill somebody?"

She was one of the few people in the world he trusted. "Yes, honeychild," he said softly, "I did."

Her eyes widened. "A white man?"

"Yes."

"*O-o-oh!*" It was a cry of pain, and for a moment her eyes pinched closed.

"Don't worry," he said. "Nobody knows. Nobody who'll tell. They can't prove a thing."

"*They* don't *have* to prove a thing, nigger! Was it Mr. Jeppson? Or one of them Bassetts? Or one of them Carstairs boys? Everybody knows how they feel about Mr. Jeb of Sabrehill and how you feel about them. Jebediah, they'll hang you for it!"

"Oh, I don't think so, Leila."

Her forehead came down on his shoulder, and for a moment she was silent.

"But you can't take any chances, can you? Does this mean you'll be leaving Sabrehill?"

"I've always told you the day would come, Leila."

He felt her tears on his shoulder. "And I always told myself that we been through so much together that, when the day come, I'd forgive you. But I ain't sure I can, Jebediah."

This was proving even more difficult than he had anticipated. His throat tightened, and the ache in his heart was worse than the one in his side.

"I'm sorry, Leila. But who knows? When I get north, when I find out what it's like, well . . ."

"No." She shook her head. "Don't want you holding out no hope for me when there ain't none. Don't want to stay down here, waiting and waiting for a call that don't never come." She sat up and wiped her eyes. "And now I got a day's work to do."

"We'll talk some more, Leila."

She got up from the bed. She shrugged hopelessly and went to the door. "I'll come by when I can and see how you are."

"Thank you. Would you send Damien to me, please?"

She nodded, and left without another word.

Was he a fool to leave her behind, he wondered. He had no doubt that Miss Lucy would let her go with him if he asked. But, for all his vague dreams, he really hadn't the faintest idea of what the future held for him or how he would cope with it. For all he knew, in a few months he would be dead of starvation. He thought of Jessie. He had hurt both himself and others quite enough by letting his heart overrule his head. But perhaps someday . . .

A few minutes later, Damien entered the bedroom.

"Came down here a pickaninny, wearing nothing but a shirt," Jebediah said, "and now he's got his shirttail tucked into a pair of pants, just like a man."

Damien grinned and came to his beside.

"Boy, about what happened last night—who have you told about it?"

"Nobody. Just Zagreus and Binnie."

"And you're not going to talk to anybody else about it, are you? Ever." He saw a small uncertainty in Damien's eyes, and he added, "Not even Cat. Not Cat, not Leila, no one."

Damien nodded.

"I mean it, son. If you ever tell them, if you ever so much as hint to them that you know something, you'll be asking them to share a burden they can't help you carry. You could hurt them badly, as well as yourself and others. You're going to have to grow up fast and carry a man's load, Damien, and I won't always be here to help you. Now, you said you wanted to do what I do?"

Damien's eyes brightened. "Yes!" He hesitated. "Are you—are you Adaba?"

Jebediah laughed. "No! What do you know about Adaba?"

"They talk about him at all the plantations 'round here. They say he's the one who steals off all the niggers. They say, as long as there's Adaba, there's always hope."

"That's true. And if you want to help him, you must do exactly as I say. And when I'm gone, you do as Zagreus says. Always."

"I will, Jebediah."

"And I hope you never have to do what I did last night."

"You cried afterwards."

"Yes. And I feel no shame for it. Did you hear what that big man with the beard said?"

"He said he'd had to do the same thing. He said, 'And there's no son of a bitch so mean or so low that sooner or later I didn't weep for him.'"

"I want you to remember those words always, Damien. I want you to remember that even if you meet a mad dog, you kill him first, but you pity him afterwards. Do you know why it's important to pity him afterwards?"

"Because maybe it ain't—isn't the dog's fault it's mad. You've got to kill him, but you can be sorry for the good dog he might have been. The good dog that can never come back now."

"Of course you know!" Jebediah said, tears of pride coming to his eyes, and in spite of the pain in his side, he sat up on the bed and enfolded the boy in his arms. There was still so much to teach him, and the time had almost run out. But he was bright and he had a good heart. He would be all right. Jebediah had to believe that.

That same day, he later learned, Philo Bassett's mule was found. Two days later, its ownership was acertained, and two days following that, the patrol, accompanied by Constable Wiley Morgan, arrived at Sabrehill.

The constable, who had learned to be nervous in Mr. Justin's presence, reported to him in the office.

"It's just the regular patrol on its regular beat, with me and a few extra people, Mr. Sabre, nothing to worry about. But Philo Bassett has been missing five days now, and ain't *no*body seen him, nobody at all! It ain't like he just went off and got drunk with his friends for a few days."

"What do you expect to find?"

"Nothing!" the constable said quickly. "I just wanted you understand about me and these extra people being here. Most everybody knew—knows old Philo."

"All right, get on with it. But I don't want my people disturbed any more than necessary."

The inspection of the nearby outbuildings and the field quarters was quiet and orderly, considering some of the people who were riding with the patrol—P. V. Tucker, the Carstairs brothers, a couple of Bassetts. When it was over, Balbo Jeppson, who was beat captain, rode his horse to the middle of the field quarters quadrangle where Mr. Justin and Jebediah were standing.

"We've already covered most of your place, Sabre," he said. "Now we're going over the rest. There ain't a nigger I don't want to talk to or an acre I don't want to see."

Justin shrugged. "Talk to all you want. Just don't abuse them, and don't damage my crops."

Jeppson's eyes narrowed and his jaw clenched, then jutted. "Mr. Sabre, you don't like me and I don't like you. But I think you know I don't go around damaging a man's crop without good reason. And I don't abuse niggers. I'm strict with them, but I don't abuse them."

"Except when you're 'breaking' them," Justin said contemptuously.

"That's not abuse. That's discipline. And it's something you could learn about. It's no secret that you've got some of the worst disciplined slaves in these parts." His eyes turned to Jebediah. "Like you, nigger. I've been watching you for a long time."

"I am aware of that . . *massa! Suh!*"

Justin motioned for Jebediah to keep quiet. Jeppson's face tightened. He gave Jebediah a long baleful look before speaking again.

"If there's anything I purely hate, it's a nigger that don't know his place."

"Jeppson," Justin said, "I suggest you finish your business here and leave Sabrehill."

Jeppson ignored him. "You set a bad example, Jebediah. Seems to me things have been getting worse in these parts ever since you got here—more killing, more burning, more slave stealing. And I ain't forgot how you raised your hand to Philo Bassett—the man we're looking for."

"I was only defending my master's property—and his daughter."

Jeppson brushed the words aside. "Philo's been out to get you ever since, boy. Him and some others have been keeping an eye on Sabrehill, and he was here the night—"

"Jeppson," Justin said, "are you telling me your friends have been on Sabre property—spying on us—"

"I'm telling you that Philo Bassett was here the night he disappeared, and I think this here nigger had something to do with it. But whether he did or not, I think it's high time an example was made of him. I think it's high time he was hoisted on my whipping post. And I swear to God I'm gonna have his hide—"

"Get out of here, Jeppson! Get off Sabrehill before I drag you down out of that saddle!"

Jeppson hauled on the reins and drew his horse back as Justin came for him. He wheeled and rode away.

If there had been any doubt at all in Jebediah's mind about what he must do, that incident decided it. That evening he went to see Mr. Justin.

But what if Mr. Justin were no different from Mr. Pinkham about keeping his promises of freedom, he thought, suddenly apprehensive, as he walked the short distance from his house to the office. He didn't want to believe such a thing, found it almost impossible to believe, and yet what

if it were true? After all, Mr. Pinkham, too, had been a
good and honorable man of abolitionist inclinations. Jebediah found he was trembling as he entered the office.

"Mr. Justin."

Justin smiled. "Yes, Jebediah. Come in. Sit down."

"Mr. Justin . . ." Jebediah groped for words.

"Yes, Mr. Jeb," Justin said after a moment, "Jeppson
scares me too. I wouldn't admit that to many people, but
he does."

"I think he's getting worse."

"So do I. He's a frightened man, Jebediah. I suppose
you're aware that the country is in a great deal of trouble.
We're having the biggest financial panic since 'nineteen,
and banks have been closing by the hundreds. *We* haven't
been badly hurt, but I understand that Jeppson is in danger
of losing Redbird. He feels as if the gods are against him,
and he's looking for a scapegoat."

"Me."

"Well, maybe not you specifically, but you'll do."

" 'Snotty Sabrehill nigger.' He's wanted to get me into
that slave jail of his for a long time."

Justin nodded. "Jebediah, I don't know how to say this.
You know you'll have a home at Sabrehill as long as you
care to stay here. But I wonder if the time hasn't come for
you to leave."

Relief flooded over Jebediah, and for a moment the
breath went out of him.

"But Mr. Justin, sir," he said weakly when he could
speak, "You still don't have a new overseer."

"Oh, you needn't worry about that. When I came down
here, I'd been away from plantation life a long time, and
besides, our crop up in Virginia is mainly tobacco, not
cotton or rice. But I've learned a lot from you and Miss
Lucy in the last couple of years, and I think I can be my
own overseer until I find somebody suitable."

"Yes, sir. Mr. Justin, you'll make a fine overseer."

Justin reached over and put a hand on Jebediah's. "Mr.
Jeb," he said, "I take that as a high compliment."

From that evening on, it seemed to Jebediah that time
flew faster than it ever had before in his life. He was going

to leave Sabrehill. He was going to go north and be a free man. But everything was happening so rapidly that he wanted to cry out, *"Yes—but not yet! not yet!"*

The procedure would be quite simple, although it entailed some circumventing of the spirit of the law. Since it was virtually impossible to free a slave in South Carolina, Justin would take Jebediah to Charleston where he would sell him to a certain trustworthy gentleman of his acquaintance for one dollar and services. That gentleman would take Jebediah north and free him there. Justin would have been glad to do the same thing himself, but it would be better if he were away from Sabrehill as little as possible. And it would be well, Miss Lucy added, if no unnecessary attention were drawn to this event. Let people merely become aware at some time in the future that Sabrehill's notorious black overseer had vanished. Jebediah and Justin would leave for Charleston in a week.

Not so soon! Not so soon!

It seemed to Jebediah that he had so much to do first. The potatoes had to be dug and the corn shucked and the fences repaired—but people kept telling him, no, that was no longer his responsibility. Then how the hell could he be sure it all got done right! He *couldn't* just go off and leave all these things that needed doing undone, could he?

He could, and must. He would be leaving tomorrow. The time had come for his private farewells.

To Cat.

"But I don't *want* you to go 'way, Jebediah!"

"Now, Cat, your daddy says maybe you'll be coming up north on a holiday, and I wouldn't be surprised if we saw each other then."

And Damien.

"Are you going away *forever*, Jebediah?"

"Boy, don't you even think about that. You just remember everything I've told you, and one day you'll come join me. You write me a letter, you hear? I'll be waiting."

And Leila.

"Take care of my boy for me, Leila. And remember me kindly when I'm up there in the cold North."

"Oh, Jebediah . . ."

And Miss Lucy and Zagreus and Binnie and all the people of Sabrehill he had worked with and sometimes fought with.

They were all in the courtyard the next morning, before dawn, when he and Justin left. There were handshakes and hugs and more than a few tears, and final words for Damien and Cat. And then the carriage was rolling down the avenue of oaks toward the gate, while somebody yelled, "Hooray for Mr. Jeb!" and Jebediah's breath caught in his throat.

Suddenly, as they approached the gate, he froze.

What the hell was he doing?

What kind of fool was he, to be leaving the only people in the world he loved—Damien, Cat, Leila, Miss Lucy? To be leaving the only kind of work he knew, the work he enjoyed and did so well? To be leaving the snug security of his own little house, so close to the safe presence of Miss Lucy and Mr. Justin?

He was at last achieving his dream—he was going to be free—but for the first time in his life, the thought of freedom was terrifying. Never again would he be assured by a master of his next meal or a coat to hold off the cold or a roof over his head. From now on, he and he alone would be responsible for himself. He would truly be his own master for the first time—and in a world of which he knew little except what he had read in books. What did it matter that Jeppson and the Bassetts and their kind were a danger to him here? Hell, he thought, he would have outlasted them the same as he had outlasted all the others. Then why was he leaving?

When they reached the gateway, he looked back and saw Sabrehill just as he had first seen it, a few lights aglow in the windows of the mansion and some of the outbuildings. He knew he would never again see this place or its people, for by law he could never return, and he wanted to cry out, *Stop! Turn back! I was wrong! This is my home, these are my people, I don't want to go!*

But he did not. The dream had to be fulfilled. The carriage rolled on.

Jebediah Hayes had left Sabrehill and was on his way north to freedom at last.

In May 1838, Mr. Jebediah Hayes, lately of South Carolina, sat on the platform in Philadelphia's new Hall for Free Discussion. Beside him sat his recently acquired friend, William Lloyd Garrison. On the podium, Theodore Weld, a brilliant speaker, was denouncing the murder of the abolitionist, Elijah Lovejoy, in Alton, Illinois, the previous November. But Mr. Hayes hardly heard a word he was saying.

His mouth was dry, his palms were damp, and every inch of his body seemed to be quivering with panic at the thought of what was to come. Mr. Garrison was right, he thought: He was not ready for this. In the past few months, he had learned to be quite at ease in talking with small groups and even in standing up before small audiences. But to have all these faces looking up at him . . . never had he dreamed that they could be so frightening.

Still, he had to do something. The money the Sabres had banked for him in the North was gone—the bank had closed, along with hundreds of others. The bonus money Mr. Justin had given him was almost gone. He couldn't exist on the charity of the wealthy Tappan brothers, who had already given so much to the abolitionist cause, when they, too, had lost a fortune in the panic. But if people would actually pay him to hear the truth about slavery . . .

He thanked God he hadn't given in to a foolish impulse and brought Leila with him. As least she was being fed and clothed. Together, they might very well have starved.

He heard applause, saw Weld leave the podium, saw Garrison stand up and go to it. Garrison was in his early thirties, a thin, hawk-faced man, whose eyes burned fanatically behind his thick spectacles. When he had finished speaking, he looked around and smiled with compressed lips at Jebediah, and Jebediah's hands grew damper than ever.

Garrison motioned for him to come forward. Somehow he managed to stand up and walk the few steps to the podium. There, at least he could support himself by grasping the lectern. He remembered what Garrison had told him: *"Just talk to them as you talk to me, Jebediah, but speak up loud and clear so that they can hear you in the back row right from the start. Begin at the beginning and talk to them as you would to a few friends."*

Jebediah didn't know *how* to begin at the beginning. He had no prepared notes, and he began the only way he could think of—with a little story. He told how he had had one grandfather named Jebb and another called Jedediah. "So my parents compromised," he said, "and that's how I became Jebediah."

Smiles in his audience. And perhaps a touch of impatience.

People often make a serious mistake about "the peculiar institution," he told them. They hear terrible stories about it and think that those stories typify slavery, whereas in fact, the worst of them are great exceptions. Why, he himself was treated almost as a member of his master's family. Companion to a white boy, he attended that boy's lessons and had full use of the family library. He was well fed and well clothed at all times. His master was such a kindly man—

He heard a murmur of discontent in the audience. A few people looked about distractedly. A man in the front row covered a yawn.

Somehow, Jebediah knew instantly what was wrong, and thinking of that master's ultimate betrayal, he suddenly lunged forward over the lectern and savagely roared out: *"Oh, yes, he was such a kindly man!"*

His audience stiffened and stared at him as if he had unexpectedly thrown a thunderbolt at them.

Jebediah smiled.

"Oh, yes," he continued, "I insist. He was such a *kindly* man, such a *sweet* man. Such a devout man, a man of honor . . ."

From then on, every statement was laced with bitter irony, as he told of all the promises, all the expectations— and the final betrayal.

"He could not free us as he had promised, you see, because he could not afford it. *Because he could not afford it!*"

He realized that he had electrified his audience. Their souls were his. He could do anything with them, anything.

And he had hardly begun.

He made them weep, as he told tales of life in the fields. He made them feel the whips. He made them feel the degradation. As far as he could—and dared—he made them see the naked woman hanging by her wrists from the whipping post. He made them watch the death of his father. He made them see the carrion eaters descending on his mother's body.

"Ladies and gentlemen," he concluded in a low voice, "I have told you but a few little stories about my life and the lives of others in the noble institution of slavery. Some of them you may have found shocking, and if I have offended you in any way, I am terribly sorry." His voice began to rise. "But I shall tell these stories again and again, and a thousand more like them. I shall shout my stories of the evils of slavery into every ear! And like my friend, Mr. Garrison," his voice rose to a roar, as he quoted the notorious words, "'I am in earnest! I will not equivocate, I will not excuse, I will not retreat a single inch! And *I WILL BE HEARD!*'"

He was heard.

Later that evening, an angry mob, incensed at seeing blacks and whites, both male and female, arriving at the meeting together, attacked the Hall for Free Discussion and burned it to the ground. Jebediah, tearing his way through the angry crowd, barely escaped with his life. The rioting continued for several days, and the mob threatened to burn Philadelphia's Temperance Hall, where he spoke next. But he was heard.

Garrison had been looking for an ex-slave orator of power, and he had found one at last. Jebediah was heard in Boston. He was heard in New York City. Then he went west across the country to Illinois and back, and everywhere, in a voice like thunder, he was heard.

"Mr. Jeb," Garrison said, using his popular name, "you have found your vocation!"

If so, the irony of his situation didn't escape Jebediah. For years he had dreamed of freedom in the north. It had been a dream of peace, safety, tranquility. And now he was living a life of almost constant danger. He had never dreamed there was so much hatred of the black man in the North—far more than in the South, it seemed to him—and in the first year he was insulted, threatened, stoned, attacked bodily, even shot at, literally dozens of times.

But he was heard!

He took his message abroad. He lectured in England and Scotland and spent an evening telling his tales of slavery to Her Majesty and the prince consort. When he visited France, he was astonished to find that his name was famous even there.

He returned to America to publish his autobiography: *My Life as a Slave*, by Jebediah Hayes. It sold thousands upon thousands of copies in the North and was forbidden in the South. It was translated into a half-dozen languages. It was also widely pirated, but, Jebediah consoled himself, at least it was being read. He was being heard.

He was heard even in the South, in spite of his book's being proscribed.

"I swear, I don't know what the world's coming to," Sam Avery said one afternoon in the summer of 1843, "when they let some goddamn nigger print up a lot of lying trash like this!" He slammed a copy of the book down on his desk.

Duke laughed. "Better be careful, Sam. You'll be tarred and feathered if anyone finds out you have that book. Where did you get it?"

"Somebody brought it down from Boston, and it's being passed around. Everybody wants to know what the hell all the fuss is about. And nobody is gonna tar and feather Sam Avery, 'cause they all know where I stand on the nigger question."

Duke picked up the book and weighed it with one hand. "So it's all right to read it as long as some nigger doesn't get hold of it."

"Or some nigger lover."

"And it's all a pack of lies."

Sam flushed. "Now, I don't say there ain't abuses, and I don't say that that nigger didn't have it worse than some others. I do say that what he tells about ain't typical. And he's spreading his lies all over the world, Duke! People are listening to him! And you think the niggers don't hear about him? My God, boy, I've been dealing in niggers all my life, and mostly they're a docile, harmless lot, but you got any idea what can happen to them when they get *hope*? Everybody down here, everybody I know, agrees that sooner or later *some*body's got to do something about that crazy nigger!"

Duke shrugged. He smiled. "Well, who knows?" he said. "Maybe sooner or later somebody will."

THREE

DAMIEN

IT WAS WELL PAST six and almost dawn on that morning in late February 1845, when Duke realized that the carriage was still there, motionless, some fifty feet away and across the street on Vendue Range. It had been there for at least a half hour. He could make out a woman and a driver, but not their faces in the dimly flickering lamps and torches of the street, yet he was under the impression that they were watching all that happened: the work gangs and the coffle that were now leaving the Range, the slaves and masters who were arriving and departing. Curious, Duke left the doorway of Avery & Avery, as the firm was now called, and walked to the carriage.

"Excuse me. I couldn't help noticing . . . can I be of help to you, ma'am?"

"Now, just exactly what do you have in mind, Mr. Avery?"

The face was still shadowed by the hood of a bonnet, but the voice was that of a young woman. It was a low, mellow, teasing voice—and hauntingly familiar. If he had heard it at any other time and place, he would have recognized it instantly, but the last place he expected to hear it was on Vendue Range.

As he peered closer, the young woman pulled the brim of her bonnet aside and leaned forward into the light. Duke saw a wealth of tawny hair, the glitter of green eyes, and a mocking smile that was almost a grin, and for an instant he *still* couldn't quite believe it was she. "Miss Catherine!" he said.

"Miss Catherine," Cat Sabre mockingly echoed him. She seemed pleased that he was disconcerted.

"But what are you doing here? You shouldn't be—"

"I've heard Papa talk about Vendue Range and Market Street and the East Bay wharves in the early morning,

157

when the city is just waking up and going to work, and he
made it sound so exciting I wanted to see for myself."
Without waiting for assistance, Cat climbed down out of
the carriage, and Duke hastened to take her arm. She must
be about eighteen now, Duke figured, or very close to it.
He didn't know if she were beautiful or merely handsome,
for he preferred a more demure beauty, but there was
something about her that made his breath catch. Everything about Cat Sabre was bold: a bold brow, bold emerald
eyes, a bold, broad mouth that drew back to show strong
white teeth. Even her laugh and her low, pleasantly throaty
voice were bold.

"But, Miss Catherine," Duke said, "the slave market is
hardly a place for a lady."

"I didn't say it was, Mr. Avery."

"But I'm sure your daddy wouldn't want—"

"My papa leaves me free to pursue my own interests,
and in any case that is obviously no concern of yours."

Duke thought he heard stifled laughter from the carriage,
and he gave a quick look at the young black man who held
the reins. He recognized the black now: a servant and
frequent companion of Miss Cat Sabre. He gave the boy a
hard, warning look, and returned his attention to Cat.

"Miss Catherine, I have considered myself a friend of
the Sabre family for many years, and your welfare is in
every respect my concern."

Cat's eyes widened. "My word, Damien," she said, still
looking up into Duke's face, "did you hear what this here
gentleman said?"

"I heard, Cat," Damien said, and the stifled laughter was
still behind the voice.

" 'Your welfare is in every respect—' Doesn't he talk
just like an actor at the Dock Street Theatre?"

This time the boy had the sense to remain silent. But Cat
Sabre wasn't having it that way. "Damien," she said with a
note of anger, "I asked you a question!"

"Whatever you say, Cat. I'se jes' a po' niggah boy—"

"Shet yo' mouf?"

Duke had a feeling that he was being mocked, but he
was confused because he could feel no real malice behind

the mockery. He even had a feeling that Cat Sabre would have been pleased if he had joined in the game, but he had no idea of how to go about it. Still, he wanted Cat Sabre's good opinion, and he sought it in the only way that occurred to him. He looked up at Damien and said, "Boy, hasn't anybody ever taught you respect? You say *Miss* Cat when you speak to your mistress!"

"That's right, Damien," Cat said, joining him in his indignation, "hasn't anybody ever taught you respect, boy? From now, on you say *Miss* Cat!"

"Ya-a-azzum, Miz Cat," the boy said in an exaggerated drawl, "fum now on I go-wi-i-ine caw you Miz—"

Duke stepped forward and reached for Damien. With one hard pull, he dragged the mocking nigger down from the carriage. He was, by God, going to teach the black bastard a lesson, because no nigger sassed a white lady in front of Duke Avery—

Then, shockingly, it was not the black boy but Cat Sabre who was before him, shaking him, holding him off from the boy. Her eyes were green fire, her lips were drawn back until he could see the needle-sharp teeth near the corners of her mouth, and from between her teeth came an angry hissing sound. Breathing hard, he pulled her hands from his coat and stepped back from her.

"I'm sorry, Miss Catherine. I don't like seeing the boy show you disrespect."

"I don't care what you like, Mr. Avery," Cat Sabre said, her voice suddenly hard. "Nobody, *nobody*, Mr. Avery, lays hands on Damien but me."

Duke took a long look at Damien, and Damien stared back with unconcealed hatred. Under other circumstances, Duke might have made him pay for that. But then he saw the smile—the grin—slowly returning to Cat Sabre's face.

"On the other hand, Mr. Avery, I am certainly beholden to yo' fo' yo' gallantry, and I am gwine teach this yere niggah somethin' 'bout respeck an' proper manners. Damien, get yo' se'f back up in de carriage!"

Again Duke felt the mockery-without-malice, but now he knew enough merely to smile and say nothing. He helped Cat Sabre back up into her carriage. Cat, to his surprise, held a hand out to him, and he took it.

"We're going back to Sabrehill tomorrow," she said. "Do you ever get out our way, Mr. Avery?"

"Why, as a matter of fact, I'll be there in about ten or twelve days. There's a plantation I want to look at. I'm meeting a man the first Monday of next month."

"Good. Come a day early and have Sunday dinner at Sabrehill."

Afterward, Duke wondered how much a fool he had looked. The invitation was totally unexpected, and once again he didn't know how to respond.

"Miss Catherine," he said finally, "I'd like that, but your daddy . . . I mean, are you sure it's all right?"

She seemed to enjoy his discomfiture. "Why, I think so. I know for a fact that we haven't anything planned. And we lack company, with my brothers away at school."

"But I still couldn't unless your daddy . . . your momma . . ."

Cat sighed. "I shall ask my momma to extend a formal invitation. Will you accept?"

"With pleasure."

"Then I shall expect to see you. Market Street, Damien!"

Damien flicked the reins, and the carriage rolled away before Duke could say another word. He stood in the street watching it until it disappeared around a corner.

The invitation came by messenger four hours later. He immediately sent back an acceptance.

Cat looked back as Damien drove around the corner. Mr. Duke Avery was still standing in the street, watching them. "Mighty handsome man," she said.

"Trash!" Damien said, wrinkling up his nose as if Duke Avery smelled bad, and Cat grinned at him.

"Just 'cause you got smarty with him and he hauled you down out of this carriage?"

"You were the one who got smarty with him. I just said what I thought you expected."

"Anyway, I still say he's handsome. Reminds me of Papa, a little."

Damien gave her a disgusted glance. "He doesn't look like your daddy at all."

"I don't mean just appearance—though they are both tall and mighty strong-looking and handsome. I mean the way Papa can seem so calm and suddenly his temper goes off, *boom!* And the way people hate Papa's abolitionist opinions and yet respect him even so."

"What makes you think Mr. Duke Avery is abolitionist? How could he be—him, a slave trader?"

"Papa says there have been slave traders who were abolitionist. But that's not what I mean. People look down on slave traders, the same as they do on abolitionists. But Mr. Avery's like Papa—he acts like he just purely doesn't give a damn. He's his own man."

"Like you."

Cat grinned. "Like me."

"I still don't like him."

Cat reached over and gave Damien a fond hug. She wondered what in the world she would do without him. Well, she would soon have to learn, because Damien was almost all grown up now, and she knew her father meant to send him north to join Mr. Jeb.

She recalled the first time she saw Damien. Having been born and brought up in Europe, where her parents had gone for her mother's health, she had, as far as she remembered, never seen any black people before coming to America. But after her mother had died of consumption in Switzerland, her father had told her and her brothers about them, so they would be prepared. However, the very idea had given her nightmares. Black people pursuing her and going *Boo! boo! boo!* The last thing in the world she wanted to see was black people, and she made the entire trip to America in fear and apprehension.

But, of course, it turned out that they were no more black than she was truly white. (She couldn't quite decide what color she was. A king of orangy pink?) Some were so brown as to appear *almost* black, but others were almost as light as she was, and many were an absolutely lovely color.

She had been at her new home in Virginia only a few hours when she discovered Damien. She was in a parlor with the grandmother she had just met when a beautiful brown-skinned child, perhaps a year older than she and wearing only a hip-length shirt, slipped shyly into the room. She had taken one look at the child and been completely enthralled.

"Who's that?" she asked.

"That is Damien," her grandmother said. "Damien, come here."

"Is it a boy or a girl?"

"It is a boy, as you can plainly see. Damien, pull your shirt down. We found Damien behind a cabbage leaf one day and decided to keep him so that you would have someone to play with."

"Is he a slave, too?" Her father had explained about slaves.

"He is 'one of our people,' " her grandmother corrected her gently.

"Can he be *my* people?" she asked with rising excitement.

"Perhaps, one day, if you treat him nicely."

Her very own slave! It was even better than having a new doll! She went to him, and when she hugged him, he giggled and hugged her back.

From that day on, they were virtually inseparable. When she had her lessons, Damien was with her, learning as fast as she, or even faster so that he could help her. When she ate in the kitchen house, as she did most meals, Damien ate with her. They played together, bathed together, and slept in the same room. She loved her brothers, Mark and Beau, but somehow Damien was very special to her. Even when they had their spats, as they frequently did, he remained special, as if he were growing to be a part of her, and when her papa got them all a new momma and took them to live at Sabrehill, Damien went with them. Never in this world would she have allowed him to stay behind.

She would always remember those first years at Sabrehill as among the happiest of her life. Even after Jebediah started making Damien wear pants—'cause he'd soon have hair growing 'round his pecker, he explained with pride, although she couldn't understand how that explained anything at all—they continued to play together uninhibitedly until one day, when they had been dipping alone in a stream, some instinct told her that there must be no more of that.

Thereafter they tended to spend less time with each other, but no matter how much they drifted apart, something always happened to bring them back together again. There was, for instance, the party in Charleston when she was fourteen. One of her friends had invited a half-dozen girls to spend the night at her house. After donning their nightgowns, the girls congregated in one of the bedrooms and vied with one another with tales of the stupidity of their "dumb nigger" servants. Cat knew quite well that they were only imitating their mothers—she had heard such conversations a hundred times before—but she found the game distasteful. Finally, one of the girls, noting Cat's silence, asked, "What about yours, Cat? Aren't they just the stupidest things?"

"No," Cat said quietly. "Leila, our housekeeper, is very smart. And I don't think Irish, our butler, is exactly dumb. And Zagreus, our stable master, is smart, and Mr. Jeb, our overseer, when he was with us, was *very* smart. And I guess Damien, our houseboy, is about the smartest person I ever met. Smarter than anybody in this room."

There was silence.

Then Edina McClintock said, "Well, what do you expect from somebody whose daddy is no better than a Yankee niggah lovah!"

"Maybe that's so, Edina McClintock," Cat said, bridling, "but at least there's no niggah-lovah's yardchildren running all over our place, which is more than you can say!"

Edina gave a squeal and threw herself at Cat.

The episode resulted in Cat's temporary excommunication from the society of her peers, which hurt her, yet changed her not in the slightest. She had no wish to change. She knew perfectly well that she was "different" from other Charleston girls, and she sensed that the difference had something to do with her parentage and the fact that she had been born abroad and raised in her earliest years in a completely different society. She would have loved to "fit in" better with her friends, but not at the cost of pretending to be something she was not. Therefore her friends had only the slightest influence over her behavior. Even the black people she loved and admired—Jebediah, Damien, Leila—had more.

"Cat," Damien said. "Cat, we're here. You said you wanted to see Market Street early in the morning."

She sat up and shook her head to clear it. "Guess I was dozing off."

"Dreaming of Mr. Duke Avery," Damien said contemptuously.

Cat laughed. "Yes. Dreaming of Mr. Duke."

After almost ten years of hard work, Duke Avery was about to get what he had always wanted. What he had earned.

First had come the education, of course, the gift of his father. Then had come the money, and that had been harder. But Sam had been right: Duke Avery had a knack for the trade. He had an eye for black flesh, and a nose for a deal, and he knew how to squeeze out every dollar. As a result, in a trade where most men barely scraped by, he had in ten years amassed a small fortune.

Small, but respectable. More than enough to buy a fair-size plantation and the people to work it. Oh, not to own it outright, of course, but to own it with a morgage he could easily handle and eventually pay off. And with the land would come respectability of the kind that only land could give, and with respectability would come a good marriage, each giving added value to the last. In a short time, perhaps within a year, his dream would be fulfilled.

Looking across the table at Catherine Anne Sabre in the Sabrehill dining room, he couldn't help wondering if he were looking at that fulfillment.

"Redbird," Cat said. "I have quite made up my mind that Mr. Avery shall buy Redbird."

"Now, Cat," Miss Lucy said, "Mr. Avery may have some other ideas."

"No, no, I have decided. We need somebody to liven up the neighborhood, and Mr. Avery is just the person. I am terribly sorry, Mr. Avery, but I give you no choice. When do you plan to give your first ball?"

"Cat, really!"

"I hadn't thought that far ahead, Miss Catherine."

"You're seriously thinking of buying Redbird?" asked Justin Sabre, on Duke's right, at the head of the table.

"It's a possibility. I've been keeping my eyes open for the right place for some time now, and Mr. McCady, the banker, suggested that we might take a look at Redbird together, so . . ." Duke shrugged.

"You sound a little dubious, Mr. Avery."

"Well, this is a little farther out from the city than I had contemplated buying. I do still have business interests there to look after, until I divest myself of them."

"Oh?" Miss Lucy said, "you plan to give up your . . . ah . . ."

"My part in the slave trade," Duke said bluntly. "Not immediately, but as soon as I'm well-established as a planter, yes."

"What's your feeling about the trade, Mr. Avery?" Justin asked.

"Justin," Miss Lucy said, "that is a tactless question."

"I know," Justin said.

"I don't mind answering. Mr. Sabre, my father believed that, whatever justification the slave trade may once have had, it has been lost. He had strong abolitionist leanings, and to a degree at least, I have inherited them. He also dreamed of the Averys returning to the land, and I have inherited that dream, too."

"So you see, Momma and Papa," Cat said, "we shall no doubt have the pleasure of a new neighbor before long."

"If that should become the case, Miss Catherine," Duke said, "the pleasure will be all mine."

"It shall become the case, Mr. Avery, or I shall never forgive you. And now, Momma, unless these gentlemen insist on lingering over their coffee, *I* shall insist on showing Mr. Avery about Sabrehill."

"Mr. Avery has been here before, dear," Miss Lucy said.

"Ah," Duke said, "but not for many years."

"Then, *come,* Mr. Avery!"

Justin and Lucy remained at the table, and silent, for some time after Cat and Duke Avery had left the room.

"Well, what do you think?" Justin asked, at last breaking the silence.

"I always rather liked Leduc, in the days when I knew him. Not that I ever knew him well. Perhaps I just felt sorry for him. Such a nice young man, and . . ." Lucy shrugged. "My father thought well of Ben Avery, his father. Sam Avery was a different matter."

"What about Cat?"

"*What* about Cat?"

"She did invite him. Or you did at her request."

"Oh, Cat is just being Cat," Lucy said, uneasily, as if trying to convince herself. "She's met the man here and there, and she's curious about him. My goodness, he must be—what?—a good twelve, fourteen years older than she? He's closer to my age!"

"I don't know, Lucy . . . there's something about this one . . . I don't think he'll scare off as easily as most of them do."

"You want her to scare him off?"

"Don't you? You yourself mentioned the age difference. And abolitionist sentiments or not, I've heard that Mr. Duke Avery can be a pretty ruthless man when it comes to dealing in slaves."

"I don't suppose there is any other way of dealing in slaves successfully. Well . . . what do you want me to say to her?"

"I don't know. Nothing. Wait and see what she says to you, if anything. Frankly, I don't know why we're making so much of this."

"Well, his age, his background . . ."

Background, Damien thought bitterly, as he listened on the other side of the doorway. A goddamn slave trader. The same slave trader who had brought Jebediah to Sabrehill in chains—had Miss Lucy forgotten that? Damien hadn't even been at Sabrehill at the time, of course, but he hadn't forgotten what Jebediah had told him. Not about Mr.

Duke Avery or the slave trade or anything else. Not one word.

He was angry with Cat. When she and Mr. Avery had come out into the courtyard and gone wandering around the west wing toward the gardens, her younger half-brother and half-sister had followed them, and Damien, too, had followed at a discrete distance. Suddenly Cat had whirled around.

"Macy and Sarah," she had said sharply, "you just go 'bout your business now!"

"But Cat," nine-year-old Macy had said, "can't we come—"

"No, you can't."

"But Momma says—"

"*I* say you stop following us! Damien! You get these here children away and keep 'em away!"

"Cat, they aren't hurting—"

Cat's eyes had flashed. "*Miss* Cat, boy! I am *Miss* Cat to you, and you better mind your mouth! Now, you take care of these here children, or *I* am gonna take care of *you!*"

Unlike the encounter on Vendue Range, this time Cat had not been joking. Duke Avery had laughed with arrogant amusement as he looked at Damien, and Damien had burned.

"Yazzum, Miz Cat!"

"And don't you sass me, Damien! Take these two inside for their rest!"

"Yazzum, yazzum!"

He could quite understand Cat's wish to be alone with a man, and it was not because she had ordered him about as if he were a, well, a slave, that he had been angered. He was used to that—that was just Cat when she got into a bossy mood. It was that she had done it in front of Duke Avery that he found humiliating. Miss Lucy or Mr. Justin would never have treated him in such a way.

After shooing the two children up the stairs, he stood in the passage for a few minutes listening, then followed them. He looked to be sure they were in their room, then went up to the third floor, under the eaves, and from there, he mounted an iron spiral of stairs that led to a trap door. He pushed the door open and went up into the big cupola that crowned the house.

It was a pleasant spring afternoon, although winter was not officially over. The sun was bright, the temperature was mild, and the lightest of breezes moved the treetops. From where he stood, Damien could see Cat and Duke Avery walking slowly over the green parkland that led down to the wooden landing and the river.

Cat sat down on the edge of the landing and looked out at the wide expanse of water. Duke Avery sat down facing Cat and leaned back against a piling that stuck up from the landing.

Damien didn't like the way Cat was behaving. It wasn't merely that she had bawled him out in front of Duke, although that was part of it—it was her manner toward Duke himself. She had expressed interest in young men before—hell, Damien thought, no simpering belle she, she sometimes positively *slavered* over them. But somehow this time it was different.

What did she really think of Mr. Duke Avery? Often it seemed to Damien that he knew exactly what Cat was thinking, but now he was not at all sure. He had the feeling that her thoughts were confused, and so were his own. Sometimes they thought the same thing so quickly that it was as if one had put the thought into the other's head, and that was all he could try to do now.

Cat, he thought, sending his words out as hard as he could, *listen to me! He's no good! Not for you, not for anybody! Someday you'll find the right person, but it's not him! Please, believe me! I can't let him have you! I can't, I can't, I can't!*

Small wonder, Duke thought later, when he had returned to the village tavern where he was staying, that Sabrehill was the very image of everything he hoped to achieve: the beautiful eight-pillared mansion overlooking the river; the vast, rolling fields; the orderly people, well cared for by the respected master and mistress. What more in this world could a man want?

That afternoon, it seemed to him, had been the happiest time he had known since that long-ago evening when Miss Lucy had so cordially welcomed him to Sabrehill and he had spent an hour or so telling Miss Dulcy his plans, his dreams. Not even his later knowledge that Dulcy had black blood could spoil that memory. And, after all, he thought generously, it was hardly her fault that she was tainted.

As he got ready for bed, he smiled, remembering his naive dreams of so long ago: that he might actually marry Amity or Dulcy Sabre, or even Miss Lucy, and himself become the master of Sabrehill. No matter. He would have his plantation yet, and now he had someone else in mind for its mistress.

Not that he was foolishly confident, but, yes, she was a possibility. He had a feeling that it had been he, and not just curiosity about the slave trade, that had drawn her to Vendue Range that morning. And it had been she, not Miss Lucy, who had first invited him to Sabrehill. He could not imagine any other young lady of her circle acting so boldly.

In fact, Duke acknowledged to himself as he slipped into bed, that was the one thing that disturbed him about Catherine Anne Sabre. She really was a little too bold. And, for the most part, her parents seemed to tolerate her behavior. He could understand her running off the children and the houseboy so that they could be alone, but he was surprised that Miss Lucy and Mr. Justin had allowed them to remain alone for so long a time.

And down at the landing, he had to admit, he had been just a little bit shocked. Lying in the dark, he experienced the moment again, all too vividly: Cat drawing up one foot so that her calf was exposed, then removing first one shoe and then the other.

"Miss Catherine," he said, his heart beating faster, "I wouldn't—I mean, that water is still pretty cold!"

She grinned. "I like it cold." And with that, she hiked her skirt up to her knees and dangled her feet in the water.

Somehow he drew his gaze away from those so-bare legs. "Do you . . . do this very often, Miss Catherine?" he asked, pretending a nonchalance he didn't feel.

She wasn't fooled, and her eyes and smile were impishly chiding. "Come on, Mr. Avery. Take off your boots. Enjoy yourself."

"Some other time, Miss Catherine."

She looked at him unwaveringly for a moment, wearing a compressed smile, as if she were both amused and disappointed in him. Then, quite deliberately, she began unpinning her hair and shaking it loose.

For the first time, his slight sense of panic was touched by anger. For Christ's sake, he thought, what'll her daddy do if he sees her here, acting like a—

Like a goddamn ignorant nigger wench!

The words came to mind before he could stop them. But, of course, he hadn't really meant them. It was just that Miss Catherine did go a little too far at times.

But you had to remember, he told himself later, as he lay in the dark in the village tavern, that she was still very young, hardly grown up. That meant she could still be trained, still be taught. Sooner or later, the firm hand of a parent—or a husband—would bring her under control, and she would become the demure and respectful young lady she was meant to be. And meanwhile, as long as no harm came of it, her youthful boldness did have a certain charm.

Yes, Catherine Anne Sabre might very well be the woman for him.

Duke Avery slept with a smile on his face.

"In my opinion," said Mr. McCady, the banker, "this is one of the nicest stretches of land in the state. Some of the biggest plantations, owned by some of the finest Charleston families, are right along in here. On this side of Redbird, for instance, you have the McClintocks and the Pettigrews, among others, and on the other side you have the Kimbroughs and the Sabres. No finer people anywhere."

Duke knew he should be paying closer attention, but he was still caught up in the happiness of the previous afternoon. He had felt a bit nervous when he and Cat had walked up the parkland toward the big piazza, she with her hair still undone and her shoes in her hand, but Miss Lucy had appeared hardly to notice, and he had begun to feel a bit silly about his worries. He was discovering that the Sabres had a graceful informality which was quite unknown to him and quite unexpected. But as the afternoon wore on, and he had chatted about his plans, and Cat had beamed at him as if she had really brought home a prize to show her parents, he had begun to feel as if some of their special quality were becoming his own. This, he had felt, warmed by their hospitality, was truly the way to live, the way to *be*.

". . . off there to our left you can see the nearest field quarters. Needs a little work, but it's in fair shape. Most of the outbuildings are just as sound as the big house."

"Is this place as big as Sabrehill?"

"Well, ah, I don't know about *that*. At a guess, I'd say Sabrehill has well over two hundred people, maybe a lot more, and if you take all the Sabre land together . . ."

Whatever Mr. McCady said next, Duke didn't hear. They passed through a grove of persimmon trees, and for the first time he got a clear view of the big house. It was a two-story brick building, painted white. On the river side, Mr. McCady had told him, it had both upstairs and downstairs piazzas, each with four columns. If it was not another Sabrehill mansion, it was nonelessless an exceptionally handsome house.

". . . only ten years old," McCady was saying, "built after the old one burned down."

But Duke was no longer looking at the big house. He had been distracted by a small outbuilding that they were approaching. It was only a couple of hundred feet from the big house and a little to one side of the road. It was of dark brick, almost black, unpainted. In contrast to the other buildings, all glistening white, it was like an evil blot, and merely to look at it seemed to darken the day.

"What in God's name is that?" Duke asked.

"Nigger jail. Some of the previous owners used to break bad niggers. Old Balbo Jeppson, used to own the place, was known as the best nigger breaker in this part of the country. 'Course, he's long gone now. Lost everything in 'thirty-seven, as I recall."

Duke stared at the jail as they rode by. In front of the building, which faced the big house, stood the whipping post. Like most whipping posts, it was actually two posts with a crossbeam at the top to which the culprit's wrists could be tied. But it was taller than most such posts, with pulleys on the crossbeam, so that the punished slave could be hoisted up high enough to be clearly seen by those other slaves who were to learn from his example. But who would want such a spectacle in plain view from the big house, Duke wondered. If he were to buy Redbird, sooner or later he would have to get rid of the jail and post.

". . . have a good overseer if you need one. The bank is very satisfied with Mr. Ferguson."

"If the bank is doing so well with Redbird plantation, Mr. McCady, why doesn't it just keep it?"

Mr. McCady smiled at his innocence. "Mr. Avery, we are bankers, not planters. I suppose you already have your own servants?"

"Yes, but some of them are due to be put out to pasture."

"Well, Redbird has some very competent people, if you should need them."

Mr. McCady reined up as they reached the house, and they climbed down out of the carriage. "We're expected, and the door's unlocked," Mr. McCady said. "Why don't you just go in and take a look around while I locate Mr. Ferguson?"

Duke took a last look at the jail and whipping post, and entered the house. It had been built, he saw at once, more or less along the classic lines of the plantation house. A high-ceilinged central hall, or passage, ran clear through the house, allowing a cooling breeze during hot weather, and two or more rooms lay on each side of the hall, which was really a room in itself. The sparsely furnished rooms, he saw, as he walked through the music room to the parlor, were reasonably large and airy, and there was no musty smell from the house being closed. He looked into the library and the dining room, then went upstairs.

The woman was in a bedroom, looking out a window toward the river, when he saw her. He was as startled as if he had been caught intruding, for he had thought he was alone.

As the woman turned toward him, he saw that she was a rich brown, and slim and lithe. Her dress didn't hide the fact that she was full-chested, long-limbed, narrow-waisted. Her brown eyes, as she looked at him, were warm and welcoming, yet her smile was shy.

For an instant, he felt as if his heart had stopped.

"Jessie!" he said.

$$\cdot\text{-}\{\ 2\ \}\text{-}\cdot$$

OF COURSE, IT WAS not Jessie. Even as he spoke the name, he saw that it was not. For one thing, Jessie would have been about thirty, and this woman was no more than twenty or twenty-one. Still, there was something in the eyes and the broad cheekbones that immediately brought Jessie to his mind, something that brought back the aching sense of loss that had once been almost unbearable.

"I'm sorry," he said haltingly. "You reminded me . . ."

"I'm Leonie, sir," the woman said in a low, pleasant voice. "I been keeping up the house for Mr. McCady."

"I'm happy to know you, Leonie. I can see that you've been doing a good job."

"Thank you. Are you the new master, sir?"

"No—that is, not yet."

"I hope you like Redbird, sir."

"I hope so, too, Leonie."

"Now, if you 'scuse me, I better go see how dinner is coming 'long for you and Mr. McCady, sir."

As the woman moved toward the door, Duke called, "Leonie," and she turned to smile at him again. "Sir?"

"My name is Avery. Leduc Avery."

"Yes, sir, Mr. Avery."

"Mostly, my people and my friends call me Duke."

"Yes, sir, Mr. Duke. We fixing you a nice dinner."

The woman left. *Jessie,* Duke thought, staring after her. *Jessie . . .*

Afterward, he wondered if he would have bought Redbird if it had not been for Leonie. For all its proximity to Sabrehill, it was farther from Charleston than he wanted to be. But it was as if he had received a sign—he had found the woman at Redbird, and now Redbird had to be his. He told himself he was a fool, that Leonie was not Jessie. He told himself that if he wanted Leonie badly enough, he

174

might be able to purchase her. But somehow he couldn't do that. This was her home, obviously she was trusted and respected here, and he felt instinctively that she would not wish to leave: She would not be happy if he took her away, and any feeling between them would be poisoned. No, if he wanted Leonie, he would have to buy Redbird.

He spent most of the rest of the day inspecting buildings, equipment, and fields with Mr. McCady and Mr. Ferguson, but Leonie was never far from his thoughts. She was a sweet presence hovering over them at the dinner table, and he took the sense of that presence with him when they returned to their work. In the late afternoon, meeting her on the piazza, he had an opportunity to speak to her again.

"Do you have much family here, Leonie?"

Her eyes were touched by sadness. "No family, Mr. Duke. My daddy, my momma, my brother, they all gone." She smiled. "But 'course we all got lots and lots of aunts and uncles here."

"I'm all alone, too, Leonie. And I've only got one uncle."

She seemed to stiffen, and her eyes left his. "I know."

So she knew who he was. And what he did. To his surprise, he felt shamed in her eyes.

"Leonie, I'm not always going to be in the trade."

He waited for an answer, for some response, but she didn't move. He wanted her to understand. "My old daddy, he always wanted me to get out of the trade. He wanted me to go back to the land, where our family always belonged. He wanted me to take care of people and treat them right and try to make them happy, if I could. Try not to blame me for being in the trade, Leonie."

Christ, he thought, here he was, practically apologizing to a nigger. And yet it was worth it, when she raised her eyes to his again, and smiled, and said, "I understand, Mr. Duke."

He had to have Redbird.

She teased him and Mr. McCady into staying for supper. "Now, you know you want to stay. I give you something so much nicer than what you get at that tavern, and it ain't gonna take me no time or trouble at all."

No time or trouble! She had started immediately after dinner, simmering the beans with the salt pork and an onion and a bay leaf and parsley and thyme. She had cooked the sausage and browned the pork and the lamb and yesterday's leftover duck. She had cooked more onions and simmered the ham hock in beef broth and preserved tomatoes. She had added the meats to the broth and onions for long simmering. She had combined the meats with the beans in a great crock, and put the crock into a hot oven for a couple of hours, until there was a golden crust on top. And at last she served it to them, along with hot cornbread and butter—enough meat and beans for at least a half-dozen prime field hands who hadn't eaten for a week. It was a dish to make a hungry man weep for joy.

When she saw them off afterward in Mr. McCady's carriage, and Mr. Duke turned to wave to her, she knew somehow that he would be back.

It was long past sundown when she took her little stub of candle from the kitchen house and, humming softly to herself, made her way through the night shadows to her one-room cabin in the field quarters. When she went in, Damien was sitting in the dark, waiting for her.

"Thought he was never going to leave," he said.

She lit another candle and looked about the room to see that all was in order. Not that there was much—one bed, one chair, one small table, an ancient cabinet, a fireplace, pegs on the walls for her clothes. But it was whitewashed inside as well as out, and she kept it scrupulously clean. For as long as she could remember, it had been her home.

"You been here long?"

"Seems like it. What about him? Did he say anything?"

" 'Bout Redbird? No, but I do reckon he serious 'bout buying it."

"Why do you think so?"

" 'Cause he been acting like a mighty happy man, not like somebody was wasting his time."

Damien made an angry sound and turned away, slapping one hand down on the other.

"Now, why you don't like him, Damien?"

"Because he's trash. And I don't want him anywhere near Cat."

Leonie felt the smile slip from her face. "He sweet on Miss Cat?"

Damien opened his mouth to answer, then hesitated. "I don't know. He sniffs after her whenever he gets a chance —which isn't often—but there's something about that man . . ." He shook his head. "Sometimes I wonder if he could ever really be sweet on anybody."

"Oh, he could be," Leonie said, relieved.

Damien looked at her suspiciously. "He after you?"

"Oh, no!" Laughing, she kicked off her shoes and threw herself down on her bed. "But I like him, Damien. I know he's a slave trader, but he don't act like no mean man, and I think he'll be good to the people at Redbird."

Damien looked down at her morosely. "As long as he keeps away from Cat."

Leonie held out her arms to him. "Now, you just forget all 'bout Mr. Duke and your Cat. You take off your boots and come here to your Leonie."

It was rare that she gave him such an invitation—it had happened only two or three times before—and, for that matter, rare that she gave in to his importunings. But she was as fond of Damien as she was of anyone else in the world, and this evening she was feeling particularly happy and loving and generous. The surprise on Damien's face and the grateful smile that followed it, brought a fresh surge of warmth to her breast, and she urged him to hurry. He sat down on the edge of the bed, and a few seconds later, not only were his boots gone, but every other piece of clothing as well, and he rolled naked into her arms.

She remembered their first time together. It had happened a couple of years earlier, when, near the end of the winter season in Charleston, the Sabres had sent Damien back to Sabrehill ahead of them to help prepare the household for their homecoming. He had just got back, when a young man and woman arrived at Redbird. They were from different plantations, they said, and their masters wouldn't allow them to marry and live together, and so they had run away. They were barely older than Leonie and Damien and so frightened that Leonie didn't think they could be trusted on their own. Therefore she took them to Sabrehill, where Damien offered to take them still further up the line.

It had seemed so simple. He had done the same thing a number of times before without the slightest difficulty. Not on that particular night, however. How he could have missed hearing the patrol, Damien had no idea, but they nearly walked right into it. He was leading the way through some woods on the Buckridge plantation, when he heard a low-pitched voice. "Hell, who was to know the nigger would die from a little whipping? And who's to know it was us that did it? I say we just hang him up from a tree and leave him here as a warning to other wandering niggers." Only a few yards away and not daring to move, Damien and the two runaways crouched in frozen horror, as they watched the patrolmen hang the corpse of the black man they had killed.

Somehow he got the young couple to a little farmhouse that was a station up the line. He rested a few hours, then started back, carrying a pass that identified him as a Sabrehill servant who was being sent home. But that didn't save him from further trouble. On the way back, as he was crossing the Buckridge place, he was seized by a patrol that dragged him into the woods, showed him the hanged corpse, and threatened to do the same to him if he didn't "tell what he knew about it." Finally, after whipping him, they let him go. He didn't stop when he reached Sabrehill that evening. He kept right on going until he reached Redbird and Leonie's cabin. There he broke down.

"Jesus, Leonie, I was never so scared in my life! From the minute we first ran into that patrol until I got back here, I was scared, and I'm still scared. Leonie, I am so goddamn scared!"

She shushed and soothed and stroked him, as he lay with her in the dark room, sobbing against her shoulder, and when, after an hour or so, he had calmed, they simply did what seemed most natural. As she continued kissing him, their caresses became increasingly intimate, and he bared her breast. He shuddered and sighed as she unfastened his clothes and reached within, and before long he swept up her skirt to return her caresses. Neither of them had done this before, and she had a moment of fear, when she thought he might hurt her. But then, without a word, they drew closer together and joined.

After that, he was the only one for her, and she thought it likely that she was the only one for him. Not that it happened often. She knew that one day he would go north, and most likely alone, and she had no intention of wasting herself on him, any more than on the poor field hands who had courted her in vain. Slave or not, she was a worthy woman, and somehow she could make a future for herself.

Meanwhile, it was good to have a friend like Damien, someone she could trust and confide in and now and then lie with. And this was such a time. She sat up on the bed and looked at his long, hard, beautiful brown body in the candlelight. She ran a hand down over him from chest to thigh. Then, with a smile and an eager little cry, she slipped out of her dress and lay down beside him.

Redbird was his.

Duke could hardly believe it. In a mere matter of days, every detail had been settled, from his bank payments to his share of this year's crop to Mr. Ferguson's contract, and he had found himself in Mr. McCady's office, bending over papers that blurred before his eyes while he signed his name with a trembling hand. His signature had been witnessed, the papers had been gathered up, and Mr. McCady had said, "Congratulations, Mr. Avery. You are now the master of Redbird plantation. This calls for a drink."

Redbird was his, and his life was changed.

He immediately hurried back to the plantation, for there was so much to be done in March and April, the season of sowing, and he wanted to take part in it all. In the last several years, he had learned everything he could about plantation management, but he had had no practical experience. With Mr. Ferguson's help, he intended to remedy that. He intended to be the best kind of working planter there was.

And then there was the house. He intended to replace

most of its few furnishings, and that would take careful planning. He also had to organize a household staff that could serve him both in Charleston and at Redbird, but that task didn't prove at all difficult. Raphael would continue to be his butler. Birdie, his Charleston housekeeper, was content to retire in favor of Leonie, as long as she retained her position of well-respected queen bee.

He had little time for social life that spring, or so he told himself, and he realized that the other planters were busy, too. In April they were all getting ready for their annual departure for Charleston and Sullivan's Island, for Saratoga and Newport, some even for Europe. But still, he did meet some of the men in the nearby village from time to time and had a drink with them in the local tavern.

By late May, most of his neighbors had left, and he pretty much had that stretch of the river to himself. But he was happy and busy. Now the growing season was well under way, and weeds and grass had to be chopped and killed and the cotton thinned to a stand, roofs had to be repaired as the rainfall got heavier, a tool shed had to be completely rebuilt—there was no end of work to be done, and he wanted to watch every bit of it and participate in it and learn. He had heard that Justin Sabre hadn't known a damned thing about cotton when he had come down here from Virginia, and now he knew as much as most men who had lived here their entire lives. Well, if Justin Sabre could learn, he thought, Duke Avery could learn too.

It was true, he had to admit, that at times he felt a little lonely. He missed the constant clatter of iron-rimmed wheels on cobblestones and the daily meetings with a dozen acquaintances. But his loneliness was sweetened, and sometimes even banished, by the presence of Leonie. Each time he returned from the fields, he looked forward to seeing her. Each time she left the house for her own little cabin, he was reluctant to let her go, and he often tried to delay her. He tried to make her feel as at ease in his company as possible, and one of his great pleasures was having a cup of tea with her in the late afternoon, sitting companionably together, more as if they were friends than master and servant.

"Leonie," he said, one afternoon, as they sat on the steps of the kitchen house, "there's something I've been meaning to speak to you about." He looked around to be sure there was no one who might overhear him. "Do you remember the morning I first came to Redbird and saw you?"

" 'Course I 'member. Said to myself, that gonna be the next master of Redbird."

"But do you remember how I called you Jessie?"

"Yes, I 'member that too."

"That was because I was so surprised. You see, you looked so much like someone I knew a long time ago who was named Jessie. And at times you still do make me think of her. So maybe sometime, without thinking, I'll call you Jessie again."

Leonie took the liberty of lightly and briefly touching his hand, and he seemed to shake within. "Oh, that's all right, Mr. Duke," she said. "I don't mind."

"No, it's not all right, Leonie. Because you're not Jessie, you're yourself. And a man should respect that and call you by your right name. Now, I've known men who called every dog or horse or mule they owned by the same name, but a nigger—I mean a person, Leonie—a person like you or me isn't a dog or a horse or a mule, and we're entitled to our own names. So if I call you by the wrong name, I'm doing you a wrong. But I want you to understand that it's not because I don't have respect for you. It's just that sometimes you remind me so damned much of Jessie. Leonie, my daddy always taught me—"

"Shush!" She dared to hold up a fingertip close to his lips. "Mr. Duke, honey, it's all right! You don't have to 'splain. I understand!"

Christ, he thought, if only a man could love a nigger!

He wanted her, of course. Sometimes at night, thoughts of her kept him awake for hours. He tried to avoid such thoughts, for they seemed degrading both to her and to himself. God, he thought, she would either hate his guts or laugh her fool nigger head off if she knew what he was thinking. But what could he do? She was not a piece of fancy goods like Jessie, brought up to believe that her main purpose was to pleasure a man. Should he try to bargain for her favors? Try to seduce her? Aside from a certain friendly attraction, she had not shown the slightest indication that she would be receptive. In any case, he was damned if he was going to be the kind of planter who pestered his black women and spread yardchildren all over the place. As a slave trader, he had never taken advantage of the women, and as a planter, he was not about to start.

One evening he asked her why she didn't have a man. "A good-looking woman like you, Leonie, I'd have thought you'd be married long ago."

"Nobody here at Redbird I want to marry, Mr. Duke."

"But you're a natural woman. Don't you get a need for somebody from time to time?"

She shrugged. "Some."

"Then there must be somebody—"

"I don't want to talk 'bout this, Mr. Duke."

"I'm sorry, Leonie."

By the end of June, he felt that he simply had to get away from her for a time, before he lost control of himself and did something foolish, thus perhaps losing any chance he might have of winning her. It might be better, in fact, since he saw no encouragement on her part, if he overcame his obsession with her altogether. A few days later, taking all the house servants but Leonie, he departed for Charleston.

He planned to stay a month or two. He stayed three.

One of his first acts was to walk up to Elliott Street and speak to Madam Lariena. At fifty, she still had a good figure and was as lusty as ever, and before long, she invited him upstairs "for old times' sake." He had little difficulty in forgetting Leonie when he was between those strong Spanish thighs, and he was a frequent visitor to Elliott Street that summer.

He also had more social life than ever before. His acquisition of Redbird had become common knowledge, and people who had turned up their noses at the young slave trader were eager to meet the rich young planter. He was invited to a dozen dinner parties and a dozen "carpet dances." But he did not fail to notice that the invitations were not from other planters but from Charleston tradesmen and their wistful-eyed daughters.

Ah, well, he thought, that would change as he became more active as a planter and gave up his part in the slave trade. Meanwhile, there was plenty to do at Avery & Avery, and as he had no current income from Redbird, he decided he might as well turn a dollar.

By October, when it was time to return to Redbird, he felt that he had quite overcome his infatuation. It had been based on the mere fact that Leonie reminded him of Jessie, and he now realized that she was *not* Jessie and never could be. And yet, as he entered the big house passage on the evening of his arrival . . .

She stood in the middle of the passage as if awaiting him. And it was as if he had never left. The entire summer he had deceived himself into thinking he was forgetting her, when in fact she was never far from his mind, and now he had all he could do not to gather her into his arms and lift her from the floor.

"You enjoy Charleston, Mr. Duke?"

"Yes, but I missed Redbird. And most of all," he said huskily, "most of all, Leonie, I missed you."

He felt, rather than saw, her slight stiffening. He had revealed too much of his feelings, perhaps had offended her. But then, to his relief, she smiled warmly and said, "Well, we all missed you, too, Mr. Duke."

There was so much to be done! The new furniture had arrived from Charleston, and with Leonie's help, he installed and arranged it. The entire house was repainted under his supervision—that was hardly necessary, but he wanted the place to shine as if new. And, of course, there was the abundant daily work of the harvest season.

He kept track of the return of his neighbors—not always an easy task, for some of the plantations in those parts were vast, and their mansions far apart. But he rode about the countryside on weekends, and the slaves passed along news of arrivals, and as each neighbor returned, he made a point of paying a call. He was always cordially received. Mr. McClintock, up the river, and Lawyer Devereau, down near Sabrehill, invited him back, and he issued invitations to one and all.

But, of course, at that time of the year, with Christmas

and the New Year approaching, most people were very busy, much too busy to visit him. Some of them gave dinner parties for the neighbors they had not seen since the previous spring. Duke knew—he heard about them from the slaves.

Had he failed, then? Perhaps not, but it certainly appeared so on Christmas Eve 1845. And sometimes, he had to admit, his long-held ambitions did seem childishly naive. To be accepted as a gentleman in the best circles of Charleston. To have the name of Avery resume its rightful place among the aristocracy. Was he a fool to have dreamed of such a thing?

He was poking at the coals in the library fireplace when Leonie entered the room. She was wearing a heavy shawl, for the night was cold, and there was even a rare hint of snow in the air. "Mr. Duke, time for you to go out to the quarters with me."

"Oh, they don't want me out there, Leonie."

Her eyes widened. "What you mean, they don't want you!"

"It's Christmas. They're celebrating—"

"And you gave them more extra rations than they had in a long time, and a pretty kerchief for every woman, and tobacco for them that wants it, and whiskey, and candy for the children—"

"No more than they deserve. I hope next year we can do better for them."

She took his hand and tugged at it. "Then you come out and say happy Christmas to your people. You come on, now!"

At that moment, he wanted to say "happy Christmas" only to her. He wanted to draw her into his arms and tell her how fond of her he was and always would be. He wanted to pick her up and carry her up the stairs to his bedroom. He wanted . . .

But he would never do that. He would never do a thing that might cost him her affection and respect.

He managed a smile, although it hurt. "All right, Leonie," He said. "Let's wish a happy Christmas to our people."

* * *

The people, even the more sullen among them, behaved very nicely toward Mr. Duke that evening—they'd have answered to *her* if they hadn't—and he appeared to be in a much better mood when they returned to the big house. There she settled him into a comfortable chair in the library and sat down on a hassock near his knees and told him jokes and stories and teased smiles out of him, until finally he even laughed aloud.

She made only one mistake. When he said something about the house being so empty and quiet, she replied that, well, one day he would marry some nice lady who would give him babies, and then the house wouldn't be so empty and quiet. She saw the unhappy look return to his eyes, and he shook his head. "Not very likely that will happen, Leonie," he said. "I'm thirty-two years old, pushing thirty-three, and I still haven't found the right woman. And I'm not a man to settle for any woman who comes along, just to have a family. I'm afraid you've got an old bachelor on your hands."

She herself had been wondering if that weren't true, but she said, "Oh, now, Mr. Duke, you just wait and see! I know a old voodoo woman, she told me you gonna have a long, happy life!" She worked hard to bring back his smiles and his laughter, and by the time she left the house, she was sure he felt that his Christmas Eve had not been wasted.

But, Lord God, she was angry and disgusted with the neighbors! When Damien came to her cabin the next Sunday evening, she told him so.

"That man, all he wants is be friends with his neighbors. He rides up and down the river and over the countryside for miles to meet people, and what do he get for it? Maybe two times somebody asks him to come back again. He asks them to come to his house, they always too busy. And then Christmas comes, and everybody having parties and balls and dinners, and do they invite him?" She trembled with indignation. "He don't get one invitation. Not one invitation!"

"He tell you that?"

"I know! I know that man!"

"Well, is *he* giving any dinner parties?"

"He don't dare." Tears came to her eyes. "He scared to ask people—and nobody come!"

"Well, what the hell do you expect, Leonie?" Damien said indifferently. "A goddamn slave trader like that—"

She slapped him, resoundingly, before she ever thought what she was doing, and he looked at her in surprise.

"Now, you listen to me, nigger," she said angrily. "Mr. Duke may be a slave trader when he's in Charleston, but out here he is the master of Redbird. And nobody, not even your fine Mr. Justin, treats his people better than *my* Mr. Duke. I reckon Mr. Duke was born to the trade, same as you and me was born slaves. And when he's trying hard to improve hisself and rise and be a good man, that's no reason for your highfalutin Kimbroughs and Buckridges and Sabres to look down their noses at him. Now, you hear me, nigger!"

"Leonie, I'm sorry! But *I* don't like the man, I don't care how hard he's trying to rise!"

Leonie sat down on the edge of her bed. "Go home, Damien."

"Aw, Leonie . . ." Damien sat down beside her and wrapped his arms around her. "After I came all this way to see you? I said I was sorry."

She allowed Damien to rock her in his arms for a moment. She was fond of him, and she was going to find it difficult to say what she must say next.

"Damien, maybe it's best if you don't come to see me no more . . . when we ain't got special business."

Damien stopped rocking her. "Now, why do you say that?"

"I been doing a lot of thinking. Someday soon Mr. Justin gonna send you north."

"Oh, that won't be for a long time, maybe two or three years."

"Maybe. But two or three years is plenty of time for you to put a baby in me, no matter what I do to keep from it. And I don't think you want to leave no baby behind."

"But, honey, I've been thinking maybe we could go north together."

She shook her head. "Now, you know better'n that. We got a great care for each other, Damien, but we each got his own life, and you ain't gonna want me following after you forever. 'Sides, even if you did, I don't think Mr. Duke ever let me go."

"Aw, Leonie . . ."

He fought her, but in his heart he knew she was right. Finally he accepted that.

"But don't make me go away yet, Leonie," he said, turning her to him in his arms and kissing her, "please, not yet."

"No," she murmured, as sweet, warm desire swept through her, "not yet."

Much later, when she lay alone in her dark room, she wondered if she would be able to keep to her decision. After all, she had hardly seen the last of Damien.

And even if she did keep to it, what would happen to her now?

For years she had taken for granted that, when the right time came, she would go north on the Underground Railroad. But now Mr. Duke was at Redbird, and that changed things.

Did she really want to go north? North, to the cold unknown? Redbird, and South Carolina, was home.

And Mr. Duke liked her. Cared for her. Wanted her. And he himself had confirmed that it was very unlikely that he would ever marry.

She could be the mistress of Redbird.

Of course, she was very nearly that now, but to share Mr. Duke's bed would assure her position. And to have such an ambition was far from outlandish—it was hardly unheard of for a wealthy white man to have a well-beloved black mistress. There was even a possibility, however remote, that someday Mr. Duke would be able to free her. And then he might very well marry her, since such marriages were allowed in South Carolina. In any case, he would certainly take good care of any children she might bear him.

But could she be a wife or mistress to a white man and still do what she had to do for the Underground Railroad?

Others had done it.

Her head was awhirl with thoughts, and she sought relief in sleep. But before long, she would have to think hard about the future—and about Mr. Duke.

On New Year's Eve, Duke Avery was again in the library, this time lounging back in a chair while he watched the sputtering fire that cast the only light in the room. He was in shirt sleeves, with a robe thrown over his shoulders, and he had a glass of brandy in his hand. He had been staring at the fire for some time, when he became aware that Leonie was standing in the doorway.

"Now, Leonie," he said, forcing a smile, "I am not going out to the quarters to wish everybody a Happy New Year. That can wait till tomorrow."

"Yes, sir," she said, stepping into the room and walking toward him on silent feet, "that can wait till tomorrow."

He suddenly realized that she was wearing a present he had bought for her in Charleston, a warm flannel nightgown. It was light gray, almost white, prettily trimmed with pink and blue lacing at the neck, and it reached almost to the floor, where her bare toes peeped out from under the hem.

She stopped beside his chair and held her arms out from her sides. "You like it?"

Smiling uncertainly, she tilted her head first to one side and then to the other. So much like Jessie, he thought. Christ, so much like Jessie. But what was she doing here with bare feet and dressed in a nightgown? Was it possible . . . ?

Her eyes gleamed as Jessie's had done when . . .

His heart lurched and began to pound wildly.

"*I* like it," she said. "I think maybe you like to see . . ."

"Yes," he said, his voice catching in his throat. "Yes."

She brought her hands up to cup her breasts. "Soft and warm, so soft and warm." As she ran her hands slowly down over her body, he could see her nipples, the shadow of her navel, the rise of her pubic mound.

For an instant, her smile vanished and doubt clouded her face. "You ain't angry with your Leonie?"

"No. Of course not."

Her smile returned, a little more certain now. Stepping closer to him, she took the brandy glass from his hand and set it aside. Bending her knees, she leaned over him until her face was above his.

"You been very good to me, Mr. Duke."

"I'll always be good to you, Leonie," he said breathlessly, "always. You mean more to me than . . ."

For a moment, she looked into his eyes as if to see what was behind them. Then she took his hand and brought it to her breast.

"So soft and warm. Feel how soft and warm it is."

"Oh, Jesus . . ." The rising nipple pressed against his palm through the flannel. He was on the verge of an erection, and he closed his eyes, fighting it, though he hardly knew why.

"Come," Leonie said.

Still holding his hand, she drew him out of his chair. He felt as if he were dreaming, as she led him through the dark passage and up the stairs. A lamp was burning in his bedroom, and when they entered, he saw that the bed had been turned down.

When she looked at him again, standing so close they nearly touched, her eyes were large and luminous and her mouth quivered as if she too were caught between fear and yearning.

"Your bed is ready, Mr. Duke," she said softly. "You don't want me, I go 'way now."

"No . . . I want . . . oh, Leonie!"

Taking her shoulders in hand, he leaned forward. She took his face between her hands. He brought his lips down on that wide, warm, generous mouth.

He could hold back no longer. He felt the savage rush of hot blood, the swift hardening of his male flesh.

He drew her into his arms.

HE AWAKENED AS IF from a dream which he could not quite remember. He lay on his side, the blankets up over his shoulder, but the arm covering his eyes felt the cold air, and as he tucked himself deeper into the bed, Duke realized he wasn't wearing a nightshirt.

The dream came back to him.

He had had Leonie. Had descended between her raised thighs, had been welcomed, had taken her.

But it hadn't been a dream, though it still seemed like one. Now he remembered that first kiss and his unleashed need as he drew her into his arms, the robe falling from his shoulders, her fingers pulling at his shirt, at his belt, at his buttons. He remembered standing naked before her, while she knelt on the bed and began pulling her gown up over her shoulders. He remembered taking her into his arms again.

Impossible, the sweetness that had followed. But it had happened. As if everything that had been taken away from him fourteen years earlier had been given back. Almost as if Jessie herself had been given back to him.

He withdrew his arm from his eyes. The lamp still glowed, its flame turned so low that the light hardly reached across the bed. He felt a stirring and realized he was not alone. When he reached behind himself, under the covers, his hand came to rest on a bare hip. He felt Leonie turning toward him, felt her move up against his back, felt her slide her arm around his chest.

He laughed quietly, pushed her away, and slid out of bed. He washed with icy-cold water, and went to a window. He had a sense of approaching dawn, but as yet there was no light in the kitchen house. A new year, he thought. The first day of a new year, and who could tell what it might bring?

190

"Mr. Duke?"

Leonie's voice was a silken whisper. He turned back to the bed, where she still lay, half-concealed by the covers, smiling expectantly up at him. Whatever the Sabres and Kimbroughs and Buckridges might deny him, he thought, however they might look down on him and cut him or ignore him, they could never take this away from him. He had not bought her, she had come to him voluntarily, without the slightest urging on his part, and never would he let her go.

"Mr. Duke?" she said again, and as she stretched her arms out to him, Duke slipped back into the bed with her.

Thereafter, she came to him frequently, always staying until dawn. He supposed his people, or at least his house servants, soon knew about them, in spite of her discretion, but he hardly cared. He was no longer in his father's house but in his own, and there were long years to be made up for. Once again, he lay in his brown woman's arms and told her his dreams. "We're going to make Redbird the finest plantation in these parts, Leonie. Never mind Sabrehill and Kimbrough Hall and all those others. You and me, Leonie, we'll show them." And then they joined again, and perhaps again, and whether you called it lust or sin or any other name, what fine lady or effete gentleman of Charleston could ever understand the sweetness between a stallion like himself and his well-cherished wench?

He felt his confidence returning, a gift from Leonie. So the chivalry still didn't accept him? Well, they would, sooner or later, and not simply because he bought a plantation or gave up the slave trade. They would know him for what he was, because he lived among them, and they would accept him on his own merits. His quality would be denied only by fools, he vowed, and to hell with fools.

It was hog-butchering time, ground-clearing time, plowing and bedding-up time, and he worked as never before. And Leonie proved more helpful than ever. Having been at Redbird far longer than Mr. Ferguson, she knew much better than he the secret hopes and resentments and fears

of the various slaves, and she knew what to do about them.
She knew who needed and deserved a new pair of boots,
who felt cheated out of a shirt or a jacket. She knew how
and when to give praise and rewards. "Mr. Duke says you
done a good job on them fence posts, Jared." Jared might
affect to sneer, but secretly he would be pleased, and he
wouldn't sneer at the bit of extra rations that might come
with the praise.

"You and me, Leonie. We'll show them."

"Yes, sir, Mr. Duke. We'll show them."

Or would they?

On the eleventh day of the year, a Sunday, Duke attended church in the nearby village of Riverboro. A number of his neighbors, including the Sabres, were there.
After the service, they lingered for a little while in front of
the church, chattering, laughing, discussing their plans for
the afternoon, the evening, the week to come. They nodded
politely to Duke. He rode home alone.

Was he deluding himself? he wondered.

How many months, in all, had he spent at Redbird and
hardly spoken a word to any white person but Mr. Ferguson and his family? And now one more Sunday was
passing, while he wandered through his silent mansion like
an exile from the race of men.

Suddenly he wanted to weep. He wanted to cry out
aloud: *"I am so lonely!"*

He wanted to take Leonie and head back for Charleston
immediately. To say to hell with the Sabres and the Kimbroughs and the Buckridges, and never give them another
thought. To put Redbird into Mr. Ferguson's hands and
never see it again, and go back among his own kind, the
tradespeople of Charleston.

Except that he had never thought of them as his own
kind. And he never would.

As wearily as if he had spent the day in the fields, he
climbed the stairs to his bedroom. Leonie, who had sensed
his mood and avoided him for most of the day, was already
there, turning down the bed. She looked at him apprehen-
sively.

"You tired, I think I best go—"

"No. Don't go." He managed a smile. He drew her to him by the shoulders and kissed her gently. "Please don't go, Leonie. I want you here with me."

Tremulously, still not quite certain, she smiled back at him.

And then came the banging at the door.

"You're Mr. Avery, sir?"

"Yes?"

There were two men at the courtyard door, both of them in their fifties, Duke judged, and both decently dressed but unshaven and travel-stained.

"Mr. Avery, my name's Pringle, and this is my overseer, Mr. Stokes. I'm terribly sorry to disturb you like this, but we're after a couple of runaways, and we'd like permission to search your quarters."

Duke looked off toward the quarters, where he saw the movement of some torches and heard some shouts.

"Looks like you're already doing it."

"Yes, sir, well, we didn't want 'em flushed out and gone before we ever started looking."

"Of course not. Two, you say?"

"Two brothers and a free black wench." Mr. Pringle shook his head. "Goddamn free blacks, they make more trouble! That boy of mine wanted to marry her, and how the hell is a slave boy gonna marry a free wench? So they ran off, and his brother went with them. And they're armed —one of them stole a pistol from me."

"Hounds?"

"Goddamn hounds lost them yesterday and couldn't find the scent again. But we know that quite a lot of runaways have headed this way the last few years—"

"Toward Sabrehill," Mr. Stokes said disgustedly, and he spat at the ground.

"So we thought we'd give it a try. My people have given me too damn much trouble lately, and this time I intend to teach them a lesson."

"That the patrol out there in my field quarters?"

"Patrol and some others—seven or eight men in all. The constable is rounding up some more."

Duke considered the situation. "All right. We'd better not wait for them. We'll leave word for them to catch up with us. If you don't find your slaves here, I suggest that my overseer and I follow the river road downriver, while you and Mr. Stokes follow the inland road, and the patrol covers the ground in between. Frankly, I don't think you have much chance of catching them at night unless they're holed up somewhere, resting, and you take them by surprise. But maybe we'll do that very thing down at Kimbrough Hall or at Sabrehill. Got everything you need? Torches, ropes, shackles?"

"We've got everything. I'm certainly obliged to you, Mr. Avery."

"Think nothing of it. I'll be with you in a minute."

He hurried back upstairs and explained to Leonie what was happening. Suddenly he felt much better, filled with the excitement of the chase, but Leonie looked as if she might weep.

"Now, don't you worry," he said, "I'll be back as soon as I can. You just keep this here bed warm for us."

At first, Cat thought she felt as she did simply because it was Sunday. Sundays, when Sabrehill had no interesting guests, had always been boring, and now that Mark and Beau were away at school, they were deadly.

Several times she had suggested that they invite Mr. Duke Avery for Sunday dinner, and her parents had agreed that, yes, they must do that soon, but somehow the invitation always got put off—as had happened that morning, when she suggested it after church.

"Oh, not today, Cat. Momma Lucinda will be angry that I didn't tell her first."

"But, Mother-r-r!"

"Now, Katie Anne . . ."

Sometimes she thought that her parents didn't really want to invite Mr. Avery, didn't really approve of her interest in him. But why not? Because he was so much older than she? But she *liked* mature men! Because he was in the slave trade? But they *admitted* that he wasn't like most other slave traders! Actually, she would have given the whole matter very little thought, except that, especially on Sundays, it was all so *boring*!

"Cat, can't you sit down?" Her father looked up from his book and glared at her when she tromped through the library the third time that evening, sighing loudly.

"I'm bored."

"Then go to bed."

"I can't. I'm too restless to sleep."

"Go see if you can help your mother with something. Help Momma Lucinda clean up the kitchen."

Cat groaned.

Damien, she thought, where was Damien? She would find him and give him a bit of hell for—for—well, she didn't know what for, but she'd think of something.

She saw no light in the little house at the head of the east lane, which he had taken over from Jebediah. Likely he's got some goddamn wench in there, spreading for him, she thought angrily, as she went toward the house. Well, she didn't care. She'd just walk in and drag them both out of bed, and kick the wench's ass clear back to the quarters. And then she would *really* give Damien hell.

"Dami*en-n-n*!" she yelled, as she threw open the door and marched into the dark house.

He wasn't there.

Then where the hell was he?

For the first time that evening, she recognized her boredom, her restlessness, for what it was—a sense that something was askew, out of joint, off-center. Somewhere, there was trouble.

She went back out onto the little veranda. Across the courtyard, Momma Lucinda was putting out the kitchen house lights and locking up, and further away, at the head of the west service lane, a light burned in the butler's cottage. She hurried to the kitchen house.

"Momma Lucinda, have you seen Damien?"

"No, I ain't, not lately."

"Well, if you see him, you tell him I want him, and he'd better move his lazy ass pretty damn—"

Momma Lucinda whirled toward her. "Now, don't you talk that way!"

"Well, just tell him——"

"Sometimes, Miss Cat, you talk like just plain trash, and I ain't gonna stand for it! I didn't stand for it from your momma, and I ain't gonna stand for it from you!"

"I'm sorry!"

"Just plain sandhill white trash!" the cook muttered, heading for the house servants' quarters at the end of the west lane.

So, Cat marveled as she followed slowly after the cook, Momma Lucinda had long ago scolded Miss Lucy Sabre for using naughty words. Cat so seldom heard her stepmother use any but the most ladylike language that she could hardly believe it.

But now she had more important things on her mind.

"Irish!" she called into the butler's cottage, and Momma Lucinda's thirty-year-old son came to the door. "Irish, do you know where Damien is?"

"Ain't——I haven't seen him since supper, Miss Cat." Irish often tried to talk house-proper, the way Jebediah had done.

"Well, if you see him . . ."

"Yes, Miss Cat."

Her anxiety increased with every step as she headed through the dark to the west gardens. Situated there were several small houses that were used only when the Sabres gave their rare large parties, or for more permanent guests, such as tutors or a long-ago nanny. Among them was a house now occupied by Leila.

"Leila," Cat said, looking into the little front room, "have you seen Damien?"

"No, but if he ain't around, maybe he headed off for Redbird. I think he's sorta sweet on that Leonie over there."

"Oh, that dumb . . . pecker!"

Leila burst out laughing. "Little Kitty-Cat, no wonder you scare off all the fine gentlemen, talking like that!"

"If they scare that easy," Cat said sullenly, "I don't want anything to do with them. Anyway, why shouldn't I talk like that? What does it hurt? And *they* talk like that—behind my back!"

"Yes, only you ain't s'pose to hear or understand."

"Leila, that is dumb!"

"I know, I know."

But where *was* Damien, she wondered, as she stood shivering in the dark west gardens. She had a feeling that Leila was right: He had, for whatever reason, gone to Redbird.

And he shouldn't have.

Not this evening. Of all evenings, not this evening. This was an evening for trouble.

Damien was in trouble.

The knowledge hit her like a physical blow.

She ran through the dark back to the house and entered the library, where her father still sat reading his book.

"Papa, I can't find Damien!"

Her father sighed. "Cat, it's late. What do you want Damien for?"

"He's in trouble! Papa, I just know that dang fool has got himself in trouble!"

Her father laid his book aside. "Now, what makes you think that?"

"I'll bet he went off to see that gal at Redbird, and something happened!"

"But what makes you think—"

"I just know!"

Her father studied her for a moment. "Cat, is there something you aren't telling me?"

"No, Papa!" Cat laced her fingers and wrung her hands till the knuckles whitened. "Please, we've got to go to Redbird! We've just got to help him!"

Justin Sabre had little faith in blind intuition, but whether Damien was in trouble or not, Cat was pleading for his help, and he knew that this was no time to ignore or laugh at her or even to reason with her.

He stood up. "Go tell Zagreus we need a carriage. I'll tell your mother where we're going and be with you in a minute."

Damien had no idea how many pattyrollers there were, but they seemed to be everywhere, milling about on their horses in the dark. He recognized the voice of Mr. P. V.

Tucker, saying, "I swear to God I seen 'em running into these here woods, all three of 'em, and maybe four!" From his other side, Caley Carstairs yelled, "Well, if they don't give up, just shoot anything that moves!" and Rowan Carstairs yelled back, "Christ, no, you goddamn fool, we'll be shooting each other!"

In seven years of working with the Underground Railroad, only four or five times had Damien felt that he was truly in great danger. Tonight, when all he had wanted was to pay a call on Leonie, he expected to have his head blown off at any moment.

With any luck at all, he would never even have encountered the three blacks, let alone the patrol. He had been taking a shortcut across the fields and through the woods, when without the slightest warning he had virtually walked into the muzzle of the biggest horse pistol he had ever seen in his life. He had backed off, throwing up his hands and yelling, "Don't shoot! Don't shoot!" and it hadn't helped at all when he saw that the big black holding the pistol was as terrified as he. Fortunately, a second, smaller black man appeared at once and shoved the pistol toward the ground. 'He'p us!" he had pleaded. "You he'p us!" "Yeah! sure! okay! ban!" Damien had rattled off every expression of assent and reassurance he could think of.

A woman had then appeared. He learned that Shango, carrying the gun, and Kwamay were slaves, and that Marcie, Kwamay's woman, was a free black. They had been on the run since Saturday evening, Kwamay said, and their pursuers were not far behind. Damien could think of no better place to hide them than Sabrehill.

They had almost made it.

If only the moon stayed under cover, he thought. If only the other three had enough sense to stay in the thick brush and not move, no matter what happened. If only Shango had done as Damien had told him and gotten rid of the gun. That gun could do absolutely nothing for them except perhaps get them killed.

"Nothing here," came Mr. Tucker's fading voice. "They musta moved on. . . ."

"Wait!" Rowan Carstairs yelled. "I've got one! Come out of there, you black—"

Shango's frightened cry and the pistol shot came at the same time. Rowan Carstair's roar of anger turned into something else: a bleat, a whimper, a sob. "Son of a bitch shot me. Son of a bitch . . . think I'm . . ."

Damien saw a shadow fall from a horse and into the brush.

"Jesus Christ," a man yelled, "the nigger shot Rowan!"

"No!" Caley Carstairs yelled, "what you talking 'bout!"

"Killed him dead, looks like!"

"No! Where is the nigger! I'll kill *him*!"

Somewhere Marcie sobbed.

There was more heavy crashing through the brush, and as the moon appeared from behind the clouds, Damien saw a dark figure run by.

A gun flashed and roared, and Marcie screamed. The dark figure stumbled and fell.

"You shot the woman, you goddamn fool!" somebody said. "It wasn't her that killed Rowan!"

"I don't care!" Caley Carstairs cried. "They shot Rowan, I aim to kill the whole fuckin' lot of 'em!"

"Look! Look there! There's one of 'em!"

The voice was coming closer, and Damien fought not to panic; but when he felt the brush move, he could only assume that he had been seen. He tore his way out and ran—ran with every last bit of power he could channel into his legs, ran as he had never before run in his life.

He had taken only a half-dozen steps when his skull seemed to explode like a bright glass ball and he fell into darkness.

This could not be happening to him, he screamed inwardly as they dragged him out of the woods and down onto the river road, this could not be happening to him. This kind of thing happened to other black people, to other slaves, but not to him! He was Damien of Sabrehill, and one day he would be sent north, and he was hardly a slave at all, "slave" was little more than a word to him, and this could not be happening to him!

But it was.

His head had exploded, and then he had found himself being dragged over the ground, his wrists bound behind him, and now he was being lifted to his feet. A couple of torches had been lit, and he saw that Shango had been wounded in the chest. The man's head hung down, and he looked as if he could hardly stay on his feet. Kwamay was there, too, looking about with terrified eyes, but the woman was nowhere to be seen. Dead, Damien remembered. Shot dead. She and Rowan Carstairs.

"I say hang 'em," Caley Carstairs shouted. His dirty face was wet with tears. "They killed my brother, and I say I'm gonna hang 'em, and I'll kill any son of a bitch that tries to stand in my way!"

"But we can't do that," one of the men said nervously. "They ain't our property, and even if they was—"

"I say Caley's right," said another. "A bunch of runaways murders a white man, we ain't got no choice."

"We're gonna hang 'em," Caley said, "right now!"

Kwamay moaned, and Damien heard a cry come from his own throat as he watched Caley Carstairs throw the coil of rope over a tree limb. "Come on," he yelled, "two more ropes! I want to see all three of these niggers dancing at once!"

Somehow Damien found his voice, though he hardly knew what he was shouting. He was no runaway! He was from Sabrehill! He had nothing to do with any runaways! He had a pass! "Please! My pocket! Look in my right pocket! I've got a pass from Mr. Justin! I was on my way to Redbird, and—"

"Shut up, nigger!" Caley Carstairs' hand struck like hard leather across Damien's face, and he tasted blood.

"He got a ticket, all right, Caley—"

"I don't give a shit what he got!" Caley grabbed the forged pass, which had been taken from Damien's pocket, tore it up, and threw it away.

Shango didn't resist, as they put the noose around his neck. Caley grabbed the free end of the rope.

"Somebody give me a hand with this."

Shango's knees gave away before they even started pulling the rope, and at first he hardly twitched. Then suddenly, when he was five feet off the ground, he began kicking wildly and his bowels came loose. Caley Carstairs's laugh was uncontrolled. "Kill my brother, will you, you son of a bitch?"

Kwamay fell to his knees, sobbing. Two men lifted him to his feet and a third fitted a noose around his neck. "Now!" Caley said. "Up! Make him dance!"

Kwamay uttered one last cry before the noose tightened around his throat. His mouth opened wide, and his eyes glistened, as they reflected the flickering torches. The men on the other end of the rope gave a single great heave, and he shot into the air, until he, too, was high above the road, bobbing from a swaying pine limb.

Then they were putting a noose around Damien's neck.

No! He tried to tell them that this was wrong, that they were making a mistake, that he wasn't a runaway, he was simply a Sabrehill nigger on his way to Redbird when he had encountered the other three, but they didn't seem to understand. They only looked at him, their eyes as bright as Kwamay's, some of them grinning, yet looking oddly sick. Caley Carstairs giggled as he tightened the noose.

Cat!

"Gonna hang you up, nigger!"

Cat, help me!

"Gonna make you pay for what you done to my brother!"

"Mr. Carstairs, I didn't harm your brother!"

"You killed him, you and these others, and now, by God, you are paying!"

"Please!"

Caley Carstairs grabbed the rope and pulled.

"Pay, nigger!"

Damien felt a tug that seemed to stretch and nearly break his neck. His feet left the ground.

Cat!

Cat saw the torches down the road and heard the shouts and knew she had been right.

"The river road, Papa," she had said. "Take the river road!"

"Cat, are you sure—"

"Papa, all I know is something's wrong, and we'd better take the river road!"

And now, as the carriage rolled closer, they seemed to be entering a kind of hell, and her eyes were seeing something they didn't want to see, and her father was saying, "For God's sake, Cat, don't look!"

But she had to look. The first of the hanged men was still, except for a slight twisting at the end of the rope. The second was kicking in a strangely erratic way. The third was—

"Damien!"

As the carriage came to a halt, her father hunched forward, his pepperbox pistol in hand, and she heard the clicking of its cock. One of the three men on the end of the rope jumped away.

"Drop him," her father said.

"He killed my brother!"

"And I'm going to kill you, Carstairs, if you don't let go of that rope *now!*"

The second man released the rope, and it slid through Caley Carstairs's hands. Damien fell to the ground and didn't move except for the heaving of his chest. One of the men hastily loosened the noose.

"Now the others."

For a moment Caley Carstairs didn't move. Then he walked to the carriage, his face twisting with a gargoyle grin. Cat shrank back from him, as he looked up at her.

" 'Evening, Miss Cat. This your first hanging?"

"Carstairs, I am warning you—"

"Mr. Sabre, I am hanging the niggers that murdered my brother, and not you nor anybody else is gonna stop me." He looked around toward Damien. "Now, get that nigger back on his feet!"

Her father raised up in the carriage, aiming his pistol. "Don't do it, Carstairs!"

"Mr. Sabre," P. V. Tucker broke in, "I wouldn't interfere, if I was you." There was now a pistol in his hand. It wasn't pointing at anybody, but it was there.

Her father ignored Tucker. "Carstairs, if I have to fire this thing, you'll be the first to go."

Carstairs shook his head. "You won't fire it. If you do, there'll still be six of us left, and one of us will kill you. But Miss Cat will still be here, and do you know what's gonna happen to her then?"

There was utter silence. One of the hanged men kicked, more like the twitch of one leg. Cat had never seen her father look so terrible. His face was bathed with sweat in spite of the chill of the night, and his eyes seemed to be sinking back into his skull. He didn't move. No one moved.

Cat heard the clopping sound of hooves and looked down the road to see Mr. Duke Avery and his overseer on horseback, coming into the light of the torches.

"Well, gentlemen," Duke Avery said, as he reined up near Damien, "I see you finally caught up with the runaways."

"They killed my brother."

"I'm sorry to hear that. What do you intend to do now?"

"Hang this nigger. And if there's any interference . . ." Caley Carstairs reached for Cat. Before she could move away, he grabbed her arm and yanked her out of the carriage, dropping her into the dirt at his feet. "When we get done with the bitch here, there's gonna be one more scar-faced whore at Sabre——"

Duke Avery never stopped smiling. He pulled the pistol from his holster. Only as he pulled back on the cock and leveled the pistol, did it seem to occur to Caley Carstairs what Duke meant to do. Then, his eyes widening with horror, he clawed at his own pistol and managed to get it out. Too late. Fire flashed from the sides and muzzle of Duke Avery's gun. Caley Carstairs fell back to the ground. He made a final desperate attempt to rise up and fire, then cursed, sobbed, and lay still.

Duke Avery pointed his gun at P. V. Tucker, then swung it around at the other men. "Gentlemen, I've got four more shots in this Colt, and I reckon Mr. Sabre has some pepper in that box. If anyone is inclined to dispute the matter . . ."

The men looked at each other.

"It was Caley's idea," one of them said, "not ours. And now he's dead."

"Then I suggest you cut those niggers down. Quick. And then we'll sort all this out."

For the rest of his life, he was certain, he would never forget: the air reentering his fire-filled lungs until they threatened to burst; the purple darkness receding from his mind; the smell of dirt under his face; somewhere nearby, the flickering of torchlight and the sound of voices. He had felt someone removing the noose and untying his wrists, but he had hardly dared to believe that it was over and they were going to let him live.

All the way back to Sabrehill, he felt, not the joy of his life saved, but the horror of the death so narrowly escaped. Never again, surely, would he come so close to death and yet live.

They rode back to Sabrehill in silence, he on one side of Mr. Justin, and Cat on the other. When they reached the courtyard, Mr. Justin said, "Damien, come into the house. I want to speak to you."

At that moment, Damien wanted only to go to his own house and escape into sleep, but he followed Justin into the library, where Miss Lucy awaited them. She looked at them questioningly, but Justin shook his head: Her questions could wait until later.

"You know, don't you," Mr. Justin said, "that Cat saved your life? If it hadn't been for her, we wouldn't have been there. A few minutes later, and you would have been dead."

Damien lowered his head. "I know, Mr. Justin."

"Damien, I'm not going to lecture you. You've been through enough hell tonight. But I want to remind you that you've been brought up to do something better than dangle from the end of a lynch gang's rope."

Miss Lucy's breath caught, but she remained silent.

"Mr. Justin, I truly swear to you . . ." Damien's voice

rose painfully, and he couldn't hold back his tears. He was a small boy again, in a world too brutal for comprehension. "Mr. Justin, I swear it wasn't my fault!"

Justin ignored his words. "I've sometimes suspected that runaways were going through our quarters. I've always looked the other way. Hell, in my day I've even helped a few of them. But I'm not going to have you—"

"Mr. Justin, I swear to you! Even if I do help some poor nigger now and then, it wasn't like that tonight! I was going to Redbird to see a friend, and I met those three, and I couldn't just say . . . what I mean is, before they could get away, or I could, the patrol was on us, and . . ."

"Justin," Miss Lucy said softly, carefully, "even if I don't yet know all that's happened, I have a feeling that you are wrong to blame Damien."

"I don't blame Damien. I accept his story. But I'm going to have a hell of a time persuading some other people to accept it. And to get them to agree that, in any case, he's been punished quite enough. And from now on, I want Damien to stay out of trouble."

"Do you understand, Damien?" Miss Lucy asked in that same soft voice, going to him.

"Yes, ma'am. Yes, sir."

"Then go to bed, dear." Miss Lucy touched one wet cheek and lightly kissed the other. "And don't cry anymore. You're home now, and safe."

"Yes, ma'am."

He left the house and went out into the courtyard. His head ached sickeningly, his neck was sore, and he could still feel the rope-burn in his flesh. But as he breathed deeply of the crisp night air, he began to savor life again. As Miss Lucy had said, he was home and safe.

He went into his house. His own little house at the head of the lane. Never had he loved it more. He continued on into the bedroom.

"You . . . God . . . damn . . . !"

She came at him out of a dark corner, fists flying and pounding on him, nails clawing at him. *"You . . . damn . . . black nigger . . . son of a bitch!"*

"Cat! Please! For God's sake!"

He tried to fend off her blows, tried to seize her arms, but she kept coming at him, jabbing, slapping, flailing.

"You . . . stupid . . . bastard! You . . . goddamn . . . !"

"Please, Cat!"

Somehow he pinned her right arm under his left, somehow twisted her left arm behind her, and held her up close against him. As she strained to escape, he realized she was weeping.

"It's all right, Cat!"

"You . . . damn . . . fool . . ."

Then her mouth was on his, and he was returning her kiss, crushing her mouth and kissing her all over her tear-wet face, kissing her fiercely, hungrily, achingly, as their arms went around each other and they fell onto the bed and he grew hard against her. Went on kissing her, as they rolled together in the darkness, thighs entangled, straining together, as if trying to be one with each other and make this moment last forever.

But, of course, that could never be. And they both knew it without ever saying it. Her mouth roved over his face one last time, and she rolled back from him, releasing him with a long shuddering sigh.

After a moment, she sat up, and he knew she was going to leave him. But first she leaned down over him again and touched his cheek.

"Oh, Damien, if they'd killed you, I'd have died too."

"I know, Cat."

"You are my heart."

She kissed him once more, gently, and left.

It was almost dawn when Duke got back to Redbird. A lamp was burning for him in the passage of the big house and he carried it up to the bedroom. He set it down on a table and quickly, silently got undressed. Sitting on the edge of the bed, he gathered Leonie into his arms. Her eyes fluttered and she smiled. "Mm," she said, "I thought you wasn't never coming back."

"I'm back, honey," he said, kissing her, "but only for a little while. Something's happened that could change everything for us here at Redbird. And I'm going to celebrate by giving you the best pleasuring that you ever did have."

But it wasn't Leonie he was thinking of as he took her. It was Cat Sabre. Cat Sabre lying in the dirt of the road. Cat Sabre staring up at him with horror and fascination as he gunned down Caley Carstairs.

I did it for you, he thought. *And you know it.*

He was as certain of it as he was of anything else in his life: One day he would make Cat Sabre the mistress of Redbird.

-◦⊰{ 4 }⊱◦-

"DAMIEN! Damien-n-n!"

Cat's voice called him up out of sleep. For a moment, all
the horror of the previous night came back to him—the
shots and screams in the dark, the two men hanged before
his eyes, the rope tightening around his own neck and
snatching him from the ground—but then, as if the memory were too terrible to bear, it receded like a half-forgot-
ten dream. He was alive. That was all that mattered. He
was lying in his own bed, and he could smell ham and
hominy on the cool, sweet morning air, and he was alive.

"Damien!"

He blinked himself further awake and saw Cat standing
over him. She returned his smile. "Momma said to let you
sleep in, but it's late now, and I brought you some breakfast. So you get your lazy carcass out of that bed before
your food gets cold."

"Thank you, Cat."

"You're welcome. How're you feeling this morning?"

"Mm." He thought about it. "Like it was my birthday.
My eighth birthday."

Cat laughed. "Well, happy birthday! When are you
going to get up?"

"When you get out of this room."

"No, now!"

Before he could stop her, Cat had yanked the covers
down off of him. Fortunately, his nightshirt preserved his
modesty. She leapt away as he tried to slap her butt, so he
tossed his pillow at her. Sticking her tongue out, she made
a jeering sound, wagged her tail at him, and left the room.

He loved her, he thought, smiling after her.

No need to tell her that, of course. She already knew it.
No need even to think about it. And as for what had
happened between them last night, he knew she would

208

never refer to it, and neither would he. But somewhere, locked away in the back of his mind, he would have the memory.

He got out of bed and washed, and when he ate his ham and hominy, no food had ever tasted better. Looking out the window, he found that the sky was marvelously blue and the day was dazzlingly bright, and why had he never before noticed how beautiful were the sheep grazing in the courtyard? Everywhere he looked, he saw a scene painted in fresh oils, glistening, not yet dry.

After dressing, he took his plate to the scullery, washed it, and put it away. When he told Momma Lucinda, the cook, that she was beautiful, he meant it.

"You must have been some real fancy wench in your day."

"In my *day*!" she said with mock indignation. "In my *day*, did you say? Are you trying to tell me my day is *done*, you rascal, you?"

Laughing, he dodged her blows and ran out of the kitchen into the courtyard. There, Mr. Justin was mounting a horse Zagreus had brought to him, and Miss Lucy was seeing him off. As Damien walked toward them, his eyes misted with love and gratitude. He was a servant in their house, but he had never felt like a servant. He had been a boy, and was now a young man, doing his fair share of whatever had to be done and trying to live up to their expectations for him. Like Jebediah and Cat, they made him feel loved.

"How are you this morning, Damien?" Miss Lucy asked.

"Oh, I'm fine, Miss Lucy." Painfully, Damien made himself think of what had happened. "Mr. Justin, last night I was so . . . scared . . . I don't think I even thanked you for—"

"Don't thank me, thank Cat." Mr. Justin reached down and ran a hand over the back of Damien's head. "And you remember what I told you, Damien, and stay out of trouble from now on."

"Yes, sir, I will."

"Oh, Papa," Cat called, as she came running out of the house. "Papa, will you be very long in Riverboro?"

"I don't know, Cat. I could be there an hour, or maybe all afternoon."

"But you will be seeing Mr. Avery?"

Mr. Justin nodded. "We agreed to meet there, so we could clear this matter up."

"Well, when you're all through, bring him back here for supper. We can have him for supper, can't we, Momma?"

Cat and Mr. Justin both looked at Miss Lucy. She shrugged. "Oh, I suppose."

"I'll ask him."

"You do that. He'll come. Now, don't you forget, you hear me, Papa?"

Mr. Justin laughed. "I won't forget."

Suddenly the day didn't seem quite so bright to Damien.

Cat Sabre's green eyes widened in the lamp light. She said, "But you might have been killed!"

"I don't think so, Miss Catherine. Unless that new-fangled revolving pistol of mine misfired, and it's pretty reliable. You were in more danger than I was."

"Until you came along."

"I suppose we were both lucky. But you mustn't think about it."

Cat had invited Duke to stay on after the other supper guests had left, and they were sitting in the north parlor. She closed her eyes and shook her head. "I can't help thinking about it. I'll never forget . . ."

No, Duke thought, she'd never forget. A lot of people would never forget.

Until he met Mr. Owen Buckridge on the main street of Riverboro that afternoon, he had thought he would have more trouble with the Carstairs's pattyroller friends than from the law, but then he had learned differently.

"Mr. Avery, sir," Mr. Buckridge had said, "I just want you to know that most of us around here are behind you one hundred percent. P. V. Tucker told us all about it. Now, Tucker and Justin have had their differences, but that didn't keep him from saying that you and Justin were dead right, and he's going to speak up for you."

"Tucker?" Duke had said, surprised. The previous night, Tucker had appeared to be anything but a friend.

"He and the others are all agreed. It's a shame about the Carstairs boys, and you can't really blame Caley for wanting to kill the niggers that killed his brother. But when he laid hands on little Katie Anne and said what he did, he went too far. You didn't have a choice, Mr. Avery. Any gentleman would have done the same thing."

Duke had remembered what one of the pattyrollers had said: *"It was Caley's idea. And now he's dead."* They wanted no part of the blame for hanging a couple of valuable slaves and nearly killing one who might have been innocent.

"My papa told me how you stood up for Damien, Mr. Avery," Cat said now.

Duke shrugged it off. "The boy was obviously innocent. He was coming from one direction, and the runaways from another, after running a full two days. It had to be plain bad luck that he ran into them. Tucker said the boy even had a pass, till Caley tore it up."

"Damien often goes to Redbird to see his friends. I hope you don't mind."

"Of course I don't mind, Miss Catherine."

"If anything had happened to him . . ." For a moment, the fire seemed to leave Cat's eyes. "You see, Damien's very special to us . . . to me. We were raised together, and he's almost like one of my brothers. Closer in some ways, though it's hard to say how."

"Well, a lot of us have special feelings for our black servants, Miss Catherine. That's something that a lot of people up north just don't seem to understand."

Cat shook her head. "I don't mean that exactly. Or maybe I do. It's so hard to explain." She smiled. "Maybe you'll think I'm making a joke, but . . . well, let's just say that when Damien stubs his toe, my foot hurts!"

"No, Miss Catherine, I don't think you're making a joke. And I know exactly what you mean, because I've had servants I felt exactly the same way about. Believe me, I understand."

Jessie, he thought.

"Yes," Cat said slowly, "I think you do."

Leila, the housekeeper, looked in through the doorway, stared unsmilingly at him for just the right length of time, and departed. It was not the first time she had done so, and Duke understood.

"Well, Miss Catherine," he said, rising, "it's getting late, and I still have to ride back to Redbird."

Cat threw a quick frown in the wake of the departed Leila, but said nothing. She accompanied Duke out into the courtyard, where his horse awaited him.

She held out her hand. "Mr. Avery, if you happen to be free Sunday for dinner . . ." She raised that faintly mocking brow. "I have already asked my momma, if that should worry you."

Duke smiled and lifted her hand. "I'd be delighted, Miss Catherine—if you could bring yourself to call me Duke."

"Most people call me Cat."

He touched his lips lightly to the back of her hand. "Cat—for Catherine. It's a lovely name."

"Good night, Duke."

"Good night, Catherine. Until Sunday."

It was long after dark the next Sunday evening, when Leonie saw Duke's horse and carriage coming through the moonlit persimmon grove. By the time he reached the courtyard, she had aroused the sleepy stable boy and returned to the house.

"It's late," she said as he sprang down out of the carriage. "I wasn't expecting you so late."

He smiled. "Do I detect a slight note of resentment, Leonie?"

"I was worried 'bout you, Mr. Duke! You had any supper yet?"

"I ate at Sabrehill. Miss Catherine asked me to stay on after the others left."

Miss Catherine again. Lately it seemed to Leonie that Miss Catherine's name was on Duke's tongue every other time he spoke.

"The others?" she asked, following him into the house. "Was there others there too?"

"Oh, yes. Your Mr. Duke wasn't the only guest, Leonie. Merely the guest of honor."

"Why, that's wonderful, Mr. Duke!"

When she had closed the door, he wrapped his arms around her and lifted her from the floor. "The Pettigrews, the Buckridges, Lawyer Devereau, Dr. Paulson—they were all there, more than a dozen of them, and all *so* interested in your Mr. Duke. Leonie, it was like all of a sudden they remembered just who the hell Leduc Avery was and recalled their manners."

"Well, it was just a matter of time, wasn't it?" she said, laughing, as he whirled her around and set her down again.

"A matter of time and little luck—being there when Caley Carstairs put his goddamn hands on Miss Catherine. I'll never forget the look in her eyes afterwards. . . ."

Miss Catherine again.

Duke picked up the passage lamp, put an arm around Leonie's waist, and led her up the stairs. "Honey, we've got a lot of planning to do. Before long, everybody will be going to Charleston for the gay season, and I already have half-a-dozen invitations. And I told Miss Catherine that I was going to give a dinner party too."

"Why, that's fine, Mr. Duke. But I'm 'fraid I don't know much 'bout—"

"Don't you worry about it, you won't have to do a thing. Raphael and Birdie gave many a party for my daddy in the old days, and Birdie'll be in her glory. We'll just leave that part to them."

Leonie felt that she should be happy for her Mr. Duke, but something was nagging at her, like a fear she hardly dared to admit even to herself: the thought of Miss Catherine.

"You got Raphael and Birdie—you gonna take me to Charleston, too?" she asked, as they entered the bedroom.

"Why, of course, didn't I just say so? You don't think I could go a whole month without my Leonie, do you, honeychild?"

Later, when they lay in each other's arms in the dark, Duke murmured sleepily, "You remember how I said everything was going to change for us at Redbird? Well, I was right, wasn't I?"

Yes, he was right. But now Leonie wasn't sure she wanted everything to change.

It was the most disappointing gay season Damien had ever experienced.

Every year he looked forward to it. Long, lazy summer days in Charleston were enjoyable, but the winter season had a special gaiety, with its trips to the race course, and the windows already lighting up at five o'clock, and the many parties and balls crowded into such a short period. The streets seemed more crowded, more filled with excitement in February than in August, and he had always loved to roam through the city with Cat.

But here it was, the night of the Jockey Club Ball and almost time to return to Sabrehill, and he felt as if in the last month he had hardly even seen Cat. Even after she had turned sixteen and started attending many more grown-up parties, they had always spent Monday, his free day, together. But not this year. This year she had spent almost every moment, it seemed to Damien, with Mr. Duke Avery. Mr. Goddamn Slave-Trader Duke Avery.

Mr. Duke was with her that night, after the ball, when the guests came pouring into the house on Lynch Street. Damien was kept busy seeing that drinks were replenished and the sideboard of food never ran out. In any other year, he and Cat would have whispered jokes back and forth, and she would have given him sly winks from across the room; this year it was: Damien, fetch more Madeira; Damien, we need more pâté; Damien, do this, do that, while she played the *lady* for Mr. Duke Avery. And while other guests came and went, Duke Avery stayed on and on, halfway through the night, as if he were a member of the family.

But at last he could find no excuse to stay any longer. Damien watched as Cat escorted him to the door. Saw the little whispers of farewell, the shared smiles. Saw Cat boldly touch a fingertip to her own lips and then to Mr.

Duke's. Saw Mr. Duke try to hold her hand, while they both laughed and Cat drew the hand away.

The few remaining guests left. The servants went to their quarters. Miss Lucy and Mr. Justin went upstairs. Cat started up the stairs, then gave him a hard look and came back down. He followed her into the parlor. As she turned to him, he could feel her hostility like a chill breeze off a cold lake.

"Well?" she said, her voice as hard as he had ever heard it. "I know you have something to say to me. You may as well do it and get it over with."

For a moment he couldn't think of a thing to say. He said the first thing that came to his mind.

"I've missed you, Cat."

Cat's shoulders slowly lowered and she looked away from him. "I'm sorry." Her voice was much softer. "I know what you mean. We haven't had much fun together this year."

"We haven't had any. Because you've spent all your time with *him*."

Instantly, Cat's shoulders were squared again, and her eyes challenged his.

"Yes, with him! And what's wrong with that?"

"Cat, you know who he is. And you know what he is. That's the man who sold Mr. Jeb to Sabrehill—"

"And it was pretty damn lucky for us, wasn't it! Tell me, Damien, was his selling Mr. Jeb to us any worse than our buying him?"

"I don't know, Cat. I just know—"

"You don't know *nothing*! All you know is to be rude to Mr. Avery every time he comes around—"

"Cat, I haven't!"

"The goddamn hell you haven't! You've sulked and glared and got in the way and dragged your ass around like a goddamn lazy nigger every time I've asked you to do something, and, Damien," her voice rose until he was certain her parents must hear it, *"Damien, I am goddamn sick of it!"*

"Jesus, Cat," he said, looking worriedly about at the lamps, "when you talk like that, you could shatter glass!"

She stared at him for a few seconds and burst out laughing.

"Oh, you bastard!" she said, tears flowing from her eyes. "Making me laugh like that!"

"Cat, please . . ." Taking her shoulders, he shook her gently until she calmed. "Cat, I'm sorry. I never thought about it, but I guess I have been acting sort of like a dog in the manger. But that's because I don't like him and I feel like he's taking you away from me."

"Have you forgotten he saved your life?"

"No. Because he didn't save my life. You saved my life, you and your daddy."

"But if he hadn't come along—"

"If he hadn't come along, your daddy would have shot Mr. Carstairs, and Mr. Tucker too, if he'd had to, and everybody else would have gone home, just the way they did. And if I'm wrong, I *still* don't like him, and I don't want him around you."

Cat pulled away from him. For a moment she walked back and forth, her eyes half-closed and a hand to her face. Then she turned to him again.

"Damien, there is something you have to understand once and for all. I'll soon be nineteen. At some time in the near future, I'll be getting married. I'll marry a man I can at least tolerate, I hope—there aren't many of them—and one rich enough so that I can live as I've been brought up to live. I shall do my damnedest to be a good wife to him, and I shall probably even love him.

"Now, I suppose that in some fashion I love you, too, Damien, and I always will. But we can't be together forever. And if you have some insane idea that I might go north with you and crusade with the Grimké sisters for women's rights and abolition, and maybe bear you a pickaninny from time to time, and likely wind up as a poor nigger pig-farmer's wife—"

"Cat!" Her words went through him like an electric shock.

She grinned. "I know. It sounds ridiculous. Not to mention insulting. I meant it to sound that way."

"But I never in the world thought such a thing!"

"Neither did I, until this minute. And I'll never think of it again." She took his face in her hands. "Damien, I'm sorry you don't like Duke. I do like him. I find him reasonably intelligent and well-spoken and *very* attractive. Sometimes a bit hotheaded, like Papa, and sometimes a little stuffy and humorless, but very gentle and very thoughtful. A *good* man, Damien. I may even marry him some day, if he asks me. And since that's true, I'm begging you, Damien, don't ever do anything that will make me love you less than I do."

He honestly didn't believe he was antagonistic to Duke Avery out of mere jealousy. He and Cat had always had better noses for each other's difficulties than for their own, and to him, Duke Avery smelled like trouble. But he realized that, if Cat was making a mistake, there was not a thing he could do about it except be ready in case she needed him.

"All right, Cat." He pulled her hands down from his face and drew her into his arms. "All right, for you I'll be nice and polite to Mr. Duke Avery from now on. Not because I like him, but because there's nothing in the world I want more than for this here catamount to be happy."

"I thank you, Damien." Cat rubbed her cheek against his shoulder. "And I promise you, when we get back to Sabrehill, we won't see nearly as much of Duke Avery. And you and I will spend much, much more time together."

But it was not to be. It seemed to Damien that Cat was now almost as busy at Sabrehill as she was in the city. Visitors, young and old, came for days at a time and had to be entertained. Cat herself was away on visits. Young men rode for hours on Sundays to come calling, for even those she discouraged as suitors continued to enjoy her company. Her nineteenth birthday celebration took up most of a week, and not once in that time did Damien find her alone.

And then there was Mr. Duke. Two and three times a week, Mr. Duke. Damien kept waiting for Cat to grow bored with him, to utter the words that would cool his ardor—"I suppose if I waste my time with a horse's ass,"

she had told one of the McClintock boys, "I can only
blame myself for not bringing a shovel"—but they never
came. On the contrary, her language was increasingly
curbed and her behavior ever more ladylike in Duke's presence.

Damien had almost given up, had almost accepted the
fact that the years of their intimate companionship were
over, when, in mid-April, Cat suggested a day of sailing.

"You mean you want me to take you and Mr. Duke—"

"No, not me and Mr. Duke! Just you and me and the
babies." Her half-sister and half-brother, Sarah and Macy,
were still "the babies," although they were now eight and
ten. "Can you have the *Celandine* ready by Monday
morning?"

He would have it ready.

Monday turned out to be a perfect day for sailing. It was
warm for April, but there was a brisk breeze to cool them
and to send the twenty-foot sloop skimming over the water.
The sky was a clear blue between the few white puffs of
cloud, and the river was a deep green under the tall over-
hanging trees.

With a lunch packed away in the cuddy, they headed
upstream, taking turns at the tiller and the jib sheets and
practicing tacks and jibes in figure eights. Macy and Sarah,
thoroughly at home in the water and burdened only by
their skimpy shirts, jumped overboard, splashed to nearby
islands and back, and trailed in the water by clinging to the
Celandine's transom and gunwales. Damien took off his
shirt and, wearing his oldest pants, torn off at the knees,
went for a swim and had to fight Cat to get back on the
boat, thus nearly capsizing it.

The morning passed quickly and with constant laughter.
But in the early afternoon, Cat's laughter suddenly stopped,
and Damien saw a distant, longing look come into her
green eyes. Following her gaze, he saw that they had arrived at Redbird. Only a few yards away was the landing,
and up the green slope stood the white big house with its
two four-columned piazzas.

He felt his face stiffen with resentment. "Redbird," he
said. "Is this where you meant to go all along?"

She looked at him quickly. "Why, no!"

"Just you and me and the babies, you said—"

"That's right, you silly, and we are *not* stopping at Redbird. Now, you just give me . . ."

Before he realized what she was up to, she snatched his shirt from the bottom of the cockpit and turned away as if to throw it overboard. He yelled "Cat!" and grabbed her from behind.

"Cat, give me my dang shirt!"

"Try and get it!"

"Give it to me, give it . . ."

Still holding her, he struggled to reach the shirt, and she to keep it away from him. Her skirt came up and he hooked one leg between hers. Macy, shrieking with laughter, abandoned the tiller to pound on Damien's shoulders, and the boat swung about and drifted until he took control again. Damien tickled Cat's ribs, while she wiggled softly and warmly against him, whooping with laughter and begging him to stop. He did stop, but only to keep the game going a little longer.

"Give me my shirt, Cat," he said again, when they were well past Redbird and she was still lying in his arms.

"Oh, all right," she said lazily. "But don't put it on yet. I'm too comfortable to move."

"Come to think of it, so am I." His lips brushed her hairline. She was his Cat, and he loved her, and now he knew the meaning of this day she was giving him. They had had many like it in the past. They would never have one like it again. They had grown too old, and their futures were claiming them. This day was a farewell.

And so there was sadness in Cat's eyes when she said, "I suppose we should turn back soon. We can stop and have our lunch on one of the islands."

Reluctantly, Damien told Macy and Sarah to head back downstream.

He was half-asleep, with Cat still lying against him in the curve of his arm, when he heard Duke Avery's voice float out over the water: "Ahoy, there!"

Cat sat up quickly. Damien saw that they were only a hundred feet offshore and approaching the Redbird landing.

"Ahoy," Duke called again. "Come ashore." His voice was friendly, yet it had an undertone of command.

"Do you want to?" Damien asked Cat.

She waved to Duke. "What else can we do? We have to stop for a minute or two, at least. We can't be rude." Her eyes were bright with anticipation, all sadness gone.

Shit, Damien thought, he should have known a day like this one couldn't last. "Put in, Macy."

"Damien," Cat said in a guilty whisper, "put on your shirt."

Damien pulled on his shirt, while Macy and Sarah brought the boat in to the landing as expertly as he had taught them, and Sarah threw Duke the painter.

"Welcome to Redbird," he said. "You're just in time for dinner."

"Well . . ." Cat's eyes begged Damien to forgive her for betraying him. Let her go, something told him, and he sadly nodded his permission.

"But I am such a *mess*!" she said, laying a forearm across her breasts. "My old straw hat and this raggedy old dress—and Momma Lucinda will never forgive us for wasting the lovely picnic lunch she packed for us."

"Let your boy eat the lunch," Duke said, as he finished securing the boat. "You're going to eat with me."

"But the way I look . . ." Cat burst out laughing, as Duke assisted her out of the boat, and Damien wondered if Duke knew it was because she didn't really give a damn how she looked—knew, in fact, that if a man had eyes to see, she would have looked beautiful in sackcloth and ashes.

The children scrambled up onto the landing after her, and Damien slowly followed. Hand in hand, Cat and Duke started up the slope toward the house. Cat paused and looked back.

"Damien, look after Macy and Sarah. See that they get fed. And see that they . . . you know." She made a waving motion that meant she didn't want the children near Duke and her. And that meant she didn't want Damien near either.

"Don't worry, Miss Cat," he said quietly. "We'll stay out of the way."

"That's right, boy," Duke Avery said, "you just stay out of the way."

Damien expected one of Duke's usual superior smiles. Instead, the corners of the man's mouth drew down and his eyes had a cold gleam. Then he followed after Cat.

Quite by chance, he had seen them. He had been upstairs when he had noticed the boat, and he had been certain that the woman was Catherine Anne. He had had a servant fetch his spyglass, and when he had looked out the window again, he had seen the near-naked boy clutching at her, his leg thrust between hers, as they rolled about together in the bottom of the boat. *My God*, he had thought, *what is that nigger doing to her?*

He had stood there paralyzed until the boat was out of sight, and then, in a rage, had hurried down to the river. He had considered following the boat, but had thought better of it. Somehow he had known that Catherine would resent his doing such a thing. But she would almost certainly stop at his landing on her way back—he would see to it that she did.

She was completely innocent, of course. She was still quite young, and being a lady, she had little idea of the feelings her fair skin and casual attire might arouse in a more animal nature. Even a gentleman such as himself might be tempted by such wanton disorder.

He had to admit, in fact, that he was disturbed by the sheer, unlaced physicality of Catherine Anne Sabre. Her movements were graceful but unrestrained, and she had the sure-footed stride of a man, thoroughly at home with her body and the earth she trod on. It was as if she had not yet learned that she was a member of the weaker and more vulnerable sex. But, then, the Sabres were not known for putting a low valuation on themselves—and that was one of the principal reasons he was drawn to her. Whatever her lack of training, she remained in his eyes the fairest prize in all Carolina.

Duke put his anger with the black boy out of mind, and the afternoon turned out to be one of the most pleasant of his life. First, he and Cat enjoyed a long leisurely dinner, then he showed her the house. She and her parents had visited Redbird earlier that spring, but this time he had the pleasure of being alone with Cat while he showed her every room.

Afterward, he showed her all the outbuildings—shops, storehouses, even the slave quarters. There was not a building he couldn't be proud of, except the dark old jail, with its high-standing whipping post.

"I suppose it's good for discipline, even if we don't use it," he said, "but I don't like having it so near the house. I'd tear it down, except that it seems a shame to destroy a perfectly good building."

"Even a coat of whitewash would help," Cat said.

They finished their tour of the plantation in a grove of trees some distance from the house, where Duke was sure they wouldn't be overheard or seen by servants or field hands.

"Well, what do you think of the place?" he asked.

"It's beautiful, Duke."

"I admit it's not quite another Sabrehill."

"It's every bit as beautiful as Sabrehill. And you have every reason to be proud of it."

Once again, the sense of her physical presence struck him. As he looked at her, she leaned back against the slanting trunk of a sycamore tree and took off her straw hat to use as a fan. A faint sheen of sweat covered her forehead, and her feet were apart. Duke had a sudden awareness of rising breasts and spread thighs, and of his own awakening need.

"If your daddy knew we were spending all this time alone together," he said, his voice thick in his throat, "he'd likely shoot me."

"Oh, I don't know. I think he kind of likes you, Duke."

"Even so . . ."

He couldn't help stepping closer to her. He waited for her to lower her eyes demurely and bring her feet together. Instead, she continued to look boldly into his eyes, and it seemed to him that her knees moved even farther apart. Then her tongue appeared at the corner of her mouth and moved slowly over her lip.

God, he thought, *if she was a nigger, I'd fuck her right now!*

He instantly went sick with shame. How could he degrade her, or himself, with such a thought? If she knew, she would despise him.

"What's the matter, Duke?"

He suddenly realized that she was suppressing a smile, a very knowing smile, as if she understood his discomfiture and was amused. But, he told himself, of course she couldn't, not possibly.

"I was just thinking . . . how pretty you are."

"I thought maybe you were thinking of taking advantage of me."

"You know I'd never do a thing like that."

"No, I don't suppose you would." Her voice was lightly mocking, but he'd grown used to that.

"I wouldn't do that to a woman I might one day ask to share Redbird with me."

Cat's smile faded. She looked at him for a moment. Then she straightened up from the tree, rose up on her toes, and leaned toward him. Before he realized what she was going to do, she kissed his cheek.

His eyes blurred. What did a man do, when his every dream was coming true? Duke swore that never again would he have a lustful thought about Catherine Anne Sabre.

She took his arm, and they walked slowly back to the house. "It's getting late," she said, "I think we'd best be getting on home. You'll come to dinner on Sunday, won't you?"

"I'd be mighty pleased to. But I'd like to see you again before then."

She smiled up at him. "You know where I live."

They found Damien and the children still playing on the slope of lawn between the house and the river. Cat called to them that it was time to go home now, time to get back on board the *Celandine*, and walked with them down toward the landing. Damien, standing near the piazza, started to follow. Duke, in a low voice, growled, "Just a minute, boy."

Damien stared at him. Duke could have sworn he saw guilt in that carefully blank face, and all the rage he had felt earlier began to return.

"Come here, boy. Face me."

Damien slowly came to him and faced him, his back to Cat. Duke purposely stroked his rage, thinking of this boy in the boat with Catherine, his hands all over her, his leg thrust between hers. He leaned toward Damien.

"Now, you listen to me, boy," he said in a low voice. "I saw what you were doing to your mistress in that boat. And if I ever see or hear of you so much as touching her or any other white woman again . . ."

He raised his right hand. Before the boy could move away, he brought the back of it down hard against the boy's crotch. Damien uttered one small choked cry of pain and shock and leapt back, covering his genitals with his hands.

Duke stepped toward him, raising his hand again. He gazed into the boy's widened eyes. He put all the venom he possibly could into his voice. "I say that if you ever touch her or any other white woman again, I'll cut off your black nigger dong and make you eat your balls!"

Their locked gaze, his and the boy's, was like an iron chain between them, and for a moment, neither of them moved. Down on the *Celandine,* Cat called, "Damien, come on!"

"All right, go on," Duke said, drawing back. "See to it that your mistress and the children get home safely."

Damien turned and hurried toward the boat, limping and trying not to show his pain. Duke followed more slowly after him. Cat waved as the boat left the landing, and he waved back.

He watched, his anger fading, until the boat was out of sight. Maybe, he thought, he had been unwise, letting his temper slip like that. The boy would probably tell Catherine Anne what had happened, and he now remembered her warning: *"Nobody, Mr. Avery, lays hands on Damien but me."* Still, he tried to believe she would understand. After all, he had only done it for her.

As he walked back up to the house, some of the desire he had felt earlier returned to him, a gently simmering warmth. Well, he knew what to do about that.

He found Leonie in the pantry, dusting. When he tried to put an arm around her, she pulled away, unsmiling.

"Now, what's the matter?" he asked, trying to tease a smile from her. "Have I done something wrong?"

She didn't answer or look at him. She continued dusting the shelves and plates.

"Leonie," he said quietly, "I asked you a question. Have I done something wrong?"

Leonie's hands shook. "You aiming to marry that gal?"

"It's possible."

"You told me you wasn't gonna get married."

"I never said that. I told you that at my age it wasn't likely. Now it does seem that there's a possibility after all."

Leonie's hands very nearly knocked a bowl from a shelf. She gripped her dustcloth with both hands and closed her eyes tightly for a moment.

"Mr. Duke, if you marry that gal, you ain't never gonna touch me again."

"Now, Leonie—"

She whipped away from him, as he again tried to embrace her.

"You ain't gonna touch me long as you even *thinking* of marrying her!"

"Leonie," he said patiently, "you don't understand. A white gentleman in my position is supposed to marry if he can. It's the only way to raise a proper family and have sons and heirs. But that won't change a thing between you and me. What you and I have together, Leonie, that's very special."

"*No!*" Again, she whipped away when he tried to touch her. "I gave myself to you! I gave myself the way I never did before to any man!"

He laughed. "You mean to tell me you never—"

"One boy!" As she faced him and held up a forefinger, he saw that tears were streaming down her face. "Just one!

And hardly ever him! And I coulda took my pick, too! But
I gave myself to Mr. Duke 'cause he need me and my heart
hurt so much for him! And now he—he—"

"Leonie!"

She turned from him and ran out of the pantry.

He felt more shaken than he would have believed. He
looked at his hands and saw that they were trembling as
Leonie's had.

Well, she would get over it, he thought. She was a black
wench, and she needed a man just as much as he needed a
woman. He had to be fair and remember that he understood her feelings and needs a lot better than she understood his. He would be patient. And sooner or later, everything would be the same between them again.

The western sky was streaked with brilliant crimsons
and golds and a soft mauve. The breeze had fallen, but
they had the current to help them, and they traveled homeward more swiftly than they had moved upstream. Cat and
Sarah joked and teased in the middle of the boat, while
Macy handled the jib sheets and Damien sat at the tiller.

His flesh still ached, and he thought he was going to be
sick.

Never before in his life had any man, white or black,
spoken to him in such a manner. Never before had he been
made to feel so inferior, worthless, vile. Never before had
he been made to feel such a nigger.

Never before had *nigger* seemed such a terrible word.

He looked at the back of his hand on the tiller. Nigger.

He thought about telling Cat what had happened. But
how could he ever tell her anything so humiliating? How
could he tell her that Mr. Duke had done such a thing to
him and he had just stood there and taken it? Like a
nigger. It would be like exposing her to something shame-
ful, something obscene.

But if he could bring himself to do it, surely she would
feel differently about Mr. Duke.

But perhaps she would feel differently about him, too.
How could she help but feel differently about someone

who had spoiled her happiness? *"Damien, don't ever do anything to make me love you less than I do."*

No, he couldn't tell her.

Anyway, he thought, she *must* have *some* idea of the kind of man Mr. Duke was.

"Damien," she said, "what's the matter? You haven't said a word."

"Nothing, Cat."

She frowned. "I don't believe it. What did Mr. Duke say to you?"

Tell her!

"He said to see that you and the children got home safely."

"Is that all?"

He had to tell her. He owed it to her, no matter what the consequences to himself. But not now. He couldn't now. His stomach lurched painfully, and he was certain he was going to be sick.

"I said, is that all?"

"That's all, Cat."

He never got a chance to tell her. Or rather, he corrected himself in order to be honest, he put off telling her for too long.

On a May evening, soon after the return to Charleston, Cat took him aside in the garden. "Damien," she said, "I want you to be the very first to know. I've let Duke speak to Papa. He asked for my hand, and Papa gave his permission."

Too late, he thought, as they embraced, too late. He wished her every happiness and held back his tears until he was alone.

The announcement was discrete, of course—no vulgar clamoring about of the news, merely the informing of other Sabres and a few good friends, who then quietly informed others who would be interested to know.

But of course there was a certain amount of celebration. The Sabres gave a party for their older daughter. Her female friends gave her another. Mark and Beau Sabre, home from school, gave a bachelor party for their future brother-in-law. And one evening Mr. Duke Avery gave a very grand dinner party and carpet dance for the Sabre family and all their friends.

As it was a considerable distance from the house on Lynch Street to the house on lower King, Damien drove Cat and her parents down. Mr. Justin said he could leave then if he wished, but Damien decided to stay. From outside the house, he would watch the lights and listen to the music and the laughter and for once be glad he was excluded.

He ate supper in the kitchen house. Mr. Duke had given orders that he was to be fed as well as any guest. Mr. Duke had never failed to be anything but courteous and considerate to Damien since that day at Redbird. No one could possibly have treated him better than Mr. Duke did.

Damien hated his guts.

The night grew darker and the music merrier. In the courtyard, Damien watched while servants hurried back and forth between the kitchen and the main house. Looking back toward the gardens, he saw Leonie also watching the house, and he strolled back to join her.

"Shouldn't you be in there helping?" he asked, merely for something to say.

Leonie didn't look at him. Her gaze, hard and unblinking, remained on the house. "Raphael and Birdie and the others, they doing everything. *He* don't need me. Reckon I'm the last person he wants to see tonight."

Then, slowly, she turned her eyes to his. She looked into them for a long moment, and he held his breath.

She lowered her head against his chest and swayed against him. He felt her thigh move up between his and press against him, beckoning desire. He slipped an arm around her waist.

After a moment, they walked slowly away from the house, into the darkness, toward the little room at the end of the lane.

-—(FOUR)—-

CAT

DEAR LORD, JEBEDIAH THOUGHT, was it possible? In a few more months it would be nine years since he had left Sabrehill and become a free man: nine years that had gone by so quickly that he wanted to protest that some mistake had been made—he *couldn't* have been traveling, lecturing, and writing his books and articles for nine years now! Why, it seemed like only four or five years since he had first arrived at Sabrehill!

And yet it had indeed been nine years, he thought, as he hurried through the streets of downtown Boston on that May evening. Nine of the best years of his life. Oh, there had been plenty of difficulties. The depression that had followed the panic of 'thirty-seven had made it hard for the movement to raise funds. Membership in the various anti-slavery societies had fallen off. Garrison had become more rigid and fanatically moralistic in his outlook with every passing year, while other leaders looked increasingly to realistic political solutions. But Adaba had been right: Despite all internecine rivalries and quarrels and differences of view, there was still no merrier band than the abolition-ists and the Underground Railroaders. Whatever their problems, their spirits rarely flagged.

He found himself outside the law offices of William I. Bowditch, and despite the hour, there was a light in the window. When he thumped with the heavy knocker, the door was opened at once.

"Good evening, Jemmy," Jebediah said, stepping inside. "I was hoping to find someone in."

"Good evening, Mr. Jeb," the young law clerk said, "and welcome back. How was the trip?"

"I'd call it a success in every way." Jebediah had just returned from a lecture tour with William Welles Brown for the Massachusetts Anti-Slavery Society. Brown, like

231

Jebediah, was an ex-slave who had worked for the Underground Railroad before turning to lecturing and writing. Increasingly, Jebediah was pleased to note, the blacks were asserting their own leadership.

"But Mr. Jeb," Jemmy said, looking out the door before closing it, "you're not alone, are you? You know you shouldn't go out alone after dark. You've been told time and again!"

"I appreciate your concern, Jemmy, but I haven't been bothered much lately. I seem to have gained a certain reputation for cracking skulls."

Jemmy smiled. "Yes, we heard about what happened the night before you and Mr. Brown left on your tour."

On that particular evening, Jebediah had been reliably informed that a young black couple had been forced to board a ship in Boston Harbor. He and Brown and a couple of friends had simply marched aboard and taken them off again—laying flat the dozen or so men who had tried to stop them. It had been merely the latest in a long series of incidents that had taught a lot of people an important lesson: If you didn't wish to get hurt, you didn't "mess" with Mr. Jeb.

"But even so," Jemmy continued, "they're still kidnapping Negroes—more all the time, with slave prices so high. And you know there are several rewards offered for you."

"Ah, yes, a few piddling thousand," Jebediah said with bleak humor. "Not nearly as much as they've offered for Arthur Tappan. Why, I understand that one state has offered three thousand dollars for his ears alone." Jebediah shook his head ruefully. "Really, much as I love Arthur, I cannot for the life of me understand what makes him so much more valuable than William Garrison or Frederick Douglass or *me*!"

"Mr. Jeb, it's not a laughing matter! If anything were to happen to you—"

"Well, I'll try to be more careful. Meanwhile, is Mr. Bowditch here?"

"No, but we do have some mail for you."

Jemmy brought him a handful of envelopes, which he quickly thumbed through. There seemed to be nothing terribly important or urgent among them—until he came to an envelope addressed to Mr. Bowditch in Damien's handwriting.

His correspondence with Damien was necessarily infrequent and discrete. The Charleston post office was not to be trusted. Mail was frequently searched for "inflammatory materials," antislavery pamphlets and the like, and if it were ever discovered that Damien was actually exchanging letters with the infamous Mr. Jeb, he would almost certainly be confiscated from the Sabres and sold out of state to a new owner. Hence his messages to Jebediah had to be sent through Mr. Bowditch, just as Jebediah's to Damien, or to Leila or any other at Sabrehill, had to be sent through Justin Sabre.

It had been almost a year since Jebediah had last heard from Damien, and he couldn't wait to reach his rooming house before at least glancing at the new letter. He sat down at one of the several desks in the front office and took the letter from its envelope.

Miss Lucy and Mr. Justin were well, as was Cat . . . Momma Lucinda and Irish were well . . . Zagreus and Binnie and Leila . . .

Oh, Leila, he thought, smiling to himself and remembering her fine-boned, delicate features. There had been other women in his life, both before and since, and in the heat of youth he had sometimes thought he could not live without one or another of them. But somehow it was Leila's memory that most often returned to haunt him.

He read on. Mr. Leduc Avery, it seemed, had bought Redbird. Yes, Damien had mentioned that in his last letter.

Perhaps, Damien wrote, Jebediah had already heard how Mr. Avery had shot Mr. Caley Carstairs. . . .

Jebediah froze as he read Damien's spare account of how he had nearly been hanged on that January night. For a moment he could read no further. He remembered the eleven-year-old boy who had said, "I want to help. . . . I'm gonna do whatever you do, Jebediah." His brave boy, the closest thing to a son he would ever have. Now more than ever he would be in Justin Sabre's debt. And in Cat's.

He read on: "After that, the chivalry began to accept

Mr. Avery as they never had before, and it seemed as if Cat couldn't see enough of him. They were together all through the season in Charleston last winter, and even after we returned to Sabrehill, Mr. Avery came calling several times a week.

"Well, I suppose you can guess the rest, Jebediah. I have a feeling that Miss Lucy has certain reservations about Mr. Avery, but Mr. Justin seems to like him well enough. So Mr. Justin has given his consent. . . ."

Oh, no! Jebediah thought. *Oh, Cat, no!*

"They plan to be married in June and leave for a long tour of Europe in July. . . ."

Jebediah read no further. *How could you, Cat?* he thought, sickened. *How could you? How could you be such a fool? Don't you know who he is, what he is? How could you throw yourself away on such a man?*

He clasped his hands and rested his forehead on them. No, he thought, be fair. You hate Duke Avery, and you always will. Because of Jessie. But the truth of the matter is that he is *not* the worst man in the world. You know in your heart that the poor bastard always wanted to be a *good* man. And whatever he did to Jessie or to you, he may still be able to make Cat happy.

Jebediah had to believe that.

Dear Lord, let me be a good wife to Duke. Let me be the best wife he could possibly have. I know I have so many faults—I'm often willful, and sometimes I talk like a common doxy, and too often I just plain don't have sense enough to keep my mouth shut—but please, Lord, help me learn to do better and to deserve his love as much as he deserves mine.

She repeated the prayer often in the weeks before the wedding, and on the evening that they left the rice-throwing guests behind and Duke drove her to her new home on King Street, she silently said it again.

He was her husband now, and most likely the only one she would ever have. She was acutely conscious that church and state gave her only this one chance at the most important kind of happiness she could imagine, the happiness of having a well-beloved and loving husband and the family that would one day spring from their union. *Please, Lord, bless us. . . .*

She already knew most of the servants who greeted them at Duke's house—first, Ebba the cook, in the courtyard, looking happy for her master; then Raphael and Birdie in the house, smiling and laughing softly, and saying that they had a nice supper all ready for Mr. Duke and Miss Catherine. Cat wasn't in the slightest hungry, but she wouldn't have dreamed of disappointing the old butler and the retired housekeeper by saying so. She and Duke spent a pleasant half hour at the table.

He showed her the house then, that part of it she had not seen before, and they ended their tour in the bedroom they would share. "If you want to, sweetheart," he said, "why don't you get ready for bed now? I'll be back in a little while."

She was grateful for his tact. She knew that some people regarded her as much too bold a young woman, but she didn't feel at all bold now. She had had no idea of how she would face this moment, and now she found that she was trembling with apprehension.

Her clothes had already been put away for her. As soon as Duke had left, she searched out her prettiest gown, the one she had bought for this night. She took off her dress, washed, finished getting ready for bed. For the first time in her life, except for cold winter nights, she pulled on her nightgown before taking off the last of her clothes. The big, canopied four-poster bed had already been turned down, and she slipped between the sheets.

When Duke returned some minutes later, he was in a nightshirt and robe. He smiled at her. "Shall I put out the lamp?"

"Not yet." She thought of a poem she had read:

> *Love's mysteries in souls do grow,*
> *But yet the body is his book.*

Soon, as passion grew and timidity fled, she would, by lamplight, read the book.

Duke sat down on the edge of the bed, letting his slippers fall softly to the floor. He slid a forearm under her head and leaned over her. "Catherine," he said, "I love you very much."

"And I love you, darling."

"Do you want me to explain . . . ?"

She smiled. "You don't have to. I think I know . . . not everything, maybe . . . but enough."

"Your mother . . . ?"

"And Momma Lucinda. And Leila."

He laughed, a little ironically. "So many teachers! It sounds as if you've been well instructed."

"I don't know. I hope so. My mother says it's criminal to leave a girl so ignorant that she's shocked and frightened on her wedding night. I suppose that growing up on a plantation helped some to learn, once I knew what to watch for. And Leila says—"

"Sh." He put a finger on her lips. "Never mind what they say. Listen to what *I* say. Darling, I just want you to know that, even though a man has certain needs that a woman may find difficult to understand, and even though he has certain marital rights, I'll never force myself on you. I'll make everything as easy for you as I can, and I'll try to understand your feelings too."

"I know you will, dearest."

He leaned down and pressed his mouth to hers. Warmth flowed through her, and her trembling stopped. She tried to put an arm around him, but he raised up from her again.

"Sweetheart," he said. "I know it's been a long, hard day for you. If you'd rather wait . . ."

Fear was ebbing now. "Oh, no," she said, with a happy laugh. "It's our wedding night. Come back to me, darling!"

Before she could stop him, he blew out the lamp.

Afterward, she thought it was probably just as well that the room had been dark.

Certainly the experience was not what she had expected. She remembered having seen him in warm sunlight, his thick brown hair tousled and his Byronic collar lifted by the gentle breeze. And there was the time she had been with him in a sycamore grove on a spring afternoon and had felt the force of his desire as she leaned back against a tree and he loomed over her. And once, when they were alone, he had seized her under the arms and lifted her over his head and whirled her around, and she had felt as if she were flying.

She supposed she had expected something like that. Not sunlight, of course, but moonlight or perhaps soft lamplight—lamplight on the strong deep chest she had sensed beneath the shirt with the Byronic collar, lamplight on his long, powerful arms and thighs, lamplight on his hard, demanding flesh.

And lamplight on herself, when she grew bold enough. Lamplight on breasts and belly and mound and thighs, making her perhaps a little more beautiful than she really was—for him.

She had thought there would be plenty of time for caresses that gradually grew bolder, plenty of time for kisses that grew ever more ardent, time even for a little laughter. And then a moment of sharp, terrible pain, her willing blood-sacrifice to him, making her his forever.

And, finally, a hint, at least, of ecstacy, of even happier nights yet to come.

But it wasn't that way at all.

He kissed her again, of course, and quite tenderly, and her warmth mounted. She tried to embrace and caress him in that absolute darkness, but that interfered with what he was trying to do. She felt him pulling her gown up and she helped him, but when she tried to pull it up off her breasts, thinking to discard it altogether, he whispered "No, no" and stopped her reply with a kiss.

He stroked her breasts for a moment, then suddenly touched her where she had been touched by no one but herself since childhood. She had expected to feel a lovely, shrinking fear, a modest embarrassment at this moment, before giving herself up to blissful intimacy. Instead, the moment had come so quickly that she merely felt shock.

It was all happening too fast, too fast!

She felt him rising up beside her in the bed and pulling his nightshirt up. More out of a sense of obligation, now, than out of desire, she reached for him, but he brushed her hand away. He moved over her spread thighs, lowered himself, and fumbled with her labia. She felt the tip of his penis between them, and pulled back in fear and revulsion.

But he thrust at her insistently and found the way again. Fortunately, she had previously been aroused enough— barely enough—to ease his entry. She felt a slight, sharp, lingering pain and had a sense that he was within her. He thrust no more than half-a-dozen times before she felt his body stiffen above her and heard the sharp intake of his breath. He remained perfectly still for a moment or so, then sighed and relaxed, withdrawing from her, and rolled off her and onto the bed.

Was that all there was to it, then?

Was that *all*?

Surely there should be something more.

And yet, she realized, at that moment she wanted nothing more. She wanted only to be left alone with her small aching wound. She felt as if she had been cheated, cheated even out of the physical pain of sacrifice. She would willingly have forgone the pain, but if she couldn't have *more* than that, she should have had that at the very least.

Perhaps he heard her muted sob. He gathered her into his arms, and she felt his lips brush a tear from her cheek.

"I'm sorry," he whispered.

"It's all right."

"Did I hurt you badly?"

"No. Hardly at all."

"It won't be so bad after this."

"I know."

He was soon asleep. She hadn't expected that, either, not on their wedding night. But, she thought, perhaps it was just as well. Rolling away from him, she let her hand wander down over her belly toward her womanhood, then stopped. No, not that. There was no real satisfaction in that, at least not the kind she wanted, the kind she was surely entitled to. She was married now, and she wanted the real sunlight, the real lamplight, the real moonlight, and not her girlish dreams of them.

And surely she would have the real thing yet. She remembered something Momma Lucinda had told her not long ago. *"Now, chile, you got to remember ain't everything gonna be perfect right from the start. Everybody thinks it's gonna be, but it ain't. That's 'cause they think they know each other's ways and needs, but they don't. You both got to take time to learn each other's ways and needs. And if you do that, if only you be patient, you find that everything gets better and better and better. That's the truth in the kitchen in the daytime, and that's the truth in the bed at nighttime too."*

Better and better and better. Yes. Momma Lucinda knew. That's the way it would be.

She awakened to find her cheek on a strange pillow, and she remembered: She was married now. She was Mrs. Duke Avery. And last night . . .

She smiled ruefully. No, last night had not been quite what she had dreamed of. But how naive she had been to think it would be. Momma Lucinda had tried to warn her, and she should have paid closer attention.

She rolled over toward Duke and sat up. He was handsome even in sleep. No awkwardly canted head, no mouth ajar, no silly snores. Just sweet repose, his dark brown hair over his forehead, his lips barely open. She bent down and lightly kissed those lips.

She slipped out of bed, stretched herself more fully awake, and washed. When she had finished, she looked at Duke again and felt her heart swell. In sleep he looked so much younger than he was, and why had she thought that he would be so much more knowledgeable than she? *You both got to take time to learn each other's ways and needs,"* Momma Lucinda had said.

Well, she thought, smiling to herself as she got back into bed, it was the first day of their marriage. What better time to start learning them than now?

She would be a little devil, she decided, slipping her hand under the sheet and feeling for the hem of his nightshirt. She would be a little dickens.

When she touched him, he awakened almost at once. His eyes rolled wildly, his head jerked from side to side, and he shoved her hand away and sat up, sliding his legs over the side of the bed. He mumbled something incomprehensible.

"Good morning, darling!"

He looked at her as if he didn't know her.

Lying back in bed, she watched in silence while he washed and dried himself. He looked out the window.

"My God, it's late!"

"Not so awfully late. Are you awake now?"

He shook himself and smiled. "Yes. All awake."

"Good." She held out her arms to him. "Come back to bed."

"What for?"

"To make love to me!"

He laughed self-consciously and returned to the bed, leaned down and gave her a quick kiss, and drew back again before she could embrace him. "Darling, thank you very much, but morning's no time for that. It debilitates a man. And we should be up and doing."

"But it's our honeymoon!"

"That's no excuse for cultivating bad habits."

She tried not to show her disappointment. "But can't we at least have breakfast in bed on our very first day together?"

He began pulling on clothes under his nightshirt, carefully keeping himself hidden. "Well . . . I'll tell you what. You're absolutely right. You've been through a lot lately, darling, and after—after last night, I'm sure you need more rest. I'll tell Raphael and Birdie to send up your breakfast and see to it that you're not disturbed."

"No," she said, getting out of bed, "that won't be necessary. It wouldn't be fun without you. We'll have breakfast together."

She would be patient and learn, she vowed. Just as Momma Lucinda had taught her.

Patient and cheerful and loving, that's what she would be. She was hanging onto his arm as they entered the dining room. Birdie gave them a smile and left. Duke carefully detached Cat's fingers from his arm.

"Not in front of the servants," he said.

"Oh." Well, he always had been a little stuffy, she thought, but she supposed he was right. Anyway, if she expected him to learn her ways and needs, it was only fair that she try to learn his.

"What are we going to do today?" she asked over breakfast.

"You rest. Do anything you please that isn't strenuous. I'm going up to Vendue Range."

"Today?" It hadn't occurred to her that he might leave her alone so soon.

"I haven't been there for several days. Since we'll soon be leaving, I want to be sure everything's going well."

"I thought you were going to give up the slave trade."

"I was. But now I wonder if that's really such a good idea. I know what people say about most traders, but they don't seem to think the worse of me for being in the trade. In fact, some say I'm the one man in Charleston who runs it in a decent manner, and if I quit, who can they turn to? And since we'll be dividing our time between Charleston and Redbird, there's really no reason why I shouldn't divide mine between the slave trade and cotton."

He was right, of course—she could see that. She had heard her own father say that Duke helped keep Sam Avery in line. And if some people would never quite accept Duke as long as he was in the trade, well, wasn't that one of the things that had attracted her to him? The fact that, like herself, he didn't quite fit in?

"I know what we can do," she said, suddenly inspired, "you take me with you!"

"Take you with me where?"

"To Vendue Range! To the slave pens!"

"Catherine, that's no place for you!"

"Oh, nonsense. Duke, I know all about cotton, and a lot about rice, and something about most crops. But I hardly know a thing about the slave trade. And I'd like to learn. I'd like to know what you do, to be able to help you."

"Catherine, that . . . that is *insane*! A woman on Vendue Range?"

"Women often go up there to buy and sell slaves."

"I know they do, but a *lady*? *My wife*? I don't know how you can suggest such a thing!"

"But I only want to understand what you do. What if something happened to you, what if you got sick? Then I could help you."

"Catherine, there is absolutely no question—"

"And I'll bet I'd be good at it, too, and do you know why? Because I *like* black people." She laughed. "Why, my goodness, sometimes I'd much rather be with the black people at Sabrehill than with the white people in Charleston. And I think they'd know that I meant them no harm and that I was only trying to help them get through a terrible time as easily as possible. Please, Duke—"

"That's enough! It's unheard of!" Duke threw down his napkin and nearly knocked over his chair as he stood up. "Catherine, I'm sure you mean well, but you haven't the slightest idea of what you're talking about. I try to treat our merchandise decently, yes, but a slave trading firm is no place for a white angel of mercy. It's a place for stripping down blacks, male and female, separating plains from fancies, field hands from house servants, and grading them for strength, flaws, and breeding equipment. Do you really think you could do that? Do you think that in a thousand years I'd let you?"

Cat tried to keep the disappointment out of her voice. "There must be something I can do."

"There is. Stay home and be the lady you were brought up to be, the lady I married."

"But I only want—"

"Catherine, I forbid this subject!"

Her eyes widened. "You *forbid* it?" Except when making a nuisance of herself, she hadn't been forbidden any subject since she was twelve years old.

"I forbid it! I don't want to hear another word about it, ever again!"

She was silent. *Be patient*, she told herself. *Be patient.*

"Catherine, I'm sorry. I didn't mean to be harsh. It's just that . . . darling, you're my *wife* now. And you've got to learn . . ."

"Your ways and needs."

"Exactly. And believe me, I know best in these matters. Just as you know best in others."

"What others, Duke?"

He leaned down from behind her chair and kissed her cheek. "How to be a lady. How to bring out the best in both of us. How to be a wife a man can be proud of. You do want to do that, don't you?"

"Of course."

"And believe me, you have already made me proud. There is no prouder man in all Carolina than Duke Avery."

He kissed her cheek again and straightened up. "Well, I'd better be on my way now."

"When will you be back?"

"I don't know. By suppertime at the latest. If you need anything, Birdie will see to it."

When he had reached the door, she turned and called to him. "Duke. Where's Leonie? I just realized, I don't think I've seen her in days."

Duke hesitated. His eyes drifted from hers. "Ah . . . Leonie. Leonie hasn't been feeling very well lately. About a week ago, I sent her back to Redbird. She'll be happier there."

"Oh."

It was just as well, Cat thought. She knew Birdie liked her. Somehow she had the feeling Leonie did not.

All day she had been waiting for this moment. She had tried to avoid thinking about it, tried to avoid anticipating what it might be like, tried to avoid expecting too much, but always it had been in the back of her mind.

Somehow she had wiled away the day wandering about the house, talking to the servants, reading a George Sand novel she had brought with her from Lynch Street. When Duke had returned at suppertime, he had refused to discuss his day or his work, but she hardly cared. The hour had arrived at last.

"Wait," she said. "Don't put out the lamp."

"Oh? What is it?" He came back to her in the bed, gave her another little kiss and a smile, and asked again, "What is it, dear?"

"I just want to see you."

She had told him he needn't leave the bedroom while she undressed, but he had done so anyway.

"*See* me, Catherine Anne?"

She returned his smile. "Yes, darling. See you."

"But—"

"While you make love to me."

For a long moment, he merely looked at her, as if trying to fathom the meaning of her words.

"Don't you want to see me?" she asked.

He stirred uneasily. "Catherine, you mustn't feel you have to . . . sacrifice yourself every time we go to bed."

"I don't." She reached up to run her fingers through his thick hair and draw her palm down over his cheek. "But this is our honeymoon, Duke."

"I know, but even so—"

"And I want to make love." She lifted her head from the pillow to kiss his lips. "Don't you want to make love to me, darling?"

His smile was uncertain. "Of course I do. More than I can say. But that doesn't mean that I'm constantly going to subject you to—"

She laughed and combed his hair with her fingers some more. "That's all right. Subject me, darling."

"You . . . really want to?"

"Yes!"

"Well . . . all right." He sat up and turned toward the lamp.

"No, don't! I want light!"

"Really, Catherine!"

She wanted to say, *"Yes, with the lamp on! Take off your nightshirt first and come here to me and hold me and kiss me and stroke me. And then in a little while take my gown off and kiss me and caress me some more. And then at last, at last join with me. . . ."*

But he had sounded genuinely aggrieved, perhaps even a little frightened, so she said nothing. *You both got to take time*, Momma Lucinda had said.

"Really, Catherine," Duke said again, as he returned to her in the darkness, "I'm sorry, but—"

"It's all right, darling. I love you. I love you so much. Just make love to me."

He did. But was this making love? It was little different from the first time: A few kisses and some groping in the dark. Her gown raised and a hand on her thigh while she begged, "Not so fast, not so fast!" He did take a little more time, but he ignored her moaned protest when he shoved her thighs apart. He thrust into her, spilled his seed, and departed.

Afterward, she lay awake in the dark for hours, feeling not loved but soiled, and filled with a vague but violent aching that was as much of the soul as of the body. For all the instruction she had been given, she still did not really know what to expect of the marriage bed, but surely it wasn't this, not this!

He'll learn, she told herself repeatedly, as she sought sleep. *We've only been married a day, after all, and he'll learn, we'll both learn.*

But for the first time an enormous doubt began to loom in her mind.

WHEN, DUKE WONDERED, HAD he first begun to suspect that he had made a terrible mistake? There were a number of incidents, each comparatively unimportant in itself, so that it was difficult to say.

There was, for example, the matter of the book. It occurred less than two weeks after the wedding and not long before they departed on their bridal trip. He came home one afternoon to find Catherine in the parlor, so immersed in a book that she hardly noticed his arrival. When he asked her what she was reading, she seemed a little reluctant to tell him. Finally, hesitantly, she handed the book to him.

"Where in hell," he asked, "did you ever get this!" The book was *La Physiologie du Mariage* by Balzac.

"From home," his bride said. "From our library there."

"But why should you want to read such a book?"

"Papa has always insisted that I keep up my French."

"But to read such trash!"

Though he had never read the notorious book, he had some idea of its contents and was aware that it expressed sympathy for unfaithful wives. But surely nothing in the world could justify or excuse a wife's infidelity, and the thought that his own Catherine Anne would sully her mind with such filth was enough to give Duke a feeling of panic.

"I think it's rather good," Cat said, as if to confirm the justice of his reaction.

"Catherine, I forbid you to read this garbage."

She stared at him, her mouth open, and he felt an instant of guilt.

"Well, do you mean to tell me your parents actually allowed you to read books like this?"

"My parents never stopped me from reading anything in my life."

246

"Good God!"

Such a small thing, and yet . . .

And then there were her feelings toward those two niggers, her Aunt Dulcy and that damned Jebediah.

Certainly Duke wanted few things more than to make his bride a happy woman. To that end, he booked them into the Irving House, on their arrival in New York City, simply because it had a bridal suite, the first in an American hotel. He did his best to keep her entertained during their short stay in the city, taking her to see Christy's Virginia Minstrels at Palmo's Opera House, a burletta at the Bowery Theater, a popular comedy at the Olympic. But nothing seemed to reconcile her to the fact that she had missed seeing Jebediah and her Aunt Dulcy.

"But, Catherine, you knew it was unlikely that either of them would be in the city when we got here."

"Oh, of course, but even so . . ."

In spite of his own undying hatred for Jebediah, he could quite understand Cat's attachment to the black man. He felt much the same way about Raphael and Birdie. But her Aunt Dulcy was a different matter. The two were not even close blood relatives, and had met only two or three times, when Catherine's family had taken her north on vacations. And yet apparently there had been an immediate sympathy and affection between them. Why? Duke wondered. Did his wife have some kind of special affinity to black blood? Or was it simply Dulcy Sabre's fame as an actress that drew Catherine to her? An *actress*, Duke thought with distaste. He felt a certain guilt in thinking badly of Dulcy when he remembered how kindly she had treated him all those years back, but he had felt betrayed on learning that her blood was tainted. And now she was an actress. Everybody knew that actresses had the morals of the poorer sort of nigger, so it was hardly surprising that the beautiful Dulcy had ended up on the stage. He was just as happy that Catherine had missed seeing the woman.

Nevertheless, to soothe her, he said, "Maybe we'll see them both on our way back home."

Incident after incident, culminating in their first real quarrel, less than two months after their arrival in England.

Cat wanted to travel to England on the steam packet, the *Great Western*, a two-week trip; but there Duke drew the line at pleasing his bride. Like most travelers, he was apprehensive at the thought of great fires burning under boilers that might explode at any moment, and tall stacks belching smoke and sparks. But in the end he had to admit that she had been right. They crossed in five weeks, not bad time for a sailing packet, but when they arrived at Liverpool, Duke felt that he couldn't have stood even one more day at sea. For some time after that, he attributed Cat's pallor to the crossing.

They were soon taken in hand by Justin Sabre's friends, Sir James and Lady Amelia Wallopp, who were intent on making their visit a success in every way. Under the Wallopp's auspices, they attended plays at the Covent Garden and the Drury Lane theaters and the opera and ballet at the Haymarket. They took a boat trip up the Thames to see the still-new Houses of Parliament from the river, and they cruised back down to enjoy a delicious seafood dinner in Greenwich. Duke explored the gaming houses of Jermyn Street and Leicester Square with Sir James, and Cat learned to play cricket—hardly a proper sport for women, Duke privately observed—from Lady Amelia. And in October, just before their departure for Hamstead, they were honored by a dinner party at the Wallopps' house in Belgravia—the dinner party that precipitated their quarrel.

There were more than a dozen guests at table that evening, and after dinner the house was crowded, as dozens more came calling, mingled for a time, and departed. It was one of those parties where one meets so many people so quickly that one has little hope of remembering more than a few names, and Duke soon gave up trying. It seemed to him that his bride's comportment under his tutelage had improved considerably during the four months of their marriage, but that evening, perhaps due to the influence of wine, she seemed to forget herself. Her pale cheeks bloomed, her green eyes sparkled, and her laughter was less than restrained. Reluctantly, Duke was forced to admit that there was something just a trifle vulgar about his young wife, and he decided to speak to her strongly, later, when they were alone.

His determination was reinforced when, toward the end of the evening, her behavior got quite out of hand. At the time, they were seated in a drawing room, chatting with three other guests. One was a lady-novelist in her fifties, a woman of lingering beauty, called Marguerite by the others. Another was a tall, slim, auburn-haired Frenchman, immaculately groomed, called Dorsey or Dorsay or something of the sort. Catherine had whispered to Duke that the Frenchman was known as one of the handsomest men and wildest gamblers in all Europe. The third was a rather ugly man of forty-odd, said to be a novelist-turned-politician. He had a high, pale forehead, flowing black locks, a long aquiline nose. He looked Jewish to Duke, who winced at the man's canary waistcoat and green velvet trousers. All in all, the three struck Duke as a rather raffish lot.

Wearied by the evening, he paid little attention to the conversation until he heard Cat mentioning some of the places on their itinerary: Paris, Munich, Zurich, Venice, and Florence, and then Rome for a rest. "And then perhaps Naples, and we'll go on to Athens before turning back."

"A marvelous trip," said the woman called Marguerite. "And you say your father has friends in all those places? How does that happen?"

"Oh, some years ago, when the Holy Alliance was causing problems for Switzerland, our secretary of state asked Papa to investigate the situation. That led to his traveling all over Europe for the president and meeting a great many people."

"I'm sure we have mutual friends—or perhaps I can recommend someone to you. Do you know anyone in Athens?"

"We hope to stay with the Theotokys. My father knows the countess—"

Marguerite threw back her head. "Oh, that woman! I wish I hadn't asked."

"Now, Marguerite," the Frenchman said gently.

"I don't care, I never could abide her. Countess indeed —she may be on her third husband and God only knows which lover, but she'll always be plain little Jane Digby to me."

"Marguerite caricatured the erstwhile Lady Ellenborough as Lady Walmer in her novel *The Two Friends*," the Jew-novelist-politician told Cat.

"It was not a caricature," Marguerite said, "anymore than your portrait of Dorsey in your *Henrietta Temple* was a caricature. It was our Jane, right down to her little round heels."

"But I do think Balzac was rather fairer to her, when he did her as Lady Arabella Dudley in his *Le Lis dans la Vallée*. Don't you agree, Dorsey?"

Marguerite shook her head. "Oh, you men! By the way, Dizzy, did I ever tell you the story of what *really* happened after Lord Ellenborough divorced Jane and she went off to join her lover?"

There followed, with much hilarity, an exchange of stories about the notorious Jane Digby, each, it seemed to Duke, more tasteless than the last. And that was the woman Justin Sabre wished him to expose Catherine Anne to? The one-time lover of Balzac, if these people were to be believed, and mistress of the king of Bavaria? Not if Duke could help it. He would have to find a way of avoiding the woman, even if it meant not going to Athens.

"Oh, the delightful gossip we would have missed," the Frenchman said, "if only Lord Ellenborough had had more youthful vigor on the honeymoon or if Lady Jane had been less than insatiable. That, of course, is what set the marriage on the road to ruin."

"Oh, but that's not true at all!" Cat said, and Duke saw an odd glitter in her eyes that should have warned him. "At least it's not true according to what my father told my mother. Do you mean to tell me you don't know what *really* happened on the honeymoon?"

"Oh, do tell us!" Marguerite said, with an eager smile, leaning forward in her chair. "Tell us what *really* happened!"

"What *really* happened was that while they were at Brighton she caught him with the daughter of the hotel's pastry cook."

"Oh, my dear! You don't mean . . . ?"

Yes, she did. Jane's parents had been doubtful about the match because Lord Ellenborough was some eighteen years older than the seventeen-year-old bride-to-be. But he was very handsome and very wealthy and swore repeatedly that he would do his utmost to give Jane a life without pain or discomfort, so they had soon given in. Imagine, then, the poor girl's dismay, after they reached the bridal suite of the Norfolk Hotel in Brighton, when he did his duty by her just once and thereafter treated her as a charming but bothersome child and never so much as touched her again.

"Do you mean to say, he never—"

"Never! Furthermore, he was constantly disappearing for hours at a time, day and night, without explanation. Finally, one evening she determined to find him if she had to search the hotel from top to bottom."

Find him she did—standing in a storeroom in the back of the hotel, with the pastry cook's daughter in his arms and his trousers at his ankles. " 'You see, my dear,' he said, tossing an embarrassed smile over his shoulder but never for an instant ceasing his endeavors, just as I promised! No pain or discomfort! No pain or discomfort!' "

The other four burst into laughter, and Duke forced a smile, but his face felt stiff. Was this *his wife* telling such a story? And really, no matter how well she had told it, what was so damned funny about it?

He was still perturbed when the last guests had left the house and he and Cat had ascended the stairs to their room.

"Really, Catherine," he said as he closed their door, "was it necessary to tell that story about Lord Ellenborough and his bride? I know you had drunk quite a lot, but that's hardly an excuse."

"The others were telling stories against Jane Digby. It wasn't fair. I wanted to tell one on her side."

Her back was to him, and as she spoke, he saw her shoulders square and her head come up, and he knew that when he next looked into her eyes they would have a glassy brightness. They had had minor quarrels before, and he recognized that she was primed for one now. Well, he thought, so be it. Although she had improved, she still had a lot to learn, and he was in no mood to be soft with her.

"I don't give a damn what you wanted, that was still about as tasteless an exhibition as I've seen you give."

When Cat turned to him, he saw that he was right: Her pallor had returned and her eyes glittered.

"I'm sorry you feel that way. The others seemed to be quite amused."

"To hell with the others. I'd say they're not much better than your Jane Digby, and after some of the things that that Marguerite woman told about her—"

"Lady Blessington, you mean. And Papa told me that most of the stories they tell about Jane Digby are simply not true."

"Even so," Duke said, taking off his coat, "the woman has certainly made a career of having husbands and lovers. And I'll tell you this: If we go to Athens, we won't be calling on the Theotokys."

Cat's eyes widened. "But I *want* to call on them. The countess was my father's friend. I want to know her."

"Catherine, I'm sorry, but I think not. Considering what we now know about the countess and what people say—"

Cat's hands clenched before her. "I don't care what people say! My sympathies are entirely with *her!*"

Duke, pulling off his cravat, paused and stared at her. He thought he at last had a glimmering of why she had told that vulgar story.

"My dear Catherine Anne," he said slowly. "You surely aren't accusing me of having a pastry cook's daughter in my life, are you?"

"Oh, Duke, of course not!"

"Then, if you will pardon my language, just what the hell is bothering you?"

Cat sank down onto the side of the bed. When she raised her head, there were tears in her eyes.

"Duke, why did you marry me?"

"You know why. Because I love you."

She looked aside, wiped her eyes. " 'But yet the body is his book.' "

"What? What are you talking about?"

" 'To our bodies turn we then,' " Cat quoted softly, " 'that so / Weak men on love revealed may look; / Love's mysteries in souls do grow, / But yet the body is his book.' "

Duke felt a trace of fear. In his heart, he knew what she was talking about; perhaps in some ways he knew better than she. But he didn't want to admit it.

"Now, what the hell is that supposed to mean?"

"It's a poem about making love. 'The Ecstacy,' by John Donne."

"I know what it is, I understand English!"

She raised her eyes to him again. "Do you understand love?"

"I told you, I love you. Catherine, what more do you want from me?"

"I don't know, I truly don't know! I thought I knew what to expect, but I didn't!"

"Well, if you can't tell me—"

"More tenderness? More time in your arms?" Her voice rose, both accusing and imploring. "Perhaps something more than your intermittant and—and *perfunctory* interest in my pudendum?' "

"Oh, Christ," he groaned, "can't you learn to talk a little less like a dictionary and more like a lady?"

"I guess what I'm trying to ask you, my love, is why you don't really like me."

"Don't like you—Catherine, I love you!"

She was already shaking her head. "You don't. You don't like the way I talk. Or the way I laugh. Or the way I behave in company. Or any number of other things. You hid it pretty well until we were married, but from the moment I said, 'I will,' it was 'Catherine, I forbid you!' Every day, something more about me you didn't like, something I had to change. And I have tried, Duke, I have tried! I have tried to change for you as I have never before tried to change in my life. But somehow, I just can't satisfy you." She laughed miserably and shook her head again. "Jesus, Duke, I used to think you wanted me. But, my God, you don't even seem to like getting into my drawers!"

The crude words brought warmth to his face. "Catherine, I have always tried to spare you——"

"Oh, haven't you, though! 'No pain or discomfort, no pain or discomfort!' Well, thank you very much, my dear, but all I know is that somehow you don't make me feel loved at all. Not out of bed, and certainly not in it. And it's driving me out of my mind."

Cat rolled over on the bed and sobbed quietly. Duke sank into a chair.

He felt sick. What had happened to his dream of marrying a lady, a *real* lady, a lady worthy of his ambitions? How had he ever been deceived into thinking that Catherine Anne Sabre was anything other than the common wench she had so often shown herself to be?

And now she seemed to be telling him that, white though she was, her animal nature was a lot more like Leonie's and Jessie's——and his own——then he would have expected or cared to believe.

But, whether he had wanted to admit it or not, hadn't he already realized that?

He remembered an evening a month earlier, when he had been out drinking with Sir James and some friends. When they had returned to this same house, he had found Catherine in bed but still awake. Perhaps due to the spirits he had consumed, he decided to make use of his husband's privilege. After all, it was a privilege he didn't abuse, he told himself, and he hadn't been with Catherine for at least two weeks. Also due to the spirits, the act was somewhat prolonged that night, and when he heard Cat moaning under him, he at first thought he was hurting her: His penis was not only a bit longer than most——or such was his impression——but also considerably thicker. He paused, looking at her almost invisible face in the darkness and thinking to say some comforting word, but before he could do so, she was clawing at him and jamming her clutching flesh tightly up against him. "Oh, Jesus," she moaned, "don't stop! Harder! Please! Do it harder!"

My God, the thought jolted through him, *she really likes it! She likes it as much as any nigger wench!*

He immediately lost his erection. She moaned and reached for him as he slipped away from her, but he escaped to her side. When she rolled away from him and he heard her half-stifled sobs, he patted her shoulder. "I'm sorry," he said. "I'm sorry I hurt you." But he knew perfectly well that that was not why she was weeping.

Well, if their marriage was a mistake, what could he do about it? Not much. Except keep on trying.

He went to the bed and sat down beside her. He put a hand on her shoulder.

"I'm sorry, Catherine," he said. "I wish I'd known before this how you felt. All I can say is, I'll try to be more the kind of husband you want. And I hope you'll try to understand and do what I ask of you. Isn't that fair?"

She nodded.

"I want to make you happy, Catherine. Believe me. And I do love you more than I can say. Now, shall we get ready for bed?"

"Yes."

"Do you . . . want to tonight?"

She shook her head. "It wouldn't be any good."

He was relieved. "We'll both make things better from now on, won't we?"

She nodded again. "Yes."

But they were not better.

Great God-a-mighty, he frequently asked himself, *what does she want of me?* He was glad to know she wasn't one of those women totally without warmth, who so hated the sexual act that it became almost impossible; and if she wanted him to pleasure her more in bed, fine, he was trying to do it. Going a little slower, taking a little more time with her. And at the same time, he tried to treat her with the respect that was owed to her as his wife.

Then why did she seem to grow more pinch-faced and pale by the day, if that were possible? Did it really take such an effort to behave more like a lady? Hardly a day passed that he didn't see her on the verge of tears—tears for no perceptible reason whatever. There were moments, he was ashamed to admit, when the quivering of her chin and the trembling of her lip made him want to slap her across the face.

Thus there were further quarrels. Silly quarrels, trivial quarrels, quarrels of which he hardly knew the cause, and occasionally a more important one.

Such a quarrel occurred in December at the Wallopps' country estate in Hampshire. They had been invited for a fox hunt. Few women rode to the hounds, and the fact that Cat insisted on doing so—to Duke's dismay—immediately brought her to the attention of the gentlemen.

In the midst of that attention, and in the excitement of the hunt, she seemed to revert to her old self. Her cheeks became flushed. Her eyes sparkled. Her lips pulled back from those strong white teeth, and uninhibited whoops of joy burst from her throat as she jumped timber on a saddle never meant for such rough riding.

"Catherine," Sir James called to her after one such leap, "you quite terrify me when you do that!"

"Let me ride astride as I did when I was a girl, Sir James, and I'll follow you anywhere!"

"My dear girl, no English lady has been seen astride a horse in a hundred years."

"Dare me, and I'll do it!"

Her behavior was even worse that evening at the hunt ball. After the display she had made of herself in the morning, every man in the room was drawn to her, and she made no effort to discourage them, dancing with one after another, flirting and teasing and trading jest for jest without so much as a blush. As he watched her, Duke's whole being seemed to jangle with alarm. Christ, he thought, didn't she know what she was doing? It was as if, knowing she couldn't get what she wanted from him, she was flagging her tail like a bitch in heat in an attempt to get it elsewhere, and doing it in front of his very eyes. And furthermore, Duke realized with dismay, there was scarcely a man in the room, from his host on down, who wouldn't have leapt at the chance to give her satisfaction.

And so in the small hours of the morning, after they had

retired to their room, they fought. He said that her behavior had been disgraceful, that she had acted like a common jade, that she had made him look like a fool. She said that any time she enjoyed herself in the slightest, he spoiled it all afteward by treating her as if she were a wicked child. They finally made up after a fashion, but she fell asleep weeping, while he lay awake, haunted by the specter of her possible infidelity. How in God's name, he asked himself, had he ever come to marry this woman?

His final disillusionment came a month later, in January, soon after they arrived in Paris.

Once again, they had been taken in hand by one of Justin's friends, who had installed them in an apartment in his *hôtel* on the rue Saint-Honoré and who was showing them the delights of the city. They had been to the opera that evening, and perhaps it was Bellini's *La Sonnambula*, with its silly but touching libretto—the tale of a sleepwalking beauty caught in another man's bedchamber by her jealous lover—and its glorious soaring arias that had made Cat turn to Duke's arms. She had wept like a child at the end when Amina's name was cleared and she was again with Elvino, his love regained. The weakness of women, Duke thought later that night, as he kissed her eyelids and caressed her between the thighs.

A small dying fire crackled in the fireplace, and by its light he could just make out Cat's face. He smiled to himself as he heard her sighs and watched her roll her head about on the pillow in pleasure at the long, slow strokes of his fingers. She had sometimes implied that he didn't know how to please a woman. Well, this time she was going to learn how wrong she was, he had decided. If it was pleasure she wanted, this time she was going to get it. This time—

He touched something—something so unexpected that for a moment he couldn't identify it.

He felt further, tried to grasp whatever it was between his fingers.

Cat opened her eyes. "What's wrong?"

"I don't know. What is this?"

Her fingers joined his between her thighs. "Oh. Oh, that. That's just the string on my sponge."

He felt completely lost. "On your what?"

"On my sponge. The silk sponge I use. It's not a real sponge, of course."

"But what . . . why . . . ?"

She seemed surprised that he should be puzzled. "To keep from getting pregnant before we're ready. We decided it would be best to wait until we got back home, remember?"

"I know, but . . . how long have you been using that thing?"

"Since after our wedding night." She smiled uncertainly and tried to make a joke. "My goodness, Duke, it certainly doesn't say much for your interest in my bottom that you haven't even noticed that string till now!"

Duke slid out of the blankets and sat up in bed. His heart was thumping, his breath was short, and he felt as if he were having an evil dream. He could not deny the thought: His own wife was using a whore's device. What kind of decent woman would do such a thing?

If a woman used such a device, she would feel free to bed down with anybody she pleased.

He felt her hand on his arm. "Duke, darling? What's the matter?"

"Nothing. It's just that . . . using a thing like that seems unnatural, that's all. If the good Lord wants you to get pregnant, you should get pregnant."

Cat laughed. "Duke, honey, if the good Lord wants me to get pregnant, he surely isn't going to let a little bitty old sponge get in the way."

The thought recurred, thunderingly: *She could fuck anyone she pleased!*

She was saying something: ". . . Momma Lucinda told me they work pretty well most of the time, but you can never be sure. And for some women they don't seem to work at all."

In which case, the poor cuckolded fools they had married would be stuck with other men's whelps.

What could he do? He had a feeling that it would be

useless to say, *"Catherine, I forbid you!"* She might even take it as a challenge.

He said, "Catherine, I know we agreed to wait . . . but I wish you wouldn't use that thing."

"But, Duke, if I were to get knocked-up tonight—excuse me, pregnant tonight—I'd be that way for most of our trip, and I'd have the baby in September, before we even started home. And a trip like that isn't good for a new-born baby."

Really, there wasn't a thing he could do, not a damned thing. He could destroy the sponge, but she could always make a new one. He could forbid her to use it when he spread her, but that wouldn't prevent her from using it when he wasn't around.

Using it with another man.

"All right," he said, hanging his head.

She held her arms out to him. "Now, you come back here, and let's finish what we started."

He did finish it—quickly and indifferently.

Long after her last unhappy whimper, when she had drifted off to sleep, he lay awake feeling sick. Now he knew when he had first begun to suspect he had made a mistake. Now he could admit the truth to himself.

He had begun to doubt his wife on their wedding night.

He remembered vividly taking her for the first time. He had expected something more or less like his experience with Jessie: the struggle, the breakthrough, and then, as her pain faded, the pleasure. But to his astonishment—his shock—it hadn't been like that at all. He had encountered very little resistance. He was big, of course, and she was tight, but . . . *now* it seemed to him that what little resistance he had met had been largely imaginary. He had *wanted* to believe it had been there. She had cried out, but not very loudly, and there had been very little blood. It had not been at all like his experience with Jessie.

Again and again, since then, though he had tried to dismiss the question as unworthy, it had floated through his mind like the whisper of a demon: *Had she been a virgin?*

Now he thought: *Maybe not.*

Who, then? Who had been the first? One of the Mc-

Clintock boys? They were known for chasing anything in skirts, from highborn planters' daughters to black tavern wenches. And they had been around Catherine Anne Sabre a great deal. Yes, there was a good chance it had been one of them.

Or, if not, who else?

His uncle's words of years earlier came back to him: "*Hell, there's black blood running all through that family. . . . Half of them Sabres is black as the ace of spades.*"

He thought of the black boy who had been Cat's constant companion for years, the one who didn't even call her *Miss.* He remembered the boy almost naked, wrestling with Cat in the cockpit of the little sloop, his bare thigh thrust between hers. He thought of the boy lying naked between her thighs, taking his pleasure.

Yes, it was possible, Duke thought.

Even likely.

HE HAD BEEN DUPED.

Being a fair-minded man, Duke was quite willing to admit that the situation was in part his own fault. He had let himself be blinded by his naive admiration of the Sabre family. He had overlooked the fact that Justin Sabre and his daughter were not Carolina Sabres at all, but from Virginia, and he had really known very little about them. He had even ignored the fact that at least one Carolina Sabre, Mr. Lewis Sabre, was known to have married black, an indication of the character of the family. Nevertheless, the fact remained that he had not gotten what he had bargained for.

He would have liked nothing more than to forgo the rest of the trip and return home at once—to be back at Redbird and in the arms of Leonie, who surely by this time had come to her senses. But Charleston knew he had promised his bride the grandest wedding trip ever, one that would last more than a year, and appearances had to be maintained. They pressed on.

In March they arrived in Munich, to find the city in an uproar. It seemed that Jane Digby's old friend King Ludwig had recently given his supposed mistress, Lola Montez, citizenship, a couple of titles, an annuity and estates, and feudal rights over two thousand subjects. In consequence of his amour, cabinets had fallen and bishops had wept, but Ludwig had vowed: "I will not give up Lola! I will never give her up! My kingdom for Lola!" For a goddamn dancing prostitute, Duke thought with disgust. Great God-a-mighty, but these Europeans were depraved!

Actually, Duke thought, they were little better than pagans. He saw the evidence everywhere. In Paris he had seen it in Delacroix's paintings—all that unbearably rich, naked flesh in *Dante and Virgil in Hell* and *Death of*

Sardanapalus. He saw it time and again in the great Gothic cathedrals, which seemed haunted by older, darker gods than the bleeding Christ on the cross. He saw it in the fountains and monuments that graced public gardens and city streets. Never before in his life had he seen so much bare-ass statuary—great stone butts, swollen breasts, and dangling phalluses exposed to the gaze of every man, woman, and child who happened by. Great God-a-mighty!

With the advance of spring, they moved on to Switzerland and then to Italy, and it seemed to Duke that the closer they approached the seat of Roman Christianity, the more this ancient world was engaged in a celebration of the flesh. In Venice they visited the Ducal Palace, ascending the Staircase of the Giants, flanked at the top by colossal statues of Neptune and Mars—nude of course. They saw Tintoretto's painting of the *Three Graces*—oh, that lovely flesh!—and Veronese's *Rape of Europa.* In Florence they saw Cellini's statue of *Perseus* and Giambologna's of *The Rape of the Sabine Women,* and secular flesh even invaded religious quarters, in the persons of Michelangelo's *Dawn* and *Dusk,* and *Day* and *Night,* in the Medici Chapels.

And there was Michelangelo's *David.* Surely, Duke thought, no man born on this earth had ever had a body like that. Christ, even his cock was pretty! Duke glanced at Cat, then looked at her again. Her eyes had narrowed as she gazed up at those long clean-lined legs, that beautiful torso, that handsome head. Her lips were drawn back in that way he knew so well that showed her eyeteeth, and he could hear the soft hiss of her breath. She was slowly rubbing her hands together, and he sensed that she would have liked to slide them over that stone flesh in an effort, however vain, to bring it to life.

In June they arrived in Rome, where they planned to rest for a time. Justin's letter of introduction took them to the address of one Conte di Loredano. The conte unfortunately proved to have died a year or two previously, but he had left behind a widow. The Contessa Antonia di Loredano was a lovely dark-eyed, olive-skinned woman of spectacular figure in her mid-thirties. She immediately took them in hand, found them a spacious apartment in the Via Sistina, and saw to it that they received a dozen invitations. Rome, she declared, was theirs for as long as they cared to stay.

But, dear God, there was so much to see! The Colosseum and the several Forums, pagan temples and Christian churches, ancient baths and Renaissance palaces—the list was endless. In Rome the centuries had not crumbled fast enough for each new one to displace the last, so they simply lay on top of each other and jumbled together, the magnificent shards of time.

And, more than ever, there was the celebration of the flesh. They found it everywhere, from the ceiling of the Sistine Chapel to the fountains of Rome to the many museums and galleries. They saw Canova's statue of *Venus Victorious*; they saw Bernini's *Apollo and Daphne*.

And there were the women. God, Duke thought, he had been away from Leonie too long. For some reason, he had always thought of Italian women as being fat and grubby, and nothing could have been more untrue. He didn't think he had seen so many desirable women before in his entire life. It was no wonder that Italian men couldn't seem to keep their minds off sex. What normal man would have been able to?

Of course, he knew perfectly well why it was that in spite of all their trappings of Christianity these people remained pagan sensualists. He had been surprised to notice that in northern Italy there were people as tawny-haired and light-complexioned as Catherine; he had not been at all surprised to see that the people were darker as they traveled southward. They were a Mediterranean people, after all, the same as the Spanish. Over the centuries there had been a lot of contact with Africa. After Hannibal's troops had come over the Alps, no doubt there had been one hell of a crop of pickaninnies in Italy.

In such surroundings it was only natural that he should turn to Cat for satisfaction, or at least relief, but he found himself doing so ever less frequently. For a time he had tried harder to satisfy her, but finally he had given up. He had to admit that ever since he had concluded that he had probably been cheated out of her virginity, he had felt a deep and abiding anger toward her and toward all the Sabres. And he had to admit that really *he did not like* pleasuring her. It simply was not true that "When all candles be out, all cats be gray," and the thought of all that writhing too-white flesh beneath his body repelled him.

God, he thought time and again, if only they could head for home at once. When they got to Carolina, he'd simply say to hell with Catherine and ignore her. Maybe he'd leave her at Sabrehill for a long visit while he went on to Redbird, and he wouldn't let Leonie out of bed for a week. But Catherine insisted that she wanted to make the full trip, all the way to Athens, even though she rarely appeared happy anymore.

Still, there were times when she lost her pallor and raised her voice in laughter, and it happened most often when she was in the company of other men. One evening when their party was wandering from cafe to cafe in the Via Veneto, he and the contessa had fallen behind the others—Cat and two other women and a half-dozen men—and he heard her laughter floating through the air. The contessa smiled teasingly at him. "Be warned, my friend. Marcello and Carlo and Aldo are the three most accomplished seducers in Rome. One or the other of them will almost certainly put horns on you."

If the contessa had known the touch of panic her words caused him, she would have been amused, but she saw only his smile. "How sad for me," he said. "But all the sweeter the consolations I shall hope to find elsewhere."

She laughed. He thought she had been joking, but even so, he had no intention of trusting anyone with a name like Marcello or Carlo and Aldo.

In July their stay in Rome drew toward its end, and Duke again raised the possibility of returning to America at once, but Catherine wanly shook her head. "I want to see all I can while I have the chance. I know you don't like it here, and we may never visit Europe again."

He sighed and let the matter go. "Well, you'd better get dressed. You haven't forgotten that we're meeting the contessa, have you? We're going to have lunch and then go to the Museo Profano."

Cat shook her head. They were in the bedroom at the time, and she threw herself down on the bed. "You go," she said. "I'm not feeling well."

"But she's expecting us both." It was true that Cat looked ill, but ill or well, he didn't like the idea of leaving her alone for any length of time. He thought of Marcello and Carlo and Aldo.

Cat closed her eyes. "Apologize for me."

"If you'd rather I stayed . . ."

"No. You have a good time."

"Well . . . I don't know that I'll be able to. I'll probably come back after explaining to the contessa."

"Whatever you like."

He shrugged. "I may be back early, or maybe quite late. We'll see."

She didn't answer.

He hadn't far to go: a few yards along the Via Sistina to the piazza of the Church of Trinità dei Monti, down the famous hundred thirty-seven steps to the Piazza di Spagna, and across the piazza into the busy Via Condotti. He soon saw the contessa looking into shop windows. It was hardly proper to meet a woman on a street corner, Duke thought, but he had found that the contessa was not altogether conventional.

"But where is Catherine?" she asked, her dark eyes widening.

"I'm sorry, Contessa, my wife isn't feeling well. She sends her apologies. I'm afraid you'll have to put up with me, but of course if you'd rather not, I'll understand."

"But I shall be delighted to 'put up' with you, Mr. Avery!" She looked at him, he thought, with fresh interest. "And now shall we have our luncheon?"

They ate in the Caffe Greco, a favorite haunt of Goethe and Byron, she told him, and all the time her eyes appraised him as if she were trying to come to a decision. While they were finishing their coffee, she leaned toward him and lightly touched his forearm with her fingertips.

"Mr. Avery, I have a suggestion to make, and I don't really know whether I should or not. You may not even think it a very proper suggestion."

He looked at the fingertips on his forearm. "Contessa, I would welcome any suggestion in the world you care to make."

"Well, you have seen so many churches and museums by now that they must be a jumble in your mind."

"That's certainly true."

"And today is not a very nice day. It's becoming overcast and it may rain. Perhaps you would rather not go to a museum today. Perhaps we could find something else to do."

He nodded. "You have something in mind?"

"It occurs to me," she said very slowly, "that you might enjoy simply coming to my apartment. You could unfasten a few buttons and stretch out and relax." Her fingertips moved up and down his forearm. "Shall I go on?"

"Please do."

"If you like, I can have my servants pour a nice warm bath for you to relax in for an hour or so. I can send them away, and you can even take a nap if you wish. It might be a very pleasant way to spend an afternoon."

They both looked at the fingertips stroking his forearm. She raised her eyes to meet his. He could feel the thump of his heart, the sensitive quiver of his flesh.

"I can hardly think of a pleasanter way, Contessa."

She flashed him a smile. "My, we are formal today! You know perfectly well that my close friends call me Toni."

"And you know that mine call me Duke, Toni."

"Shall we go now, Duke?"

Well, now maybe he could keep his health and sanity until he was with Leonie again, he thought, as he fitted his key into the lock back at the apartment in the Via Sistina. They still had a long way to travel, and with stops in Vienna and Berlin on their return, it would be almost Christmas before they reached Carolina. But at least he would be able to savor the memory of this afternoon and evening for a long time to come.

He supposed he was still naive in some ways, but, until they had reached Toni's apartment, he had hardly dared to believe that she meant what she seemed to be suggesting. After all, what did he really know about these people and their customs? What if he had discovered that all she had meant was that he really was welcome to relax for an afternoon and be on his way? But, no, it seemed that even in Italy a woman didn't invite a man into her home to take off his clothes with nothing but that in mind. And she didn't help him to undress and then climb naked into bed with him simply to take a nap. "But I can't, Duke!" she had said, laughing hysterically, when she had seen it. "I can't! Holy Virgin, it is simply too big!" But she had, and when the storm broke outside, they were making their own thunder and lightning.

It had been one of the great afternoons of his life. He hadn't had one like it since he was a nineteen-year-old stud, all balls and no brains, with Jessie. Later, he and Toni had gone out to dinner and strolled about the city before returning to her apartment for another couple of hours. She had tried to tempt him into prolonging his stay in Rome, even suggesting that, if he were interested, she knew two or three other couples who might share their pleasures, but there Duke drew the line. No witnesses, no depravity. Just good, healthy pleasuring.

Well, he thought, as he stood within the dark apartment, maybe he could manage another time or two alone with Toni before they left; but he had to admit that, no matter how much fun and pleasure it had been, it hadn't been the same as with Leonie. Maybe it wasn't all thunder and lightning with Leonie, but there was something else between them, something they shared. . . .

He shrugged the matter off. It didn't do any good to think about such things and pull them apart and try to understand them. All he knew was that, even now, after having screwed Toni half-a-dozen times in a single day, he still would have given his left ball to be back home with Leonie.

As he continued through the apartment, he saw that a light showed from the half-open bedroom door.

It suddenly struck him how very long he had been gone. Jesus Christ, he thought, what if she hadn't been alone all this time? What if she wasn't alone right now?

He hurried to the door and shoved it open. Cat lay face down on the bed, much as he'd left her. She looked as if she had hardly moved. Her eyes were hollow and red from weeping, and she was biting her thumb like a child.

"I'm sorry I'm so late," he said. "I had dinner with the contessa, and we saw some of Rome by night. I took her home—"

"It's all right," Cat said without looking at him. "Duke, I've changed my mind."

"About what?"

"I want my momma. I want my papa. I want Damien and—and Leila and—"

"What do you mean?"

"I want to go home. Oh, I want to go home!"

Duke could scarcely believe she meant it. Was it possible that after all this time the gods were smiling on him again at last?

"You'll change your mind tomorrow."

She closed her eyes and shook her head. "No. I've decided. I want to go home."

"All right, Catherine, if that's what you want, we'll go home. We'll start packing in the morning."

There would be no Naples or Athens, no Vienna or Berlin. He nearly laughed aloud, as he threw off his clothes. "We'll get there the fastest way possible, and this time, if you like, we'll take the *Great Western*. Don't worry, sweetheart, we'll be home in a matter of weeks!"

He would be back at Redbird and in Leonie's arms. He felt as if they were already on their way.

On a September evening in 1847, Mr. Jebediah Hayes sat on a chair in the stage-left wing of the Broadway Theater in New York City, watching a performance of *The Merchant of Venice*. Poor old all-too-human Shylock was one of his favorite villains, but he was not here tonight to enjoy Shylock. He was here to witness Miss Dulcy Sabre in the role of Portia, and his eyes misted over as he listened to that low, clear, bell-like voice that had held audiences across America entranced:

> *The quality of mercy is not strained.*
> *It droppeth as the gentle rain from heaven*
> *Upon the place beneath . . .*

The Divine Dulcy, they called her. Most critics agreed that she was the greatest tragedienne alive and the finest actress America had yet produced, rivaled only by the great Charlotte Cushman. And who would have dreamed fifteen years ago at Sabrehill that one day she would be acting with the likes of Edwin Forrest and Junius Brutus Booth and William Charles Macready?

The performance was approaching its end. Portia, disguised as a doctor of laws, had won her case, and Shylock had slunk off, muttering, "I am not well." Portia and Nerissa, still in disguise, had teasingly demanded rings from their husbands as their fee. And now, in the happy last scene, identities were revealed, the merchant learned that his ships had come in, and on Gratiano's final jest, the curtain fell.

And rose again to the audience's cheers and wild applause.

Dulcy came running off stage, threw Jebediah a quick smile, and, head held high, strode back onto the stage again. Queenly, Jebediah thought. Regal. She returned to the stage again and again for her curtain calls, sometimes alone, sometimes with her fellow actors, bowing low and throwing kisses, accepting flowers, and it seemed as if the audience never would let her go. But finally she swept off stage, seized Jebediah's arm, and, laughing, declared, "That's enough!" Suddenly the backstage area was mobbed by cast and crew and a hundred strangers, most of them crowding in to congratulate the Divine Dulcy, but somehow they managed to press through to her dressing room.

"Mignon," she said to her maid, "you may go for now, but stand guard! Let nobody in until I tell you!"

The instructions were unnecessary. The maid knew her

mistress wanted no other guest until she was out of costume and had had a few minutes rest. She left the room.

"How was I tonight?" Dulcy asked, going behind a screen.

"Magnificent. But why should I tell you? You'll only say I must be insane, because you were terrible and you'll never be able to play Portia right."

Dulcy laughed. "I know, and it's true! But I like to hear the praise anyway."

Jebediah settled down on a couch she used for resting between scenes. A moment later, she emerged from behind the screen clad in a loosely belted peignoir of black lace lined with black silk and, aside from her black slippers, apparently nothing else. She sat down at a dressing table, made a face at herself in the mirror, and began slapping some white sticky substance on her cheeks. "God, I hate grease paint," she said. "Of all the ways to make a livelihood, I had to choose one where I had to spread this—this *merde* on my face!"

"You know there's nothing else in the world you'd rather do."

She gave him an arch, impish look. "Oh, I don't know. I can think of one thing I like almost as much. It doesn't require grease paint, and some women make it pay very well."

"I know, my dear, and as I recall, you're marvelous at it—but after your performance, you'd miss all that applause."

"Oh, you dog!" In a fit of laughter, Dulcy turned and hurled a paint-stained towel at Jebediah.

She was a lovely woman and a lovely person, he thought. At thirty-two, she had attained the quality of agelessness. She could widen her eyes and cast an innocent smile in a way that made her a sunny seventeen again. Or she could frown and purse her lips and suddenly become a middle-aged harridan. She was Juliet. She was Lady Macbeth. She was Woman. And she was, and always would be, one of his dearest friends.

"What are your plans?" he asked. "Have you decided yet?"

"Oh, I don't know, Jebediah. Mr. Barnum wants me to tour the West again, but I'd rather like to go abroad. Can you see me playing *Phèdre* or *L'Ecole des Femmes*—in French? I'd make a complete fool of myself, of course."

"You'd have Paris at your feet."

"Yes—rolling with laughter. Just the same, I'd like to try it. And what are your plans?"

"Oh, more lecturing, another book, and whatever I can do for the cause."

Dulcy scrubbed vigorously at her face with another towel. "Poor Jebediah. Always so busy, yet so often lonely, I suspect."

"Occasionally. Would you believe me if I told you that at times I actually miss Sabrehill?"

"Of course. I loved Sabrehill, and I think you came to love it too. It was our home, Jebediah, and they'll never let us go back. We're exiles."

Her makeup removed, Dulcy threw down the towel. She arose from the dressing table, crossed the little room, and settled herself on Jebediah's lap. Her belt had come loose, and he pulled her gown back across her bare breast.

She said, "I think you need a family, Mr. Jeb."

"My! Is this a proposal, Miss Dulcy?"

"You had your chance a long time ago, you brute, and you sent me away."

"Wasn't I right?"

"Yes, I suppose you were. But just the same, I'll always have a kind of love for you, Jebediah."

Jebediah recalled those early months at Sabrehill, when Mr. Turnage had been intent on breaking him, and the ever-jealous Amity Sabre had made life a kind of hell for all within her reach. Small wonder that for a brief period he and Dulcy had found solace in each other's arms.

"And I shall always have love for you, Dulcy, dear," he said. "Always."

She put a hand behind his head and, leaning toward him, placed a kiss aslant his mouth.

At that moment, the door opened.

Dulcy was instantly off his lap, her robe flying open. She blocked his view, but he heard footsteps and then the maid saying, "I'm so sorry, madame! I told the gentleman he must not—"

"That's all right, Mignon. You may go now."

Jebediah stood up. Dulcy was hastily rebelting her robe. Near the door, a young woman at his side, stood Mr. Duke Avery. He stared at Dulcy. The faintest of smiles came to his face, and his gaze shifted to Jebediah.

"Katie Anne!" Dulcy said. "Cat!"

It was indeed Cat, could be no one other than Cat, and yet with those hollow eyes and that white, twitching face, Jebediah hardly recognized her.

"Aunt Dulcy," she said, coming forward, "oh, Aunt Dulcy!" Her face screwed up, and she went into Dulcy's arms, weeping. Duke, looking at them, seemed to be suppressing laughter.

"Oh, Jebediah!" Cat said after a moment, coming to him. "Oh, Jebediah, I am so happy to see you again!"

She continued to weep as he drew her into his arms, but her tears were less those of happiness than of a wounded child. "It's all right, Cat," he said softly, as he stroked her head, "it's all right. Yes, you're back with your Jebediah."

Looking over Cat's head, he impaled Duke Avery with his gaze. *You bastard,* he said silently, *what have you done to my girl!*

That lovely ivory body, so swiftly glimpsed . . . the full, plump-nippled breasts and the black spearhead of pubic hair . . . she was almost as white as Cat, but Duke knew she had black blood, and that made all the difference. He could envy Jebediah. Jebediah and Dulcy were lovers, of course, but Catherine hadn't seemed shocked or even surprised, almost as if she had known about it all along. And that seemed to confirm every suspicion Duke had ever had about her.

"Tell me, honeychild," he said as they rode back to the hotel in a hack, "I've heard that there's more than a little black blood here and there in your family. Just as a matter of curiosity, is it possible that you have some yourself?"

"Why, no." She stared at him. "Why in the world do you ask?"

"As I said, curiosity—aroused by the display you made of yourself with those niggers back there. How do you know you don't have black blood?"

"Because I asked Papa. He said something about there being reason to believe Damien had white blood—Sabre blood—and since Damien and I were so close, I wondered if I had any black blood. Like Aunt Dulcy."

"That nigger boy of yours," Duke burst out laughing, "that boy is a *Sabre*?"

"I guess he might be. But I don't see what's so funny about that."

Neither did Duke, actually, yet he found it difficult to stop laughing. My God, he thought, what kind of family had he married into?

He wiped his eyes. "I'm sorry, Catherine. It was just the thought of all you Sabre cousins, black and white, scrambling about and multiplying like rabbits . . . in and out of marriage."

She continued to stare at him. "Would it matter to you if I did have black blood?"

"Should it?"

"I hope not!"

But of course it would have. A Madam Lareina or a Contessa Toni might have black blood, but not his wife. Not his wife.

And how could he be sure that what she said was true, even if she believed it? He thought of the day she had looked at the stone *David* through narrowed eyes and rubbed her hands together. He thought of the intensity of her desire in bed on certain nights. *"Oh, Jesus, don't stop! Harder! Please! Do it harder!"* He thought of her wallowing in the cockpit of the little sloop with the near-naked black boy, his thigh shoved high between hers.

Was that boy the one? He had asked himself the question a hundred times. Was that black bastard laughing his head off at Duke Avery right now? At the thought of having put horns on Duke even before the wedding? *"Yeah, you got her now, massa, but I had her first. And how she loved it!"*

He would pay. They would all pay, sooner or later.

They arrived at the Astor Hotel and went to their suite. Cat immediately went to bed, but for a long time Duke stood by the window in their dark sitting room and looked out at the dimly lit City Hall Park. Cat had arranged to meet with Jebediah and her Aunt Dulcy tomorrow. Duke didn't care. Let the happy niggers play together. He and his wife would be in New York only a few days, and he had plans to make and people to see. Old friends, people he could trust.

Yes, he had been duped. But his turn was coming.

─◦❦{ 4 }❦◦─

SHE WAS HOME AT LAST. As they drove up the long avenue of oaks toward the lights of the Sabrehill big house, the past year seemed to recede in memory like an unhappy dream.

Momma Lucinda saw them first. She was standing on the east steps of the kitchen house, hands on hips, staring into the darkness as if wondering who in the world could be arriving at this hour of the evening. When Cat waved and called, "Halloo, Momma! We're back, Momma Lucinda!" she stiffened, then threw up her hands. "Oh, my Lord, they're back!" She ran down the steps and toward the big house. "Miss Lucy! Miss Lucy, come out here! They're back! Miss Cat and Mr. Duke, they're back!"

As Cat got out of the carriage, she found herself surrounded. First, the children came running out of the house —"Oh, Macy Aaron, you've grown so big! And Sarah, I'd hardly know you!"—then Irish appeared, and Leila was in her arms embracing her, and they were all practically carrying her into the house, where her mother came running down the stairs.

"Catherine? Oh, Katie Anne! Cat!"

She found herself weeping in her mother's arms.

"Cat, darling, how are you? Oh, you look so pale! Have you been ill?"

"No, I'm just tired from traveling. We thought we might as well stop by here—"

"But of course! And stay as long as we can keep you. Oh, I wish your father were here, and Mark and Beau!"

"So do I! And Damien—where's Damien?"

"Why, look behind you, dear."

Cat withdrew from her mother's arms and turned. Damien was standing by the piazza door, his arms folded across his chest, smiling at her.

275

"Oh, Damien!"

She went to him. Went to him, unfolded those arms, and entered into their embrace.

"Oh, Damien, how I've missed you!"

"I've missed you, too, Cat."

Hugging him, she pressed her wet face against his warm throat. "I was so afraid you'd be gone before I got back. And then maybe I'd never see you again."

"Mr. Justin said I should go, but . . . I just had to see you first, Cat."

"I'm so glad . . ."

She felt his sudden wariness in a stiffening of his body, the lift of his head, the stillness of his hands on her body. She looked up to see him gazing over her shoulder. Turning, she saw Duke watching them from a dozen feet away, a little smile on his face, a gleam in his eye. Suddenly she felt awkward.

"Duke . . . you . . . you do remember Damien, don't you?"

"Of course," Duke said softly. "I do indeed. Yes, I remember Damien."

They had arrived in Charleston early in the week. While resting for a few days in the care of Raphael and Birdie at the King Street house, they had learned that her mother had only recently made an early return to Sabrehill. They had followed after her, arriving on Friday evening.

"Your father is in Virginia on family business," her mother said, "and he should be back in a few weeks. But with Beau in school and Mark off on his own now, goodness knows when we'll see them again!"

"Well, they'd better not stay away too long!" Still, there were quite enough people at Sabrehill to make her feel welcomed and comforted and loved.

She slept late the next morning, happy to be back in the bed she had known since childhood, though she now shared it with Duke. When she awakened, Duke was already up and gone, and Leila took it on herself to serve her breakfast in bed.

She had a lazy day and hardly saw Duke. When she

arrived downstairs, he was out in the office talking with her mother. The three of them and the children had dinner together. Afterward, Duke returned to the office to read the past year's agricultural magazines, and Cat spent the afternoon visiting with old friends and telling Damien about her trip.

"He's made you unhappy, hasn't he?" Damien said, as they sat together down on the landing, watching the river flow by.

"Oh, no . . ." She realized that Damien had been staring intently at her for some minutes.

"He has. I can tell. Your face has a funny sick look, and your lower lip has a little twitch at one corner. I had a feeling last night, even before I saw you—"

"Damien, he's my husband. He does the best he can. Momma Lucinda told me that a man and wife have to learn each other's ways and needs, and we're both still learning."

"You've had over a year."

"Please, Damien. Don't say something to make me cry."

She looked away from him, but she could feel that he was still staring at her.

"I only want to help you, Cat."

"I know that."

"I'll do anything for you that you want me to do," he said slowly. "Anything."

"Then please . . . please don't say anything more."

At supper Duke said he thought he had better go on to Redbird in the morning. Her mother looked disappointed and urged them both to stay at Sabrehill longer, but Duke said, no, he was eager to find out how things were going on his plantation.

"But Catherine may stay if she wishes," he said. "In fact, I think it might be a good idea. She's been away so long, it'll be good for her to spend some more time with familiar faces."

Cat would have liked nothing better than to remain at Sabrehill. But her mother, like Damien, was already beginning to question her suspiciously, and Cat didn't want to burden her with the knowledge of how unhappy her life had become. No, she would go on with Duke to Redbird in the morning. "But it's not as if we were going a long way off this time, Momma. Why, we'll be seeing each other a lot from now on!"

After supper Duke returned to his magazines in the office, and Damien busied himself with some chore for her mother. Left to her own devices and hearing music in the field quarters, Cat wandered out through the dark to listen for a while, then returned to the kitchen house, where she found Momma Lucinda sitting on the steps, a cup in her hand.

"What's that?" Cat asked, sitting down on a step below her.

"Now, what you think it is, chile? This is Saturday night, and this here is my Saturday night cup."

"Give me some."

Momma Lucinda handed her the cup, and Cat sipped from it. It was, as she had thought, whiskey from Momma Lucinda's privileged jug, mixed with water. She remembered how shocked Edina McClintock had been to see Damien and her passing a cup back and forth—Edina McClintock, who had sucked milk from her mammy's breast, yet refused to drink from the same cup with her. But how could you refuse to share a cup with someone you loved? Tears rushed to Cat's eyes, and she couldn't hold back her sob.

"What's the matter, chile?"

"Nothing." Cat wiped her eyes and calmed herself.

"Why are you crying?"

"I don't know. I cry a lot lately."

"I see that. He ain't treating you right?"

"Oh, he doesn't treat me badly. He's really a very nice man."

"Sometimes they is the worst kind." Momma Lucinda took the cup back and sipped from it. "He giving you satisfaction?"

"Oh, Momma!"

"Well, is he?"

"Oh . . . of course. Why do you ask?"

" 'Cause you don't look like a woman getting her satisfaction. *No kind* of satisfaction. There is all kinds of satisfaction, chile, from pleasuring and making a baby to bringing it up right, and from doing good work to sharing some whiskey on Saturday night. And if a body ain't getting her satisfactions, and ain't got no hope of getting them, she might as well lay herself down and die."

"I haven't given up hope."

Momma Lucinda took another sip of whiskey. "I tried to teach you right, chile, and you know I never told you you wasn't gonna see no troubles. Everybody got troubles. You just think 'bout the troubles your momma and daddy had."

Cat took the cup, sipped, and handed it back. "What troubles?"

"Why, that time way back before you was born when your daddy fought the duel with Mr. Vachel Skeet and near got hisself killed."

Cat had only a vague idea of what Momma Lucinda was talking about. She did know that, shortly before marrying her natural mother, her father had visited Sabrehill and had nearly lost his life in a duel, but she had never heard the incident discussed.

"Over my mother? You mean . . . my mother Lucy?"

"Oh, they was something wonderful together, Mr. Justin and Miss Lucy. As I rec'lect, she was 'bout nineteen that spring, the same as you was when you was married. And wasn't two people ever more in love."

Cat had a feeling of confusion. What Momma Lucinda was saying couldn't be true. She knew that soon after the duel her father had come home and married her natural mother. And she knew that her father had loved her natural mother.

Momma Lucinda sipped again. "Chile, I ain't sure I ought to be telling you 'bout this."

"Tell me."

"Oh, like I say, they was beautiful together. I rec'lect your momma said something 'bout your father was handsome as David out of the Bible, but real, 'stead of stone like a statue—"

"*David?*"

"And your daddy was always talking 'bout your momma being like flowers. But to me they was like two wild things that thought the world wasn't made for nothing but loving." Momma Lucinda laughed. "Why, I couldn't hardly keep your momma's drawers on her that spring! And you know what a gal's got on her mind when she's in love and she don't want to wear her drawers."

"My *momma*?"

"Oh, chile, I shouldn't be telling you these things."

"Tell me!"

"Well, like I say, I couldn't hardly keep your momma's clothes on her, so after her daddy said they could get married, I didn't even try. And they was off in the woods alone together 'most every day. I don't suppose any two people in the world ever enjoyed their loving more than them two, and every day Miss Lucy just got more and more beautiful." Momma Lucinda sighed. "I think I been drinking too much of this here whiskey."

"But what happened?"

"The duel is what happened. 'Cause a jealous man thought your daddy done stole Miss Lucy away from him. Your daddy near died. But when he was getting better, your momma was in his bed every night, 'cording to Leila, and Aunt Zule, the conjure woman, she said it was your momma that breathed the life back into him."

"But if they were so much in love . . . ?"

"Whyn't they get married? I don't know. Your daddy went home to Virginia and married Miss Rosellen and didn't come back here for twelve long years. But I never doubted that he truly loved Miss Lucy. Oh, chile, I shouldn't tell you such things."

"I'm glad you did."

She was glad, because the story seemed to draw her closer to than ever to her stepmother. It was not that she had not loved her natural mother or that she doubted her father's love for Rosellen Sabre. She had seen his love during Rosellen's life and his grief at her death. Nevertheless, there had been a time before that when he had loved Lucy, and Cat was glad that he had had that love to return to.

Why couldn't she have had such a love, Cat wondered.

Why couldn't she be a wild and beautiful thing with a wild and beautiful lover?

What had happened that her life had turned out to be a thing of such grayness and despair?

She put her head against Momma Lucinda's breast and wept.

She awakened the next morning feeling tired and logy and troubled by a dull, thudding headache. She hardly touched her breakfast. When the time came to depart, she tried to put on a show of cheerfulness, but she failed to dispel the look of worry she saw in her mother's and Damien's eyes.

They arrived at Redbird in the early afternoon. Mr. Ferguson, the overseer, gave them a cheerful greeting and sent for the housekeeper, and Duke showed Cat the room they would share.

"And now, Leonie," he said, when their room was ready for them, "do you think we could have something to eat?"

The housekeeper had shown no joy at their return, and her face was expressionless. "There ain't much, 'cause we didn't know you was coming. But Fenella has got a soup pot on, and she can make you some biscuits."

"That will be fine."

A little later, old Fenella, lazy and sullen but a good cook, thumped their dinner on the table, and Cat sipped at the deliciously brothy, soothing soup with the poignant gratitude she often felt for small blessings in the midst of misery.

"I'm going to look the place over," Duke said, when they had finished. "I don't suppose you'd care to come with me?"

"No. I still don't feel well. I'm going to take a nap."

Returning to the bedroom, she kicked off her shoes and slipped out of her dress. She pulled down the counterpane and, with a whimper, threw herself facedown on the bed.

Her headache was fading, but another kind of ache seemed to pervade her in both body and soul. She lifted her pelvis from the bed, then pressed it back down hard. She felt as if she were filled with a hundred different longings that would never be fulfilled. Again she lifted her pelvis, again pressed it down, still harder, but she only felt worse. Tears came to her eyes. She took one corner of her pillow, stuffed it into her mouth, and bit on it until her teeth ached. She curved the fingers of one hand into claws and slowly drew them over the bed as if to rip the mattress apart. The wretched dream of the last year was not over after all. It would never end.

Twice Duke came to the door and asked if she were asleep. The second time, she didn't bother to answer.

Now he knew what it was to have the reality surpass the dream. A hundred times in the past year he had told himself that memory always betrays and that Leonie couldn't possibly be all that he remembered her. Then she had come to the house to prepare the bedroom, and once again he had seen the face of Jessie—the sweet round face, the full mouth with the delicate corners, the lightly dimpled chin. He had wanted to reach out and touch that face, but of course he hadn't dared. Leonie had quietly done her work and departed.

He had waited, hoping she would return, almost fearing the first time they would be alone together. Now he could wait no longer.

He was at a dining room window when he saw her enter the kitchen house. When he went outside, the sun was staining the western sky crimson and purple, and the moon was high in the deep blue. The faint sounds from the field quarters and the call of a mockingbird only emphasized the evening silence that hung over the plantation.

The only light in the kitchen came from the fire Leonie was building up in the fireplace. He watched its play on her face, framed by a brightly flowered silk kerchief he had given her, and on her long-fingered, delicately boned hands. It had never before occurred to him that she had beautiful hands, but they were the most beautiful he had ever seen.

"It's a little early to be starting supper, isn't it, Leonie?"

"Got to keep up the fire under the soup pot, Mr. Duke,

so it don't go bad. We'll finish off the soup tonight." She straightened up from the fire and gave him a quick, meaningless smile. "There! Now, if you 'scuse me—"

"Wait, Leonie. Don't go. I want to tell you how much I've missed you."

"Well, we all missed you, too, Mr. Duke."

"You, Leonie? Did you miss me?"

Her delicate fingers met, intertwined, and tightened on each other. "We *all* missed you."

"No, Leonie. You."

" 'Course, Mr. Duke. Now—"

As she tried to step by him, he took her by the shoulders. "Leonie—"

"Please, Mr. Duke."

"I've missed you every day I've been away. I started missing you long before I left. Can you truly say you haven't missed me?"

Leonie closed her eyes. "Please."

"Mr. Ferguson tells me you still haven't taken a husband. At your age. He thinks you're one of those women without much natural feeling. But we know better, don't we?"

"I want to go now, Mr. Duke."

"God, how I've missed you. How I've dreamed of you. You have no idea. Leonie, in a year and a half, not once have I had the happiness you gave me. Not once."

"Mr. Duke, this ain't doing no good."

"Is there anyone you ever loved more than you loved me, Leonie?"

A tear trickled down her cheek. "No."

"Then you love me still. Isn't that so?"

She shook her head.

"Yes, you do." His voice broke. "And I guess I must love you. In a way that I could never love any other woman. God, yes, I never thought I'd hear myself saying it, never thought it was possible, but I love you, Leonie. I love you, and I want you more than life."

He tried to draw her to him, but she lowered her head and braced it against his chest.

"Mr. Duke, I told you a long time ago, you got to choose 'tween her and me. And you chose."

"Well, I was wrong! I was wrong, and I've suffered for it every day and night since! Don't make me go on suffering, Leonie!"

"I don't want you to suffer, Mr. Duke. I just want you to leave me be. Mr. Duke, I got somebody else now!"

"I don't believe that." He forced her head up, forced his body against hers, forced his kisses on her wet cheeks. "You belong to me, and you know what I want. I want my Leonie the way I used to have her. I want her naked in my arms. Don't you remember how it used to be, Leonie, how we used to pleasure the night away, holding, kissing, touching every living part of each other until we were both crazy with want and then—"

"Please, Mr. Duke, don't do this to me!"

"I want you now, Leonie, God, how I want you." As she struggled to escape, he forced her back against a table and held her with his body. "And you're going to want me, because I know how to make you want me, and you won't be able to help yourself."

"Please, please, Mr. Duke!" Tears were streaming down Leonie's face. "You always said you wouldn't never take me 'gainst my will!"

His hands moved up and down her back as he rolled his body against hers, feeling the softness of her breasts and the hardness of her mound. "I don't have to take you against your will, because you're going to want it, Leonie. And once I've had you again, you'll be mine forever."

"Oh, Mr. Duke, Mr. Duke . . ."

Her body was beginning to answer his in spite of herself. Duke knew that the body carried its own memories, and he did everything in his power to awaken those memories by touches, strokes, kisses, whispers. He felt her body going limp against his, felt her nipples rise, felt her thighs tremble and part. Her breath came in short, shuddering gasps as he stroked her. "I love you, Leonie. And I want you and I'm going to have you. Right now. Are you ready, sweet Leonie? Because I am, you can feel how ready I am. Now, you just lean back and we'll get your skirt up . . ."

The voice that rang out behind his back was like lightning tearing through the darkness of the room: *"YOU BASTARD!"*

It was as if the voice seized him and tore him away from Leonie. She uttered a little cry and ran out the door, and he found himself facing Cat.

"You bastard! You son of a bitch!"

"Catherine—"

"You goddamn shit-ass—"

"Catherine, please listen to me."

"All this time you've left me alone on my bed, chewing my pillow for the want of a fuck, and *you're* down here trying to stick your goddamn pizzle into the housekeeper!"

"Catherine, I forbid you to talk that way!"

"*You* forbid *me*! You forbid me nothing, you nigger-humping mutt! You forbid me nothing ever again! Do you hear me, Duke Avery, you shit-ass, pig-turd bastard? You, God damn your eyes, you forbid me *nothing*!"

"Catherine!"

Her words were like fire across his face, and he found himself raising the back of his hand to her. Instantly, she leapt aside, reached out toward a table, and a nine-inch knife appeared in her right hand, its gray steel shining dully in the firelight. As he stepped toward her, her left hand slashed clawing through the air, and the knife darted out. He jumped back and looked down in shock as he felt a searing sensation and saw a red stain spreading on his shirt.

"You—you cut me!"

"Duke Avery," she said, her voice abruptly soft, "if you *ever* again raise your hand to me, I swear to God I'll kill you. In fact, if you ever so much as raise your *voice* to me, I'll likely cut your goddamn throat."

She meant it. He saw in the glitter of her green eyes, heard in the softness of her voice that she meant it. Under the right circumstances—and they were very close to those circumstances now—Catherine Anne Sabre was quite capable of killing him.

"If you'd only listen to me," he said as calmly as he

could manage. "If you'd only try to understand that a man has certain needs—"

"Needs! You dare speak to me about your needs? When you've never given a thought to anything but your own stinking needs? When have you ever once given the slightest thought to *my* needs? What about that damn nigger wench you were abusing, what about *her* needs? Your needs, my ass, Duke Avery, I say fuck you and your goddamn needs, and you can go to goddamn hell!"

Cat turned and, knife still in hand, strode out of the kitchen.

For a time Duke remained right where he was. He seemed to be trembling in every part of his body, and he had trouble comprehending what had happened. His gentle, soft-spoken wife had turned on him. Had reviled him in the evilest language and had threatened him with a knife. Had actually threatened to kill him. Had even drawn blood.

But surely the cut had been accidental and those words had been produced only by the heat of anger. She couldn't have really meant them. She couldn't have.

Fenella arrived to fix supper, and he couldn't remain in the kitchen. He hurried across the darkening courtyard to the house. Inside, he could hear footsteps upstairs. Going up, he found Cat crossing the upstairs passage with an armload of dresses.

"What are you doing?"

"Moving to another bedroom. The farthest one from yours."

He felt the trembling coming on again. "Catherine, you are still my wife, and I will not have closed doors between us."

She threw back her head and laughed. "Oh, what do you care, Duke? You never have had much interest in my fair white body, and I'll have to admit that I've kind of lost interest in yours."

He followed her into her chosen bedroom. "Do you have to talk like a whore?"

"You bring out the best in me."

He watched in silence as she hung up the dresses in a

clothespress. Never before in his life had he had such a feeling of impotence and futility.

"What do you plan to do?" he finally asked.

"I don't know. As far as the laws of South Carolina are concerned, we're sort of stuck with each other, aren't we? But what the hell, Duke, it's a big world, and I think my next tour of Europe will be a little more fun. I remember three dagos, as you would call them, that I met in Rome. They were named Marcello, Carlo, and Aldo, as I recall—"

"You bitch!"

He was on her before he realized what he was doing, on her with his hands tightening on her throat, on her and looking into her startled eyes as he shoved her back onto the bed. But then her claws were tearing across his face, and his testicle and guts seemed to explode in pain and nausea as her knee drove up, and he fell to the floor. When he looked up, the knife was back in her hand, and he knew she was ready to use it.

"Bitch," he sobbed, "you bitch! You—you goddamn—hellcat!"

"That's right, Duke," she said hoarsely, "hellcat! I am the goddamnedest hellcat you will ever meet, and from this night on, you had damn well better never forget it!"

When she appeared for supper, it was as if he were looking at a different woman, one he had forgotten had ever existed. She entered the dining room with a confident step, her head held high, and her cheeks seemed to have a fresh glow. Her gaze, as she sat down at the table, was once again firm, direct, and commanding.

"I take it," Duke said, "that you have decided to grace my board if not my bed."

"One must eat. But if you'd prefer me to have a tray in my room—"

"Of course not."

Fenella slouched into the dining room and thumped a platter of pork cutlets down on the table.

"Fenella," Cat said, "pick up that platter."

Fenella looked at her uncertainly.

"I said, pick up that platter."

Fenella picked up the platter.

"Now, put it down again, and this time do it properly. Put it down gently, evenly, and silently."

Fenella put the platter down as she had been told.

"That is how you will serve from now on. Do you understand?"

"Yes, ma'am."

"Good. You may leave now."

Fenella left the room.

Duke smiled. "I see you do know a thing or two about being a lady."

Cat gave him a long, level, unblinking gaze, as if considering her response.

"Duke, let us be clear. You are the one who aspires to the condition of the chivalry, not I. The truth is that, except in the most superficial way, you don't even know how to recognize a woman of the breed when you see one. Or to put the matter differently, my dear, you are still, and probably always will be, knocking at the door, while *I* have always dwelt within. A mere upstart tradesman does not gives lessons in quality to one who is to the manor born."

"God, I don't know why I married you."

"Don't be dull, my dear; we both know perfectly well. You married me because you thought I'd give you a passport to social acceptance. And I married you because I thought you were one hell of a man. And to give you all due credit, of the two of us, you were the more correct."

"I'm sorry I've disappointed you."

She gave him a brief smile. "We're both sorry."

"I have always tried to be a good husband to you. I have always tried to be the kind of gentleman a real lady would appreciate."

Cat laughed. "Oh, you have that, all right. And you know all the things a gentleman is supposed to do, don't you? Learn a little Latin and Greek and go to college. Gamble, dabble in politics, and fight duels, but only with other gentlemen. Own land. Marry well, but never burden his lady fair with his animal appetites. After all, God gave us the lower classes and the lesser races for that. And certainly a lady has little such appetite, or she is by definition not a lady at all, but a mere peasant wench. Isn't that right, Duke?"

Duke shrugged. "You're the one giving the lecture."

"Actually, Duke, I don't think you're any worse than a lot of other men. You all think that if you can just get certain things—a fine horse, a suit of armor, a lady's silk to wear on your helm—you will perforce become Sir Gawain. It never occurs to you that you're just little boys playing a game. You never realize that you'll never achieve Camelot if you don't look for it first in your heart. And even a poor nigger boy has been known to find it there, while the rest of you fine gentlemen search in vain."

"I didn't realize I had such an eloquent wife."

"Only because you've rarely listened to her." Cat started to take a bite of cutlet, hesitated, and put her fork down again. She stared at her plate. "And it's really too bad you didn't listen, isn't it? Because I think I might have been able to help you find what you're really looking for. You would have had to start by throwing away some of your silly rules, of course, but then the ones you kept would have come to mean something. You would have been Sir Gawain to me, whether the rest of the world knew who you were or not. It's just possible." She looked up at him. "But I don't suppose we'll ever know now, will we?"

For an instant he was seized by a huge doubt, a feeling that he might unwittingly be throwing away treasure. But that could not be true. He could not believe it. He had had a dream and he had been cheated out of it.

"No," he sighed, "I don't suppose we ever will."

"I don't seem to be hungry anymore. If you'll excuse me, Duke, I think I'd like to go to bed."

Duke didn't answer. Cat got up and left the room.

Whatever had become of happiness, he wondered, as he lay alone in his bed in the dark room. How had the dreams he had dreamed with Jessie in his arms gone so wrong? What had happened to the hopes and plans he had whispered into her ear?

His testicles still ached, and he couldn't sleep. It seemed to him he had lain awake for hours. He didn't really care

that Catherine had found out about Leonie and him—to
hell with Catherine, he thought; he had given up all hope
of finding happiness with her. But he had so much looked
forward to this homecoming, and to have it turn out so
badly . . .

Of course, it was his own fault. He could blame Leonie
for nothing. He had forgotten how badly hurt she had been
by his marriage to Catherine. He had assumed that a year's
separation would have been more than enough time to heal
her wounds. He had forgotten that she was a black woman
of dignity and pride, and in his eagerness for reconciliation
with her, he had allowed himself to be carried away. Hell,
he thought, maybe Catherine was right. Sometimes he *was*
a thoughtless, selfish bastard. He was man enough to admit
it.

But now, somehow he had to set things right.

Well, he could do it. He would start out by asking Leonie's forgiveness for the way he had behaved this evening.
He would make her understand that he had been carried
away by his feelings for her, feelings he could never have
for any other woman.

And then he would court her. Never again would he give
the appearance of trying to force himself on her. He would
ask her only to allow him to be in her presence, to listen to
his plans for Redbird and their people, and to accept those
small gifts he had always enjoyed giving her—a kerchief, a
bangle, a fancy sweet from Charleston. He would let her
see for herself the source of his unhappiness—and that his
only real happiness lay with her.

And then one evening, perhaps when Catherine was
away at Sabrehill, it would happen. Leonie, knowing he
belonged only to her, would come to him. And once again
they would ascend the stairs to his bed chamber.

It had to be. He could imagine no other happiness.

Sleep had never seemed more distant. He got up from
his bed and walked about the dark room. If only he could
talk to Leonie now. If only he could explain. He wouldn't
even touch her. He would tell her that he only wanted to
sit with her for a little while, to be in her presence. That he
wanted to tell her about London and Paris and Rome

and all the marvels and miseries of the past year. And that he wanted to hear what she had done and felt and thought while he had been away.

But when could he do it? Would he ever find a better time than now?

He looked out into the passage. No light showed beneath Cat's door.

Tomorrow he might never have a chance to speak to Leonie alone. His wife would be present, and Leonie would almost certainly avoid him. But tonight he could at least make a beginning, even if it consisted only of a few whispered words through her barely open door: *"Leonie, forgive me. I meant it when I said I love you. And I'll never again do anything that might hurt you."*

He would do it. He would go to her right now.

Quickly, he dressed in the dark and pulled on a coat against the night chill. Walking carefully, he managed to get down the stairs and out of the house without making a sound. Cat's window, as he had expected, was dark. The moon was low, and the old jailhouse, with its tall whipping gallows, seemed to crouch in waiting like something from an evil dream.

He walked past the jail toward the field quarters. The rows of neatly whitewashed cabins, pale as ghosts, seemed to be sleeping. Except for one cabin. A glimmer of light showed through a crack in a shuttered window.

It was Leonie's cabin.

He came to a halt. He stared at the sliver of light, wondering why she would still be awake at this hour, why wasting a candle.

As he walked on toward the door, his hands were suddenly damp, and he had a sick feeling in his guts. Faintly, he heard Leonie's muffled voice. She was not alone.

One of the other women might be with her, he thought, not for an instant believing it.

He heard another voice. A black male voice, soft and intimate.

His mind churned, trying to stave off the truth. That very day she had said that there was no one she had loved more than him. She had wept for their love, and he had held her in his arms and felt the longing in her body. Never in this world would she have been just any man's woman, and hadn't Mr. Ferguson told him that she still hadn't taken a husband?

Then who was with her, and why?

He put his ear against the door. He heard her laughing. Her companion said something and laughed with her.

He recognized the voice instantly. Catherine's favorite nigger boy. The one she called Damien. The one he had seen half-naked wrestling with her in the sloop.

And now he was with Leonie . . . in Leonie's bed . . . in Leonie's arms. She had told Duke there was someone else, but he hadn't believed her. And right now that boy was probably lying between her thighs, having her.

He sank to the ground by the door. No, this couldn't be, not when he had dreamed for so long of being with Leonie again. He had dreamed his way across Europe and back, he had dreamed his way across the sea. He had long ago lost Jessie to one treacherous nigger, he couldn't lose Leonie to another.

But he was losing her. He had lost her already. He covered his mouth, trying to stop the sounds that were coming from his throat.

His head against the door, he heard laughter again. Damien, laughing at him.

Well, he wouldn't laugh for long.

He felt the old anger coming to him in a hot crimson tide. Too much had been taken from him. Someone was going to pay. And this time his father was not here to stop him from collecting what was due.

He recalled the warning he had given Damien: *"I'll cut off your black nigger dong and make you eat your balls!"* Perhaps the time had come.

He stood up. His impulse was to charge into the cabin and take vengeance with his bare hands. But, no, he could do better than that.

First, however, he had to get help. Mr. Ferguson and a foreman or two should be enough. He turned away from the cabin and silently left the field quarters.

* * *

Damien!

Even before Cat heard the first scream, she knew he needed her. Somehow the sound of the whip had pierced her dreams, and she had felt his pain and his struggle not to cry out, and she called to him.

Damien!

Instantly awake, her eyes wide open, she threw herself to the edge of the bed.

Damien!

Then she heard the crack of the whip, distant but clear, followed by a scream that welled up like sheer animal agony. As she raced to the window, the whip cracked again, and again the scream tore through the night and seemed to lodge itself in her soul.

The single torch did little to hold back the darkness, but she could see the naked figure hanging spread-eagled on the whipping gallows, and she knew it was Damien. As he kicked one leg loose, Mr. Ferguson and a male slave grabbed it and resecured it to the post. A woman was clinging to Duke, trying to pull him away from the gallows, and he turned and gave her a shove that sent her sprawling. Then he raised the whip and sent it ripping across Damien's back again—and again that terrible scream tore through the night.

Cat knew at once what had happened. Duke had caught Damien with Leonie. And for that, Damien might die.

There was no time to be lost. Clad only in her cotton gown, she ran from the room and down the dark stairs. As she threw herself out the front door of the house, Damien's cries came to her like a voice from hell.

"Mr. Avery, the boy is bleeding." The overseer sounded frightened. "You can't cut up other people's property that way."

"The hell I can't."

To Cat's horror, Duke reversed the whip and brought the butt up in a hard blow between Damien's legs. Damien gave a final strangled cry, his head fell forward, and he hung limp from the overhead beam.

"Water," Duke said. "Throw a whole bucket on him. I'm not through with him yet."

As Duke raised the whip again, Cat seized his arm, and she saw the madness in his eyes.

"Duke, you can't—"

"Bitch! Let go of me, God damn you, or by God I'll have you up on this gallows beside him."

"No!"

She heard her gown tear, then Duke's free hand swept across her face, a searing, blinding blow that sent her flying backward. All the breath shot out of her lungs and her head seemed to explode as she slammed into the ground.

"Mr. Duke, please!"

As her head cleared, Cat saw Leonie throw herself at Duke, only to be thrown to the ground again and have that whip come down once, twice, three times across her buttocks as she screamed and tried futilely to crawl away.

"Hold them off of me, goddamnit!" Duke ordered. "Break their goddamn legs if you have to!"

And he turned once again to Damien.

How many lashes Duke gave him, she had no idea, but every blow seemed to tear into her own soul. She heard herself screaming Damien's name as she struggled to her feet. Then Mr. Ferguson grabbed her from behind, holding her and whispering into her ear.

"Please stay 'way from him, Miss Catherine. He's gone crazy, crazy, and he'll likely kill you too!"

"Then stop him! Stop him!"

Duke turned and grinned at her. "How do you like your nigger boy now, hellcat?"

Cat moaned.

Mr. Ferguson thrust her aside. "Mr. Avery, I'm begging you. You got no call to kill that boy. Now, please, let him down."

"I sent a boy for a carriage. I'll let him down when the carriage gets here."

"Then where the hell is that goddamn carriage? I'll whip that damn stableboy myself!"

The threat was enough to bring the wide-eyed stableboy and the horse and carriage into sight. Mr. Ferguson rushed to help bring Damien down from the gallows.

"Damien," Cat sobbed, trying to get to him, "Damien!"
But Duke's hard hand across her face drove her back.

Duke threw Damien into the carriage and climbed in
with him.

"I'm delivering this property to its owners, Mr. Ferguson," he said, "and I do thank you for your assistance."

Cat tried to climb into the carriage. She saw Duke raise
a big, booted foot. The boot shot out at her, catching her
squarely on the right side of the face, and as she fell, hot
blood rushed from her nose and mouth.

When she looked up from the ground, the carriage was
rolling away on the road from the big house courtyard.

"Damien!" she cried.

She rose to her feet and ran after the carriage.

"Damien!"

The carriage pulled farther away, but still she pursued it,
her tortured cry ringing out over the night-shrouded fields.

"Damien! . . . Damien! . . . Damien! . . ."

⫸ 5 ⫷

HOW LONG IT TOOK her to reach Sabrehill, she had no idea. When the carriage disappeared into the darkness ahead of her, she left the road and went the shortest way, crossing fields, wading streams, running through woods. Her bare feet were soon cut, bruised, and bleeding. The right side of her face was so swollen she could hardly see from the eye, and the taste of blood was always on her tongue. Her throat ached from crying Damien's name. Tree branches and brushwood lashed at her face and body and tore at her gown until she was half naked, but still she kept running through the night, running toward Sabrehill.

At last she forded the final stream and broke through the final patch of woods. She stumbled through the kitchen garden and past the seed house toward the courtyard. The big house, the kitchen house, the office, all was in darkness. As she staggered toward the big house, she saw something lying near the door.

It was Damien.

At first she was certain he was dead. Weeping, she fell to her knees beside him. She sat, and drew his head into her lap. Then she threw back her own head and began screaming his name again, as if somehow she could call him back to her.

A few minutes later they found her there, her arms still around Damien, still weeping and calling his name.

And now it was his turn, Duke thought. He would take no more threats, no more sneers, no more defiance from Catherine Anne Avery. Redbird plantation and everything on it, including her, was his, and she would never again be allowed to forget it. He hadn't yet decided how he would punish her for her rebellion, but he would find a way. And as for Leonie . . .

296

He couldn't believe she was entirely lost to him. He couldn't give her up as he had given up Jessie. But could anything ever be quite the same between them?

He took his time returning to Redbird, and there was a hint of dawn in the sky when he got there. Leaving the horse and carriage with a sleepy stableboy, he entered the dark house. When he called Catherine's name, she didn't answer, so he went upstairs. She was in neither the bedroom he had chosen for them nor the one she had taken for herself. He looked about the latter, wondering . . .

When he went back downstairs and outside, he found the overseer approaching the house.

"Mr. Ferguson, have you seen Mrs. Avery?"

Mr. Ferguson came to a halt and stared at him, stony-eyed. "The last I seen of Mrs. Avery, she was chasing after you. Far as I know, she never come back."

"I see." She had probably gone to Sabrehill, then. Well, he would go after her later. Meanwhile, he wanted to talk to Leonie. "All right, thank you, Mr. Ferguson."

But the overseer wasn't ready to be dismissed. "Mr. Avery, I just want to tell you . . ."

"Yes, Mr. Ferguson?"

"Well, I just want to tell you I never seen a nigger whipped like that before in my life."

"Let's hope you never have to see it again."

"I don't like whips, I don't believe in them, and you know I don't let my foremen carry them. My people don't get whipped if I can help it, Mr. Avery, and . . ." The overseer's voice shook. "I'm just telling you it ain't gonna happen again as long as I'm in charge."

"That boy wasn't one of your people, Mr. Ferguson. It was a personal matter."

"Then you had no right to drag me into it."

"You're right. I didn't. I apologize. Do you want to quit?"

The overseer looked at the ground and clenched his fists a couple of times. "No. I need the work. And besides, if you'll excuse me saying so, Mr. Avery, when a master has got a temper like yours, his people need an overseer like me."

Mr. Ferguson turned and walked off quickly, as if fearful of saying more than he should.

Duke continued on toward the field quarters. This time he was going to say what he had to say to Leonie, and she was going to listen to him. He was determined to win her back, no matter what or how long it might take.

The door of her cabin stood open.

He whispered her name and stepped inside. There was no light now, no lamp or candle.

And no Leonie.

Nothing much hung on the wallpegs, only an old apron. The drawers of the much-repaired old chest were open and mostly empty.

She was gone, he realized, as he sank down on the edge of the stripped bed. She had bundled up all she could carry and had left him. She had run away.

Well, she couldn't have gotten far in such a short time. He would get a slave catcher with some hounds and put them on her trail. He'd have her back in a day or two.

Then why did he have this feeling that he would never see her again?

He drifted in and out of consciousness. He was aware of being led and half-carried into his house and being laid facedown on his bed. He heard the voices of Miss Lucy and Momma Lucinda, and he heard Cat sobbing his name: "Damien . . . Damien . . ." When he opened his eyes, the lamplight blinded him for an instant, and then he saw that Cat was kneeling by his bed. The right side of her face was purple and swollen, the eye almost shut, and blood had run down her face onto her torn gown and bare breasts. He forced himself to speak. "Cat . . . what . . . he do to you?" Oddly, she smiled. "Never mind," she said, stroking his head. "You're home now. We're both back home." He closed his eyes and slipped back into darkness.

The next time he awakened, it was to the touch of Momma Lucinda's hands on his back and the sound of her voice as she whispered comforting words. "You're gonna be all right, now, boy. Momma Lucinda is here to help you. You're gonna be all right." Her hands were like fire as they spread her unguents over his cuts and welts, yet at the same time they were deeply comforting.

He opened his eyes. Cat was sitting in a nearby chair. She was cleaned up and dressed now, but the right side of her face still looked awful—like a piece of battered eggplant.

"Well, about time," she said through swollen lips. "I asked my momma, 'Are you going to let that boy lazy away the whole day?'"

He asked again: "What did he do to you?"

"Oh, nothing much. I just got careless and ran into his oncoming bootheel. I'll be all right in a few days, and so will you."

"You ain't cut too bad," Momma Lucinda said. "That man was whipping you more for hurting than for cuts, and may the good Lord forgive him, 'cause I can't."

"You mustn't go back to him, Cat."

"No, I'm not going back to him. Mr. Duke Avery and I are finished."

Damien closed his eyes. He felt Momma Lucinda's hands leave his back and draw a blanket up over him. "Sleep, boy," she whispered. "Sleep is the best thing you can do."

Once again, Damien drifted into sleep.

Cat folded her arms over her chest and looked at him, unmoving. Momma Lucinda went to the bedroom door.

"You coming?"

Cat shook her head. "I'm going to look after him. You just tell me what to do, Momma Lucinda, and I'll do it. Everything."

Momma Lucinda frowned. "Now, you and a young buck like that, I ain't sure it's proper—"

"Momma Lucinda, I remember when I was seven years old and first saw Damien. I took one look at him and said, 'He's mine!' I've been looking after him ever since, and he's been looking after me, and that's not going to stop until the day he leaves Sabrehill. So you just tell me what to do."

The frown left Momma Lucinda's face. She laughed and shook her head. "I 'member your Aunt Dulcy saying the same thing 'bout Mr. Jeb, all them years back when Mr.

Turnage near killed him. Almost the same words. And I 'member Miss Lucy saying them 'bout Mr. Justin. Can't nobody say the Sabre ladies don't take care of their own people, black and white. And I'll bet your Momma Rosellen was something special too."

Cat nodded. "Yes, she was, near as I remember. Very special."

Momma Lucinda left. Cat remained sitting where she was.

Twenty minutes later, Duke Avery arrived at Sabrehill.

From where Cat was sitting, she could see through the little house out into the circular courtyard. She happened to glance that way when Duke, in a carriage, came driving around the far side of the circle. She got up and walked out onto the little veranda. When Duke saw her, he continued around the circle and reined up in front of the house.

He got out of the carriage and started toward her, then came to a sudden halt, his eyes widening.

"What's the matter, Duke?" she asked, turning the right side of her face to him and drawing her hair back from it. "Don't you like the sight of your own bootprint?"

"My God, Catherine, I never meant . . . Catherine, believe me—"

She didn't know if it was anger or disgust she felt. "Catherine, Catherine, always Catherine—who the hell do you think you are, my father? My name is Cat Sabre. What's the matter, can't you say it?"

He came toward her. "Catherine—Cat—I've come to take you home."

"I am home, Mr. Avery. Home to stay."

"Now, Catherine, I'm sorry about what's happened. But I'm still your husband—"

"As far as I'm concerned, you severed that relationship last night."

"We'll talk about it on our way home."

"No!"

She pulled her arm away as he reached for it, but then he had her wrist and was dragging her down from the porch, and she saw his eyes heat with anger.

"I said, you are coming home, Catherine."

"And I say, you can go to goddamn hell!"

A third voice spoke, almost unrecognizable in its fury. "And I say, you take your hands off my daughter, Leduc Avery."

Looking around, Cat saw that her mother had come out of the office and was advancing on them with a six-barrel pepperbox pistol held before her in both hands.

Her mother came to a halt ten feet away from them, and Cat realized that in her anger Lucy Sabre might almost be an older mirror-image of herself. The hair was blonder, and the eyes were pure blue fire instead of green, but her lips were drawn far back, her breath hissed between her teeth, and her entire body shook with the strength of her fury.

"You get back in your carriage right now, Mr. Avery, and you ride out of here. And if you ever dare lay your hands on my daughter again, I swear to God I'll blow your guts out."

Duke's hand tightened on Cat's wrist. He smiled faintly. "Now, you know you're not going to use that pistol, Miss Lucy."

"You think I won't? You take one look at my daughter's face and see if you dare to think I won't. In fact . . ." Lucy Sabre's blue eyes widened. "You bastard, I think I may just shoot you anyway."

The pistol steadied as she took aim.

Cat spoke very softly, very carefully. "She means it, Duke. In about one minute, my momma is going to kill you."

Duke was very still. After a few seconds, his fingers slipped from Cat's wrist. His smile faded. He leaned away from Cat. Slowly he turned away from her. He climbed into his carriage. He shook the reins. He rode away without looking back.

Her mother began to cry.

Cat began to laugh.

Her mother threw her arms around Cat and began to laugh with her.

Still embracing, laughing and crying together, they walked back toward the office.

"Anybody ever tell you you have a pretty butt, Damien?" she asked one morning.

"Oh, Cat!"

"Well, you do," she said, giving his bottom a little slap, but avoiding the cuts and welts. "I've seen half the statuary in Europe, and I've never seen a prettier ass than yours."

"Jesus!"

She was the first person he saw in the morning and the last at night. She brought him his meals, and on the first day, when he still couldn't sit up, she fed him. She spread Momma Lucinda's soothing ointment over his back, slowly rubbing it in from his shoulders to his thighs, and after his first embarrassment, he enjoyed the touch of those gently kneading fingers. She brought him his chamberpot, teased him at first by refusing to leave the room, and then emptied the pot for him. Later, when he could walk without too much difficulty, she put a nightshirt and a robe on him, and helped him get to the "necessary house" and back. It was at the end of one of these trips, while he was still leaning on her shoulder, that he realized her bruised cheek was fading to saffron and would soon be well. Impulsively, he drew her to him and kissed the cheek. "Oh, I like that," she said, wiggling against him, "do it some more."

Didn't he know then what might happen? What in their secret selves they both wanted to happen?

That evening after supper, she ordered him to get back into bed, facedown as usual, so that she could rub the ointment into his back.

"Oh, Cat," he said as he stretched out and pulled the blanket up to his waist, "I am so tired of lying on my belly. If I don't lie on my back again soon, I'll go crazy."

"It won't be long."

He helped her work his nightshirt up to his shoulders, and she took it off of him, saying she would get him a fresh one. She sat down beside him on the bed, and he closed his eyes and felt the glow of the lamp against his eyelids. After a moment, he felt the chill plash of the ointment on his shoulders, followed by the warmth of Cat's hands, and he sighed and relaxed.

She laughed. "You really like this, don't you?"

"Oh, yes."

"Well, tonight we'll make it real nice for you."

It was very nice indeed, he thought, as her hands worked over his shoulders and down over his back. There was still an ache in the deep-bruised muscles and a hint of pain in the cuts, but somehow her hands transformed the ache and the pain into a kind of pleasure, and he moaned his delight in it.

"You like this?" she asked again, working her hands up his sides to his armpits.

"Oh, yes, yes."

"Then what about this?"

She slipped her hands between his chest and the bed and, flexing her fingers, slowly worked them down his body until they were probing his belly. A muscle fluttered, and he laughed.

"What's the matter?"

"Nothing. It tickles."

She withdrew her hands and pulled the blanket down. He felt a trickle of ointment on his buttocks and thighs and then her hands again.

"I've said it before, Damien, and it's still true. You have a beautiful backside."

"Cat, if your momma knew you were massaging my tail—"

"If she asks, I'll tell her. Meanwhile, your tail belongs to me, and I've loved it since I was a little girl."

A hand slipped between his thighs, and he felt the swift stab of desire. The hand moved up, stroking him lightly, and his flesh suddenly hardened. He groaned.

"Anything wrong?"

"No."

Those hands kept on working on him, still higher and, Jesus, didn't she know what she was doing to him?

She paused, one hand resting right where it was, idly scratching him.

"Had enough?"

"I could never have enough. But I don't think I could take much more."

She laughed, gave his rump another little slap, and got up from the bed. "I'll get you a clean nightshirt."

He felt he couldn't bear to remain lying face down another hour, especially not in his present condition, so he took advantage of her departure to the front room to turn over onto his back, moving very carefully, and he pulled up the blanket, tenting it over his raised knees. He had just managed to cover himself when she returned.

"Why, you're on your back!"

"Cat, I just couldn't stand to lie on my belly any longer."

Slowly a grin came to her face. "Why have you got your knees up like that?" she asked, putting the folded nightshirt on the nearby table.

"Just being comfortable."

Suddenly, before he had the slightest inkling of what she was about to do, she whipped the blanket down, dropped onto the bed at his side, and—

"Cat!"

—grabbed his rigid prong.

"Careful, Damien, don't move, it might break off!"

"Cat, please," he said in horror at the thought that she might really damage him, "please, let go!"

"I just want to look at him. My, he's grown since I last saw him! Fine, upstanding little feller now, isn't he?"

"Cat, you're hurting me!"

"No, I'm not. You want to know something? Yours isn't as big as Duke's, but I'll bet it's a lot prettier. Duke's is maybe an inch or two longer and a *lot* thicker—at least that's the way it feels in the dark. But that's all he's got—just a big, dumb old pizzle."

Damien was suddenly distracted from his fears. "You mean to tell me you've never even seen his?"

"Nope. He only wants to do it under the covers in the dark with our nightclothes on. And pretty damn seldom even that way."

"Lord-a-mighty! Don't you have any fun?"

She wiggle-waggled his penis and drew at the foreskin.
"Nope."

He sighed. "Cat, I wish you wouldn't do that."

"Doesn't it feel good?"

"Of course it feels good!" he said miserably.

"You used to let me do it."

Misery turned to indignation. "Oh, Cat, we were hardly
more than babies then!"

"I can remember the very last time I saw this little
fellow. I couldn't have been more than ten or eleven years
old. He got hard then too, and for the first time he sort of
scared me, and we never went skinny-dipping together
again. We're going to have to remedy that."

He threw a forearm back over his eyes. "Oh, Cat, Cat,
Cat, Cat . . ."

"Kind of enjoying yourself now, aren't you?"

" . . . Yes."

She laughed. "Damien, how many women have you
been with?"

Once, even knowing he couldn't fool her, he would have
lied, and bragged about his many conquests. Now he could
only tell the truth.

"One. And her not often."

"Leonie."

He nodded.

"I guess we're both practically virgins." She played with
him for a minute. "Damien, what does a man like?"

"What do you mean?"

"You know what I mean. Making love. Pleasuring.
What does a man like?"

"I don't know. About the same things a woman likes, I
reckon."

"Sometimes I think I hardly even know that. Does a
man like this?"

He felt her light kiss drifting over his face, her tongue
barely touching his mouth, his ear, his throat.

"This, Damien?"

"Mm-hm."

The kiss drifted on, and her lips and tongue played with
a nipple.

"This?"

"Mm-hm."

. . . And on and on, while his flesh trembled, and she never ceased fondling him, and he felt her hot breath and the flickering of her tongue, until he thought he could stand no more, and he opened his eyes and thrust her away.

She lifted her head and looked at him with drugged eyes.

"Wait a minute."

While she left the room, he covered his eyes again and tried desperately to calm himself. He heard her return, and after a moment the rustle of clothing. When he looked again, her dress was off and, her back to him, she was slipping out of her drawers.

"Cat," he said, aghast, "what are you doing!"

"What does it look like I'm doing? I'm getting naked with you."

"But if anyone caught us—"

"No one will. I fixed the door, and the windows are covered."

"But . . ."

He broke off as she stepped out of her drawers and turned toward him. The sheer loveliness of her pink-nippled breasts, the tapering to her waist and the swell of her hips, the long, graceful thighs cut through his fear, and he looked at her with awe. He raised up on an elbow as, her eyes now bright with excitement, she walked to him and put a knee up on the bed.

"Do you like me?"

"You're beautiful."

Guiding his hand to her breast, she leaned down and kissed him on the mouth. Then she slid onto the bed beside him, lying on her back. Her eyes narrowed, and a little smile played on her lips.

"Now," she said, "my turn. Be nice to me."

He was as nice to her as he knew how to be, considering his inexperience. Assuming that she had given him more or less what she wished to receive, he followed her lead, and when he found that he was pleasing her, he grew even bolder than she had been. Such was his success that, whooping with joy, her heels pounding into the mattress, she very nearly knocked him off the bed.

His fear returned, however, when after some twenty minutes she asked him to couple with her. "Aw, Cat, we shouldn't!"

"Just for a minute or two," she said, laughing a little crazily, "and you don't even have to finish if you don't want to. But I never had his in me for more'n about fifteen seconds, and I want to find out what it's like."

"But Cat—"

She insisted. Sitting up, she straddled his hips and, before he could stop her, guided him into her vagina and settled on him. She brought the palms of his hands to her breasts and leaned forward against them. Her eyes were nearly closed, and her lips were full and heavy with desire, and he tried to concentrate on how beautiful she was, rather than on his own sensations.

"Damien," she said, her voice little more than a murmur, "I need you tonight. God, how I need you, and how *long* I've needed you. But I want you to know, and never forget, I'm not doing this only because of the need. I'm doing it because I love you. I may never tell you again, but I love you as I'll probably never love any other man."

Then she began, and somehow he stayed with her, even through the height of her frenzy. At last she slowed, and sighed, and threw herself off him to lie at his side. After a few minutes, her hand slid over his belly to grasp his still-erect penis.

"Poor little fellow," she said lazily. "Leila says that when he doesn't get his satisfaction, it can hurt something awful. You better bring him back here again and get his satisfaction."

He had no more resistance. He rolled over her spread thighs. She raised her thighs to his waist, and he thrust back home again. Still hazy-eyed, she grinned up at him, clamped hard around his man-part, and started moving her hips. And he got his satisfaction as never before in his life.

* * *

Afterward, he dozed a little, that being in the nature of the human male, as he pointed out to Cat, and not a reflection on her charms. He heard her pottering about his room, and eventually smelled burning tobacco. When he opened his eyes, Cat was sitting on the edge of the bed, back in her dress, though her other clothes were still on the floor, and she was puffing on his old seldom-used corncob pipe.

"Well, that was fun," she said. "What do we do next?"

Damien laughed.

"It's a funny thing, Damien. I knew I was missing something, and I had some idea of what it was, because between them, my mother and Momma Lucinda and Leila told me just about everything. But some things are hard to describe. And I guess loving is sort of like a foreign country. You can listen to all the travelers that come your way, but you'll never really know what it's like until you've been there."

"And now you've been there."

"I certainly have." She sighed. "But I surely didn't expect to make the trip tonight. I didn't even have my sponge in. Be funny if I got knocked up the very first time we did it, wouldn't it?"

"I can hear the laughter." At the moment, Damien was feeling too good to worry about it.

"Oh, well. Papa can always send us north to live with Jebediah and Aunt Dulcy. Our own little colony of happy niggers." She reached over and tickled his shriveled penis. "Cute little thing. Why haven't you washed him yet?"

"It's only us on him. Why should I?"

"I don't know. All I know is that, whenever Duke did it to me, and I hoped to be hugged and pleasured some more, he could just hardly wait to hop out of bed and wash his dong. Like I'd dirtied it up for him somehow."

"Well, truth to tell, Cat, it does feel kind of sticky."

"If that bothered my sweet loving man all that much, I'd be glad to lick it clean for him, just so he could stay in bed with me."

Damien laughed some more. "Thanks, but you needn't bother."

Then, as she fondled him, something wonderful happened. Like Damien himself, the little fellow seemed to wake up. He began to stretch and grow, as if to stand up and take a fresh interest in life.

"Oh, my God!" Cat said in surprise. And then in delight: "Oh, my *Go-o-od*!"

She tossed down the pipe, whipped off her dress, and crooning with pleasure, threw herself back into the bed with him.

It was two weeks after Cat ran off to Sabrehill that Duke finally learned the truth about her. Since that first day, he had made two more trips there and quietly tried to persuade her to return home. Now he would never ask her again.

He learned the truth from old Fenella, the sullen, vindictive sometime cook. A couple of times she had asked if "Miz Catherine coming home from her visit soon?" as if she knew more about that visit than Duke did. The third time she asked, at breakfast that morning, he said, exasperated, "All right, Fenella, out with it. What have you heard about Miss Catherine's visit to Sabrehill?"

Fenella shrugged her shoulders elaborately and muttered. "Why, I ain't heard nothing." Of course she and every other black for miles around knew that Catherine had run off in the middle of the night after he had whipped the nigger boy.

"Fenella, I want to know."

"Ain't gonna get whipped for spreading no fool darky tales."

"You're more likely to get whipped for not telling me, and you'd better, right now."

Fenella shrugged again in her massive, lazy way. "Well, all they say is, she spend a awful lot of time in that Damien boy's cabin."

His heart quickened. "That's all they say?"

"They say she's in there night and day. And him all well now, and the windows closed and the door . . . locked."

She looked at him sideways, and he saw the malicious gleam in her bloodshot eye.

"They say that, do they? What else do they say?"

"I don't want to get in no trouble—"

"Fenella!"

"They say her and that nigger boy go off all day long together. He don't hardly do no work no more. They say . . ."

"Yes?"

She looked at him carefully, looked down at the floor again. He could see her calculating how far she dared to go. He had commanded her to speak, but she was, after all, saying these things about her master's wife.

"They say the things she doing with that boy, she ain't no better than Miss Dulcy was."

The blood pounded in his ears.

"That'll be all, Fenella," he said softly. He pointed out the window. "And if I hear of your spreading these tales, I'll have you up on that whipping gallows."

Fenella hurried off.

He thought of Dulcy Sabre and Jebediah in the dressing room in the Broadway Theater: that glimpse of lovely nakedness and the sense of the intimacy between the two. He had asked questions since his return to Redbird, and, yes, there had been stories about Dulcy and Jebediah.

And now Catherine Anne Avery, his wife, had followed the same path.

Often in the previous two weeks he had thought of his last conversation with Catherine at the supper table. He had remembered the huge doubt that had assailed him, the feeling that perhaps he was totally wrong, had somehow made a terrible mistake, did not even know how the world and Cat Sabre really worked.

Now he knew he was right, had always been right.

There had been no way to hide the disgraceful fact that his wife had left him—had run off in the middle of the night because he had whipped a slave who was particularly dear to her. The blacks had quickly carried the story to every family and every plantation around. Similarly, there would probably be no stopping the rumor that she had taken a slave as a lover—that he, Duke Avery, had a nigger-fucking wife. Perhaps everyone knew already.

All he had most wanted to achieve, had virtually had in his hand, was being taken from him.

But he wasn't beaten yet. He would show them. One way or another, he would have their respect, even if he was giving less of a damn for it every day. And in the process he would have his revenge on the whole damn Sabre clan, Catherine Anne and all the rest of them.

But why hadn't his plans worked out before now? He was tired of waiting. He might have to take further steps. In any case, he decided, it was time for him to return to Charleston.

She thought of those weeks as the honeymoon she had never had. "Momma Lucinda says most people make love more in the first month they're married than any month after, and more in the first year than all the rest of their lives," she told him one afternoon as she lay in his arms. They were in the *Celandine*, drifting lazily downstream. "And she says that no matter how many husbands a woman has, it's likely she'll have that kind of month only once in a lifetime. But that doesn't matter, she may not even want it again, as long as she has it once. Because if that month is truly good, it becomes part of her, something she can carry with her and treasure for the rest of her life. And that's what I feel cheated out of, Damien. I want to have that first month that Duke never gave me. In fact, after what he did to me in the last year, I feel like if I don't get my month, I'll go crazy."

"I wish you wouldn't talk about him so much, Cat."

"I'm sorry. I can't help it. It's like he was a sickness in me, and I can't be rid of him till I talk him out. So please let me talk some more, Damien, and then I'll never mention his name again."

"All right," he said, sweeping his hand up her thigh and raising her skirt, "but I know one way to take your mind off him."

She tugged at his belt. "Oh, yes, you do!"

She knew they had to be careful. As Damien's back

healed, it became less permissible for her to spend long
hours alone with him in his house. Still, they always found
ways to be together—floating in the *Celandine,* stopping at
favorite islands, visiting remote groves, even meeting in his
house late at night, long after the rest of Sabrehill was
asleep.

It seemed to Cat that she was compelled to explore and
experience sex as she might never have done if it hadn't
been for Duke. Years of waiting for something wonderful
to happen, followed by fifteen months of profound disappointment—a disappointment that itself suggested some
tantalizing and mysterious possibility that always eluded
her—had produced a hunger that was almost insatiable.
She lived to make love. She wanted to experience every act
and emotion associated with love. She wanted to make love
on her back, astraddle her lover, standing up, on her knees,
in every imaginable way. One afternoon she would want to
give herself to Damien in the profoundest way, entering
into his very soul. The next, she might prefer to treat him
as a mere amusing sexual toy and to have him treat her the
same.

The fact that she spent so much time with Damien could
hardly be hidden, and she saw the thought that had come
to her mother's mind, the worry that lodged in her eyes.

"Oh, I wish your father would get home!"

Her father was still in Virginia, along with Zagreus and
Binnie, and for the time being Cat was content that he
should remain there. She wanted nothing to interfere with
her love for Damien.

Leila was the first person to speak to her about Damien.
It happened one morning while Cat was waiting for him in
a flower garden gazebo.

"Miss Cat, child, I don't want to interfere in something
that ain't none of my business, but are you fixing to run off
with that boy again?"

"Why—we were only going for a sail."

Leila looked at her gravely. "You mean disappear with
him for hours at a time, and not even the children with
you?"

For the first time, Cat began to worry. "Has anyone been talking?"

"Not yet. Not that I know of. But, honey, your Leila ain't the only one with eyes to see."

Cat tried to shrug the matter off. "Leila, it's only Damien. He's always been my own servant, in a way—"

"Honey, don't say that to Leila. I think I know what you been going through, God love you, and I'm just saying, please, be more careful. For that boy's sake, as much as your own."

All right, she would try to be more careful, for Damien's sake. But it was difficult when she was having so much pleasure, so much tenderness, so much love, so much sheer good fun.

" 'Once more unto the breach, dear friend!' " she said that same day, as she lay naked in Damien's arms on one of their favorite islands. " 'Once more!' "

"But Cat," Damien wailed, "I can't! Not again!"

"Oh, yes you can," she said, her deft fingers arousing him. "Observe our little grenadier! Ready for man's work!"

"But that doesn't mean—"

"It means 'The game's afoot! / Follow your spirit! And upon this charge / Cry "God for Catherine, England, and Saint George!" ' "

Somehow, by dint of mighty effort, Damien produced the desired results for both of them, and afterward she gave him all the tenderness she could find in her soul.

By early November, her mother could no longer refrain from speaking to her about Damien. Cat saw the moment coming and, since it was inevitable, did nothing to avoid it. It came late one evening while she was wondering if there were any way she could safely steal another hour with Damien. Her mother called her into the north parlor.

"Catherine, there is something I must ask you." Her tone was soft, almost pleading. "Perhaps I should have asked you before. It's about you and Damien."

Cat had already considered how she would answer. Quietly but firmly, she said, "Momma, ask me no questions, and I'll tell you no lies."

For a moment her mother stood perfectly still. Then her hands flew to her mouth. "Oh, my God!"

"Before you pass judgment on me, Momma," Cat went on in the same tone, "think about Papa and you when you first met—and some of the stories I've heard."

"Darling, I am not passing judgment on you. But I am so frightened for you. And for Damien. Oh, Catherine, how could you do such a dangerous thing?"

Cat smiled. "Now, what have we done that's so dangerous? Spent a few hours together? Shall I tell you about those hours, Momma?"

"Only what you wish to tell me."

"Think about a time when you thought a part of your very soul had been lost or destroyed, and then you found it given back to you. Given back and even enriched."

". . . I see."

"And for that, even though we both know we must part, I shall always love Damien."

"Then I must always love him, too."

Cat started for the door, then paused. "One thing."

"Yes?"

"It's up to you, of course, but I wish you wouldn't mention any of this to Papa. It's my own affair, mine and Damien's. Maybe someday I'll tell Papa."

Her mother closed her eyes. She was still deathly pale, her voice faint. "I understand, dear."

Cat started out the door. Behind her, she heard her mother say, "I love you, Katie Anne."

"I love you, Momma."

"They're home," Leila's happy voice rang out. "Mr. Justin and Zagreus and Binnie, they're home!"

She entered the passage just as Cat came out from the parlor.

"They are? Where are they? Momma, did you hear?"

"They're coming up the avenue right now."

All worry and unhappiness had been swept from her mother's face when she joined them. "How can you tell it's them in the dark?"

"Why, Miss Lucy, I'd know that carriage anywhere. And you can see Binnie's white face plain as day! Come on out."

They followed Leila out into the courtyard just as the carriage came to the circle, and Binnie's face, as light as Cat's, was easily seen. Zagreus drove around the circle and reined up before them. There was no third passenger.

"Why—welcome home," her mother said, her smile vanishing, "but where is Mr. Justin?"

"Stayed on in Charleston, Miss Lucy." Zagreus climbed wearily down from the carriage. "He sent us on ahead. Said he didn't want you to hear the news from no strangers."

"News?" Cat said. "What news?"

"'Bout Jebediah. They got him back here. He's in Charleston right now."

"But how could he be?"

"In chains, Miss Cat. In chains."

--◈{ FIVE }◈--

THE FURIES

HE HAD IGNORED HIS friends' warnings and been careless once too often. Perhaps he had dodged so many sticks and stones, had fought off so many attacks, that he felt invincible. They taught him that he was wrong.

They took him at dusk on the Boston Common, near Park Street. Jebediah was thinking about the lecture he was to give that evening at Faneuil Hall, when he realized that, although he seemed to be walking alone, there was an odd coordination among the shadowy figures around him: It was as if their movements had been planned and practiced.

Instantly, he knew what was going to happen, even knew why there was a carriage waiting on Park Street, the driver looking his way. He stopped dead and raised his arms to beat off his attackers, but it was too late. An arm came around his neck from behind, a hip drove into the small of his back, and both of his arms were seized. Roaring his defiance, he struggled to stay on his feet and throw his captors off, but he felt himself being born backward. Another figure appeared in front of him, and a hand slammed a thick wad of cloth over his face, smothering his cries. The smell of the cloth was so hideously vile that he couldn't breathe. Sulphuric ether, he thought. He had never smelled it before, but he had heard of it and knew what it could do to a man, and somehow he knew that this could be nothing else.

Then he had to breathe, and the vile odor, like a poison, rushed into his lungs, sickening him. He tried to blow it out, to be rid of it, but he couldn't, couldn't get his face away from that wad of cloth, couldn't help inhaling again.

His head swam. The world faded. He fell into darkness.

He came out of a strange welter of frightening dreams to find himself lying on a wooden floor. He could see

319

nothing. His head pounded, the vile odor was still in his nostrils, and his mouth was bitter and dry. He allowed himself to slip back into merciful sleep for as long as possible, but was awakened when his stomach heaved and hot liquid shot out of his throat.

The floor seemed faintly aslant. He felt it lift slightly, and he heard distant creaking, straining sounds. He lay still, and wept, and sought sleep again.

The sharp crack of an overhead hatch being flung open awakened him, and he looked up into the blinding glare of a lantern.

"Jesus," a Yankee voice said, "it stinks in here."

"No wonder," said another. "Your damn nigger has puked all over hisself. Looks like he's soaked through."

"Well, at least he's alive," said a southern voice. "Christ, he was out so long I thought he was gonna croak."

"No, not a big strong fellow like Mr. Jeb," said the first voice. "How are you, Jebediah? Feeling better now?"

Jebediah stared into the light. He said nothing.

"Say, listen," the first voice continued, "we can't let the poor bastard lie around in his own puke like that. Can you get some clean clothes for him?"

"For a price," the second voice said. "And he's got to clean up that mess he made."

"Oh, sure, he'll do that. And—Jebediah? Anything you want?"

"Water." Jebediah had to force the word out through his painfully constricted throat. "Water to drink."

"Water—of course! We'll get you some fresh water to drink, and you'll need water to swab yourself and this place up with. Get you some food, too, any time you're ready for it. Anything else?"

"Why have you done this?"

There was some laughter, and the southerner said, "Oh, shee-it!" The first Yankee spoke again.

"Well, you might say we're just doing it for the hell of it, Jebediah. For the challenge. People are always talking about stealing you abolition-preachers south and making you pay for your sins, but they never take back anybody important. Now, you, you're Jebediah Hayes, author, lecturer, self-appointed Black Wrath of God. Hell, you've got a name that's known all the way 'round the world."

"And when we put you back in the fields where you belong, boy," the southern voice said, "that is going to be something for the world to see."

"You intend to humiliate me and my race."

"Oh, don't take it hard, Jebediah," the northerner said. "Just think of it as material for a new book."

"If he ever gets to write one."

"Aw, now, don't you go trying to frighten Jebediah. He isn't going to come to any harm if we can help it."

"Who are you?"

"You'll never know. Just some old school chums—"

"That's enough," said the southern voice. "Nigger, you're going home. Just be thankful you're still alive."

The lamp vanished, and the hatch slammed down.

Jebediah sat on the starboard deck, his back against the cabin wall, and shivered. He could hardly squeeze into the ragged old pants and shirt they had given him, and the jacket did little to stop the wind that swept off the cold gray waves.

"So you're taking me home," he said. "Does that mean this ship is putting in at Charleston? Georgetown? Or Beaufort perhaps?"

The southerner was seated on Jebediah's right. Jebediah had carefully memorized his features: mid-thirties, thick dark-blond hair and mustache, slate-gray eyes as cold as the sea. He seldom smiled or spoke, and he did neither now.

"I am curious as to why you think you can do this and go unpunished. There are laws against kidnapping, you know."

Still, the man said nothing, but merely stared toward the unseen shoreline.

"I suppose," Jebediah went on, "it is most probable that the ship will put in at Charleston. The sheriff will then come aboard to seize and jail any Negro seamen until the ship departs. I shall identify myself to him and be sent north. And you, if you don't get away very quickly, will be jailed—both for kidnapping and for illegally bringing a black man into the state. Does that sound accurate?"

"Mr. Will, nigger. Or sir."

"Does that sound accurate, Mr. Will, sir?"

"Sounds like we could be in a heap of trouble and you haven't got a thing to worry about."

Jebediah knew better, however confident his own words might be. He had reason to worry, both at being transported back to South Carolina and in being in the hands of men such as these.

"How many people are with you in this, Mr. Will, sir? The captain of this ship, of course. But who else? Who had the idea? Who is paying the bills?"

As Jebediah spoke, his other captor approached and sat down on his left. He also was in his mid-thirties. He had hazel-green eyes and curly black hair already flecked with gray, and was clean-shaven.

"God," he said, grinning, "I sure get tired of this wind, even if we do need it to get there."

"Get where?"

"Charleston."

"Shut up, Frank."

"Hell, he knows where we're taking him."

"Nigger's been asking a heap of questions."

"Well, why not answer them, as long as he's going to find out anyway?"

"South Carolina," Jebediah said, "won't allow me to remain in the state."

"Well, then," Will said in a hard voice, "I reckon your owner will just have to sell you *out* of the state, won't he?"

Owner?

Frank was laughing. "Now who's telling him more than he's supposed to know?"

Jebediah thought of the various owners he had had before leaving the South. Pinkham. Osborn. Wingate. Briefly, Leduc Avery. Sabre.

Leduc Avery.

Any of hundreds, even thousands, of men might hate

him enough to arrange for his kidnapping. But surely none
of them hated him as much as Duke Avery.

"Are you working for Mr. Duke Avery?"

"Never heard of him," Will said.

"Aren't really working *for* anybody, except ourselves,"
Frank said. "Anyway, it's a surprise."

Duke Avery. Surely it could be no one else.

"Hey, Jebediah!" Frank gave him a friendly slap on the
knee. "Hell, I know this isn't any fun for you, but nothing
so bad is going to happen. Before long, the whole damn
world is going to know what's happened to you and exactly
where you are. And do you think your friends aren't going
to do something about it? All those crowned heads of
Europe you're supposed to be so friendly with? Isn't that
right, Will?"

Will slowly turned his cold gray eyes on Jebediah. "All I
know is that this nigger is going back to where he belongs.
And I don't give a damn if he's shaken President Polk's
hand and kissed Queen Victoria's ass and scratched the
balls of King Louis Philippe. He could even have broken
bread with Jesus, for all the good it's going to do him."

For the first time, Jebediah seriously considered the possibility of throwing himself overboard.

"Welcome back, Jebediah."

From his seat in the boat, Jebediah looked up at Duke
Avery, standing hands on hips and grinning down at him
from the torchlit wharf. He had several whip-bearing
guards, both black and white, with him. Though it was not
yet dawn, the wharf was crowded, and there had been
cheers when the boat had appeared.

"All right, nigger," Will said, "get out of the boat and up
the ladder."

How naive he had been, Jebediah thought, to believe
that the law might actually rescue him. The sheriff and
the harbor master had probably long ago agreed to cooperate in this venture.

He had been tied hand and foot, but enough slack had
been left in his bonds to allow him to climb in and out of

the boat. As he reached the top of the ladder, hands grabbed his arms and pulled him up onto the wharf.

" 'Bye, Jebediah," Frank yelled from the boat. "You take care of yourself, you hear? And good luck!"

A prank, Jebediah thought. It really was just a prank to him.

He looked around. There were as many black faces as white in the crowd, all of them straining to get a look at him, as if he were one of Mr. Barnum's freaks.

"Well, Jebediah," Duke said, "here we are again, right back where we started. Sort of like we've come full circle."

"We have not."

"No. You're right. Things are a hell of a lot different this time. You haven't even begun to find out how different." He turned to one of the guards. "Muley, untie Jebediah's hands and then tie 'em again behind his back. Just the way he was when you first saw him. We want to give him a proper welcome home."

Jebediah hadn't even recognized Muley, who went to work with a grin. "Now we see who get a whip up his ass," he said, and Jebediah remembered that not all of his enemies were white.

Once he might have fought, as Muley tried to retie his hands. Once he might have damned their whips and their souls and made them pay for every ounce of dignity they tried to take away from him. Now he couldn't. He could only feel the futility of resistance and a great weariness, as if he were being aged far beyond his years.

"Now," Duke said, "tie a rope to his wrists and bring me my horse."

At first Jebediah thought Duke merely intended to take him to Vendue Range in the same way that Wingate had taken him on that February morning almost sixteen years earlier. Then, when they turned south on Bay, he thought Duke intended to take him to the house on King Street. He was wrong.

Though the day was just breaking, working people were up and awake, and all Charleston seemed to be aware of what had happened. People stood on the sidewalks and hung out of almost every window. Duke rode down the middle of the street, prodding Jebediah ahead with his toe. Now and then a guard jabbed him ahead with the butt of a whip. Before long a youth with a large bass drum joined them, leading the way while pounding out a lively march rhythm. They went down to the Battery, then up King Street, past Duke's house. Jebediah Hayes, renowned black abolitionist, was being marched through Charleston for all to see.

"Well, how does the old town look to you, Jebediah?" Duke asked. "How does it feel to be back home again?"

Jebediah didn't answer. He was trying to summon up the old anger, the old madness that had served him so well for so long. But it was no longer to be found. All he felt was humiliation and despair.

Dawn broke red, as bloody red as he had ever seen it, and the march seemed endless. Small boys followed them up King Street, occasionally throwing stones at Jebediah until shooed off by a white guard. His crippled left foot, which rarely bothered him, began to ache. Repeatedly he told himself that the indignity was not his but his enemies', that they could not make him less a man than he was, that his head was still held high. And yet he had to fight back the tears that came to his eyes.

And then, near Market Street, he saw Zagreus and Binnie.

Zagreus's face was twisted with pain. Binnie's was whiter than ever, white with shock. Her eyes seemed to beg Jebediah to tell her that this wasn't happening. At Sabrehill, he had been close to both of them, and now they saw him on a leash, being led through the streets of Charleston like an animal. *I mustn't let them see weakness,* he thought, and he tried to smile at them. But he knew he was producing only a ghastly parody of a smile, so he turned his face away.

He stumbled on, to the everlasting pounding of the drum.

After that, he paid no attention to where he was being led until they reached Vendue Range and the sign AVERY & AVERY. Duke got down from his horse and led Jebediah

into the courtyard, where Sam Avery and a black man
stood waiting. The black man, in a leather apron, stood by
an anvil, a couple of heavy iron chains lying at his feet.

Sam laughed and shook his head. "By God, he is *still*
one of the biggest sons o' bitches I have ever seen!"

"Yes, but not so proud now, I think. When the mighty
fall, they fall hard."

"You want to inspect him?"

Duke looked at Jebediah.

Jebediah looked at Duke.

And now some of the old madness began to come back,
a flickering of fires that were not altogether dead after all.
Perhaps Duke saw it. His eyes widened and he stepped
warily back from Jebediah. After a moment he shrugged
and said, "Hell, what for? I'm not going to sell him. He's
my favorite slave. That's why I'm going to put the heaviest
chains on him a slave has ever worn."

He walked over to the leather-aproned black and picked
up the chains. "See these, Jebediah? This is more chain
than you'll ever need to hold you. But I want you to feel
their weight. More than that, I want them to hang down
from your wrists and be seen. I wouldn't be surprised if
people came from all over the South to see you, and maybe
the North too, and when they look at you, Jebediah, I
want them to know they are looking at a *slave*."

The guards prodded him to the anvil, and the iron bands
were riveted to his right wrist and ankle and padlocked to
his left. He didn't resist. Nor did he resist when they led
him to the same little room he had occupied sixteen years
earlier, shoved him to the floor, and slammed the door
shut. This time he didn't even test the door's strength.

"Mr. Sabre is here, sir. Mr. Justin Sabre."

The little bookkeeper's eyes were bright behind their
spectacles, and he was having difficulty hiding his excitement. Expecting fireworks, no doubt. Like a large part of
Charleston, he had probably heard that Duke was having
problems with Justin's daughter, and he certainly knew
that the famous Jebediah Hayes had once been Sabrehill's
black overseer.

"Well, show him in, Clytius. Show him in."

A moment later, Justin entered the office. Duke stood up smiling but stayed back from his father-in-law and didn't offer his hand. Nor did Justin offer his.

"I heard yesterday you'd just got back, Justin. A good trip, I hope?"

Justin ignored the question and didn't return the smile. "Duke, a couple of my people have told me that you have Jebediah Hayes back in Charleston. They say you were parading him through the streets this morning."

Duke sank back down into his chair. "Why, yes. Sorry you missed seeing it. We gave Jebediah quite a welcome."

"How did you get him here?"

"A couple of gentlemen, perfect strangers, came to my house last night and said they had him. Well, I couldn't let our Jebediah remain in the hands of perfect strangers, could I?"

"What do you plan to do with him now?"

Duke shrugged. "Oh, I don't know. He's a mite past prime to fetch the best price, but I figure a big fellow like that still has some good years left in the fields. I think I'll just keep him."

Justin's voice softened, not always the best sign with him. "Duke, this is no joking matter."

"I assure you, Justin, I am not joking."

"He's not a slave, and you can't treat him like one."

"He is, and I can."

Justin's deep-set eyes bore into Duke as if trying to read his full intentions. "You sold Jebediah Hayes to the Sabres," he said slowly. "I believe it was in the spring of 'thirty-two. In 'thirty-seven I sold him to a man who transported him out of the state and freed him in the north."

"Well, now, it appears to me that you sold a piece of property that wasn't yours."

"Would you please explain that?"

"You're perfectly right about our selling him to the Sabres—I sold him to Joel Sabre myself. The trouble is that I can't find any record that we were ever paid for him. I've even gone over the clerk of court's deed book, and I haven't found anything recorded there. Now, if you can show me some kind of bill of sale, that'll put the whole matter in a different light. But as things stand, it does appear that the Sabres just kept putting off making payment until the whole transaction was lost. Justin, why don't you sit down? You can't be comfortable standing there."

Justin didn't move. "Even if what you say is so, do you really think you can call in a debt like that after all this time? And in this fashion?"

Duke threw up his hands. "I don't know. I do know I'm doing it, and if we're going to have an honest difference, you can always take me to court."

Justin's voice became softer yet. "Duke, Jebediah Hayes happens to mean a great deal to us. I'm sure you know he once saved Cat's life. If the simplest, easiest, fastest way to get him back in the North where he belongs is to pay you for him, I'll be glad to do it. And we need never speak of the matter again."

Duke shook his head. "Oh, I'm afraid it's not that simple. You see, Justin, you and I take entirely different views of Jebediah Hayes. And I am just too purely overjoyed at having him back in my hands again to let him go that easily."

"Is it because of Cat? Miss Lucy wrote to me that you two were having trouble. Is this your way of getting back at my daughter?"

"Justin, my differences with Jebediah Hayes go way back, even before his Sabrehill days. What they are needn't concern you. But even if I'd never met your daughter, I'd still be doing exactly what I'm doing now."

"Then why did you sell him at Sabrehill at all?"

Duke hesitated. He hadn't intended to reveal so much of himself, but it was too late to stop. "Because at that time Sabrehill had about the meanest, orneriest, most nigger-hating overseer I'd ever known. Just the kind to break the likes of Jebediah Hayes. Well, maybe he didn't succeed, but I, by God, am going to."

"I see."

Justin looked at Duke as if his son-in-law were a bad taste he would have liked to spit out. Well, to hell with him, Duke thought. He no longer gave the slightest damn for any Sabre's opinion.

"May I see Jebediah before I go?"

"Why not?"

Justin stared through the small, barred window in the door. He could hardly believe that this was the same Jebediah he had known for so many years. The black man lay in rags and chains in one corner of the room, looking battered and diminished like a monument that had crumpled in on itself. The face, unshaved for days, had a scraggly beard, and the hollow eyes lacked any gleam of hope.

Justin uttered no word of greeting. He said, "Jebediah, we'll get this matter straightened out as quickly as possible."

Jebediah nodded.

"I just want you to know you aren't going to be here one minute longer than I can help."

Jebediah closed his eyes and nodded again.

Justin turned away from the door. "Why is he in chains?"

"Because I want him that way."

Justin left without saying another word. He liked to think he was a cool, controlled Virginia gentleman and not one of those Carolina hotheads, but he did have a temper, and he didn't trust himself in the presence of a man who had put a boot in his daughter's face.

He went directly to the offices of Paul Devereau, a Broad Street lawyer who also happened to be a Sabrehill neighbor. The lawyer was a solidly built man of about Justin's age, with intelligent, calculating eyes and a somewhat theatrical manner. He listened to Justin's story of his interview with Duke, and asked a few questions in order to understand every detail.

"Surely you do have a bill of sale," he said,

"Paul, I'm sure there was nothing in the slightest irregular about the purchase of Jebediah. But why did Duke even mention a bill of sale when he made clear that he has no intention of giving Jebediah up?"

"Because he knows there is no bill of sale," Paul said,

giving voice to Justin's thought. "Because he has eliminated it. Could he have done that?"

"Perhaps. He and Cat have been home for some weeks now, and he has access to our office at Sabrehill." Justin's smile was twisted. "He is, after all, a trusted member of the family."

"No bill of sale." Paul leaned back in his chair and ran his fingers through his thick mane of white hair. "Well, look for it anyway. Nothing could be more helpful. Meanwhile, I really don't think Duke Avery has much of a case."

Justin breathed a sigh of relief. "Then we shouldn't have any trouble—"

"Wait a minute. I didn't say that. Duke Avery doesn't *need* much of a case. The fact is that he did once own Jebediah, and he claims he still does. And he has *got* Jebediah, and you can't prove with legal paper that you ever completed his purchase. And the good people of Charleston and South Carolina are going to like it that way."

"But we have witnesses—"

"Who? Joel and Aaron Sabre? Turnage? They're all gone."

"We have Lucy—"

"Good! We can get a statement from Dulcy, too, though it'll probably be discounted because she has black blood. I myself am prepared to swear to God Almighty that I know Mr. Jeb was legally yours, and maybe some of your other neighbors will do the same. But I want you to understand, Justin, that this isn't something we're going to win overnight. It's going to take weeks, possibly months."

"But there are laws! Blacks who have been in the North aren't allowed in South Carolina!"

"Justin," Paul said patiently, "if South Carolina can attempt to nullify the laws of the central government, it can certainly nullify its own laws. And do you really think the governor won't be tempted to go along with popular sentiment and pardon Duke Avery for his little peccadillos?

"You make me feel it's hopeless."

"No, it's not hopeless. But we're going to have to work

like hell, and keep on working for a long time, and I am going to start today by appealing to Governor Aiken. I suggest that you stay in Charleston for the time being. I may need you."

As soon as he reached the Lynch Street house, Justin sent for Zagreus and Binnie.

"I'm going to stay here for the time being," he told them, "but I want you to start back to Sabrehill in the morning and get there as quickly as possible. Tell Miss Lucy and the others what's happened. I don't want them to hear it from strangers."

Each morning, long before dawn, Duke sent Jebediah out to labor for the City of Charleston. Each day, crowds gathered to watch him wrestle with the paving stones. Sometimes the white foreman had trouble keeping them back.

"Sorry, mister, but you can't talk to that nigger."

"But I only want to ask a question or two. I represent a Philadelphia newspaper—"

"No talking to the niggers! Now you all stand back and let 'em do their work! You talk to them or get in the way, they the ones that get punished!"

Duke smiled with satisfaction. He frequently stopped by to watch Jebediah and to listen to the crowds and he liked what he heard.

"Now, that's what a bad nigger should look like," said a northern voice. "In chains and at hard labor."

"You a Yankee?"

"Born and bred. But I own a plantation down near Savannah."

"I came all the way from Columbia just to see this."

"*I* came down from Norfolk," said another voice. "I been waiting for years for that evil son of a bitch to get his comeuppance, and I wouldn't miss seeing it for nothing."

Jebediah hesitated in his struggles with a paving stone for a few seconds too long, and Duke heard the crack of Muley's whip.

"That's right, keep that nigger working."

"Make that nigger pay!"

"Make him pay for every abolitionist word he ever said."

Perhaps encouraged by the comments, Muley brought the whip down a second time, and then again. Duke considered warning him not to go too far, then changed his mind. It wouldn't hurt Jebediah to have a bad day, and he'd speak to Muley this evening. He turned and walked away.

Behind him, he heard Muley's whip crack down a fourth time.

And heard Muley scream, heard the whip come down again, again, again, heard the crowd yelling in excitement, and Muley still screaming. He turned and fought his way back through the crowd.

Justin was standing over Muley, the whip in his hand. Jebediah was on his knees nearby, leaning against a large torn-up paving stone.

Good, Duke thought, as he went to them. Fine. Now he'd show Charleston how to handle a Sabre.

"Mr. Duke," Muley sobbed, "he was trying to talk to the nigger."

"Justin," Duke said, "you know you can't talk to—"

In the next instant, Duke had the sensation of being charged by an enraged tiger. He saw Justin wheel toward him, a large hunched shoulder raising, the whip coming up and then cracking down so close to his legs as almost to singe the flesh. Duke jumped back, but not fast enough, and Justin's big fist gathered up his shirt front, twisting it, and yanked him to those rage-filled eyes.

"What did you say?"

"I said—"

"Avery, don't you ever tell me whom I can or can't speak to." The words came out slowly and distinctly for all to hear. "Don't you ever speak to me in that way again, or by God, you'll feel this whip. I'll give you a public whipping that neither you nor Charleston will ever forget."

I can take him, Duke thought. *He's older than me, and I can take him.*

And knew that at that moment he could not.

"Now, do you have anything further to say?"

"Justin, that is my slave—"

"Mr. Sabre to you, you ignorant bastard. Don't you know how to address a gentleman, you filthy-handed, wife-beating slave trader? Do I have to teach you manners?"

"Mr. Justin," Jebediah said softly, "it's all right. It's all right."

Justin disposed of Duke with a shove that sent him reeling back.

"It's not all right. This man says you're his slave." Justin's voice rose for all to hear. "I say this man is a goddamn liar. I say that Charleston and South Carolina and the whole country now knows Duke Avery is a goddamn liar."

"Justin," Duke said, "I am going to call you out."

"You're calling out nobody, Avery. And I'm giving you fair warning. There are a lot of good people in Charleston who aren't going to have you abusing Jebediah Hayes, no matter what they personally think of him. And if I ever again hear of you allowing such a thing, I swear to God I'll make you pay."

Justin turned to Muley, who had risen to his feet. "And you." He touched Muley's chest with the whip, and the guard cringed back. "You're never again going to touch Mr. Jeb with a whip, isn't that right?"

"Oh, massa—"

"Because Mr. Duke may own your body, but Mr. Justin will send your miserable soul straight to hell. Understand?"

"Oh, yessuh, massa, yessuh!"

Justin turned to Jebediah. "Jebediah, I just wanted to remind you that we're working for you, and we'll never let up."

Jebediah nodded.

"And as for you, Avery, whenever you see me coming, you just stand aside."

Justin threw down the whip. He dismissed Duke with a contemptuous toss of his head, averting his eyes. He came walking toward Duke.

Without thinking about it, Duke stepped aside.

Justin kept on walking, as if Duke had never been there. Duke looked around. The crowd was dispersing. A few people were looking at him covertly; all were avoiding his eyes. He felt as if all Charleston had seen what Justin had just done to him, and he wanted to be sick.

Behind him, Duke heard a low chuckle. When he turned around, Jebediah was still laughing softly and shaking his head. For the first time since his arrival, he wore a slight smile, and Duke had to fight the impulse to kick that smile off his face.

"Laugh all you want, Jebediah," he said quietly. "Tomorrow morning we're forming a coffle, and in a few days you'll be at Redbird. Right where I want you."

✦{ 2 }✦

HE HAD FORGOTTEN THAT chains could be so heavy. Each morning he rediscovered their weight, and all through the day it grew. The chains dragged his feet so that each step became more difficult. They pulled his arms toward the earth until the ache in his shoulders became unbearable. Their weight bent his back and dulled his mind, so that long before the day was over he was reduced to a creature of animal pain, to a mere beast of burden. Even in sleep, as he turned on the floor of his small cell-like room, he could not entirely escape their weight.

And now, as Duke Avery's men assembled the coffle in the torch-broken darkness of early morning, they added still more weight: an iron collar around his neck, attached to the coffle section ahead of him by a heavy ten-foot chain.

"This time you'll enjoy yourself, Jebediah," Duke Avery said. "The weather will be cooler, and we'll take an extra day or so to reach Redbird. A lot of people are going to want to see you. Oh, yes, you've got a lot of friends in South Carolina."

So it seemed. Whenever they passed a field where hands were at work, all labor stopped and all eyes turned toward the coffle. Often the hands came to the side of the road to stare at him, the black abolitionist who had been brought south and reenslaved. They knew who he was. Tens of thousands of abolitionist pamphlets smuggled into the South had spread his fame, and word had been passed ahead: "He coming! Mr. Jeb coming! Him they brought back! He coming in chains!" A lesson for the niggers: There was no escaping the harsh justice of their masters, not even in the North.

He tried to walk by them with dignity, his back straight

335

and his head high. But hour by hour, mile by mile, his chains bore him down.

The second day, he wondered if he would live to reach Redbird. He was still an exceptionally strong man, but he was now almost thirty-eight years old, and at times he felt as if his heart wanted to quit. *Endure,* he commanded himself, as he had in the old days. *Survive. Remember that you are still a half-crazy nigger, mean as hell, who can't be broken.* But he had lived a civilized life for too long. He didn't feel like a half-crazy nigger any longer. So he told himself that it made no difference, that this was just a passing incident in his life, that Justin Sabre would soon have him free.

Then he looked at his chains and saw that they were real, and felt them growing heavier.

On the third day, in the afternoon, they passed Sabrehill. The field hands saw them long before they were in sight of the big house or even the field quarters, and he could see boys being dispatched to carry the news: Mr. Jeb was coming. "All your old friends, Jebediah," Duke Avery said, riding beside him on horseback. "Ought to make you feel right at home."

He didn't want the Sabrehill people to see him like this, but of course there wasn't a way in the world of avoiding it. He was on exhibit, and Duke Avery would have no mercy. By the time they were near the main gate and he could see the big house, dozens of black people, hundreds of them, were lining up along the road. Before, the crowds had been silent. Now, though no one spoke to him, he heard a moaning in the crowd, and occasionally someone said his name. He tried desperately to walk standing tall, all the time praying that Miss Lucy would not appear in the crowd, or Damien, or—

The young man standing not thirty feet away, speechless, looking helpless as a child, could only be Damien.

And there, once again, were Zagreus and Binnie, looking as stricken as they had been in Charleston.

He heard Cat cry out, "Oh, Jebediah, Jebediah!" and saw her, just as Leila let out a wail of grief and turned to weep on her shoulder.

He turned his head away from the people of Sabrehill and closed his eyes. He followed blindly at the end of his chain leash. He would see no more, would hear no more, if that were possible, but would escape into the solitude of his mind.

The coffle moved on. For a time, he could hear some of the crowd following. He prayed to God that those he loved most would not.

"Do you know what this is, Jebediah?"

"I've seen it before."

They were standing in front of Redbird's dark jailhouse. The torches of the courtyard did little to illuminate it, and it seemed to lie crouched in the shadows, an evil brick beast, with the tall whipping gallows standing nearby like the beast's toy.

The coffle had arrived at Redbird after dark. It had been fed, led to the latrine ditch, and quartered in a barn for the night. Jebediah had been detached from his chain, but the iron collar remained around his neck. "In case it's needed," Duke Avery had said. "Besides you look good in it, Jebediah. It suits you." Now Jebediah painfully raised his hands and clutched at it with his fingertips: anything to change the position of his arms and relieve their awful aching.

"I always wondered why I didn't tear the damn thing down," Duke Avery said. "Never even bothered to white-wash it, because I was going to get rid of it. But now I know why I didn't. This is your home, Jebediah. It's been waiting for you all this time."

Jebediah considered whether he could kill Duke Avery —how long it would take. Could he do it before the guard, standing a few feet away, stopped him? Perhaps, and then Cat would be free of Duke. In New York, she had loyally refused to discuss her husband, but her misery could not be hidden. Was that why she was now at Sabrehill rather than at Redbird?

Duke walked over to the jail. Mounted on the door were two pairs of iron hooks, and through each pair lay a heavy

plank, which prevented the door from being drawn open
from the inside.

"I'm told nobody has ever got out of this jail without
having help from outside," Duke said, as he removed the
planks. "And after tonight, not even that will do him any
good. Tomorrow I'm going to have the biggest damn hasp
and staple you ever did see bolted to the door and wall,
and they're going to have a padlock that nobody is ever
going to break. Just so you'll feel safe at night, Jebediah."
Duke shoved the door open. "Now, would you like to step
inside?"

Jebediah measured Duke. Yes, in spite of his weariness
and the cumbersome chains, he just might be able to kill
the man. But aside from freeing Cat, what good would that
do? He himself wasn't afraid of dying, but if he were
hanged for killing Duke Avery, the odds were that he
would be seen as a murderer and not a martyr, and that
could only hurt the cause of abolition. He had no choice
but to endure.

Duke's voice hardened. "I said, would you care to step
inside?"

The guard shoved him toward the open stairway. Merely
lifting his chains to step up into the darkness of the jailhouse seemed to drain his strength, and he wondered if he
could have killed Duke Avery after all. Behind him, Duke
said something about blankets, and they were thrown in
after him. He heard the door close, and the first plank fall
into place, and then the second.

He looked about. He could see the night sky through
four small barred windows, all of them unglazed and un-
shuttered. He went to a window and, lifting his chains,
grasped the bars to test them. They were all set solidly into
the brick walls.

He tested the bars at the other windows, wondering why
he bothered. All were firmly in place.

He went to the door and tapped it here and there. The
wood was thick, sound, and solid. He could believe Duke
Avery when the man said that nobody had ever escaped
without help from the outside.

On his knees, he groped in the darkness for the blankets. There were two, and he would need them both, as the night grew colder. He rolled up in them, grateful for the partial relief from the weight of the chains.

He closed his eyes. *Survive*, he told himself. *Endure.*

To his surprise, he was given three days' respite in which to regain his strength. He was well fed, allowed to bathe in a stream, and given fresh clothes. The clothes were little better than rags, but at least they were clean. Most of the time his left manacle was taken off and the chain fastened to a post of the whipping gallows. He spent his time either lying down or sitting with his back against the post, while he watched the big open courtyard. He was constantly looking for Cat, but he never saw her.

"Having a nice rest, Jebediah?" Duke asked. "I hope so. We don't want anyone to think we're abusing you in any way."

"You don't consider these chains an abuse?"

Duke grinned. "Hell, no. You've earned them."

The slaves sometimes stared at him from a distance, but they never spoke to him—except once. A young whip-carrying guard was conducting him to the latrine. Jebediah asked, "Do you know who I am, boy?"

The guard said, "Massa say we no talk."

"Have you ever heard of Mr. Jeb of Sabrehill?"

"Massa say you talk, I whip you. I s'pose warn you once."

"But I only asked—"

Instantly the whip cut its fiery path across Jebediah's back. He gasped in pain and twisted around to face the guard.

"Why did you do—"

The guard's arm came up, and again the whip seared Jebediah's back. His impulse was to throw himself at the guard, but he saw that the man was waiting for that. After a moment, he continued on, the guard following.

On Monday morning, his fourth day at Redbird, his holiday came to an end. He was awakened before dawn, and after he had eaten breakfast, his whip-carrying guard led him to the little one-room office building on the east side of the courtyard. There three white men awaited him.

"Well, Jebediah," Duke Avery said, "ready to earn your keep?"

Jebediah said nothing. The man he'd heard called Mr. Ferguson looked unhappy. The third man bared crooked teeth in an angry grin. Jebediah knew him.

"Your master asked you a question, nigger."

"Oh, now, Mr. Bassett," Duke said, "we mustn't be too harsh on Jebediah. We must remember that he's more used to the lectern than to the fields. He's going to have to learn the rules all over again."

"He'll learn."

"I'm told that you and Mr. Tag Bassett have met before, Jebediah."

"Mr. Bassett," Jebediah said, "has often visited Sabrehill with the patrol. Some years ago he was instrumental in the death of a young black girl he was trying to rape—"

"You son of a bitch!"

Before Jebediah could move, Taggart Bassett's fist came hurling at him like a rock. He caught it on his chin, tripped backward on his chain and fell to the ground.

"Mr. Avery," Mr. Ferguson said, "this just ain't gonna work right."

"I'll instrumental him," Bassett said. "I still say it was this nigger that killed my cousin Philo."

"Easy, Mr. Bassett, easy." Duke Avery was grinning, as he patted Taggart Bassett's shoulder. "I already told you we can't have this kind of thing. Now, do you want to oversee Jebediah or not?"

"You're damn right I do. I'll oversee his ass right into the ground."

"You see, Jebediah, Mr. Ferguson doesn't like whips, and ordinarily neither do I. But Mr. Bassett does, and you're a kind of special case. You may be a mite hard to keep working. Given half a chance, I reckon you'd sit down in the shade by a pleasant stream and enjoy a book of poetry.

"But just the same, you're going to work and work hard.

In fact, you're going to be a kind of assistant to Mr. Bassett here—his foreman. And whatever your gang is assigned to, whether its digging potatoes or spreading manure or mauling fence posts, *you* are going to see that the job gets done and done right. Do you understand?"

Bassett snatched the whip from the guard's hand. "Answer, nigger," he said, "and answer right."

"I understand. Mr. Avery. Sir."

Duke smiled. "Then why don't you get up off the ground Jebediah. You're through resting. It's time to go to work."

Duke's neighbor, Colonel Kimbrough, and Mr. Owen Buckridge, from farther down the river, were the first to come view the spectacle. They arrived at Redbird together that afternoon, two men in their sixties, mustachioed and graying.

"Jebediah Hayes, back in Carolina and working in the fields," Buckridge said wonderingly. "This is surely something I never dreamed I'd see."

Duke had taken the two men out to watch Jebediah and his work gang put up a new fence. They stood a hundred feet away, almost as if afraid to go closer. Jebediah never looked up at them.

"Did you know him, sir?" Duke asked.

"Not really. But of course we all knew about him. Justin might say he was acting as his own overseer, in order to comply with the law, but he didn't know a thing about cotton when he came down here, and we all knew who really ran Sabrehill."

"Jebediah and Miss Lucy," the colonel said. "It scandalized a lot of people when they were alone together at Sabrehill, before Justin came down."

"Including me, I must admit," Buckridge said. "But they did keep Sabrehill going, and they took good care of their people."

"Still," the colonel said, "Justin was absolutely right to send Jebediah north."

"To preach abolition?" Duke asked mildly.

"Hell," Buckridge said, "you don't think he waited until he was up north to preach abolition, do you? We all came to be grateful to him for Miss Lucy's sake, but just the same, we were damn glad when we thought we'd seen the last of him."

"That's the one thing that worries me now," the colonel said. "Having him here, spreading his poison among our people."

"He isn't spreading any poison," Duke said. "Tag Bassett doesn't let him say a word that hasn't to do with his work. He eats his meals alone, and he's locked up alone every night. His days of spreading poison are over, and now he's getting his just reward."

The next day, a dozen people came to see the captive Jebediah, and the day after that some fifteen or twenty, and thereafter there was always a small crowd. There was hardly a planter from up and down the river, or a yeoman farmer from the region, or a shopkeeper from the nearby village who did not stop by to see him, and some returned repeatedly. A number of them brought slaves and pointed out to them what could happen to a black, even a free one from the faraway North, who didn't know his place and stay in it.

"How do you like it, Jebediah?" Duke asked one evening after he had been at work for a couple of weeks. "You are now serving as an example to our people of what happens to upstart darkies. Chains. An iron collar. Give you a good feeling, Jebediah?"

Jebediah gave no sign that he had even heard the question. He seldom spoke unless it was necessary, and his face rarely showed any trace of emotion.

Watching Jebediah at work, Duke freely admitted to a certain admiration. The big black quickly reacquired the good field hand's knack of never wasting an ounce of energy. When those big shoulders and that broad back weren't working, they were resting, restoring themselves. Although his chains could not have been easy to carry, he learned to manage them in the easiest possible way and even make their weight work for him at certain tasks. And, like the best kind of slave driver, he always tried to do more than his share and, if necessary, suffer his overseer's whip rather than let it fall on lesser shoulders. It was usually easy for a slave to hate his driver. It was difficult for a slave to hate Mr. Jeb.

Colonel Kimbrough and Mr. Buckridge returned.

"I don't like it," the colonel said, frowning, as they watched Jebediah use his manacles as a tool to help grub a stump. "I know you say he isn't spreading his poison, but I'm not sure this business is having quite the effect we want it to have, Avery."

So he was Avery again. For a time he had been Mr. Avery or Leduc or even Duke. But at least they made no reference to his missing wife or the public quarrel with Justin. Except, of course, behind his back.

"I'm not sure either," Buckridge said. "Seems to me my people have been kind of restless ever since they heard about Jebediah being brought back. And some of them are acting downright resentful."

"Some of mine," the colonel said, "act like they're in mourning. You'd almost think that Jebediah had become a hero to them."

"Don't worry, gentlemen," Duke said, "he's not going to be a hero for long. A nigger in chains and an iron collar, with the Carolina sun ahead of him each day and a whip behind him, doesn't make much of a hero."

Buckridge shook his head. "I don't know. At first I was glad to see this happen, but there's something about it that gives me a bad feeling. And I hate like hell to think of what Justin and Miss Lucy must be feeling. They truly love that nigger."

Duke nearly laughed out loud.

From where he lay in the brush, Damien could see the redbird gin house. He dared move no closer, for fear of being seen by Mr. Bassett or one of the dozen or so other white men who stood about watching. Though Miss Lucy and Cat were frightened that he might be caught, he visited Redbird almost daily, hoping to learn that Jebediah was still all right.

Now, as he felt a hand on his shoulder and another across his mouth, he thought his heart would burst.

"Easy, old son," a deep voice murmured. "It's just your old traveling carpenter friend."

Looking back over his shoulder, Damien saw a familiar face. The black muzzle of beard had a few more gray hairs then when they had last met.

"Johnny Dove," he said breathlessly, "does anyone go through the woods quieter than you?"

"Yes. My woman. Goes through the woods like a god-damn haunt, and faster than hell. But never mind that—how's Jebediah?"

"About as well as can be expected, I guess. You'll see in a minute."

As he spoke, Jebediah appeared at a corner of the gin house. Bassett, whip in hand and a pistol in his belt, was with him.

"Son of a bitch," Adaba said. "I wish I could have got here sooner."

"Can you get him away?"

"If I can't, my woman will never forgive me, son. She always was just a little bit in love with old Jeb. Isn't that Mr. Taggart Bassett guarding him?"

"His own personal overseer."

"If it was only Mr. Bassett, I'd just send him on a permanent holiday with his cousin Philo and steal our friend away. But I think I might be a touch conspicuous in front of a crowd of white spectators."

"There's always a crowd."

"I'm sure there is. Jebediah is now about five times as famous as he was before. Where is he kept at night? In the jailhouse?"

Damien told everything he knew about Jebediah's confinement.

"So," Adaba said, "there's no way out of that jailhouse and no easy way in. And there's dogs to be silenced, and likely he keeps some ass-licking nigger sleeping nearby, maybe in the office, to hear any racket." Adaba shook his head. "Son, this may take some time to work out."

"I just hope there is time. I'm scared for Jebediah."

"Don't be. Mr. Duke Avery won't be in any hurry to end his fun, and sooner or later he'll give us our chance. If we can just find a way to get Jebediah out of that jailhouse, we can make him disappear."

"Yes, but I'm scared of what might happen first. They say that Mr. Duke has sworn to break Jebediah, and that just makes me want to cry."

Adaba gave Damien's shoulders a comforting hug. "Son, not so many years ago, I saw Mr. Jeb carrying five-hundred-pound bales of cotton on his back for the amusement of his friends. And I have known him to survive beatings worse than any man should ever have to take. I don't think Mr. Jebediah Hayes is going to break easily. Now, let's get back to Sabrehill and give this matter some thought."

They gave it a great deal of thought, that evening as they sat in Zagreus and Binnie's room over the coach house, but they found no answers, and Damien found himself resentful when Adaba announced that he was leaving in the morning and would be gone at least a week or two.

Adaba saw it. "Son, I know how you feel. But it's not going to be easy getting Jebediah north again, and I've got some arrangements to make. Your task is to find a way to get Jebediah out of that jail and then hide him good—because a lot of people are going to be looking for him awfully hard, and that whip-blazed face is well known.

"But don't worry! If worst comes to worst, we'll simply burn goddamn Redbird to the ground and murder Mr. Duke Avery in his bed! Might be more fun doing that anyway."

Damien felt only slightly cheered when Adaba left.

A couple days later, Mr. Justin arrived from Charleston. The news, he said, was not good. It appeared that the process of freeing Jebediah was going to be long and tedious, just as Lawyer Devereau had warned him. Therefore he had returned to Sabrehill to try another tactic.

The next evening, a meeting was held at Sabrehill.

Duke heard about the meeting the next day, on Sunday morning. Fenella said it had had something to do with Jebediah, but he could have guessed that, and he was not particularly surprised when carriages began to arrive at

Redbird that afternoon. First came Colonel Kimbrough and Mr. Buckridge with their sons, Quentin and Royal, followed by Mr. McClintock and Mr. Pettigrew, who shared a carriage. Dr. Paulson arrived a few minutes later, and Mr. Haining and Mr. Harmon drove up right behind him. In all, there were nine of the most prominent men in the district, representing seven plantations.

"I hope you'll forgive us," Mr. Buckridge said, "for coming like this, without warning—"

"Not at all, Mr. Buckridge, happy to see you all at any time. Just let Raphael take your hats and coats, and we'll pour some drinks to remove this December chill."

"First of all, Mr. Avery," Colonel Kimbrough said, when they were all settled in the parlor, glasses in hand, "I don't have to tell you how we all feel about your bringing the famous Mr. Jeb home for a visit."

There was approving laughter, and Duke noted that once again he was *Mister* Avery.

"Now, gentlemen," he said, smiling, "don't give me more credit than I deserve. Two other men brought Mr. Jeb home. I merely recognized a slave I had never been paid for."

There was more laughter. *You can laugh your fool heads off*, Duke thought. *Whatever you want, you'll get nothing from me.*

"Well, whatever the precise facts," Colonel Kimbrough went on, "all of us here are very grateful. That darky boy has been impugning the dignity and honor of the South for far too long. It was time we got back a little of our own, and you have demonstrated to the entire world that if a nigger doesn't mind his manners, he may just find himself slapped back down into his proper place."

"The fields of Redbird, by God," Mr. McClintock said, slapping his thigh, and the laughter became louder than ever. Louder and yet just a little strained, Duke noted, as if his guests were not really altogether in a laughing mood.

Mr. Buckridge cleared his throat. "The question is, how shall we handle this situation now?"

"Situation?" Duke said innocently. "We?"

"Yes," the colonel said, "this has been an awfully good

thing for the South, and we certainly wouldn't want it to go wrong."

"Why, what could go wrong?"

"Well, it's pretty delicate," Mr. Pettigrew said.

"It certainly is," the colonel agreed. "Strictly speaking, it's a completely illegal state of affairs, and it cannot be maintained indefinitely. Naturally, we'd like to know if you have any particular plans."

Duke, standing before the others, shrugged. "Run Redbird. Cultivate my own garden, I think is the phrase."

"You mean," Mr. Pettigrew said, "more or less allow events to shape themselves?"

"You put that very well, Mr. Pettigrew."

"But Mr. Avery," Colonel Kimbrough said, "very soon now we are all going to feel a great deal of pressure—and you most of all. In the North there is a great deal of anger against us. And not only there. It takes only a couple of weeks for news to cross the Atlantic on a Cunard liner, you know, and apparently Jebediah's kidnappers sent word of what they were up to just as soon as they laid hands on him. Maybe even before."

"Interesting."

"And we now know how the English feel about this affair."

"Do we?"

"I'm sorry to say that the reaction has not been good. In fact, the English have been outraged, Mr. Avery. Completely and utterly outraged. It seems that Jebediah Hayes is a very popular figure abroad, and the English are taking this as proof that we Americans are no better than barbarians."

"Colonel Kimbrough, do you really give a damn what the English think?"

"Yes, I do. Because we sell cotton to English mills. And, furthermore, if it ever comes to a war between the states, we're going to need English friends."

"The secretary of state," Mr. Pettigrew said, "has sent word to us that he wants Jebediah Hayes freed."

"Secretary Buchanan is a northerner."

"Well, Senator Calhoun is not," Colonel Kimbrough

said, at last showing a trace of anger, "and Calhoun says he wants that Nigra sent north immediately."

"Now, you've got to give some consideration to the wishes of John C. Calhoun," Mr. Buckridge said.

"Do I?"

Dr. Paulson sighed and spoke for the first time. "Mr. Avery, you must know that sooner or later a court is going to order you to send Jebediah out of the state. At the very least. We would like to know what you will do then."

Duke shrugged. "Why, send him out of state, I suppose. Put him in the next Avery coffle that goes by and send him to Louisiana, perhaps. Sell him into the cane fields. A big fellow like Jeb, he should be good for another three or four years, even in the worst of them."

The room was silent, all eyes on Duke. Finally Mr. Pettigrew shook his head. "What you do not seem to understand, Mr. Avery, is that, whether we like it or not, we are dealing with someone that a large part of the world regards as a *hero*."

"And we've got to keep this situation from turning against us," the colonel said. "So far, we've made everybody who believes in slavery feel mighty good, and we've taught the abolitionists a badly needed lesson. Now, what can we do that will resolve the situation in a manner that's favorable to us? What can we do that will make us—and Mr. Leduc Avery—look even better?"

"I think," Mr. Pettigrew said slowly, "that the time has come to make some kind of grand gesture."

The colonel nodded. "Show the world that, no matter what the abolitionists say, the South has a great heart. Generosity. Magnanimity."

"Having soundly spanked Jebediah's behind," Mr. Pettigrew said, "send the darky north again with our fondest, best wishes."

"For Christmas!" Mr. Buckridge said excitedly. "A Christmas present for Jebediah!"

"Exactly," the colonel said. "We've proved our point— that we won't put up with abolitionist nonsense forever. Now we prove that we are not heartless barbarians, as our enemies claim, but men of good will like any others."

"Better than others! We'll even celebrate Jebediah's departure! Give parties for him, all over the state! Load him with Christmas gifts to take north with him! Ha!" Mr. Buckridge burst into laughter at the thought of such a jest, and the others joined in with him.

And these were the men he had so much admired, Duke thought. These were the gentry whose ranks he had sought to join. These fools.

"Gentlemen," he said, as the laughter died, "do you honestly think that Jebediah Hayes would ever accept a goddamn thing from any of you?"

"Well," Mr. McClintock said uncertainly, "he *is* a nigger."

"He'll accept his freedom fast enough," the colonel said.

"Where did you get all this information about England being outraged and Calhoun wanting Jebediah sent north? From Justin Sabre?"

Colonel Kimbrough looked uncomfortable. "Well, yes. He just got back from Charleston a couple days ago."

"And you believed him? An abolitionist?"

The colonel raised his eyes almost defiantly. "Justin Sabre may have abolitionist sentiments, sir, but he is not a liar."

Duke remembered the words Justin had flung at the crowd in Charleston, and he knew that every other man in the room was remembering them. His impulse was to damn them all and run them off Redbird. But somehow he produced a smile.

"Maybe not. But now that you've delivered his message, you can run back to him with my answer. Tell him that Jebediah is mine and I'll decide what to do with him. Hereafter he can speak to my lawyers."

The colonel's face stiffened. "Mr. Avery, we are here to speak for ourselves, not for Justin Sabre."

Duke shrugged. "Happy to hear it."

"Mr. Avery," Mr. Buckridge said, "won't you at least consider—"

"Oh, hell, yes," Duke said expansively, "of course I'll consider. I'm not going to let Jebediah go for Christmas, but in the spring, who knows? Maybe at Easter. The resurrection of Mr. Jeb. Has a nice ring about it, doesn't it? Now, why don't you gentlemen join me for another drink?"

His guests left soon after that.

Jebediah lay shivering on the jailhouse floor. He had rolled up in his blankets, but the cold December breeze seemed to penetrate everything. It flowed through the barred windows, seemed to flow through the very bricks of the jailhouse, and entered his bones. Sometimes it seemed to Jebediah that he would never be warm again.

He heard the carriages arriving, but he didn't get up to see whom they brought. He had to use ever hour, every minute he wasn't being worked to recover his strength. His body had grown leaner and harder in the first weeks of his captivity, but now he had a sense of both body and spirit being slowly and methodically eroded.

The afternoon waned. He heard the carriages depart.

It was after dark when he heard the clatter of the padlock. He was surprised, because he thought it was not yet time for supper.

The two thick planks made a scraping sound as they were removed, and they thumped against the side of the jail. The door opened, and he saw Duke Avery, a dark figure against the lights of the big house.

" 'Evening, Jebediah. Getting your rest, I see."

Jebediah said nothing.

"I suppose you know I've had visitors."

Jebediah didn't move.

"Not interested? I think you should be. You might be surprised to learn how many friends you have in the South."

Had Avery come here merely to bait him? Or had something significant really happened?

"They seem to think I'm going to have to let you go before long. They think that sooner or later you're bound to walk away from here a free man."

I shall!

"But they're wrong, aren't they, Jebediah? It's never going to happen, is it? We know what's going to happen to you, don't we?"

Jebediah closed his eyes.

"Good night, Jebediah."

He heard the door close, the planks fall into place, the lock snap shut.

Endure, he commanded himself for the thousandth time. And perhaps, just perhaps, survive.

—◦⊰ 3 ⊱◦—

IT WAS NOT YET dawn when Duke unfastened the padlock and Bassett opened the jailhouse door. They heard the clanking of chains, and after a moment Jebediah appeared, his big body filling the doorway.

" 'Morning, Jebediah," Duke said cheerfully. "Ready to do a good day's work?"

As usual, Jebediah didn't answer. He merely looked about with a dull, brutish gaze, all fire gone from his eyes. Bassett lifted his whip and started to speak, but Duke shook his head. Let him be. Save the discipline for the fields.

Jebediah slowly sat down in the doorway, resting his chains on the ground between his thighs. A kitchen wench came over and handed him his breakfast on a wooden plate: boiled cornmeal, molasses, and salt pork.

"Eat hearty," Duke said, "and keep your strength up. If you do good work, maybe next week we'll give you Christmas day off."

Slowly Jebediah began to eat.

God, Duke thought, how the nigger had changed since that night in New York at the Broadway Theater. Changed, for that matter, since he had arrived in Charleston. Changed most of all since he had come to Redbird. Certainly he was no more than a pathetic shadow to the defiant young black he had been sixteen years earlier. *Jebediah*, Duke thought, *I am putting out your fires forever*.

When he went out to the fields later that morning, he found Jebediah and several other blacks cleaning out a drainage ditch. It was a miserable job, made more so by the cold gray day: It entailed the slaves' taking off their brogans and climbing down into the cold water and mud to pull out the debris. Before long, their clothes were soaked through and filthy, and their very guts seemed to be frozen.

352

People were still coming to see Jebediah, Duke noted with satisfaction, and that morning a half dozen were standing about watching. His neighbors, however, rarely came by anymore. Since Duke had made clear that he wouldn't cooperate with them, their eyes had grown hard and they seldom spoke to him. Duke could hardly have cared less.

"You!" Bassett yelled. "Nigger! Get to work!"

Duke looked around. Jebediah's skin had toughened, but the iron still bit into it sometimes, and now he was trying to clean the dirt and blood from under a manacle with his tongue.

"I said, get to work!"

Bassett's long whip came down across Jebediah's shoulders with a loud crack. Jebediah's back stiffened, and he threw his head back. His eyes bulged, and his face was distorted from the effort of holding back a cry. Bassett started to raise the whip again.

"Better let him take care of that wrist," an onlooker said. "You can lose a good nigger by not taking care of something like that."

"That's right," Duke said. "Let him be for now, Mr. Bassett. Give him a few minutes, and see if you can find something to wrap around that wrist."

Bassett grinned and lowered the whip. Duke had him well trained. At first the man had wanted to lay on the whip at any excuse, or none at all. Duke had taught him how to hold off until the right moment. "You want to space out those stripes, Bassett. You don't want to give him six or seven bad ones and maybe ruin him for the day. You want to keep him at work by going easy—and giving him eight or ten stripes or even more." Duke didn't say it, but what he meant was, *You don't want to put the poor bastard out of his misery. You want to torment him until he begs you to put him out of his misery.*

That afternoon something happened that Duke had been waiting for.

Jebediah and his work gang were still cleaning drainage ditches. As Duke was approaching them, Bassett turned his attention to a woman standing knee-deep in water. Evidently she had been dawdling, because he walked up behind her and snaked his long whip across her back. She screamed. Bassett flogged her again. She screamed again, and as her scream went on, he flogged her a third time.

By then, Jebediah was up on the bank and, insofar as his spancel permitted, was running toward them. Bassett saw him coming and, his eyes big with fear, he shot his whip out at Jebediah with all his strength.

The blow seemed to spin Jebediah around. Bassett drew back the whip and struck again, just as hard, and Jebediah's cry drowned out the woman's. Forgetting in his fear all that Duke had taught him, Bassett struck again and again, a frenzy of blows. Duke ran to stop him. Then he saw that Jebediah, too, was running. Not running away, simply running about wildly, swinging his chains, like a blind, maddened animal, a long, hoarse animal cry coming from his throat, until he fell facedown on the ground, kicking and pawing the earth like a fallen bull with a broken back.

Broken, Duke thought, as he grabbed Bassett's arm. Broken.

And, hidden in a patch of weeds a hundred yards away, Damien wept.

It was suppertime when he arrived back at Sabrehill, and he went directly to the kitchen house. Momma Lucinda and Leila turned to him as he came through the doorway.

"Did you see him?" Momma Lucinda asked.

"I saw him."

"Well, tell us."

"I want my supper, Momma Lucinda."

"What was he doing?" Leila asked. "Is he all right?"

"He was cleaning ditches. I don't want to talk about it."

"But is he—"

"*Leila, I don't want to talk about it!*"

Leila's eyes grew larger and her voice was hushed. "What they doing to him?"

"What do you think they're doing to him? They're killing him, that's what they're doing!"

Leila gave a muffled little cry and ran out of the kitchen.

"Boy, be careful how you talk to Leila," Momma Lucinda said, as she filled a plate from an iron pot. "She don't love Jebediah no less than you do."

Damien didn't answer. He took the plate and a spoon from Momma Lucinda and carried them across the courtyard to his cottage. There, in the dark, he put the plate on a table and sat down to eat. Supper was chicken fricassee and hominy johnnycake, and it should have been delicious, but he hardly tasted it.

He was just finishing when Cat appeared at his door. She came in and sat down at the table with him.

"Momma Lucinda said it was so bad that you don't even want to talk about it."

He shoved his plate away and sat with his head down and his eyes closed.

"Cat," he said, "Mr. Duke isn't ever going to let Jebediah go."

Cat took his hand. "But he'll have to. Damien, Papa headed back for Charleston this morning to see what more he could do. He said he'd be back here by Christmas. Why, I wouldn't be surprised if he had Jebediah free by then. I'll bet Jebediah spends Christmas day right here with us at Sabrehill."

Damien shook his head. "He's going to die, Cat. He's going to die at Redbird."

He was silent for a moment, and Cat's hand tightened on his. Then he yanked away from her and smashed his fists down on the table.

"Unless I can find a way to get him out of that damn jail!"

"Get him out?" Cat said, startled.

"Yes! Johnny Dove says that if I can get him out, he can get Jebediah north where he'll be safe."

"Johnny Dove? Who's Johnny Dove?"

He stared at her. *Oh, shit,* he thought.

"Who is Johnny Dove?" she asked again.

"Nobody. Just an old nigger man I know. A traveling carpenter."

"How come you never mentioned him before?"

"Never had any call to." *Oh, shit.*

"How can *he* get Jebediah north?"

"I don't know. He just says he can. He's pretty smart."

"The Underground Railroad?"

"I guess. If you want to call it that."

"You have a friend in the Underground Railroad? One you never told me about?"

Oh, shit.

"Johnny Dove, Johnny Dove," she mused when he didn't answer, and he could almost see her mind working. "Johnny *Dove*?" Her green eyes suddenly seemed to grow very bright in the dark. "Adaba? The Brown Dove?"

"Oh, Cat, there isn't any Adaba. That's just a fairy tale."

She burst out laughing. "Oh, you bastard! For years they've told stories about how runaways disappear when they get near here, it's caused Papa and Momma no end of trouble. And that time the pattyrollers nearly hanged you, and you played so innocent—it all fits! Bastard, why didn't you tell me?"

"Jebediah said not to."

"Jebediah too? Oh, God!" Cat burst into fresh laughter. "And you never let me in on the fun!"

"Jebediah said it could only get you into bad trouble."

"How long have you been doing this?"

"About ten years. Since just before Jebediah went north."

"Ten years! How could *you* ever keep a secret from *me* for ten years?"

"Hardest thing I ever did. And I didn't get to eleven years, did I?"

"You and Jebediah," Cat said, still laughing. "Who else?"

"Leonie. And that's all you have to know, Cat. So don't ask anything more."

Cat shook her head and laughed, "Bastards! Bastards!" and Damien felt a little better than he had when he had arrived home. He was glad to be sharing his secret with Cat after all this time.

"How are we going to get him out, Damien?" she asked, when her laughter had died.

"I don't know."

"There's got to be a way."

She put her hand back on his, and for a long time

they were silent, but he knew she was thinking about Jebediah.

"Remember when we were little," she said at last, in her softest voice, "how he hid sweets in his pockets for us?"

"You always took the candied apricots."

"They were my favorite. And remember the time we hid in the supply wagon? And Philo Bassett threw us out, and Jebediah fought with him?"

"Nearly got himself killed for us."

"Nearly got himself killed for *me* the time I got into the paddock with that crazy horse. He was like an extra daddy to me."

"He was like a daddy and a momma and a big brother to me."

"We had our own special little family. Always took care of one another."

"Always."

"But you really should have told me about the Underground Railroad, bastards!"

Damien laughed, and yawned. "Cat, I'm so tired. I think I'll take my plate to the scullery and then lie down for a while."

Cat squeezed his hand, then stood up. "I'll take care of your plate. You go get your rest."

"Thank you, Cat."

"You're welcome." She took the plate and spoon and went to the door. "And Damien . . ."

"Yes?"

"Nothing. Good night."

Perhaps her mind was made up even then, as she crossed the courtyard to the kitchen house. Perhaps it had been for a long time, but the thought was so dismaying, so sickening, that she didn't want to put it into words, didn't even want to acknowledge it. *Tomorrow*, she had told herself repeatedly, *maybe tomorrow. Or maybe something will happen and Jebediah will be free, and I won't have to do it.* But nothing had happened. The bill of sale had never been found, and Damien was probably right: Jebediah would die at Redbird.

A lamp still burned in the kitchen, but no one was in it. Cat had just put down the plate in the scullery when she heard a quiet sobbing. She followed the sound to the west door of the kitchen.

"Leila!"

The housekeeper was sitting on the steps, almost hidden in the outer darkness. Cat sat down and put an arm around her.

"I can't help it, Cat, child. Damien said tonight that they was killing Jebediah."

"Damien should keep his damn mouth shut."

Leila shook her head. "No, I got to know the truth. But, oh, it hurts so much."

"I forget that you knew Jebediah even before I did."

Leila rested her head on Cat's shoulder. "I remember when he first come here. How me and Miss Dulcy took care of him after Mr. Turnage whip him so bad. And one time when Miss Amity pushed me down the stairs and broke my arm, how Jebediah held me on his lap and rocked me like a baby on these here same steps, giving me comfort."

"You loved him?"

Leila nodded. "Even more than I knew at the time. That's why I never took me a husband. Oh, I know he had wenches 'sides me—and likely plenty of 'em after he left Sabrehill. And I was no fool, I knew I hadn't no chance with him, so after he left, I had me some men. But each time I got to thinking 'bout jumping over the broomstick with one of them, I decided, no, it wouldn't be fair to the poor man. 'Cause too much of my heart still belonged to Jebediah."

"Seems like everybody loves Jebediah. Except people like Mr. Duke and the Bassetts."

" 'Course they do. 'Cause he's a runner and a fighter. Don't let nobody take 'way his self-respect. Lot of people, black and white both, don't know a nigger slave can have self-respect till they meet Mr. Jebediah Hayes. You was too young to understand all the things he was doing for our people here at Sabrehill, Cat, child, and he's still doing them up north. Or was, till they brought him back. And I reckon that's why white folks hate him so."

"They don't all hate him, Leila. I love him."

"I know. And you got more reason than anybody ever told you."

"What reason is that?"

"Ain't for me to say. Ask your momma. Ask her how Jebediah Hayes saw her through times so bad that you are just plain lucky there is still a Miss Lucy alive to be a momma to you. Ask her sometime."

At that moment, Cat knew that her mind was made up and that there could be no more delaying.

"All right," she said, "I'll ask her. Now, don't you cry anymore, Leila. Everything is going to be all right. Good night, now."

" 'Night, child."

She went back across the courtyard and down the east service lane to the coach house. In its dark interior she climbed the stairs and knocked on the trapdoor that led to Zagreus and Binnie's room.

"Zagreus? Are you awake?"

The trap door opened and she dimly made out Zagreus's face.

"Zagreus, I'm sorry to disturb you, but I need a carriage. Just for myself. The cabriolet will do."

"Now?" He sounded surprised.

"Right now. Bring it to the house."

She went back along the lane to Damien's cottage. When she opened the door and softly called his name, there was no answer. She went inside and felt her way through the darkness to the bedroom. He was lying face up on the bed, already asleep. He was still dressed, so she eased off his boots, careful not to awaken him, and covered him with a blanket. She stood watching him for a few minutes, then kissed him gently on the mouth and left.

In the big house, she took a lamp that was burning in the passage and went up to a storeroom on the top floor. There she found a small valise, which she brought down to her bedroom. Most of her clothes were still at Redbird, but there were a few things she wanted—a nightgown, some shoes, an underskirt. She was packing when her mother came into the room.

Her mother stared at her. "I thought I heard someone upstairs. What are you doing?"

"I'm going back to him, Momma. I'm going back to Duke."

"But you can't!"

"Isn't that where everybody says a wife's place is? With her husband?"

"But after what he did to you—"

"I don't care. Momma, I think he's holding Jebediah mostly because of me. I'm going to tell him I'll come back to Redbird and stay with him if he'll let Jebediah go."

"And if he won't do it?"

"Then I'll stay with him anyway. Maybe, living at Redbird, I can find some way to get Jebediah out of that damn jailhouse."

Her mother shook her head and put her hands over the top of the valise. "Oh, Katie Anne, don't do this."

"Momma, Jebediah once saved my life. I owe him just about anything I can do to save his. So don't try to stop me."

"At least wait until your father gets back."

"No. He might try to stop me, too."

"Then wait until morning. You can't go out at this hour of the night!"

Cat shook her head. "No. I'm a coward. By morning I may lose my nerve."

"Do you want me to go with you?"

"Oh, Momma!" Cat laughed and gave her mother a hug. "I can't go back to him and say, 'Here I am, but I've brought my mother and her pistol along in case you want to plant another boot in my face.' No, this is something I've got to do all by myself."

Her mother wrung her hands. "Oh, but I wish you'd wait!"

"The longer I wait, the harder it'll be for Jebediah. No, I'm going tonight."

She pulled on an old coat and tied a scarf over her head,

and, carrying the valise, went back downstairs. Her mother followed, carrying the lamp.

Outside, the cabriolet and horse were waiting. Cat dismissed Zagreus, put her valise into the carriage, and turned to her mother.

"Now, don't you worry, I'll be all right. I can't say I like doing this, but that business with the boot was an accident, and I wouldn't be surprised if we wound up living happily ever after. We're not the fiirst young couple to have a spat."

"I don't care, I don't trust him. After what he's done . . . Oh, Katie Anne!"

They embraced and kissed, and kissed again. Then Cat turned to the cabriolet and climbed into it. She looked around and smiled.

"Momma, Duke always wanted to marry a real lady. Would you say I was anything of a lady at all?"

"Katie Anne, my darling, you are one hell of a lady."

"Thank you, Momma."

Cat drove off.

Her mother stood watching her as she went around the courtyard circle and down the avenue, until she disappeared into the darkness.

I shouldn't have let her go.

She went back into the house. Common sense told her that Cat would probably be all right, but she couldn't stop her growing sense of dread. When she happened to look into a mirror, she saw that her face was drawn and her eyes were wide with fright.

I shouldn't have let her go!

Cat!

Something was disturbing Damien's sleep—a thought, a dream, he wasn't sure exactly what.

"And Damien . . ."

"Yes?"

"Nothing. Good night."

He should have known what she was going to do. But sometimes they did succeed in hiding things from each other, and he had been so tired. He had gone into the bedroom and thrown himself down on the bed, and now . . .

Cat!

Something was wrong—he knew it. Why hadn't he listened more carefully? Why hadn't he understood?

"Remember when . . . apricots . . . Bassett . . . that crazy horse . . .

"And, Damien . . ."

"Yes?"

"Nothing . . ."

Damien sat bolt upright, eyes wide open, and yelled, "Cat!"

No one answered. The room was dark, and empty except for himself. But she had been in it, he was sure. He had a blanket over him now, and his boots were off, and he could still feel her kiss on his mouth. Or had the kiss been part of his dream?

"Cat, goddamnit!"

Still no answer. He threw the blanket aside and found his boots and pulled them on. When he went outside, he saw that there was still a light upstairs in the big house. He hurried to the door and banged the knocker. Then, finding the door unlocked, he stepped inside.

"Cat?" he called in the dark passage. "Miss Lucy? Somebody?"

He heard a door open somewhere, and after a moment Miss Lucy appeared on the stairs in a robe, a lamp in her hand. Her eyes looked frightened.

"Damien, what is it?"

"Miss Lucy, please, where is Cat?"

Miss Lucy came down a few steps before answering. "She went back to Redbird."

The words went through Damien like a galvanic shock. "She did *what*?"

"She went back to her husband, Damien. She felt she had to, for Jebediah's sake——"

"Oh, Miss Lucy, how could you let her do that!"

"I couldn't stop her. She was determined."

"But, Miss Lucy, that is a crazy man! We can't let her go back there, and all by herself!"

"She was certain she would be all right——"

"No! no! no! She *won't* be all right! I *know* she won't! How long ago did she leave?"

"Not long. About an hour, an hour and a half."

Damien turned to leave. "Miss Lucy, I've got to go get her right now."

Miss Lucy hurried down the rest of the stairs. "But you don't dare go there, not after what that man did to you."

"Ma'am, all I know is that I have got to get Cat. It's like I just *know* she's in bad trouble and she's calling to me for help and I can't live if I don't go bring her back."

"You really do think . . . ?"

"Yes!"

"Oh, God! Then wait for me. And, Damien, you know where the key to the office is?"

"Yes, ma'am."

"The pistol we keep in there—get it."

There was no moon, and the night was as dark as any Cat remembered. She didn't see a light anywhere until she rode through the persimmon grove and saw one in the big house. It was just as well that he was still up, she thought, and she didn't have to awaken him. But she felt a cold knot of fear in her stomach, as she thought of what was to come.

When she passed the jailhouse, it occurred to her that this might be her one chance to speak to Jebediah, so she reined up and got out of the cabriolet. She looked at the tall whipping gallows. At least, from what Damien had learned, Jebediah had thus far been spared that punishment.

She went to a window and whispered: "Jebediah? Are you awake?"

She heard the clanking of chains. After a moment, two hands appeared, and the fingers gripped the bars. She could just make out Jebediah's forehead leaning against them.

"Katie Anne," he said softly, "what are you doing here? I thought you must have left him."

"I did. But I've come back."

"No. Go back to Sabrehill. Right now. Before he finds out—"

"Jebediah, we're going to get you out of here. Papa went back to Charleston to see about it, but I couldn't wait."

Somewhere a dog started barking.

"Katie Anne . . . Cat . . . go home."

"No, Jebediah, not without you. Never."

A black man started shouting: "Mr. Duke! Mr. Duke, somebody messing 'round the jailhouse! Mr. Duke!" Cat looked around to see the man running from the office toward the big house, still shouting Duke's name.

"Cat, go now, quickly, before it's too late."

Cat didn't answer. She watched as the big house door opened and Duke's tall figure, pistol in hand, stood silhouetted in it. He said something to the slave, who disappeared into the darkness, and after a moment the dog stopped barking.

Duke stuck the pistol in his belt and came walking across the courtyard. In shirt sleeves, he made a ghostly figure against the darkness. Cat went to meet him, and they came to halt a few feet apart.

"Duke," she said, "let him go."

"Is that why you're here? To beg for him?"

She was silent for a moment, trying to think what to say. All the way to Redbird she had rehearsed speeches, but now they deserted her.

"Duke, I know I wasn't the kind of wife you wanted me to be. I tried, but maybe I didn't try hard enough. And I'm sorry for some of the things I said to you. I said them out of hurt, but I know that's no excuse. I shouldn't have said them, and I should have tried harder to understand your . . . your needs."

"Well, now, it's mighty thoughtful of you to say so."

"I was wrong, Duke. And if you'll just let Jebediah go, I'll come back to you, and for the rest of my life I'll try to be the kind of wife you want me to be.

"You know, I think you really mean that."

"I do. Darling, we loved each other once. I know I loved you. Surely if we both try——"

"But what the hell makes you think you could ever be the kind of wife I want?"

"I can be, believe me!"

"God, when I think of how I used to look up to the Sabres! Real chivalry, gentlemen and ladies all, even that damn bitch Amity. The height of my ambition was to have people know that I was as good as any Sabre. How the hell was I to know that when I married one of them, I'd get a nigger-fucking whore for a wife?"

She lowered her head, put her hand to her face, and closed her eyes. "Please, Duke, don't say things like that."

"Well, isn't it true? I suppose everybody knows by now."

"No—"

"Don't bother to lie."

"Duke, I am begging you—"

"Where the hell did you ever get the damn-fool idea that I'd want you back? That I could stand to have you around?"

"Please!"

"Do you really think you could ever be a lady?"

"I can be, for you! The kind of lady you want me to be!"

"Cat! They sure named you right. You've got all the instincts of a cat and all the morals. I guess they come with your share of the Sabre nigger blood, don't they?"

She couldn't hold back her tears. "Please, Duke, don't try to hurt me. We've hurt each other enough."

"The only thing you care about right now is that nigger in my jailhouse. You don't give a damn about me. Tell me, honeychild, how many times have you spread for him?"

Cat shook her head. She couldn't stop her tears. "Don't say that!"

"And you think you could be a lady. As if a bitch in heat, a goddamn rutting animal, could ever be a lady. Because that's what you are, my dear, no better than a French Alley whore, a filthy barnyard animal, a bitch in heat."

She could take no more. The pain, the injustice of his words was too much. She had come to Redbird prepared to humble herself, to accept her lot with him as her husband, to be whatever he wanted her to be. But he had gone too far. And, whatever her intention, she was still, in her heart of hearts, Cat Sabre.

She raised her head and opened her eyes. She drew back her lips, and her breath hissed between her teeth.

"And that's just the way you love it, don't you, Duke? Bitch-hot and barnyard filthy! But not with your wife, oh, no—"

Swift as a whip, his arm snapped out at her and his big hand cracked across her face. "You shut up, bitch!"

"Not with your wife, but with some defenseless little nigger girl—"

"Shut up!"

The hand cracked across her face again, struck her so hard that her body arched, but she refused to back up, refused to retreat.

"Bitch-hot and barnyard filthy, because you've got dirt in your soul, Duke Avery—"

"She wasn't dirt! She was worth a thousand of you, if only I'd known it!"

"You've got shit in your very soul, and you'll never get it clean!"

"Shut up! Shut up!" His left hand came out to grab her coat. He balled up the right into a fist. She saw madness in his eyes. "She wasn't dirt! Shut up!"

She had no idea of what he meant. But as the fist came down on her face, she knew she might not live through the night.

She found herself lying facedown in the grass, the familiar taste of blood in her mouth. She heard Jebediah sobbing. Then light flared—someone had lit a torch. She struggled to her knees and looked around for her carriage. She tried to crawl to it.

"Oh, no, bitch!"

Duke grabbed her ankle and dragged her back. She could see his twisted face clearly in the torchlight, and when she tried to fight him, she saw the big, hard hand once again come down like leather across her face. Then the hand grabbed the neck of her dress and ripped at it.

"Mr. Avery!" came the overseer's shocked voice. "My God, what are you doing!"

"Get away from here, Ferguson. Just get the hell away!"

Again she tried to struggle against him, and again and again his hand flashed down, and through the pain she heard his curses. She was aware of her clothes being torn away, and then aware of nothing at all until she felt herself being lifted by a wrist, her entire weight dangling from it. As her feet left the ground, the cold December air brought her back to consciousness, and she looked down through dimmed eyes at her naked body.

Duke grinned up at her. "It's a fine old Carolina custom, publicly whipping women like you. If it wasn't so late, I'd get all my niggers out to watch, but I guess your Jebediah will have to do."

He anchored the rope he had used to hoist her up, then pulled tight another that had been tied to her other wrist, so that she hung from the cross beam. When he grabbed her ankles, she tried feebly to kick him away, but he easily tied each ankle to a post.

For a moment he disappeared from her sight. She saw Jebediah at a window, tears streaming down his face, and one arm extended between the bars as far as his chain would allow, as if by some supreme effort he might bring her down from the gallows.

Duke reappeared. In one hand he held what appeared to be a bunch of long, knotted cords.

"I found this old cat-o'-nine-tails," he said. "It seemed like the right thing for you. Are you ready for it?"

As he walked around behind her, she found the strength for one last curse. "You can go to hell, you shit-souled slave trader! And kiss my ass—"

"I'll kiss it with this, bitch."

She screamed as the whip raked across her buttocks.

She hated herself for that—for screaming at the very first blow. But she couldn't help it, and she screamed again at the second, screamed at the third, kept on screaming, as she writhed on the gallows, and the blows kept coming, and she knew at last what it was to be consumed by the fires of hell.

A torch was still burning, and sitting in the office near the open doorway, Duke could see Cat hanging uncon-

scious from the whipping gallows. The night had grown
cold, and he supposed he should bring her down, but there
was no hurry. In the morning he would take her back to
Sabrehill, and then he didn't care if he never saw her
again.

The nigger in the jailhouse had stopped moaning, and
the night was quiet. Duke had a glass of whisky in his
hand, but he didn't need it. He felt almost at peace, like a
man with nothing left to lose. He still had his plantation,
of course, but he found that it didn't really mean much to
him anymore. He knew he had thrown away any last
chance of salvaging his reputation with those aristocrats he
had so admired, but he didn't really care. He had lost his
wife, but he didn't want her. His only regret now was the
loss of Leonie.

How the hell could everything have gone so wrong, he
wondered, as he sipped his whisky. He wasn't a bad man.
He knew he had an evil temper now and then, but he had
never really wanted to hurt anybody, except those who had
wronged him. He had always wanted to be the best kind of
man he could be. Then why had a couple of niggers and
a white woman done this to him? Why had God let them?
If there was any fairness in the world, why couldn't he
turn the clock back a year and a half and make a different
kind of life?

He smiled a little, remembering that spring afternoon
when Catherine had visited him at Redbird and Leonie had
been so angry. What if he had answered her differently?

"You aiming to marry that gal?"

He might have teased her a little, of course. *"It's possible."*

*"You ain't gonna touch me long as you even thinking of
marrying her."*

What if he had been wise enough to give a sigh for what
might have been, and then say, *"Now, Leonie, you know
I'm not going to marry her. I've got you, what do I need
her for? You and me, what do we need besides each other?"*

She'd have said, *Oh, Mr. Duke!* and thrown herself into
his arms. And tonight she would still have been safe in his
arms, and if he had been wise enough to keep her there,

surely he would have been wise enough not to give a damn what the world said.

But that hadn't happened, and she was gone, and he knew now that he would never see her again.

A sound caught his ear, and he set down his glass and looked out the door again. He could barely make out the horse and carriage that had come through the persimmon grove. But who would be coming to Redbird at this hour of the night?

The carriage passed the jailhouse and came to a halt near the cabriolet. Duke recognized Miss Lucy's voice, as she cried out at the sight of her daughter hanging naked from the gallows.

She leapt from the carriage and ran toward the gallows, and her black driver followed. She cried, "Help me, Damien! Help me get her down!"

Quickly, they each untied an ankle, and Damien slowly, carefully lowered Cat into her mother's arms.

Damien.

. . . In the boat with Catherine, he half naked, his thighs entangled with hers . . .

. . . In Leonie's cabin, a black male voice, soft and intimate . . .

". . . *All they say is, she spend a awful lot of time in that Damien boy's cabin.*"

If there was anyone left in the world for him to hate, it was the nigger fancy boy who had spread both his black woman and his wife. Damien.

Duke's pistol lay nearby on the desk. He picked it up. Checked the action. Went out the doorway and walked toward the gallows.

Miss Lucy was the first to see him coming. She was sitting on the ground under the gallows with her daughter in her arms, and when she raised her face, tears shining in the torchlight, she let out a wail that was part anguish and part an everlasting curse.

Damien looked around. He, too, appeared to be weeping. His hand moved toward his belt buckle, then stopped.

Duke recognized the butt of the six-barrel pepperbox sticking out of his belt.

He laughed. A slave with a weapon. It was just the excuse he needed, if he needed one at all.

He flicked his pistol up, a gesture of invitation. "Well, what are you waiting for, boy? Use it."

Duke saw the realization of what was about to happen coming into Damien's eyes.

"Use it!"

Damien's hand jerked spasmotically over the pistol butt.

"Damien, don't!" Miss Lucy cried.

"It's your only chance, boy. You know that."

Duke leveled his pistol at Damien. He thumbed back the hammer. Slowly. He watched the fear growing in the black boy's eyes.

He said, "Die, nigger."

Even then, he waited. Waited until Miss Lucy screamed, as the boy's hand closed on the pistol butt and, his face a mask of terror, he threw himself back and away from Duke. *Then*, at last, finally, he pulled the trigger. And saw the bullet pick the boy up and throw him onto his back to lie unmoving in the dust.

The only sounds were Miss Lucy's sobs, and they were the most despairing sounds Duke had ever heard. Well, he thought, now she knew what it felt like. For his part, it was all over, all finished, and he could breathe a sigh of relief. Justin would probably try to kill him, of course, but what the hell, that was Justin's problem.

"It's all finished, Jebediah," he said loudly. "Do you hear me? It's all finished!"

Miss Lucy's sobs faded, and the night was silent.

He didn't recognize Jebediah's voice when next he heard it. The sound started as little more than a low animal growl, but in an instant it became a giant denial, a roar of pain, a great cry of unleashed rage. And in that same instant, Duke saw that something was happening to the door of the jailhouse. He could see it, but it happened so fast that he could not at first comprehend it. The door appeared to be bowing out. He heard a vast splintering sound, a groaning, a creaking, ripping, crashing sound of wood being torn apart. And the door exploded. It shattered. The splintered boards flew. A great shoulder appeared, a bulging thigh, a maddened face. Jebediah Hayes was coming through the door.

He came through, eyes ablaze, teeth bared, manacle chain swinging. He was still spanceled, and Duke might have turned and run, but it never occurred to him to do such a thing. Instead, he stepped forward, cocked his pistol, and fired. He thought he saw the bullet hit Jebediah's side and twist him, but Jebediah kept coming, swinging his chain. As Duke fired again, Jebediah grabbed the chain in both hands, swung it high, and brought it down like a sledgehammer. Duke felt his forearm shatter and saw his pistol fly away.

He tried to back away, to run, but it was too late. Jebediah swung his chain high again and brought it down on Duke's left shoulder. The shoulder crumpled. The chain swung up and came down again, this time at an angle, and Duke's left knee splintered. Even as he fell backward, the chain came down again, crashing into his ribs.

Then Jebediah was standing over him and still bringing the chain down. He felt the right side of his face being torn away, felt one eye go. He felt his right arm being broken again. He felt more ribs caving in, and blood rose in his throat.

The chain hung still. Jebediah stood over him, slouch-shouldered and breathing in huge, painful gasps. Somehow Duke managed to get up on one elbow. Somehow managed to point at Jebediah. Somehow even managed a kind of grin.

"Jessie," he mumbled through the blood in his throat. "You took Jessie away from me, nigger . . . but I made you pay, didn't I? . . . I made you pay."

With another anguished roar, Jebediah raised his chain again and brought it smashing down, and Duke could no longer see. But he could still feel the blows, tearing him apart. Then he could no longer feel the pain, although the blows were still coming, but they didn't matter any longer. He was leaving them, rushing away through darkness. And this, Duke knew, was death.

❈❱{ 4 }❰❈

THEY WANTED TO HANG HIM.

It didn't matter to them, the Bassetts and the Carstairs and their ilk, that he had been kidnapped, and a lot of highly respectable people agreed with them. It didn't matter that a slave had been shot. It didn't matter that Miss Lucy, with her daughter in her arms, and Mr. Ferguson, standing off in the dark, had seen it all and had sworn that Jebediah had merely been defending lives and property. The fact remained that the nigger had killed a white man. Had actually flogged Duke Avery to death with his chains. And some of them swore that if the nigger were ever caught, he would never see the inside of a court of law. If he did, there was always a chance that he would be sentenced to something less than hanging, perhaps even be freed, and if he ever got north again, he would never be extradited. No, it would be far better if they seized Jebediah Hayes and took matters into their own hands.

But where was he? All the world wanted to know.

Fortunately, his wounds were superficial, if nonetheless painful, and he had little difficulty in hiding in a hollow wall upstairs in the coach house, when the patrol came riding in search of him. Mr. Justin, when he returned to Sabrehill, could honestly swear that he had no idea of where Jebediah was, and as for Miss Lucy, well . . . as she put it, she did the lying for the family. She swore up and down that Jebediah had disappeared at Redbird, just as Leonie had done some weeks earlier. Cat, she said, had revived sufficiently to drive the cabriolet back to Sabrehill, and she herself had driven the other carriage. Mr. Ferguson, a decent man, did not contradict her.

And so it was that, as Cat had predicted, Jebediah spent Christmas day at Sabrehill, where he dined on roast goose

and baked ham and candied yams and all manner of fine
things, in an upstairs coach house room, with Zagreus and
Binnie and Leila.

By February he was sufficiently healed, and the hunt
had died down enough, to make the trip north. By that
time, he was spending his nights with Leila in the old
"voodoo house," avoided by most of the Sabrehill people,
out at one corner of the field quarters. On the last evening,
he held Leila in his arms and found that it was as hard to
leave her this time as it had been ten years earlier.

"Maybe someday, Leila . . ."

"Now, don't you make me no promises you can't keep,
or hold out more hope than I need. Having you safe again
and telling the truth about slavery, that's what I want. You
never stop telling them the truth, Jebediah."

"I swear to you, Leila, I'll never stop."

There was a tap at the door, and Leila opened it a crack.
Adaba looked in.

"All aboard," he said softly. "We travel light and fast on
the Brown Dove Line."

A few weeks later, the world got the answer to its question. MR. JEB ALIVE! shouted the newspaper headlines.
Not only alive, but back in the North and more a legend
than ever. Even in the South he was cheered by many as a
hero, but most slaveholders groaned. Would no one ever
shut that nigger up?

Soon after his reappearance, Jebediah addressed an
audience at Fanueil Hall.

"I apologize for being somewhat late to this meeting,
ladies and gentlemen," he began, "but on my way here a
few months ago, I found myself temporarily detained."

When the laughter had died, he continued. "As most of
you probably know, I recently spent an enforced holiday in
the South, visiting old friends—and enemies. The details
will have to wait for my next book, but I can tell you this
right now. The evil I have faced is not confined to any one
part of this great land, or any land. It is universal. To live a
life on the basis of demeaning and degrading another life
in any way is to live by a lie—the lie of pretending superiority in the eyes of the Almighty. And a people that

lives by a lie must suffer and die by that lie—the guilty and the innocent alike."

Once again, he was a mighty voice heard throughout the nation and throughout the world. *You never stop telling them the truth, Jebediah,"* Leila had said to him. He never would.

"You're not going to die. I won't let you go away from me, Damien. You're mine, and I'm going to keep you with me always."

Her whisper was the first thing he heard, and her hand on his was the first thing he felt, and then the pain struck, like a hook tearing out his side, and he lost consciousness again.

Later, he was aware of the doctor's presence, and of Miss Lucy and Leila and Momma Lucinda coming and going. Cat always seemed to be nearby.

"I don't know," the doctor said, when he returned. "He may survive yet, but he's got a bad fever."

"He is *not* going to die," Cat said, "I forbid it!"

All right, Cat, he thought, trying to say the words, *then I won't die.*

"What? What did you say, Damien?"

". . . won't . . . die."

"No, of course not. I've got you with me, and we're both going to live forever."

When he opened his eyes, it was morning, and his fever was gone, and although the pain was bad, he felt that he was indeed going to live forever. Cat, holding his hand, smiled.

"Well, boy, you surely caused us a peck of trouble, getting yourself shot like that. Aren't you ever going to learn to stay away from that damn Redbird plantation?"

There was no trip to Charleston for the "gay season" that year. Justin had to make a short trip to see his cotton in and to confer with his factor, but Miss Lucy elected to remain at Sabrehill. "Let the scandal run its course," she said. "I have no wish to afford entertainment to wagging tongues and prying eyes."

Cat put the matter more succinctly: "To hell with them."

Just as she had done before, she nursed Damien tirelessly. He was weak for a very long time, still weak when Jebediah came to say good-bye before departing with Adaba. But with healing came need, and one evening when Cat peeked under his blanket, her eyes brightened and she said, "Well! I see you're, ah . . . up to it!" Thereafter, they made love from time to time, but Damien sensed a change in Cat. Though she was accommodating and even eager, the erotic frenzy of their first weeks had waned. She had had her honeymoon, and they were both healing, he in body and she in spirit.

In April, Mr. Justin ordered Damien into the library, shut the door, and told him to sit down. Justin's face and voice had a hardness Damien wasn't used to, and he wondered how much the man knew, or suspected, about Cat and him.

"Damien, you know that early next month we'll be going to Charleston."

"Yes, sir."

"I think it's time for you to go north."

Damien felt a sinking sensation. He had known that this day had to come, had in a part of his soul longed for it to come. But Cat had said, *"You're mine, and I'm going to keep you with me always . . . and we're both going to live forever,"* and for a little while, they had pretended it was true.

"Well, do you agree?"

"Yes, sir." Justin's tone brooked no argument.

"Good. I'll make the arrangements just as soon as we get back to the city. You'll soon be safely under Jebediah's wing."

"Yes, sir. Thank you." Justin suspected something, all right. Damien sensed that, genuinely fond of him though the man was, he would be glad to see this black boy's tail gone from South Carolina.

Justin's face and voice softened, and he sat down. "We'll miss you, Damien. All of us."

"And I'll miss all of you, Mr. Justin. After all, except for Jebediah, you're the only family I have."

Justin nodded. "And that brings up something I've been meaning to mention. You've never had a family name, a surname, and you're going to need one. I suppose you'll want to use Jebediah's name?"

"No, sir. I figure I might just get to be as famous as Jebediah one day. And it seems to me that one famous Hayes is enough."

"Well . . ." Justin, suddenly diffident, glanced away and fidgeted in his chair. "I don't want you to feel I'm trying to push you into anything, Damien. The decision is entirely yours. But I'm told there's good reason to believe you're entitled to the Sabre name, if you should want it."

"Would you mind if I used the Sabre name, Mr. Justin?"

"Damien, I'd be honored."

"So would I."

He would be Damien Sabre, then. And Damien Sabre was heading north to a new life.

She was the Widow Avery now, and a rich young widow at that. She owned part of a slave-trading firm, a fine house in Charleston, and a plantation. When her father suggested that she sell them all, she asked, "But why?" She could do without the slave-trading firm, but she enjoyed having her own house, and the plantation was paying itself off and making a profit. And she liked thinking of herself as the mistress of Redbird. She felt that she had earned it all, and, for the time being at least, she would keep it.

Especially since she couldn't keep the one thing she wanted most.

But she had long before accepted the inevitable, and that made their parting easier. They said their private farewell one evening in the gardens behind the Lynch Steet house.

"I feel like I'm never going to see you again," she said, as they clung together in the dark.

"Oh, you will, Cat. Next summer, or the summer after that, you'll come north, and you'll see your Aunt Dulcy and Jebediah and—"

"And you won't be there. You'll have gone off some-where, and another year or two or three will go by—"

"And you'll meet some good man who can handle a catamount like you."

"But I won't ever forget you, Damien."

"And I'll never forget you, Cat. Because leaving you is like leaving part of myself behind."

"Think of me, Damien."

"I will, Cat. I promise. And you think of me."

He left the next morning.

The young Widow Avery—she still thought of herself only as Cat Sabre—found herself very popular that summer. Considering how Duke Avery had treated her, no great period of mourning was expected of her, and she discovered that wealth forgives many faults, especially in a good-looking woman. Her wicked tongue was now deemed witty, and her occasional saltiness a charming eccentricity. All the unmarried bucks surrounded her, particularly those younger sons who could not expect to inherit a plantation or any great wealth of their own. They knew a woman who needed a protective husband when they saw one.

They amused Cat, but they didn't fool her. And no matter how cheerful her days and gay her evenings, in her secret heart she remained lonely. Because she knew she was still "different." She knew she did not really "fit in."

But she was strong, she could bear that, and she still had no wish to be anything other than what she was. And at certain times her loneliness vanished altogether. That happened at those moments when suddenly she felt Damien's presence near her. Then she would smile and silently speak to him. "You're thinking of me, aren't you, Damien?" And he would answer, "Yes, Cat, I am."

That night, she might dream of him. She sometimes dreamed that she was crossing a moonlit field, calling his name: "Damien! . . . Damien! . . ." And with a surge of joy, she would hear him, distantly, calling back: "I'm coming, Cat! . . . I'm coming! . . ."